WANT A

Sign up for my newsletter and get your copy of Chasing Stacy.

River: One look at the stunning waitress carrying the weight of the world on her shoulders, and I'm a gonner. I wasn't looking for a sweet little thing with auburn hair and more baggage than I can fit on the back of my bike, but there's no going back now. She's mine. I'll prove to her I'm more than capable of handling her past and making her feel safe again.

DI SALVO CRIME FAMILY

THE COMPLETE SERIES

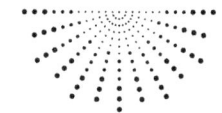

CAMERON HART

CONNECT WITH ME!

Check out my website, <u>cameronhart.net</u>, for sneak previews on my latest projects.

Follow me on social media:
   <u>Facebook Page</u>
   <u>Facebook Group</u>
   <u>TikTok</u>
   <u>Instagram</u>
   <u>Goodreads</u>
   <u>Bookbub</u>

ROMEO

Blurb:

I didn't get to be the head of the Di Salvo crime family by showing mercy. Just the opposite, in fact. Until I meet her. Thalia.

My girl witnessed something that could get her killed, but it's my job to protect her now. She's not just a loose end to tie up, she's a shy, curvy goddess with a silent strength she's not even aware of.

In my line of business, love is a liability. A weakness. Yet, every day Thalia is under my protection, I'm drawn closer to her warmth and soft-spoken words. This woman might just be my salvation.

When our enemies come knocking, I'll be ready to scorch the entire earth if it means keeping Thalia safe. They have no idea who they're messing with.

CHAPTER ONE

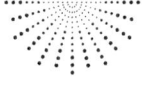

THALIA

I shouldn't have come here.

That thought replays in my mind as I curl into a tight ball behind the dumpster, trying to make myself invisible. A rancid garbage smell permeates this small alleyway nestled between two large warehouses, and despite the chill of a New York City winter, the scent hangs heavy in the air. I cover my mouth with my hand to block the smell and muffle the sound of my heavy, panicked breathing.

I know better than to be in this neighborhood alone at night, but I was on a mission. My older brother, Thomas, forgot the dinner I packed him for his night shift at the meat processing plant.

I don't bring much to our relationship, and I know Thomas resents me for moving in after Dad ditched me. I've been pulling in some extra income through my online crochet store, but it's never enough. The least I can do is make sure Thomas gets three meals a day and comes home to a tidy apartment, even if it's in the slums.

Someone kicks an empty soda can in my direction before wrenching open a side door and stomping inside one of the buildings. I hold my breath, willing this to be over soon. I had no idea what I was walking into when I searched for a back entrance to the building where my brother works. Tears sting my eyes, and I strain to hear the nearby conversation over the thundering sound of my heart.

"Thomas, you fuckin' idiot," an older man spits out. I peer through the sliver of a window between the dumpster and the brick wall, hoping to see who is yelling at my brother.

The man is short and round, with a cheap toupee that isn't fooling anyone. I've seen him before, but I can't remember his name. Mark? Matt? He's somehow involved with the union all the meat packing plant workers are in. Thomas has been hanging around him more and more lately.

"Chill, Martin. I'll get the money by the end of the week, and no one will know."

Martin. That's right.

"That's not good enough," Martin grinds out. "I don't know if I can protect you from this, kid."

Why does my brother need protection? What money?

I had my suspicions that Thomas was doing something shady on the side, but I thought he was making illegal bets or selling stolen goods. Not that those things are excusable, but they are par for the course around here.

This sounds more serious, though. *What has he gotten himself into?*

"What are you saying?" my brother asks, a hint of worry creeping into his voice. "You know I'm good for it. Plus, I thought you said we'd be getting a shitload more money soon from that business transaction you've been so secretive about."

"Yes, *soon* being the operative word," he mutters. "But you may have ruined that. Destroyed our credibility. Do you have any idea how fragile the balance of power is right now?"

Martin paces back and forth, waving his hands in the air

as if that will help drive his point home. He pulls out a cigarette and lights it, taking a long drag before coughing it out.

Silence blankets the alley while Martin and Thomas face off. The two men square their shoulders as they stare each other down. It's not just quiet; it's the complete absence of sound as if Mother Nature herself is holding her breath for what happens next.

The bitterly cold wind scrapes against my cheeks and nose until I can't feel them anymore, but I don't dare try to cover my face with my scarf. Any movement would break the almost supernatural stillness surrounding us.

Thomas is the first to speak, his voice coming out nasally and tinged with rising fear. "If you'd looped me in earlier, maybe this wouldn't have happened," he whines. He's never been known to take responsibility for his actions, so I'm not surprised at his response.

"Maybe this wouldn't have… Jesus, kid. You fucked up."

I watch my older brother's face turn from a heated red to a ghostly white. It's finally sinking in that he's in real danger. I have no clue what kind of danger, but the sinking sensation twisting up my insides says it's the fatal kind.

The men grow quiet, and I try to calm my erratic breathing.

When I first heard shouting, I didn't think much of it. The plant isn't in the best part of town and our apartment, which is only a few blocks away, is even deeper in the slums than this place. People fight all the time, but they usually keep their rage focused on the conflict at hand. I learned early on the safest thing to do was to mind my own business. Then I recognized my brother's slurred voice and knew he was in trouble.

If only he was drinking on the job again. This sounds much more serious.

"They're here," Martin whispers harshly.

My brother doesn't say anything, but for the first time in my life, I see genuine fear flickering in his green eyes.

A few moments later, three men dressed in crisp black suits and long trench coats appear. Ice creeps down my spine, filling my veins with a chill down to my bones. The dark figures carry an air of strict, ruthless authority. Dread knots my stomach as I watch the men approach Martin and Thomas.

"Leo, there you guys are," Martin says, trying to sound jovial. His voice is tinny and hollow, too strained to be believed.

"Do you have the missing funds?" one of the foreboding men asks.

Martin peers at Thomas, who has a deer-in-the-head-lights look on his face. My older brother may be a drunk and a petty criminal, but it's obvious he's never looked true evil in the eyes until now.

"I can get it by next–"

"No," the man clips out, cutting Thomas off. He turns back to Martin, eyeing him up and down. "I thought we were on the same side, Mr. Branson, but perhaps I misjudged you."

Martin's gaze dips, and I follow his line of sight to the gleaming metal gun in the man's right hand resting at his side. For now.

"We are on the same side," Martin insists. "It's just... it was..." The portly man with thinning hair scrambles for something to say to save his life. "It was Thomas! Thomas stole the money and thought you wouldn't notice."

Thomas glares at Martin, betrayal painted over his features, before he turns his attention to the man with the gun. "I can explain–"

A gunshot cracks through the inky black sky, followed by a sickening thud.

My mouth drops open, and the air drains from my lungs as I watch thick, dark red blood pool around my brother's body. He's looking away from me, but I know the source of the bleeding—a bullet between the eyes.

Staring in shock, I can't comprehend what's happened. A life has just ended, cut short by nothing more than the twitch of a trigger finger.

I finally drag air into my burning lungs, but the tears won't come. Blinking rapidly, I force my attention on anything but my brother's body. Even though we lived together, we were never particularly close. Thomas was eighteen years older than me and moved out before I turned two.

Still, he took me in when I showed up on his doorstep two years ago. Our relationship has been rocky ever since, and his drinking was getting out of control, but it wasn't all bad. I've been focusing on my online crochet business, trying to scrimp and save as much as possible to get a place of my own.

But now nothing seems real, and my brother is just… gone.

The click of a gun cocking has me whipping my head in that direction.

"Now, gentlemen," Martin starts, holding his hands up in surrender. "Let's not get any ideas here. Thomas' death is inconsequential, but if you shoot the head of the fucking UFCW union, you'll draw a lot of attention."

"Attention we can handle," one of the previously silent men says, his voice gritty and terrifying. "Traitors, on the other hand…"

He lunges toward Martin, grabbing him by his shirt collar and pulling him up, up, up until his toes are barely touching the ground. Martin whimpers as the man shoves a gun to his temple, the metal digging into his skin.

"I-I-I'm not a t-traitor," Martin stutters. "I swear it. Thomas got himself tangled up in the money laundering we were doing and thought he could skim off the top."

"Bullshit. You're working with the Di Salvos, aren't you?"

"What? No. Not since your initial offer."

Di Salvo… I've heard that name before, but I can't remember where or in what context. Probably something Thomas went on a drunk rant about at some point.

"What do you think, boys?" the man calls over his shoulder. "Do we believe Mr. Branson?"

Without waiting for an answer, he squeezes the trigger, sending a bullet tearing through Martin's skull. He drops to the ground next to my brother in a crumpled, unnatural state. I try shutting my eyes, but I can't look away from Martin's dead stare. His brown, lifeless eyes bore into me as terror wraps itself around my body in a suffocating blanket.

I'm vaguely aware of three sets of footsteps fading into the background, followed by the subtle start of an engine as a car pulls out of the gravel parking lot, but I can't bring myself to move. To blink. To breathe.

I'm suspended in this moment as it stretches on for eternity. My vision grows fuzzy around the edges, and a few black spots dance in front of my eyes. Only then do I realize I've been holding my breath for too long, and I'm on the brink of passing out.

Pulling ragged breaths into my lungs, I try not to choke on the rotting garbage smell mixed with the metallic scent of blood.

I need to get out of here.

That thought seems to reset my brain, and my fight-or-flight response finally kicks in. I carefully uncurl myself from my hiding spot and crawl a few feet down the alley before standing on wobbly legs.

One foot in front of the other, I tell myself.

It feels like I'm wading through mud, and I try picking up my pace, only to trip and fall on my hands and knees. Biting my lips to contain my whimper of pain, I continue crawling until I can stand again.

Every muscle in my body is tense to the point of trembling, but I know I can't stop. I can't look back. Nowhere is safe anymore, yet I don't know where else to go except back to the apartment.

I swear every step echoes louder than the gunshots from earlier, but I keep going. Adrenaline pumps through my veins, making my heart hammer against my chest in an attempt to break free.

When I stumble onto the porch steps leading to our apartment door, I reach into my pocket for the keys, dropping them three times before finally getting the right one.

Once inside, I frantically search for anything to block the door. No one is after me now, but I'm not stupid. I know they'll come. Whoever they are.

We don't have much furniture in our studio apartment, but I shove the little kitchen table against the doorway, as well as the chairs, coffee table, and bookshelf.

As if on cue, my body collapses as soon as I have the last piece of furniture in place. I have nothing left. No energy. No tears. No fight. No family.

I'm utterly alone in the world.

Crawling over to the bed shoved in the corner of the room, I grab a blanket and pillow and huddle up at the foot of the bed, squeezing myself between the corner and the old, lumpy mattress.

As amped up as I was a few minutes ago, I can barely keep my eyes open now. Fear still courses through my body with each beat of my heart, but I don't have the energy to do anything about it.

Just a little rest, I reason. *Then I'll come up with a plan.*

CHAPTER TWO

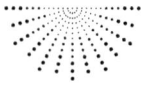

ROMEO

"*A*nd you're sure it was a hit job?" I growl at my second-in-command, Dante. "Martin Branson wasn't exactly the smartest man. He could have pissed off any number of punks with an itchy trigger finger."

"This was too clean," Dante responds in his crisp, no-nonsense tone. "And they did it out in the open to send a message."

"Fuck," I mutter, resting my head in my hands. "Do we know who did it?"

Dante shakes his head, not even blinking when I utter a string of curse words. He's used to my wrath and takes it all in stride. As the underboss of the Di Salvo crime family, he's my closest ally. He'd be my best friend if men like me could afford to have friends.

"What will this do to our day-to-day operations?" I ask, leaning back in my chair and crossing one leg over the other.

Dante gives me a breakdown of the ramifications, and I nod along while piecing together a plan.

Martin is the head of the UFCW union, which is in charge

of the many workers employed at the meat packing plant in north Brooklyn. The Di Salvo family has had a long-standing arrangement with him. More specifically, our ill-gotten gains are laundered through the union pension fund, which can only happen if management is on our side. In return, the Di Salvo family offers their protection and guarantees fair pay, plenty of sick leave and vacation time, as well as a generous health plan, including maternity and paternity leave.

But all of that disintegrated overnight after Martin caught a bullet with his temple.

"Do we know who his replacement will be?" I ask sharply, cutting Dante off.

"No, Boss. I have Valentino working on getting intel since that's his territory."

I grunt, sitting up straight and resting my elbows on my desk. Looking at my second in command, I sense there's more he's not telling me. "What else, Dante?"

"It's likely nothing–"

"Out with it," I growl, my patience wearing thin. This is not how I wanted to start my Monday morning, and now I have a shitstorm to deal with on top of the meetings I was already drowning in.

"Martin's body was found alongside someone else. Thomas Brooks. Thirty-eight, plant worker for over a decade, and a sloppy drunk by all accounts. We've ruled him out as nothing more than a wanna-be thug who got caught up in a much bigger game than he could handle."

"And?"

"He has a twenty-year-old sister. Thalia. They live together in a block of apartments behind the plant. She's no threat, but she is a loose end. Even if she doesn't know what's going on, she's bound to question her brother's whereabouts if she hasn't already."

I grunt in acknowledgment, swallowing past the unfamiliar knot of tension in my throat.

"Honestly," Dante continues, "whoever took Martin and Thomas out is probably already on their way to find and deal with her, so we shouldn't have to worry about it."

The tightness in my throat migrates to my chest, filling my veins with restless energy. Something in me recoils at the thought of harm befalling the mysterious Thalia, even if it's not at the hands of my men.

It's true, even though I'm the ruthless mafia king of the New York City underworld, I don't take pleasure in ending innocent lives. I try to conduct my business with as few casualties as possible, especially when it comes to women and children.

But this…. this… this *feeling* is something more.

I clench my fists, trying to focus back on Dante. I don't know this woman, and I shouldn't care about her well-being any more than any other stranger I cross paths with.

"Would you like me to send someone to her residence and scope it out?"

"No!" I shout, pounding my fist on the solid oak desk. I'm as shocked as Dante at my outburst, but I don't let it show. As the head of the Di Salvo crime family, I must always be in control of my emotions.

"But–"

"I'll do it."

Dante blinks a few times, opening his mouth before closing it again. Good man. He knows I've made up my mind, even if he doesn't understand why. Fuck if I know, but I can't take it back now.

Dismissing Dante, I call my head of staff to have my black BMW waiting for me out front in five minutes. I guess I'm heading to Brooklyn this morning.

Half an hour later, I make my second drive around the

apartment block where Thalia Brooks lives. I knew it was in a rough part of town, but I get that same tightness in my chest when I think about a defenseless young woman staying here alone.

Parking in a discreet location behind a few overgrown bushes, I silently climb out of my vehicle and check my surroundings before making my way to the woman's apartment. It's on the ground floor, which once again has something protective twisting up my insides.

Keeping my back to the wall of the building, I slink along in the shadows, taking note of everything around me. It's barely ten in the morning, yet a junkie is shooting up around the corner from Thalia's apartment in broad daylight. I also notice a hastily done drug deal a few doors down. Loud music blasts from an upstairs unit while a screaming match takes place in another.

I don't need to sneak around. I bet I could walk up to any of these apartments with my weapon drawn, and no one would look in my direction. Still, old habits die hard, and I can never be too careful, especially since I took on this recon mission alone.

I still can't explain it, but I'm drawn to this Thalia woman. Maybe I'm just getting soft after nearly twenty years of being the Don, but my gut tells me it's something more. Something deeper. Something worth risking everything for. I didn't get this position and keep it for so long by ignoring my instincts, so here I am.

Creeping up to what appears to be the only window in the entire apartment, I peer inside, squinting my eyes to adjust to the dim lights. I don't see anything at first, and I fear I'm too late. But then a movement in the corner of the small space catches my eye.

Long auburn hair glitters in the tiny beam of sunshine filtering through the window, drawing my attention there.

The woman turns her head to the side, allowing me to see her profile. My gaze wanders down the slope of her delicate nose, taking in her rounded cheeks and pouty lips as I let my eyes dip down to drink in her curves. Even in a ratty old bathrobe, I can tell this woman is full-figured, though I try not to eye-fuck her like a perve.

Snapping my attention back to her face, I can make out the shape of her wide, doe-like eyes as she blinks. I'm mesmerized by every inch of this angel, from her slightly upturned nose to the gentle sway of her hips as she prepares herself a mug of tea.

The more I study her, the more I realize her movements are tentative and jerky, like she's scared of her own shadow. I watch as Thalia brings the mug to her lips, her hands trembling so badly she can hardly take a sip.

Thalia whimpers as hot liquid splashes over the rim of the mug, burning her hands, and I have the strongest, strangest urge to… comfort her? No, that can't be right. I wouldn't even know how to do that.

Yet, my hands twitch to help her clean up the mess before tending to her wound. Jesus, I must be losing it. First, I drag my ass out here on a mission better fit for a captain than the goddamn Boss, and then I go all soft for a curvy goddess in a heap of trouble she doesn't even understand.

Thalia sets the mug on the counter and stands there, staring at it. No, she's staring *through* it, right into the void that's opened up in her life. I know that look all too well.

I tear my eyes from the confounding woman to examine her living quarters. The studio apartment can't be more than four hundred square feet, with a mini kitchenette and a small bathroom off to one side. All the furniture is piled up in front of the door in a weak attempt to keep the boogeyman out. The table and chairs leaning against the door are older than the building itself, and I have no doubt I could burst through the door, furniture and all, without even scuffing my Italian leather Oxfords.

A twin mattress and box spring are stacked up in the corner on the other side of the room. The blankets and pillows are at the foot of the bed as if she feels safer curled up in the corner.

What is this tightness in my chest? This sinking feeling twisting up my gut? I don't like the thought of Thalia being afraid of anything, and in this case, her fears are entirely founded.

She saw something, all right. And I need to figure out exactly what she knows.

The hairs on the back of my neck stand up, sending awareness prickling down my spine. Someone else is here. Someone else is watching her.

I dart my eyes to the left and right, catching a glimpse of a sleek navy-blue car before it turns the corner. I register the vehicle as one that drove by a few minutes ago, and I'm immediately on high alert.

Slinking back into the shadows, I keep close to Thalia's apartment and watch as the blue car pulls into a parking spot in an abandoned lot across the street. Logically, I know this sketchy character could be here for any of the tenants in this building, but every instinct I've honed over the years tells me he's looking for the same woman I am.

When I see his face, I know it to be true.

"Fucking hell," I mutter under my breath. I recognize that low-life as one of the enforcers for the Colombo family. I've been in this business for too long to believe in coincidences. He's here to grill Thalia and then dispose of her.

But I can't let that happen.

I need her. Well, I need her answers. I need to know what she knows, and that's it. What else would I need her for?

A fleeting image of Thalia smiling up at me appears and

then evaporates before my eyes, and I shake off the feeling that this woman is about to change everything. She can't. I won't allow it. Men like me weren't made for soft, doe-eyed, innocent little lambs like Thalia. I'd ruin her the same way my father ruined my mother and spend the rest of my life in a loveless marriage surrounded by opulence and an endless parade of extravagant gifts.

Or maybe I'm projecting.

Looking over my shoulder, I catch another glimpse of Thalia. She's cradling her burnt hand against her chest, her eyes closed as she folds in on herself. I can fucking *feel* the weight of her entire world resting on her shoulders, the fear pumping through her veins, and the exhaustion tugging at her soul.

I can't keep Thalia as mine, but I can protect her in exchange for her honesty about what she saw last night. That's all. It has to be all.

Then why does something in me break when the first tear falls down her cheek? Why do I want to wipe it away and hold her in my arms?

The rustling of leaves draws my attention back to the present, and I know I don't have much time to act before the Colombos get to her. Fuck me, this isn't going to end well, but I have no choice. I can't let anyone hurt her. I won't stand for it.

Tucking my piece into the waistband of my pants, I cover it with my jacket and knock on Thalia's door.

CHAPTER THREE

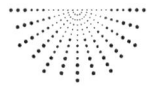

THALIA

I drop to the floor as soon as I hear the knock, barely registering the mug falling from my hand and cracking against the cheap linoleum. My knees are still bruised and bloody from when I fell last night, but the pain burns away in the face of sheer panic.

Squeezing my eyes shut and holding my breath, I curl into the tiniest ball I can manage. Another sharp knock lands on my door, and I can't suppress the whimper that falls from my lips.

I passed out last night for a few hours after the adrenaline drained from my muscles. I crashed into an all-consuming, almost drugged sleep filled with gruesome, bloody nightmares. It was still dark when I woke up, but my anxiety wouldn't let me fall back to sleep. I've been shuffling around the apartment all morning, trying to make sense of what I saw and heard and how much danger I'm in.

"Thalia," a deep voice says, clipping out my name like a command. Every muscle in my body locks up, my entire being frozen in place except for my jackhammering heart. "Let me in if you want to live."

Yeah, right. Only someone who wants to kill you would say that.

The man on the other side of the door sighs heavily as if searching for the right words. I stay huddled up in the corner of the kitchen, peering at the door and silently praying for the molecular structure of the cheap wood to miraculously transform into impenetrable steel.

As it is, I have no doubts the stranger could huff and puff and blow this whole building down without much effort. Something about that softens me toward the man outside. If he truly meant me harm, I'd be dead already.

"I know you have no reason to trust me, but I give you my word, no harm will come to you under my protection."

He's absolutely right. I have zero reason to trust him. And yet, hearing him say he'll protect me... A spark of hope dares to light up my chest, tentative though it may be.

It's not like I have a lot of options. If he's not here to kill me, someone else will be soon. I'm a sitting duck with nowhere else to go. I have nothing to lose.

As I uncurl myself and slowly stand, I search around the small space for something to use as a weapon. I know Thomas keeps a gun around here, but I've never cared enough to look for it. Something silver and shiny draws my attention, and I see one of my large crochet hooks. It's made of metal and has an ergonomic handle.

All the better to stab with, I reason.

Picking up my weapon of choice, I take a deep breath and roll out my shoulders. I have to be limber in case I need to defend myself.

Dragging the tables and chairs away from the thin, cracked door, I realize how vulnerable I am. It takes me all of thirty seconds to shove them out of the way, which means anyone could have easily done the same.

Pausing with my hand on the doorknob, I take one last grounding breath and let it out before opening the door.

I'm face to face with a broad chest, covered in a sleek black button-up and adorned with a red tie. I tip my head up, up, up, gasping softly when I'm met with brutally beautiful eyes. They are dark, nearly black, and filled with passion and power.

A jagged white scar slices through his left eyebrow, making him look even more severe. His hair is midnight black, shaved close on the sides and left longer on top. A slight stubble litters his chin and cheeks, giving the man a rugged edge to his otherwise pristine appearance.

He reaches out for me, but I recoil on instinct and then thrust my crochet hook in his face. "Don't m-make me use th-this," I say with a trembling voice, waving the hook in front of him.

His eyebrows shoot up to his hairline, and those dark eyes go wide as he stares at the weapon in my hand. The man turns his attention to me, studying me more intently this time. I'm shaking from head to toe, my breaths coming out in short bursts, but I stand my ground.

The tall, muscular man with an air of power and authority lifts his hands, palms out, in a sign of surrender. I wasn't expecting that, but I'll take any wins I can get at the moment.

"I'm not here to hurt you," he says in his deep, velvety voice. It's almost a whisper, but not quite. Like he's trying to calm me down. "Though it appears the same can't be said for you. I haven't come across such a weapon before. Tell me, how would you use it?"

I can't tell if he's mocking me, but I answer him truthfully. "I could stick it in your eye," I say with more confidence this time. "Or poke it in your ear," I add. He nods but doesn't look convinced. "If you're really a threat, I might shove it up your nose and hook out your brain."

His left brow, the one with the scar, ticks up slightly in amusement. "You've thought about this quite a bit," he observes.

I shrug. "I've had to since moving here."

The man furrows his brow as if he doesn't like the thought of me living here. Then he snaps out of it, nodding once again. "While resourceful, I don't know how much good it would do against a gun."

Terror seeps back into my veins, and anxiety wraps around my lungs, making it hard to breathe.

"Not me," he's quick to add. "I promised to protect you, remember?"

I nod, but the words float in and out of my brain.

"But you do have some powerful enemies after what you saw last night."

That's what pushes me over the edge, sending me diving headfirst into a panic attack. I step back, but my feet tangle in one of the discarded kitchen chairs. The man lunges for me, and I let out a pathetic cry as my crochet hook falls to the floor with a clang.

The next thing I know, I'm being crushed against the stranger's chest as his arms come around me and hold me close. I try fighting my way out of his embrace, unsure if he's trying to comfort or kidnap me.

"I've got you, Thalia," he whispers. "I'm not going to hurt you."

"No," I whimper, tears streaming down my cheeks as I suck in air. I'm not sure what I'm saying no to, but it's the only word I can come up with at the moment.

"Breathe for me," he commands softly, never letting me out of his embrace.

His low voice, rich timbre, and surprisingly sweet words

course through me, loosening the grip of panic. Still, my fight or flight has been engaged since I saw my brother get shot in the head, and my first instinct is to run. I shove against his chest and rear my head back, only to have him cup the back of my neck and tuck my head under his chin.

"You're safe, Thalia," he murmurs repeatedly as he gently massages my neck. "Stop fighting me."

Every confusing emotion from the last twelve hours bursts out of me at once, and my tears soak this stranger's shirt as I fall apart in his arms.

I have no idea what's going on, only that my life is in ruins, and I'm apparently at the top of a hit list. I haven't had time to process my brother's death, the bloodshed I witnessed, or the things I heard. I'm furious with my brother, yet also coming to terms with the violent way his life ended right in front of my eyes.

All these thoughts swirl and clash inside my head as I heave out ugly sobs and collapse into the arms of the tall, dark stranger who showed up on my doorstep.

"Who… who a-are you?" I manage to squeak when the worst of my crying is over.

"Romeo," he states matter-of-factly.

I tilt my head back, taking in his sharp features and angular jaw. His dark eyes bore into me with an intensity I feel down to my toes. Squinting my eyes at him, I try to decide if he's telling me the truth or if this is some messed up pickup line.

"It's a family name," he continues. "Trust me, I'm no Shakespearian knight in shining armor."

"Neither was Romeo. He killed himself when he thought his true love was dead. Then she woke up, saw his lifeless body, and killed herself, too."

I'm not sure why I felt the need to correct him, but Romeo must find it amusing. His left eyebrow arches slightly, and he gets that same almost playful look in his eyes as when I explained how I could use my crochet hook to end his life.

"And people regard that as a love story?" Romeo frowns slightly, and his eyes narrow as he replays my words in his head. "Jesus," he mutters. "And I thought I had a fucked up view of love."

I'm not sure he meant for me to hear that last part, but I tuck that piece of information away. For what, I'm not sure, but it feels important.

I pull myself away from my mystery man, though I feel increasingly vulnerable the further away from him I get. When a crack sounds from right outside my window, I collapse onto the floor, instinctively covering my head with my hands and curling up into a ball.

Part of me knows it's not a gunshot, though it wouldn't be the first time I've heard that noise. But I'm hanging on to my sanity by a dangerously thin thread, and I've just been told I have powerful enemies looking for me.

I'm shocked when Romeo kneels in front of me, his index finger hooking under my chin and tilting my face toward his. Deep brown eyes search mine as he strokes my throat in a barely there touch. "We don't have much time. I know it's a lot to ask, but you have to trust me, *bella*."

I watch his lips form the last word, and my heart stutters in my chest at the almost reverent tone he uses.

He's right. I know he's right, yet this tiny studio apartment is all I have left. Something tells me that once I leave, I'll never be back.

"We both know you're not safe here," Romeo says, holding out his hand for me to take.

"But I'll be s-safe with you?" I whisper, tripping over my words.

"I will protect you with my life," he vows, those dark brown eyes latching onto mine as he clenches his jaw.

Everything about this man is severe, from his chiseled physique to his intense stare. I have no choice but to believe him. I peer up at the man who holds my life in his hands, then slide my palm against his and let him help me up. Romeo keeps his fingers wrapped around my hand, his gaze giving nothing away.

One thought keeps replaying in my mind; *Did I jump out of the frying pan right into the fire?*

CHAPTER FOUR

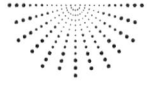

ROMEO

*H*er touch ruins me. Her soft skin and tender trust cast a spell over me, and I have a hard time letting go of this angel once she's standing on her own.

Green eyes filled with vulnerability blink up at me, and I struggle to take a full breath. What is this woman doing to me? Why do I have the sudden urge to burn the whole fucking world to the ground if it meant she never had to shed another tear?

Focus, I reprimand myself.

Ripping my gaze from Thalia, I take a step back, shuddering at the chill running down my spine. I find I don't like it when I'm not touching her in some way, but I can't dwell on that. First, I need to get her to safety. Then I need to find out what she knows.

As for the rest of my insanely possessive thoughts? I'll shove them down into the depths of my blood-stained soul. Pretty young women like Thalia don't belong in my world. There's no place for infatuation, especially for the fucking king of the underworld.

I know all too well what happens to the unlucky mafioso

bastards who get trapped with a woman. My parents were a prime example. They must have been in love once, but by the time I came into the picture, that love was replaced with cold shoulders, formalities, and a life of luxury to make up for a lack of affection.

I wipe a hand down my face, snapping myself out of whatever dark place I was in. None of that matters, and I'm not sure why I'm thinking about it now.

"Pack a bag," I tell Thalia, my tone brooking no arguments.

She searches around the small space, presumably for a duffel bag, while I peer out the living room window and check the surroundings. I haven't forgotten about the enforcer for the Colombos, but I also know he's likely taking his time to plan Thalia's torture to ensure he gets the answers he wants.

The thought of that motherfucker putting his filthy hands on Thalia makes something in me break loose. A snarl rumbles up from deep in my chest, but I cover it with a cough as best I can.

"Hurry," I grunt, needing to get this woman out of here before I lose my shit and hunt down our enemy's enforcer. I would do it in a heartbeat with no regrets, but that would make things more complicated and dangerous for Thalia. Apparently, my new goal in life is to make sure she's never in harm's way again.

Glancing over at the confounding woman making me feel all sorts of uncomfortable things, I notice she has a garbage bag clutched in one hand and is shoveling in all kinds of yarn, hooks, bobbles, and craft things I don't recognize.

"Are you making your own clothes?" I say before I can stop myself.

I shouldn't care what she brings with her. I promised her protection in exchange for information, but I was planning on placing her in a safe house with a few of my men guarding her. I have a contact in the real estate business who helps me find vacant properties for such occasions.

But that doesn't sit right with me anymore, though I'm not letting myself think about why. It can't be jealousy. Preposterous.

"Just concealing my weapons," she says over her shoulder.

My lips pull into a smirk at her sassy response, and something warm blooms in my chest. I think I'm... am I happy that she's comfortable enough around me to joke? It makes no sense, but then again, this whole interaction is throwing me for a loop. The sooner I get her out of here, the sooner I can get what I need and figure out what to do with her.

Keep her.

I shake my head at the thought. Impossible. It would never work. I don't want a relationship, and I sure as fuck don't need love in my life.

A few moments later, Thalia stands in front of me, holding the garbage bag so tightly that her knuckles are white. She nibbles her bottom lip as she looks down at her feet, which are now adorned with tattered old sneakers that won't stand a chance against the biting cold northeastern winter.

"Do you have better shoes? A hat and gloves? A coat?" I ask with a frown.

I want to punch myself in the face when I see her shoulders drop. Thalia curls in on herself, shaking her head no. I reach out on instinct, then pull my hand back. I need to stop touching her. It's becoming an addiction, and I don't know what to do about it.

"I'll get you set up with everything later today," I tell her, nodding once as I make a note to call Dante and have him work out the details. I can't get attached to her, but I can provide for her in this small way.

"No, I don't need—"

"Let's go," I say, cutting her off. Her protests are pointless. No woman of mine will walk around in ratty shoes and no coat.

Shit. Not that she's *mine*, per se. She's just under my protection. For now.

Motioning for Thalia to get behind me, I open the door, keeping my gun cocked and at my side. Peering into the dirt lot across the street where I saw the Colombo enforcer, I sigh with relief that his car is gone. I'm not sure if he saw me enter Thalia's apartment and ran or if he gave up without a fight, but I don't care. I'm just thankful there won't be any bloodshed in front of the traumatized woman trailing behind me.

As I make my way to my car, I keep a keen eye out for anyone staking out this place. I note my surroundings, logging the information away for later. It's been a while since I've been out in the field, getting my hands dirty with tasks such as collecting a witness, but old habits die hard. Every detail is important. It's where you find the devil, after all.

A soft warmth wraps around my left hand, and I look down, stunned to see Thalia's delicate fingers laced through mine. She's shaking, but her shoulders are square and her chin is up, broadcasting courage and determination even when she's scared out of her mind.

I ignore the sense of pride welling up in my chest at the thought of giving her confidence amid what has undoubtedly been the worst few days of her life.

Thalia tries to jerk her hand away from me as if realizing she's holding a stranger's hand, but I don't let her go. Not until I have her settled in the front seat with her seatbelt fastened over her lap. I know she's capable of doing it herself, but she's under my protection. It's now my job to ensure she's secure in every way, including car rides.

It's a flimsy excuse to touch her, to be closer to this intoxicating woman, but I don't have time to worry about that. This will all be over soon.

Climbing into the driver's seat, I start the car and begin winding my way through the city to the Di Salvo compound. The trash-filled streets littered with shacks and condemned buildings briefly turn into an industrial landscape before giving way to the Brooklyn Bridge.

Thalia is silent the entire ride, and I glance at her, wondering what she's thinking. She still has the garbage bag in her lap, and her fingers nervously pick at the plastic tie at the top as she stares out the front windshield.

I force myself to pay attention to the road instead of letting my eyes follow the slope of her nose or taking in her full curves. She's beautiful in a way I don't understand. A quiet strength resides inside this woman, and it somehow shines through with every blink, every breath, and every word from her lips.

"Where are we?" she breathes out as I pull up to the gate surrounding my house and the compound beyond it.

The guard standing post nods at me before opening the gate, his eyes lingering on Thalia longer than I can stand. I glare at him when he turns his attention to me, and a satisfied huff leaves my chest when I see the color drain from his face.

"My home," I tell her matter-of-factly.

I expect her to ask a few questions, like who the hell am I, and why do I own a fucking four-story mansion guarded by a wrought-iron fence and four heavily armed men? Instead, Thalia nods, her inquisitive green eyes taking in every inch of the immaculate garden, stone path, and fountain in the front yard. I probably should have blindfolded her or something. Hell, if she were any other witness, and I had one of my men collect her, she would likely be tied up in the trunk.

A sharp pain cracks through my chest, and I cough as I rub the heel of my hand over the spot. Jesus, I'm losing it. My first thought is that I'd rip the head off of anyone who shoved my Thalia into a trunk.

Once I pull my car into the empty spot in my six-car garage, I hop out and collect Thalia and her bag of yarn. I try taking it from her, but she clasps it to her chest like a safety blanket or a cherished stuffed toy.

Guiding the gorgeous and terrified woman inside through the back door, I usher her straight into my office. I need to discover what she witnessed so I know how I can protect her.

Thalia stands in the doorway, shuffling her weight from foot to foot.

"Take a seat, Thalia," I say in the calmest voice I can muster. "And start from the beginning."

She stares at the ornate couch upholstered with deep red velvet adorned with golden silk embossed pillows, then looks down at her clothes. It takes me a second to figure out what's going through her head, but then I realize she thinks she's going to get it dirty.

I try not to feel my heart breaking for this young woman. I don't know her story, but I can tell she hasn't had a lot of love or affection in her life. I mean, shit. I haven't either, so I'm not sure why I suddenly want to comfort her and reassure her she can sit anywhere she goddamn pleases. I'm not sure that would help, though.

"Come on," I encourage as I take a seat. "Not many people get to enjoy this rare antique couch. It would be a shame for you to pass up the opportunity."

A shy smile graces Thalia's lips, and my confused cock springs to life. It's so beyond inappropriate, let alone baffling.

I can't remember the last time the fucker rose to the occasion.

Thalia sits a foot away from me, and I barely resist the urge to wrap my arm around her waist and pull her closer. When I see the trepidation and conflict in her eyes, I know I need to give her space for what she has to say.

"Tell me what happened last night," I say softly, sitting forward with my elbows on my knees.

Thalia inhales deeply, and her eyelids flutter closed as she exhales. "I knew I shouldn't have gone to the plant so late at night," she starts, her voice barely above a whisper. "But Thomas forgot the dinner I packed, and I wanted to find a back entrance so I could give it to him."

I nod, listening to every word and weighing it in my mind. There's no doubt she's telling me the truth. I hardly know this woman, yet I can picture her packing a meal for her brother, who likely doesn't give a shit, and going the extra mile to ensure he gets it.

Thalia goes on to tell me about Thomas and Martin getting into an argument over missing money, which I make a note to check on later. Her breath hitches as she describes the three men who joined them, all of whom undoubtedly work for the Colombos.

"It all happened so fast, and yet it felt like an eternity," she murmurs, sniffling slightly before continuing. "They sh-shot Thomas first, and there was... so much blood. Dark red, seeping over the concrete, coming right for me..."

She shudders as she trails off, and I find myself placing a hand on her thigh to comfort her. It's a strange instinct to have, comforting someone. Then again, it shouldn't surprise me. This woman is bringing out all sorts of desires I've suppressed for so long.

"What happened next?" I ask softly, pulling her out of the dark spiral she was heading toward. I remember the first execution I saw. It's seared into my blackened soul. I was eleven.

Thalia blinks, then looks down at my hand resting on her leg. She rests her hand over mine and takes a calming breath.

We spend the next ten minutes picking apart the conversation between Martin and the Colombo goons, and somehow, Thalia ends up curled into my side, her head nestled in the crook of my neck while my arm rests around her waist. I'm unsure how it happened, but I can't bring myself to scoot away from her.

"Thank you for telling me what you saw," I whisper onto the top of her head.

Thalia doesn't say anything, so I lean back to get a better look at her. A soft snore rises from where she's buried against me, and that same sense of pride from earlier threatens to explode from my chest. She's sound asleep, the full weight of her voluptuous body pressed against me.

I take a moment to drink in her features, my fingers finding her silky auburn hair and tucking it behind her ear to give me a better view. Her porcelain cheeks are tinged with pink, and her pouty lips are parted slightly as she takes deep breaths.

The poor girl is drained, as if it took every last drop of energy to tell me what she saw. I have no doubt that it did. I still have no idea what I'm going to do with her now I have the information I need, but for now, she needs rest.

I stand with Thalia in my arms, unreasonably satisfied when she curls up against my chest. Fuck, it feels good having her right here, her supple curves and soft body pressed against the hard slats of my muscles.

As I carry her through my home and up two flights of stairs, I contemplate tucking her into my bed. However, I don't want her to assume I want any kind of *payment* for her protection. Not only would I never disrespect her like that, but I don't deal in that kind of business. Neither do my men.

Ultimately, I decide to place her in the room next to mine. I pull the blankets back before gently laying Thalia on the queen-sized canopy bed. I carefully slip her sneakers off, tossing them into the hallway so I can throw them out with the garbage. She'll have a new wardrobe when she wakes up.

Tucking the comforter around her, I have a difficult time not smelling her hair or kissing the side of her neck where I see her pulse thrumming. It takes a considerable effort to tear myself away from Thalia, but I manage to walk the fifteen steps into the hallway before closing the door.

I rest my forehead against the cool, polished wood, wondering what the hell I've gotten myself into.

CHAPTER FIVE

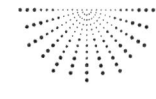

THALIA

$\mathcal{I}$ roll over in bed, my eyes still heavy with sleep, as I gather the blankets and secure them around me. The soft silk sheets are cool and comforting against my skin, which is the first sign I'm in an unfamiliar place.

Freezing, I try to remember where I am and how I got here as I slowly blink my eyes open. I'm surrounded by dark gray silk sheets, a warm, heavy comforter, and a mountain of plush pillows scattered about.

I cautiously sit up, taking a moment to stretch my sore, aching muscles. The bed is gorgeous, with four posts and a sheer white canopy draped between them. I feel like a princess as I settle back into the luxurious nest I somehow woke up in.

The small smile tugging at my lips drops as the memory of the last few days seeps into my fantasy.

Gruesome images flash through my brain, skyrocketing my heart rate. Thomas was shot. I watched him bleed out. I have nothing and no one left except the mysterious Romeo, who promised me his protection.

I try taking a calming breath, only to choke on the panic crawling up my throat.

Powerful men are looking for me and want me dead because of what I saw. I'm pretty sure I can trust Romeo, for now, at least. I already told him what he wants to know, though. Maybe I should have strung him along and given him a reason to keep me under his roof.

I wasn't exactly thinking clearly when the massive man knocked on my door earlier this morning. In fact, I don't remember coming into this room at all. My last memory is telling Romeo about the conversation I heard between my brother, Martin, and the three men who showed up.

My face flushes when I think about the way his hand stretched out over my thigh, grounding me yet making me jumpy and tingly at the same time. I faintly remember leaning against Romeo when I finally confessed everything that had been tangling up my mind. As the last word slipped from my lips, the final drop of energy evaporated, and I needed his strength to hold me up.

He must have carried me into this room.

My body flushes at the thought, but I immediately dismiss it. I don't know much about Romeo other than he has some sort of stake in Martin and my brother's death, and he lives in a freaking mansion with armed security guards. A man like that doesn't busy himself taking care of damsels in distress. I'm sure he got whatever he needed and told one of his presumably dozens of staff members to find a room to stick me in.

Still, I can't help but close my eyes and breathe in the remnants of his sandalwood and spice scent. It clings to me and calms me in a way I don't understand.

My stomach makes an angry sound, alerting me that I haven't eaten in almost twenty-four hours. I'm not sure what to do with myself or if I'm welcome here anymore. For all I know, I fell asleep in Romeo's office and he put me some-where until I woke up and he could kick me out.

Something tells me he isn't like that, however. If he wanted me gone, he wouldn't have offered his protection, right? And he wouldn't take me deeper into his opulent home and let me dirty up his pristine furniture.

Speaking of…

I groan as my fingers attempt to comb through my knotted hair. I'm suddenly aware of every grain of dirt resting on my skin, every particle of dust and grime, and every salty tear that has dried on my face over the last day and a half.

Springing from the bed, I'm terrified of leaving traces of myself and my mess on the expensive bedding. I notice an en suite bathroom and make my way over there, pausing when I see several outfits laid out on a couch across the room.

I'm drawn to the pastel colors and soft-looking material of a cozy-looking sweater, and my fingers brush over the fabric in a barely there touch. Out of curiosity, I examine the tag, surprised to find it's my size. My eyes drift to the rest of the clothes, and I'm shocked to see a variety of shirts, dresses, pajamas, and even a coat, all in my size.

There's a beautiful gift bag with pink tissue paper sticking out of the top, and I can't help but peek inside. My eyes go wide when I see all kinds of silk and lace panties and bras. With heated cheeks, I examine their tags, my face turning fuchsia when I realize that these, too, are all my size.

Romeo mentioned that he'd get me a coat when he saw I didn't have one, but I assumed he meant he'd lend me one of his old ones or something. The coat is sapphire blue and filled with down feathers. The hood is removable and lined with fur, and it's the softest, warmest, most expensive thing anyone has ever given me.

As for the rest of the clothes? I had no idea the man was

going to order a whole new wardrobe for me. Is he expecting me to pay him back? He has to know I don't have any money.

My stomach growls more insistently this time, and I quickly decide to shower and throw on some of my new clothes. If I'm going to be indebted to Romeo forever, I might as well look good while doing it.

Twenty minutes later, I feel human again. I haven't had a hot shower in longer than I can remember. The shower in my apartment was lukewarm at best, and that only lasted for the first five minutes. Don't even get me started on the satiny body wash and delicate floral shampoo and conditioner. I don't think my hair has ever been this shiny or my skin this smooth. I also had no idea how scratchy my cotton blend shirt and ancient jeans were until slipping into a pair of fitted leggings and the cashmere sweater I was first drawn to.

I've learned that good things don't last long for me, so I plan to enjoy this slice of the high life.

After slipping on a pair of thick wool socks, I open the door enough to poke my head through. The hallway stretches endlessly to the left and right, so I pick a direction and start walking. Passing numerous closed doors, I wonder how many rooms this place has and what Romeo does with them all.

Eventually, I find a staircase. Placing a trembling hand on the dark wood of the railing, I descend, following my hunger as it hopefully leads me to the kitchen.

A few moments later, I wander through what appears to be a study of sorts and then a dining room. On the other side is a door leading to a massive kitchen with high-tech, restaurant-grade appliances.

No one is in sight, which I appreciate. I'm not sure if I'm supposed to stay in my room, but my hunger won out in the end. Surely Romeo will understand. Eyeing up the fridge, I decide against it, not wanting to use the microwave or oven to heat anything.

"Bingo," I say to myself when I spot what I hope is a pantry.

I make my way over to find some crackers or cereal or something. Like everything in this house, the pantry is huge and well-stocked. It's nearly as big as my room upstairs and filled with enough food to feed an army.

I'm busy scanning the shelves for something to grab and take upstairs when a door across the hallway swings open and slams against the wall. Gasping, I hold my breath and stand completely still, praying that whoever it is doesn't come into the kitchen.

"Jesus, Armando. Take it easy," comes Romeo's deep voice.

"Sorry, boss," comes the reply. "Don't know my own strength."

Romeo grunts, and then another man speaks up.

"Are you clear on your mission?" he clips out.

"Yes, Dante. Same as every mission," Armando answers. "Crack some skulls, get some names, and further the Di Salvo reign."

Di Salvo. That sounds familiar, but where have I heard it before?

"Smart ass," Dante mutters.

"Emphasis on smart. Only the best for Romeo Di Salvo, right, boss?"

Boss. It's not that strange, I suppose, but it's the second time Armando has referred to Romeo as boss. I'm on the verge of putting the pieces of a very confounding puzzle together, but I don't have the original picture to work from.

The men shuffle further down the hallway, their voices still raised enough for me to hear.

"I don't know what you saw in him or why he's made it so far up the ranks," the man referred to as Dante says.

"I can hear you, you know," Armando sing-songs.

"And yet you're still here and not out doing your job."

"Enough," Romeo commands. Silence blankets the entire floor. "Armando, you have your orders. Dante, you know not to question who I bring into the family."

"Yes, boss," both men mutter. It's the last of the conversation I can make out before it fades away completely.

Family. Boss. Di Salvo.

Didn't Martin accuse my brother of working for the Di Salvos? He made it seem like that would be a fate worse than death, though in the end, death came for him anyway.

The realization of whose house I'm in hits me square in the chest. I grow light-headed, and little dots float in and out of my vision as I place my hands on the shelf in front of me to keep from collapsing to the floor.

Romeo Di Salvo, of the Di Salvo crime family.

A freaking mafia man.

A criminal mastermind.

What the fuck have I gotten myself into?

The pantry shrinks in size, the walls closing in as my breathing grows shallow. Once again, my world is thrown into chaos, and I don't know who to trust, if anyone.

I close my eyes and force the panic down, taking a few deep breaths to get the oxygen flowing again. Loosening my grip on the wooden shelf, I stretch my cramped fingers and try to come up with a plan.

First things first. I need to find my way back to my room.

Summoning all of my courage, I slowly open the pantry door and peek around the kitchen, relieved to see the coast is clear. Carefully and quietly, I step out of the pantry and gently close the door before tiptoeing across the room and into the hallway.

I'm almost to the winding staircase when a hand clasps my shoulder from behind and spins me around. Terror rattles through me, and I let out a silent scream as my back is pressed against a wall.

Familiar dark eyes meet mine, and even though I can feel my pulse pounding against the side of my neck, some part of me is comforted by Romeo's sandalwood scent.

"Spying on me?" he whispers, half of his face cast in shadows.

Romeo lifts his left brow in question, and my eyes are drawn to the scar there. God, this man is all sharp angles and darkness, yet I know down to my very soul he wouldn't hurt me.

I shake my head no, then gulp as I blink at him. Romeo's fingertips trace along the neckline of my sweater, making me tremble, though I'm not sure if it's from fear or anticipation. Every part of me is extra sensitive, seemingly aware of his presence on a molecular level.

"I love this on you," he says mostly to himself as he continues to run his fingers along the scooped neckline of the shirt I'm wearing. Romeo shakes his head slightly as if remembering to focus. "What exactly did you hear, *bella*?"

"N-nothing," I stutter.

Romeo's brown eyes snap to mine, and a smirk twists one side of his lips. He leans forward, his lips barely grazing the shell of my ear. "You're a terrible liar, Thalia."

I automatically tip my head to the side to give him more access, apparently starving for any attention this man is willing to offer. My back arches as he scrapes his stubble against the sensitive skin of my neck, my body rolling forward and seeking contact with his. Romeo lets out a tortured groan, resting both hands on my hips and anchoring me in place while he presses his large frame against me.

"I'll ask you again," he hums, the sound low and gravelly in his throat. "What did you hear?"

I squirm under his attention. My hands find his chest and travel up, up, up, studying every chiseled muscle along the way. I have no idea what I'm doing, only that I can't stop. Spreading out my fingers over the flat of his chest, I peer up at him, my breath catching in my throat when I see the feral look in his eyes.

"J-just your name," I breathe.

Romeo narrows his eyes at me, letting me know he's not buying it.

"Your last n-name," I clarify.

"Ah," he says with a nod. "And that scares you?"

I'm not sure how to answer because, yes, it should scare me. But truthfully? Some twisted part of me likes having a monster on my side. I've been pitted against them my whole life, and now I have the biggest, baddest one promising me his protection.

"Are you in the mafia?" I whisper, nibbling on my bottom lip as I wait for his answer.

Romeo chuckles darkly, the deep vibrations rolling through his body and into mine. Every nerve ending sizzles and pops as his body moves against me.

"I *am* the mafia, little girl," he rasps, dragging his nose and lips down the column of my throat as his hands tighten around my hips.

He nips at my pulse point, causing me to shudder and let out a breathy cry. Romeo presses his warm, wet tongue against the sore spot, licking once before placing a kiss on top.

I shouldn't be this turned on. I shouldn't feel this all-consuming pressure in my lower belly or the incessant throbbing between my thighs. My hands ball into fists, and I clutch Romeo's shirt as he scrapes his teeth down the other side of my neck.

"You taste too good, *bella*," he whispers onto my skin.

"I… I-I…"

My body is buzzing, my breath caught in my lungs as my eyes flutter open and closed. This man is barely touching me, and yet I swear to God I'd melt into a puddle of lust if he weren't pinning me to the wall.

"It's okay, angel," he murmurs. "You need never fear me. I am a powerful man, yes, and the commander of a mighty army. But I will only ever use my strength to keep you safe. Do you believe me?"

Romeo leans back slightly, and I sway toward him before catching myself. I'm surprised when he cradles my face in his large hand, making me feel so precious with his tender touch.

Brown eyes lock onto mine, but for the first time, I see something other than the carefully constructed persona Romeo projects. He lets me in for a brief moment. Whether or not he knows it, Romeo is showing me his heart. This man is filled with contradictions, but his word is his bond. I know that to be true in an instant. He's loyal, fierce, and crushingly lonely, though he'd never admit it to anyone.

Still, he's a criminal. He's involved in my brother's death somehow, or at the very least, he knows more than he's letting on. I shouldn't trust him. I shouldn't let him touch me like this. I shouldn't feel safe and seen, and I definitely shouldn't be so freaking turned on.

"I want to," I finally answer. "I want to believe you. I just…"

"I know, sweet Thalia. Life hasn't been kind to you."

I nod, once again caught up in his hypnotic gaze. Romeo peers into the depths of my being, soaking up everything about this shared moment.

Someone clears their throat, and I jump back, only to bang my head against the wall. Romeo growls and glares at the man who appeared a few feet away.

"Sorry to interrupt, boss," the man I now recognize as Dante says. His sharp eyes flit from Romeo to me, then back to Romeo. "We've got places to be."

Romeo straightens and takes a large step away from me, straightening his shirt and jacket. One look in his deep brown eyes, and I know the mask is firmly back in place. Whoever he was a moment ago is gone, and he's back to being in control.

"I know," he snaps at Dante. "I'm tying up loose ends."

Dante grunts as my heart sinks. I'm the loose end. I don't know what else I would be, and I feel like a fool for getting caught up in Romeo's games. That's all this is. It has to be.

I slip away from the wall and make a break for the stairs, taking them two at a time.

"Thalia," Romeo calls after me, but I don't stop.

"I'll be in my room," I tell him over my shoulder, unsure what else to say. I'm a naïve idiot, a stupid little girl with a misplaced and totally inappropriate crush.

Romeo mutters something, and Dante offers a half-hearted apology before the two walk out of sight.

Sprinting to my room, I shut the door and rest my back against it before sliding down and sprawling out on the carpet.

What the hell was that? And what am I supposed to do now?

CHAPTER SIX

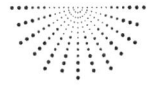

ROMEO

"*B*rent Carmichael was voted in as the replacement for Martin," Dante informs me as he paces my office.

Leaning back in my chair, I cross my arms over my chest as I wait for him to continue. My second in command is nothing if not detail-oriented. It's almost pathological at this point, and it'd be annoying as hell if it didn't make him so damn good at his job.

Sure enough, Dante rattles off Mr. Carmichael's resume, the names of his family members, which grade school he attended, and every known address he's had in the last twenty years. It's all good information, and as I look around the room at my most trusted men, I know they are listening and storing it away for later.

Good thing, too, since I haven't been able to concentrate since Thalia ran away from me yesterday afternoon.

What the hell was I thinking, cornering her like that? Touching her like that? Fuck, tasting her sugary-sweet skin and feeling her pulse beneath my lips as I pressed them to her sensitive flesh…

"But we all know Martin's death isn't the real issue here," Dante continues.

His eyes dart to mine, silently asking permission to brief everyone on the latest update. I give him a subtle nod and pretend to be focused while he tells the men what they're up against.

"Colombos again?" Armando grunts. The massive man leans forward from his sitting position on the couch in my office, resting his elbows on his knees. "I knew I shouldn't have given that last fucker a warning. Shoulda ended his pathetic life then and there."

Dante stops his fidgeting and glares at Armando. The two of them but heads all the time, but I need both men in my inner circle. Dante is calculating and methodical, while Armando would rather bash in faces first and ask questions later. Left in Dante's hands, nothing would get done, and if the decisions were solely based on Armando's wishes, we'd all be dead in a bloody war by this time next week.

It's all about balancing power and delegating tasks to the right person.

"Believe it or not, the answer to everything isn't *punch it until it stops talking*," Dante snaps.

"We could try it on you first and see if we get the desired results," Armando fires back. He's mostly joking to get a rise from the admittedly up-tight Dante, but I have neither the time nor patience for their squabbling today.

I clear my throat, and both men fall silent as their eyes meet mine. "We know the Colombos were trying to get Martin to go into business with them instead of us. He fucked up and got himself and his accomplice killed. Brent is a wildcard, but the Di Salvo captain of that area, Valentino, is working on a deal with him. The bigger problem is the motherfucking Colombos thinking they can waltz onto our territory and take over our contracts."

"Yes, Boss."

"Sorry, Boss."

I grunt, then nod at Dante to keep going. He knows I'm distracted and have other things on my mind, but like the good second-in-command he is, he doesn't question me. At least not in front of the other men.

Ten minutes later, however, the room is empty, aside from Dante and me.

"It's that woman, isn't it?" he says as soon as we're alone.

I glare at him but don't deny the accusation. "She's a loose end," I tell him yet again. The words taste bitter on my lips, and my stomach twists into a knot when I think about Thalia's face when I said the same thing yesterday.

"Yeah, and I believe you as much now as I did when you first said it," Dante counters. "Come on, Romeo. What's really going on?"

I sigh, rubbing a hand down my face. Dante is a good man, the most loyal I've ever met. Still, can I trust him with these insane thoughts plaguing me? I don't know how to feel, let alone how to articulate the spell Thalia has cast over me.

"She's under my protection," I hedge, buying time to find the right words.

Dante narrows his eyes, but thankfully his concentration is broken when his phone buzzes in his pocket. He takes it out, frowning when he looks at the screen.

"Your father?" I venture, noting the irritation and heaviness in his gaze. Dante is an extremely private man—we all are in this business—and I don't know much about his family besides his father being unwell and has been for some time.

Dante grunts, typing away furiously on his phone. "The new nurse," he mutters. "She has some frou-frou ideas about meditation and yoga to help my father manage his pain."

"Interesting," I offer, glad to have the spotlight off me.

"No, it isn't," Dante clips out. "I'm not paying her to sit

cross-legged and chant. I'm paying her so I don't have to deal with my old man."

I nod, though my second-in-command doesn't seem to notice. He groans and shakes his head when his phone buzzes with a returning text. Dante turns to leave my office, and I'm almost in the clear when he looks at me over his shoulder, his dark eyes meeting mine.

"I'm not sure what kind of infatuation you have with that woman, but it's my duty to remind you what this life is really like and what it would be like for any… *romantic* partners." He stumbles over the last few words, his distaste for relationships evident in his tone. "There's a reason we're both single."

I grunt in acknowledgment, though I don't say anything. He's right, of course, but he doesn't need to know that. Dante gives me a final warning look before focusing his anger on the yoga-loving nurse he's been texting all morning.

After Dante shuts my office door, I get buried in work. Despite what Hollywood would have you believe, the life of a mafia king involves a lot more phone calls and business appointments than clandestine meetings and territory wars. The dirty work is left to those beneath me while I sit at the top, untouchable.

And lonely.

No. Alone, but not lonely. At least, not until one little miss Thalia Brooks showed up in my life.

Bright green eyes fill my vision, surrounded by auburn hair. I swear I can smell her rosemary and peppermint scent. Try as I might to shove thoughts of the voluptuous vixen from my mind, she remains ever-present.

Unfolding myself from my desk chair, I take a moment to stretch out the kinks in my neck and back. I've been hunched over my desk for hours now and blown right through lunch and dinner. No wonder everything aches.

I close out my computer and put everything on lockdown

before heading downstairs to my home gym. A few rounds with the sand-filled punching bag should ease some of my tension.

Stripping down to a pair of sweatpants, I forego the boxing gloves and land a crushing blow to the bag. It rattles in its chains, absorbing the hit along with my pent-up energy. Over and over, I let out my frustration, my confusion, and my chaotic emotions one swing at a time until I'm drenched in sweat.

"Fuck," I exhale, holding the punching bag between my palms as I rest my sweaty forehead on the cool surface. My shoulders heave with labored breaths, and my heart hammers against my ribcage in a staccato rhythm.

When my breathing has somewhat returned to normal, I grab a towel from the shelf in the corner, wiping down my face and chest. I have every intention of going back to my room, showering, and ordering a late dinner before retiring to bed. Yet, I somehow find myself approaching Thalia's room, my feet shuffling forward with a mind of their own.

Her door is cracked open slightly, and like the predator I am, I fade into the shadows as I continue my hunt. Thalia is propped up in bed, surrounded by several balls of yarn, throw pillows, and a pile of blankets. She's busy crocheting something tiny in her hands. I can't explain my need to find out what it is or my insane jealousy that she's caressing the yarn instead of me.

"Jesus," I mutter as I step closer to the ray of sunshine beaming from inside the guest room.

Her reddish-brown hair is gathered to one side in a soft braid, her cheeks dusted with freckles and a slight blush. I watch as Thalia nibbles her bottom lip and tilts her head to the side, examining what appears to be a little stuffed dog in her hands.

Adorable. Precious. Ethereal.

All words I've never used to describe another human being, but Thalia epitomizes each one. With her slightly upturned nose, flushed cheeks, and green eyes narrowed in concentration, she looks like a delicate little angel weaving magic and happiness into her current crochet project.

I move forward, then stop, squeezing my hands into fists at my sides. I want to scoop her up, cradle her against my chest, and finally, fucking finally, claim her sweetness.

Dante's words echo through my head, giving me pause.

It's my duty to remind you what this life is like and what it would be like for any romantic partners.

Thalia is a beacon of innocence who fucking crochets stuffed toy animals. She's shy and beautiful and precious… far too precious for a man like me to know how to handle. She doesn't belong in my world. She doesn't belong with *me*.

I grunt as the tightness in my chest grows to an unbearable level. Thalia freezes, causing me to do the same. Slowly, so slowly, she lifts her head, those emerald eyes drawn to mine as if following some invisible string.

She doesn't startle, doesn't gasp, doesn't seem frightened or freaked out that I'm staring at her. She simply blinks, and her gorgeous eyes drink me in. I forgot I'm only wearing sweatpants, and I suddenly feel exposed and vulnerable in a wholly unfamiliar way.

Our eyes remain locked, and Thalia's gaze turns inquisitive as she sets down the yarn and crochet hook. In slow motion, she swings one leg over the edge of the bed and then the other, approaching as if I'm a wild animal.

When she stands, something in me snaps back to reality.

I take a step back, spin on my heel, and sprint to my room next door, shutting the door with a bang. Leaning against the solid oak, I bury my head in my hands, trying to keep my racing thoughts from spilling out.

I don't know how to talk to her or what to say, yet I can't let her go. For now, it has to be enough that she's under my protection.

CHAPTER SEVEN

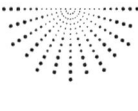

THALIA

"*O*ne... more... stitch... and... done!" I whisper to myself in the early hours of the morning.

Reaching over to grab my small scissors on the nightstand, I snip the yarn and weave the end back into the previous stitches to hide it.

I lean against the headboard of my luxurious bed and admire my handy work. It took me all night to finish this project, but it's not like I was going to get much sleep anyway. Between nightmares about my brother's execution, the uncertainty of my future, and the big, brooding mafia king brushing me off and ignoring me the last two days, my racing thoughts have made for restless nights.

Aside from being lonely, I can't complain about how I've been treated during my stay with Romeo. Not only is my room equipped with a big screen TV and all the streaming channels, but I also have a full en suite bathroom with a clawfoot tub and a freaking towel warmer rack. I didn't even know that was an option, and here it is, sitting in a guest room that, as far as I can tell, has been unoccupied for a long time before I showed up.

Meals are delivered to my room three times a day, as well as a small snack and a cup of tea around three in the afternoon. I've tried talking to the older woman who drops off the food, but she either doesn't hear me or doesn't care to respond.

The first day I was here, I was able to knock out all the orders in the queue from my online shop, Cute Crochet Creatures. I even made little beds for each animal and added them for free, so hopefully, I'll have some happy customers who want to keep doing business with me.

I was alone the second day, and my anxiety kicked into high gear. Am I a prisoner here? Romeo never told me I had to stay in my room, but he didn't seem too pleased when he found me sneaking around the kitchen. Plus, it's not like I want to waltz around the mansion of a crime lord all willy-nilly. Who knows what conversations I might overhear? I learned my lesson about eavesdropping, *thankyouverymuch*.

I run the tips of my fingers over the small crochet stitches, letting the feeling ground me back into this moment. I didn't have a pattern for this project, only a vision of what I wanted. It turned out pretty adorable, if I do say so myself. I just hope Romeo likes it.

My heart kicks against my ribcage, causing the butterflies in my stomach to swarm. God, I'm pathetic.

I keep replaying the last thing I heard Romeo say. I'm a loose end to tie up. I'm the leftovers from a problem far beneath his pay grade. I'm inconsequential.

Then why hasn't he tossed you out yet? My unhelpful brain asks.

I've been wrestling with that question all night, which is why I decided to crochet away my angst in the first place. Romeo promised me his protection, but for how long? Am I supposed to stay here indefinitely? And do what with my time? Will he eventually tire of having me around and send me on my way?

Closing my eyes, I take a few calming breaths, forcing the whirlwind of unanswered questions to cease with each inhale and exhale. Dark brown eyes fill my mind, sharp, exquisite, and tinged with unbearable sadness. Just like the night he waited outside my door, watching me crochet.

I can't explain it, but I sensed his presence before I saw him. Every cell in my body was aware of him, every nerve ending firing the longer he stood there, looming in the doorway. I could only see what the light from my small bedside lamp illuminated, but I could tell he was shirtless. Breathless, too.

My eyes wandered down the contours of his physique, rippling with muscles, tattoos, and old wounds. I wanted to ask him if his scars still hurt or if covering them up with ink helped numb the pain. I wanted to reach out and smooth my hands over the canvas of his skin, tracing his tattoos as he told me the story behind each one.

I cautiously moved toward the confounding man of secrets and sorrows, but he got spooked and ran away. It's almost laughable that Romeo Di Salvo, revered Don of the Di Salvo crime family, could be spooked by little old me, but I don't have any other word for it. He was like a panicked bunny rabbit caught in the crosshairs.

Who made you afraid of kindness? I wonder for the hundredth time since that evening.

Something in his eyes revealed a truth I'm not sure even Romeo is aware of. It's obvious he doesn't trust anyone, and probably for good reason. That night, however, the longing in his soul was so clear. He *wants* to be seen. To be known. Possibly even to be... loved? He just doesn't think he deserves it.

Romeo's aching soul was revealed, and I wanted nothing

more than to cradle it in my hands and promise him he was safe with me. Like he keeps promising I'm safe with him.

He ran away before I could say anything, though, and I haven't seen him since. I want to help him, to ease the heartache he's been carrying around for so long, but I don't have much at my disposal. Just yarn and a few crochet hooks.

Sighing, I look at the clock on the nightstand, seeing it's past six in the morning. I suppose now is as good a time as any to deliver my gift to Romeo. Not face to face, of course. I don't even know where to find him, let alone what to say to the man.

I get out of bed and throw a robe over my pajama shorts and tank top, hoping I won't run into anyone this early in the morning. Gathering up my gift and all of my courage, I open the bedroom door and peer out into the dark hallway. Empty, like I had hoped.

My plan is to leave the present on Romeo's desk or possibly in front of his office door if he keeps everything locked up at night. It's such a small thing, and he'll probably think it's silly, but my customers tell me my little crochet creations always brighten their days. That's what I want to give Romeo. A reason to smile.

As I tiptoe down the spiral staircase, I question my decision-making skills. Is it a good idea to be sneaking around this place? The last time I tried doing something nice for someone, I witnessed a terrible crime and put my life in danger. Do I have a death wish or something?

Still, my feet move forward despite my brain's protests. When I reach the bottom of the stairs, it takes a moment to remember which way the office is. I was only there once when I arrived at the Di Salvo compound.

A memory of that day floods my mind. Romeo was so gentle with me, encouraging me to sit, resting his hand on my knee when I broke down, and holding me while I told him every-thing I had witnessed. There's so much goodness, so much kindness buried deep inside. He just needs a reason to show it.

Gliding along the hardwood floor, I let the cool surface calm me and refocus my thoughts. I'll pop into Romeo's office, set down the little present, then hightail it back to–

"Thalia?"

I squeak at the raspy voice, startled when I look up to see Romeo himself sitting at his desk. It's only six in the morn-ing, yet he's dressed in a crisp black suit and white button-up. Though he's not wearing a tie. Must be casual Friday or something.

"Uh…"

"What are you doing here?" he grunts, furrowing his brow.

I'm about to tell him I got lost and sprint back up to my room, but Romeo stands from his desk, holding his hand out to welcome me inside.

"Sit," he commands.

He closes his eyes, a flustered look taking over his features. I didn't think a man like Romeo could be caught off-guard, but it appears I've done the impossible.

"If you want," he adds.

I relax at his tone, finally understanding that he's trying to soften his usual gruffness for me. That thought has heat rising to my cheeks and trickling down my spine, making me aware of every single one of his movements.

"It's okay, I won't be long," I tell him as he walks around his desk, coming to a stop in front of me. I tilt my head back —way back—to meet his gaze. Sandalwood and spice permeate my senses, and the heat from his closeness warms me all the way down to my core. "Are you always up this early?" I ask, my voice breathless for some reason.

Romeo doesn't say anything for a moment, his deep brown eyes flitting between mine. He's trying to decide if I'm worthy of the truth. I hold my breath, begging him to trust me.

"I couldn't sleep," he finally answers, his dark gaze never leaving mine.

His words are heavy with exhaustion, and I know he's telling me the truth. It's a small win, but I'll take it.

"Do you have trouble sleeping a lot?"

Romeo shakes his head, and his eyes wander to the part in my robe before darting back up to meet mine. "No, *bella*," he finally answers, his voice low and raspy. "In all my years as a made man, I've rested easy, despite the bloodshed and horrors I've inflicted on this city."

I watch his lips form each word, and though his confession should startle me, it only draws me closer to him.

"But then you came into my life, and—" He cuts himself off, clearing his throat and taking a step back.

I sway back and forth, his sudden absence leaving me bereft.

"What are you doing up at this hour?" Romeo asks, leaning against his desk.

He crosses his arms over his chest, trying to close himself off from me, but it's too late. I know his secret now, though I'm not sure what to do with it.

"Couldn't sleep either," I answer, squeezing my fingers around the crocheted gift in my hand. Romeo frowns, but I press forward before I lose my courage altogether. "So I made these. For you. Uh… here."

I shove the two crochet skulls awkwardly into Romeo's chest, watching as his eyes grow wide in confusion. The two little skulls sit facing each other in the palm of his massive hand. One has a scar over its left eye socket, right where

Romeo's scar is. The other is wearing a crown of red and black roses.

I thought they were cute, and yes, some part of me was fantasizing about the scarred skull and the rose skull being an adorable goth couple representative of us, but obviously, that's all in my head. Looking at my gift now, I feel small and silly.

Romeo is a mafia king. His world is filled with violence, blood, and power. What is he going to do with two tiny, stupid crochet skulls?

"On second thought," I rush to say, fumbling to grab the pathetic offering, "I'll just–"

"They're mine," Romeo grunts, closing his hand and yanking it away from me so I can't reach it. "I'm keeping them forever."

This man. Even when he's being ridiculously sweet, he's still a growly beast.

I can't hide my smile as Romeo uncurls his hand and studies each skull individually. He traces the scar with his fingertip, and the corner of his lips twitch in an almost-smile. When his eyes finally meet mine once more, they are filled with vulnerability.

"I don't understand," he murmurs to himself. "No one has ever given me anything without wanting something in return."

My heart breaks for him. Romeo is six and a half feet of pure muscle and sin, yet the darkness in his soul evaporates the longer his brown eyes study mine. I sway closer to the enigmatic man, everything in me needing to comfort him, to show him the world isn't as cruel as he's experienced.

I rest my hand on his chest, right over his heart, surprised to find it racing. Romeo closes his eyes and tilts his head back, breathing in this moment, this connection between us.

"I just wanted to give you a reason to smile," I whisper.

A tortured sound rumbles up from his throat, and a fierce, feral glow emanates from his nearly black gaze when he lowers his head. "You're too good for me," he rasps. "I'll ruin you."

"Or maybe I'm perfect for you," I counter, unsure where this confidence is coming from. "Maybe we'll heal each other."

Romeo tentatively reaches out, tucking a few strands of hair behind my ear before trailing his fingertips down my neck. I shudder at the barely there touch, tilting my head up to give him better access. Every time this man touches me, my body cries out for more.

"I tried staying away from you," he rasps, those dark eyes softening as they follow the tender caresses of his fingertips. "Tried protecting you from myself and my life."

"You can protect us from everything else in this world, but I want to be the one to keep your heart safe. Don't hide from me anymore," I whisper, my eyes locking with his.

Romeo slowly wraps his hand around the front of my throat in a gentle yet firm grasp and pulls me closer, our lips inches apart. He closes his eyes and inhales deeply, letting the breath out with a contained growl. When he opens his eyes, they are filled with a need that matches mine.

"I can't live another second without knowing how sweet you taste," he murmurs right before squeezing my throat and closing the distance between us.

Romeo claims my mouth, stealing my first kiss and giving me more pleasure than I ever imagined. He pries my lips apart and pushes his tongue inside my mouth, licking and sucking on my tongue at a desperate, almost frantic pace.

I moan and press my thighs together to relieve some of the unbearable pressure building up between my legs. Romeo's other hand drifts over my hip and grips my ass, squeezing my sensitive flesh. Hard. I gasp into his mouth and automatically roll my hips against his.

He groans, trailing the hand at my neck down my body and into my open robe, cupping my breast and pinching my nipple through my thin tank top. I cry out, breaking our kiss as I tip my head back, exposing my throat to Romeo's greedy mouth. He scrapes his teeth down my neck and sucks a super-sensitive spot below my ear.

"Fuck," he mutters into my skin, trailing kisses lower and lower until he's nipping at the tops of my breasts. "I can't get enough of you. Knew I'd be addicted if I gave in…"

Romeo trails off, his nose and lips tracing a line from my breasts up to my neck, where he nips my pulse point before licking away the sting. I'm a trembling, wanton mess, and I know for sure I'd collapse if not for Romeo's large, capable hands holding me up.

He rests his forehead on mine, our heavy breaths mingling and slowing down little by little.

"Sweet Thalia," he whispers, stroking a hand down my spine while the other combs through my hair. "Can I thank you properly for my gift?"

"Wh-what do you mean?" I whisper, a lightning bolt of pleasure zapping through my veins and traveling to my core.

Romeo gives me a devilish smirk, leaning forward and brushing his lips against my ear. "Can I taste you everywhere, *bella*? I want to kiss every inch of your flesh and feel you shake with pleasure as I slide my tongue between your thighs."

"Oh, god," I moan as his hands open my robe and push the fabric off my shoulders, letting it pool at my feet.

"Tell me to stop, and I will," he grits, though he sounds like he's in pain. I have no doubt that Romeo could over-power me and take whatever he wants, but I know he would never harm me.

"Don't stop," I whisper. "Don't ever stop."

"Jesus, fuck," he groans. "What you do to me…"

He takes my lips in a searing kiss, the passion and need overwhelming me in the most intoxicating way. I fist the sides of his shirt, pulling him closer, needing more of his body rubbing against mine.

Romeo breaks our kiss only to nibble and lick his way down my body. Staring down at him, I can't help but feel powerful as the head of the Di Salvo crime family kneels before me, practically salivating as he stares at my core.

"Tell me how much you want it," he commands, his thumbs massaging little circles up the insides of my thighs.

"S-so much," I stutter.

"More," he growls, cupping my pussy and rubbing lightly back and forth.

God, it feels incredible, and yet it's not enough. He's not touching me where I need him most.

"Please, Romeo. I need you to t-touch me," I manage to breathe. "Everywhere. I ache. I ache for you," I beg, my breath catching in my throat as I mindlessly rub myself against him.

"Such a good girl," Romeo praises, his tone dark and filled with satisfaction. "And good girls get exactly what they ask for."

CHAPTER EIGHT

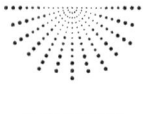

ROMEO

I rub my nose against the fabric covering her pussy and groan when I smell her arousal. I can feel her juices soaking through the material and wetting the tip of my nose as I nuzzle deeper into her.

I know I'm crossing a line, but I can't hold back. Can't contain my obsession, my addiction to this woman. One taste and I was hooked. Once I finally sink inside her sweetness, I'll never be able to let her go.

She shakes with anticipation as I caress her curves, anchoring her in place so I can worship her properly.

"Romeo…" she gasps when I replace my nose with my tongue, licking the wet fabric and then sucking on it.

When I can't stand it anymore, I hook my thumbs into the waistband of her panties and little sleep shorts, pulling them down in one swift move. She steps out of them and spreads her legs wider for me, causing a growl to rumble up from deep in my chest. It's all the permission I need.

I spread her pussy lips with my thumbs, which allows me to see her pretty pink folds, glistening with her juices. I can't wait another second. I dive right into her, lapping at her clit, spearing my tongue into her tight little hole and nipping at her outer lips. Her taste hits my tongue, the flavor exploding in my mouth and making me crazy with need. She's fucking delicious, and I know I'll be on my knees like this for her every damn day.

My hands slide up her curvy body and hold her by her hips, keeping her steady as her legs tremble. Thalia moans loudly when I guide one of her legs over my shoulder, opening her up even more for me.

"Lean against the desk, my beautiful girl," I tell her, my voice deeper than I've ever heard it before.

She obeys instantly, and my cock strains against the fabric of my pants, leaking precum like a motherfucker. I'm so hard it hurts, each beat of my heart making me throb and ache even more for my sweet and sexy Thalia.

She tangles her fingers in my hair as she grips me tightly and grinds herself against my face. I growl and lick her clit over and over until my tongue is numb. My sweet, filthy angel is riding my face like a goddess, her hips jerking, her eyes closed, her head thrown back in ecstasy as she cries out my name. I scrape my teeth over her little bundle of nerves and her muscles lock up, full of tension that so desperately needs to be released.

I suck on her clit, biting down one last time, and Thalia lets go of every-fucking-thing as she comes on my face. I lap up her juices as they pour out of her little hole. Spearing my tongue deep inside her still spasming channel, I growl when her walls pulse around me.

My angel releases more of her sweetness, screaming her pleasure while she shakes in my arms. I flick her clit with my tongue, making her leg slip from my shoulder as her other leg gives out. Holding her tight, I pin her to the desk and continue my assault, not stopping as she rides out the last wave of her orgasm.

Thalia slumps against the desk, then slides into my waiting arms, where I hold her close while she comes down from her high. I feel her ragged breaths and thumping heart as I cradle her in my arms and rub her back in calming circles.

Everything in me is screaming to tear off my clothes and claim her hard and fast, but I take a deep breath and focus on the precious woman in my arms.

"So perfect, angel," I whisper into her hair before placing a kiss on the top of her head. "Thank you for trusting me with your beautiful body."

Thalia sighs and looks up at me, her face flushed bright red from her orgasm and her eyes shining with lust and adoration. Damn, what I wouldn't do to have her look at me like that every second of every day.

"Thank you for being trustworthy," she replies before chewing her bottom lip nervously.

Something about her words hits me deep. I want her to trust me with her heart, her future, every single thing, not just her body. Could someone as pure as Thalia ever love a man with a stained soul? There's only one way to find out.

I kiss Thalia briefly and then stand with her in my arms. I grin down at her and kiss her cute little nose.

"I can walk," she insists, though she makes no move to get out of my arms. "I don't want you to hurt your back or something."

I stop in my tracks and look down at my gorgeous girl. "What?" What the hell is she talking about?

Thalia rolls her eyes, a look of annoyance and embarrassment flitting across her face. "I mean, you know. I'm..." She lifts her eyebrows and looks off to the side as if I'm supposed to fill in the blank, but I honestly have no idea what she's talking about. "Do I have to say it? I'm fat."

Rarely have I been blinded by rage, but hearing my angel

disparage herself has red clouding my vision. I don't think yelling at her to be nicer to herself is going to help, however. I guess I'll have to give her so many compliments and truths about herself that she'll forget every negative word anyone has ever spoken to her.

Does that make me crazy and obsessive? Probably. Ask me if I give a fuck.

"Thalia," I say as calmly as I can. "I don't know who hurt you or filled your head with lies, but you're mine now, do you understand? You're perfect as you are. Jesus, I love your thick thighs and soft curves. Love that there's more of you to explore. Will you let me show you?"

Her sharp green eyes pierce through me, tearing me apart and examining my words and motives one by one. I may have been distant the last few days, but I thought I was protecting her. I've come to my senses, however. The safest my Thalia will ever be is right here, in my arms. I'll stand here all damn night while she comes to her decision. I've never meant anything more in my entire life.

I watch as her eyes go from skeptical to hopeful. Finally, warmth and desire flood back into her gaze, and she leans up to kiss me.

Thank fucking god. I return her kiss and continue my path upstairs, toward my bedroom suite. When we get inside, I gently set Thalia on her feet and cradle her face in my hands. I kiss her forehead, her eyes, her nose, and finally, her soft, welcoming lips.

When we break apart, Thalia follows me like we're two magnets. I grin at her and give her one last chaste kiss.

"I love your pajamas, *bella*, but I think I'm going to love what's underneath them more," I tell her, my voice low and full of lust.

Her eyes twinkle with a devious spark, making my

painfully hard cock surge and twitch in my pants. "I guess we better find out, huh?"

I growl and spin her so her back is facing me. Slowly, so damn slowly, I slip my hands under her tank top, grazing my fingertips over her soft, supple skin. I peel the fabric off her body completely, then drag my lips and nose up her spine and kiss the back of her neck, making her shiver.

"Turn around for me," I purr.

She hesitates for a second, then slowly spins, showing off her breathtaking body. I don't even think she realizes how seductive she's being, which makes me want her all the more.

I can see her fighting off the urge to cover herself, but I'm so damn proud when she doesn't. She lets me see all of her. I can't get enough of her large, perky breasts, wide hips, and the soft curve of her belly.

I let my fingertips wander over the soft, creamy skin of her shoulders and down the sides of her breasts. Then I take one in each hand, squeezing them gently. Thalia moans softly for me and then gasps as I tease her already hard nipples.

"Perfect. You were made for me, my beautiful angel," I whisper before capturing her lips in a wild kiss.

I walk her back to the bed, kissing her the whole way. When her calves hit the edge of the mattress, I give her a slight push, making her laugh quietly as her back hits the soft sheets.

Thalia crawls up the bed and sits up on her elbows, watching me with an excited heat in her eyes. "I wanna see you too."

I growl and begin ripping at my clothes, needing her skin on my skin as quickly as possible. "Touch yourself, baby. Make that sweet pussy come."

Her cheeks turn pink and then red, but her hand slides between her legs. I love that she trusts me, even though she's a little nervous and out of her element. I want to push her boundaries but ensure she feels safe the whole time.

I watch, mesmerized, as Thalia circles her fingers around her clit and stares right at me. Fuck, she's so goddamn sexy. My curvy little vixen spread out for me. I peel my shirt off, and I can *see* her pussy throb as a wave of her juices trickles out of her.

"Oh my god, Romeo…" she breathes. "You're…" She bites her lip and turns bright red again, the blush spreading to her chest.

"What am I?" I ask as I undo my pants and let them drop to the floor.

"You're perfect. I can't believe you want me."

It pains me that she doesn't see her beauty. I plan to fix that, starting right the fuck now. I shed my boxer briefs and grin when her eyes nearly pop out of her head.

Gripping my cock, I squeeze the fucker in long, hard strokes to relieve some of this pressure building up inside. "See how much I want you, angel? You did this to me. Swear to Christ, I've been hard for you since you first stepped foot in my home."

"Show me," she whispers, still rubbing her clit. "Show me how much you want me."

"Anything for you, my queen," I grit before climbing on top of her. I replace her hand with mine, rubbing her and groaning when I feel her warm honey drip all over my hand.

Thalia reaches down and strokes my dick, spreading the steady stream of precum up and down my shaft. "I need you, Romeo. Please, please…"

I remove her hand and rock my thick, hard cock up and down her slit, gathering her juices and bumping her clit. I position myself right at her entrance and hover there, feeling her pulsing little hole massage the head of my dick.

"Ready for me, my beautiful Thalia?"

She looks me right in the eye with equal parts trust and trepidation. I kiss her softly, hoping to ease some of her worry.

"I'm ready, Romeo. I want to feel all of you. Please make love to me."

Her words course through my veins and settle deep into my heart. A month ago, I would have scoffed at the idea of making love. It's an archaic and troublesome term, mostly because I don't know how to love. Or, rather, I didn't think I was capable of it.

But looking at Thalia now, her luscious body spread out beneath me, her pink lips pulling into a gentle smile, and her green eyes filled with longing… I know I'm fucked. She's it. She's *mine*. And now it's time to claim her.

I ease my way into her tight little channel and swallow her whimpers in an all-consuming kiss. "Relax, beautiful. Let me take care of you," I whisper onto her lips. I circle her clit with my thumb as I gently stretch her open in shallow thrusts.

When she's nice and relaxed for me, I pull back all the way and fill her up to the hilt, groaning when I break through her virginity.

"Thalia," I say through gritted teeth, trying not to move. "Why didn't you tell me I was your first?"

"I didn't want you to stop," she whispers bravely through the lone tear falling down her cheek. I kiss it away, hoping to ease her discomfort. "I still don't. I want this. I want you, Romeo."

"Thalia, my sweet girl…" Her confession floods every cell of my body. She wants me. "Mine. All fucking mine," I growl, my eyes never leaving hers.

"Yours," she whimpers.

I hate that she's in pain, but I can't help the caveman that comes out in me. I want to beat my chest and roar to the universe that I've found my mate for life. Instead, I stay completely still, buried deep inside her perfect cunt, letting her get used to me.

Thalia wiggles beneath me, the movement lodging my cock deeper inside her and making us both groan.

"Shit, beautiful, you feel so good."

"I need more, Romeo. Please?" She leans up to kiss me, her arms looping around my neck and pulling me down on top of her.

I want to be gentle, but I'm only so strong. Her perfectly warm, soaking channel is wrapped around me so tight, sucking me back in even as I pull out of her and thrust back inside.

"Oh god, oh god, yes, more," she moans, bucking her hips slightly and testing out how we fit together.

It's too damn good. I snap my hips a little more forcefully than I intended and worry for a second that I hurt her sensitive, swollen, freshly broken in pussy.

"Don't stop," she cries out, putting all my worries at ease and making me growl at her eager, desperate tone.

There's a quiet, reverent rhythm to how I move inside her body and how she receives me. She strokes my back and kisses my neck.

And then something switches. Her fingernails drag down my back and she bites my shoulder, marking me and making me snarl into her mouth as I take her lips in a punishing kiss. I respond with a rough thrust that makes her breasts bounce.

"Don't stop," she cries out, louder, more forcefully this time.

I don't. I lose myself in her, fucking her hard and dirty, our skin slapping together, her wet pussy making deliciously sloppy sounds as I pull out and slam back into her again and again.

"Fuck, Thalia. So tight and perfect for me," I grunt.

Thalia gasps as her pussy chokes my dick. She's about to come. I can feel it. I pick up my speed and lean down to suck on her gorgeous tits. She lets out a jagged moan and tangles her fingers in my hair, holding me to her breasts as I feast on them.

"Romeo, oh god, I'm… I think… Oh fuck, I'm gonna…"

"Come for me," I growl, looking at her beautiful face as she races toward her climax.

Thalia sucks in a sharp breath and holds it, her body going still, her muscles straining and tensing as I pound into her sweetness.

All at once, she lets go of the tension coiling in her body. Thalia spasms around me, her cunt squeezing the life out of my cock while she writhes beneath me and arches her back. I fuck her through it, sucking on her nipples and grabbing her juicy ass, holding her in place so I can drill her into the mattress.

My angel keeps coming and coming, releasing her sweet honey all over my dick. Her pussy is still throbbing when I pull out of her. She whimpers at the loss, but I flip her over on her stomach and position her on all fours.

"Jesus, fuck. So beautiful like this," I praise her.

My dirty angel wiggles her voluptuous ass, and I smack it, growling as her cheeks jiggle. Thalia moans and bucks her hips back.

I spank her one more time and then grip her cheeks in my hands, prying her open so I can see her dripping wet opening. Without warning, I plunge back into her, hitting home in one rough thrust.

"Oh, fuck, Romeo. You're so, so deep," she cries out.

I grip her hips and bounce her curvy body off my cock while she moans and grips the sheets. My sweet, filthy girl screams and lets go, her orgasm rippling through her body and pulsing around my dick. I can't hold on much longer, but I want to feel this, feel her wrapped around me as long as I can.

"One more, Thalia, give me one more," I demand, my voice low and urgent as I snap my hips and spank her hard enough to leave a bright red mark. Good. I want her to be reminded of me every time she sits down tomorrow.

"It's too good, too much," she whimpers, her arms and legs shaking with the effort of holding herself up.

"Not enough, angel, not nearly enough," I snarl. "I've got you, Thalia. Let go for me."

One arm loops under her hips, holding her up as I fuck her savagely. I reach out with my other arm and fist her hair, riding her with every goddamn thing I have. Thalia sobs her release, gushing all over me, jerking in my arms as I hold her up. I grind my cock deep inside her, feeling her pussy massage me.

Finally, I permit myself to let go. With a roar, I empty rope after rope of sticky, hot cum inside her. My dick hurts so good with the force of each new wave. I fill her up to the brim and then keep going, my orgasm stretching out longer and harder than I've ever experienced. My seed dribbles out of her, coating her thighs, my balls, and the bed below.

With one last thrust and a primal grunt, I empty the last of my cum deep inside her. She collapses on the bed, effectively dislodging my shaft from her warmth.

I look down and see the evidence of her virginity smeared over my softening cock. Only then do I come back into my body and realize I just tore her apart viciously, almost violently, during her first time. Panic lances my heart and I find it hard to breathe.

I lie next to her and cup her face gently, the way I should have treated her all along.

"Thalia, god, are you okay?"

She opens her eyes and smiles at me, half-dazed. "So, so good," she mumbles, turning her head to kiss my palm.

"Thank fuck," I breathe before wrapping her up in my arms and holding her close. "Jesus, you're amazing. I've never experienced anything like that, Thalia. Only you, only you, baby. Only you can do that to me."

She sighs dreamily, easing more of my worry until all I can feel is whole and happy. Thalia snuggles deeper into my chest while I run my fingers through her hair and kiss the top of her head.

My woman drifts off to sleep, and as I hold her tightly, caressing her curves with my fingertips, I can't think of a time I've ever been so happy or content. I vow to myself and to Thalia that we'll end every day like this, with her resting peacefully in my arms.

I watch Thalia's eyelashes flutter against her rosy cheeks, a sweet smile kissing her lips as she sleeps. She's the softest, most precious thing in my life… and I'm terrified that my dark world will swallow her whole.

"I won't let anyone harm you," I whisper, kissing the top of Thalia's head.

"I know," she sighs contentedly, never opening her eyes.

This woman trusts me to take care of her, and fuck if I've ever backed down from an important mission. She will be safe. She will be mine. Forever.

CHAPTER NINE

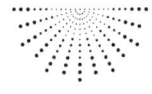

THALIA

$\mathcal{R}$omeo had to leave for a meeting at eight this morning, and I won't lie, I was disappointed that he didn't spend all day in bed with me, especially after I gave him my virginity.

He felt terrible, but I understand. I mean, I don't have much of a choice. Was I expecting the mafia boss to play hooky for the day? The man obviously has a demanding life, and if I want a fighting chance at keeping Romeo forever, I need to get used to that fact.

Plus, he sent two female staff members to pamper me all day. I've had a massage, a lovely hair mask, several moisturizing facial treatments, a manicure and pedicure, and I'm now relaxing in a bubble bath with a glass of cucumber and mint water.

So, you know. Things aren't so bad.

"Anything else I can get for you, miss?" Angela, one of the staff members, asks through the bathroom door.

"I'll get her anything she needs from now on," a booming voice sounds from right outside the slightly ajar door. "You and Margaret are dismissed for the day." There's a slight pause, and then I hear a muffled, "Thank you for taking care of her."

I can't see Angela's face, but I can imagine her eyes are bugging out of her head. I get the sense that Romeo isn't one much for compliments or gratitude, but he seems to be changing. At least when it comes to my care. He takes it so very seriously, which only endears him to me more. No one has ever cared this much or this intensely about my happiness.

A moment later, Romeo barges into the bathroom, his eyes roaming up and down my naked body even though it's mostly covered in water and bubbles. The lust is palpable, his need for me rippling off his body in waves. But when his gaze meets mine, it's surprisingly tender.

"I shouldn't have left you this morning," he says, his tone soft and full of regret.

He loosens his black tie and tosses it behind him before undoing the top buttons of his shirt. He gets frustrated and claws at the fabric, making the buttons pop off and bounce around the room.

I giggle at his eagerness, the warmth from his confession filling me up and making me glow. I didn't have to tell him I was sad to be alone after our intense encounter; he just knew. And he's more than ready to make it up to me now.

"Are you joining me?" I ask, sitting up and exposing my breasts. Romeo's eyes lock onto my chest, watching the bubbles slowly slide down my skin to reveal my hard, sensitive nipples.

He groans, biting his bottom lip as his nostrils flare. His belt is off in the next second, his dress pants and boxer briefs coming off a moment later as he stalks toward the tub. "I'll have to get a bigger one for both of us, but for now..." He trails off as if he's too preoccupied thinking of all the things he wants to do to me to finish his thought.

"What are you…?"

Romeo scoops me up from the tub and stands with me in his arms, water and bubbles splashing everywhere. He carries me toward the bed, and I giggle and kick my legs out, gasping when he tosses me on the soft mattress. His massive frame falls on top of me, but he catches himself with a hand on either side of my head. I automatically wrap my legs around his hips, moaning when I feel his thick, heavy cock lying across my slit.

"I need you, Romeo," I murmur, leaning up for a kiss.

He opens up for me, letting me take control. "Fuck, I need you too, Thalia. I should have been here with you all day, getting lost in your sexy fucking body and showing you how much I need you."

"It's okay," I murmur, running my fingertips over the slight stubble on his cheek. "You're here now."

"It's not okay, *bella*. You come first, always." I'm unsure how to respond to that, but I don't have to. Romeo sees how much his promise means to me and seals it with a kiss on my forehead. "I'll make it up to you, angel. I'll make you feel so good you forget all about it."

I whimper and nod, spreading my legs wider. I'm bracing myself for his monster cock, but Romeo surprises me by flipping our positions. He grips my hips in his large hands, steadying me and getting me into position.

I look into his obsidian eyes, so deep and full of emotions that are new to both of us. I can't believe he wants me. The look of awe on his face lets me know he thinks the same about me. I think he loves me. I think I love him, too.

"Romeo…" I whisper, unsure of how to voice my thoughts.

"I know, angel. I feel it. I feel you."

He lifts me, guiding me over his hard length. I sink down a little, gasping when the head of his cock spreads me wide open. My pussy spasms at that small contact, and a wave of wetness coats his dick, which helps me slide down a little more.

Romeo hisses and groans in pleasure, giving me the confidence to take all of him. "God, Thalia," he half whispers, half groans. "You feel so damn good, baby. Take it slow."

Romeo cups the back of my neck and draws me down for a kiss. It starts sweetly, almost reverently. I rock against him, making him growl into my mouth and pull my bottom lip through his teeth. His hands slide up my bare back, his fingertips leaving a burning trail as they roam back down. Romeo grips my ass, spreading me wider and helping me circle my hips.

"Fuck," I moan when the base of his shaft rubs against my clit. My pussy contracts as pleasure rockets through my body. Sitting up, I steady myself with my hands on his chest, clawing down his chiseled muscles as I lift on my knees. I circle my hips again and rub the head of his dick through my folds, using it to massage my clit.

"Thalia…" Romeo grunts, tipping his head back as he slides his hands up my torso, cupping my breasts.

I cry out when he pinches my nipples, surprised when my entire pussy throbs and gushes at the slight pain. I drop back down, needing more of him, more of this connection. Romeo continues kneading one breast with his hand while his other leaves teasing little touches down my ribcage and tummy until he reaches my center. He slips one finger into my folds, rubbing my clit as I grind against him.

"Oh God," I gasp, throwing my head back.

Romeo grunts and pinches my clit, sending sharp currents of electricity throughout my body. "That's it, Thalia. Jesus, that's so fucking it."

His words pull a moan from my lips as I lift my hands from his chest to tangle in my hair. Romeo grunts in approval, rubbing furious circles around my clit while I ride him, taking him as deep as possible. Each time he hits the end of me, the breath is stolen from my lungs. I'm panting and writhing and so, *so* close to falling apart.

My thighs tremble and my muscles lock, bracing myself for what's to come. My entire body is strung tight, teetering on the sharp edge of ecstasy. Romeo senses my need and takes my hips in a punishing hold. He anchors me in place and fucks up into me in powerful strokes, taking control. I gladly let him.

I can't stop the desperate, wanton whimpers falling from my lips as he tears me open with each rough stroke. I inhale sharply and hold my breath, the intense pressure in my core throbbing and consuming me, nearly choking me as my orgasm slams into me all at once.

I freeze and then spasm violently, collapsing on top of Romeo as my climax tears through me. He growls and cups my ass, holding me in place while he fucks up into me, shoving his cock so damn deep, forcing me to feel every ounce of pleasure he's offering.

I'm a sweaty, shaky mess by the time I come back down, but Romeo gives me no reprieve. He flips me onto my back and hammers into me, hooking his hand under my left knee and spreading me wide open.

It's impossible, but I feel an orgasm fighting its way to the surface, threatening to swallow me whole. I cry out, twisting the sheets in my fists and bowing my back. "I-I can't… can't come again…" I moan breathlessly.

"You can, baby. You can take it. Do you trust me?"

"Yes," I answer without hesitation.

Romeo's eyes grow dark and determined at that one word. "Then take what I give you."

With that, he picks up his speed, stroking into me savagely as I whimper and writhe beneath him. He's keeping me right there, so close, each rough thrust bringing more blissful agony than I thought possible.

Romeo takes my lips in a searing kiss, licking into my mouth and taking control. I'm completely at his mercy as he fucks me with his tongue and huge cock. I love being taken by him, filled by him, ruined by him.

He growls into my mouth, the sound almost painful. "Fucking hell, I'm gonna come. I'm gonna come so damn hard. Come with me, baby. Come with—"

I cut him off with a scream as I splinter apart. I wrap my legs around his torso, locking my ankles behind his back. I cling to him as every nerve ending vibrates with deliciously sharp pleasure. Ecstasy courses through my veins and drips out of me as my pussy snaps around his cock.

He swells inside me, stretching me impossibly wider. Romeo roars his release, his bulging muscles tensing and releasing as he fills me up with his cum. Our combined orgasm stretches on for long moments as we hold each other close.

Romeo holds himself deep inside me, even after we're both completely spent. He buries his face in the side of my neck, kissing me there and letting out a huge breath. I comb my fingers through his hair, loving this tender, almost fragile moment. Romeo sighs and relaxes even more. I love the weight of his body on top of mine.

He lifts his head, resting his forehead against mine. I didn't think it was possible, but his cock is still hard. I whimper as he rolls his hips slowly. Aftershocks of my intense orgasms spark through me.

Romeo cups the side of my face, gently stroking my cheek. He's making love to me. That's what this is. Slowly, so slowly, he enters me and pulls out. I feel every ridge and vein in his thickness as he pushes inside me once more.

He rocks into me, his forehead never leaving mine, his

hand never leaving my cheek. We come together silently, holding each other's gaze. I swear I see tears in his eyes, but Romeo leans down to kiss me before they fall.

I feel so precious at this moment. Surrounded by his strength as my limp body melts into the mattress, making me feel so thoroughly loved and protected.

Romeo gently rolls us over, draping me across his body. "Tell me what's on your mind, *bella*." He trails his hand down my spine, tenderly caressing my skin and lulling me into a fuzzy, post-climax haze.

Maybe that's why I decide to confess my fears and why they snowball into a near meltdown. "What happens next?" I ask softly. "With me, I mean. Or, I guess, with… us?" I glance at Romeo before looking away again. "I'm not expecting to stay here forever, I know that. You'll get tired of me at some point, and I'll outstay my welcome. I just… I don't think I can go back to that apartment. And my crocheting business is doing well, but it's not going to pay the rent for a while until I can grow it more, and–"

Romeo presses a finger to my lips, silencing me. "You never have to worry about money again," he says firmly. I try protesting, but he raises his scarred eyebrow, giving me a dark look. "As for getting tired of you…" Romeo shakes his head, his dark eyes searching mine for something. "How could you even think that? Have I not made it clear that I'm obsessed with you? I didn't want to scare you off with my intensity, and truthfully, I hardly understand it myself."

I blink at him, my runaway thoughts coming to an abrupt halt. How did he know exactly what I needed to hear? It's like he reached into my soul, found my deepest heartache, and spoke healing words directly into my pain. Tears sting my eyes as they rush to the surface.

Romeo starts to panic. "Shit, I'm screwing this up," he mutters. "I'm not good with words, Thalia, but–"

This time, it's me who stops his rambling with a finger on his lips. "You didn't screw anything up," I promise. I try looking away from his dark gaze, but he cups my chin and draws my face back toward his. "I just... I can't believe you want me like that," I finally whisper. "You sound like you want to keep me."

Romeo flips our positions, pressing me into the mattress as he looms over me and cages me in with his arms. His black hair is wild, matching his deep brown eyes as they bore into mine. I feel safe and protected, yet completely exposed to this man. I'm sharing my body, opening up my fragile heart, and inviting him to either soothe me or break me apart completely.

"I *am* keeping you," he vows, his voice both commanding and gentle. "You're *mine*, Thalia. Every part of you. I want your sweet smiles and sexy moans, your calming presence, and your kind heart. I want it all, including your secrets and pain, sweet girl."

"Romeo..." I say with a sniffle as he brushes away a few tears with the pad of his thumb.

He presses a kiss to my cheeks and my lips, then settles next to me before pulling me into his arms once more. "Tell me who made you feel unworthy," he murmurs. "Who made you think you were an inconvenience?"

I shrug, but my man isn't going to let me get away with that. I sigh and snuggle closer, tracing his tattoos as I spill my heart out to the only man who has ever asked. "I was a late-in-life surprise for my parents, who thought they were done raising kids," I start, my voice soft and unsteady. "My mom left when I was five. My dad made sure to remind me it was my fault."

"Asshole," Romeo grunts, tightening his hold on me.

I grin, kissing his chest right over his heart. "It is what it is," I say, repeating the line I've been telling myself for years. "At least my dad stuck around for most of my childhood."

"Most?"

"My brother, Thomas, is—*was*—almost two decades older than me. I guess my dad had enough of raising me, so when I was seventeen, he dropped me off at Thomas's apartment. I've been there for a few years, trying to build my crochet business so I could move out. We didn't have a perfect life, but we made ends meet, you know?"

Romeo nods, giving me space to say whatever I need to say.

"His drinking was getting a little out of hand, but it wasn't horrible. Not like my dad's addiction. I thought I could help him get better, but then…"

"Sweet girl," Romeo murmurs, wrapping his arms around me and holding me close. "I hate that you've gone your whole life feeling forgotten and abandoned."

I give an awkward shrug once again. "It is what it is."

"Not anymore," Romeo says firmly. "I'm going to spoil you like crazy until you believe you are worth every penny, every ounce of attention and care."

I smile through my tears, reaching out to trace a line down Romeo's nose and lips. "I don't care about money or what it can buy. I just care about you, Romeo. I want you in my life, whatever the cost."

He furrows his brow, studying me intently before capturing my lips in a slow, sensual kiss. "I don't know what I did to deserve you," he whispers into the shell of my ear. "But I'm keeping you. You're mine now, Thalia."

"Yours," I repeat, finally resting my head on his chest.

Romeo cradles me in his arms, soothing every broken piece of my past.

CHAPTER TEN

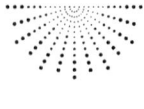

ROMEO

I woke up over an hour ago, but I've been content to lie here and count each one of Thalia's freckles in the early morning light. The sun kisses her cheeks and tangles in her auburn hair, making her glow like the angel she is.

Gently combing a hand through her hair, I let the silky strands fall through my fingers as I inhale her sweet, peppermint scent. She's the most precious thing in the world, and she somehow ended up right here in my bed.

"Are you being a creeper?" Thalia sasses, her lips curling into a grin even though her eyes are still closed.

I can't help but smile at how adorable she is. "I'm simply appreciating the work of art I woke up next to," I murmur, pressing a kiss to the side of her neck.

Thalia hums her approval, tilting her head and arching her back to give me better access. I nip at her skin, then lick a stripe up her throat before diving into her perfectly plump and pouty lips. My girl opens up for me, welcoming each demanding stroke of my tongue and matching my passion with her own.

She pulls away, gasping for air, and I growl with impatience as I focus my attention on her big, perky breasts. Thalia laughs breathlessly, then moans as I lap at her nipples, licking them into tight peaks before sucking one into my mouth and then the other.

"Need something from me?" Thalia half whispers, half groans.

I roll her on top of me in one swift motion, guiding her legs to straddle me as she steadies herself on my chest. I cup the back of her neck and pull her down so her face is inches from mine.

"I'll always need you, my sweet Thalia," I murmur, letting her see my truth.

I don't give her a chance to respond. I take her lips in a possessive kiss, hoping to convey all the unspoken promises of forever. We get lost in each other, every touch, every kiss, every soft moan binding my heart to hers.

Thalia leans back and props herself up on her knees, positioning her soaking little pussy over my raging cock. Fuck, the way she looks at me, her heart on display, her strength and desire shining through, her large, perfect breasts, soft belly, and thick, creamy thighs... Goddamn, this woman is mine, my forever, my precious, sexy as hell, future wife. The mother of my children. I feel it deep in my soul, the rightness settling in my bones and washing away everything that came before her.

Never breaking eye contact, Thalia slowly slides down my hard shaft, engulfing me in her perfect, wet heat. I groan at the sight of my dick disappearing into her ripe little cunt, precum leaking out of the tip as I think about being inside of her every damn day from now until forever.

"So good," I tell her, my voice gravelly and laced with need.

When she's fully seated on me, we both take a moment to

catch our breath. Thalia curls her fingers into my chest, her nails digging into my flesh and making me grunt with pain and pleasure. She bounces up and down my cock, crying out and twisting her hips when the angle is just right to hit her G-spot.

"That's it, angel. Use me up, fuck me until you come all over me."

Thalia moans in response, but that's not good enough for me. I spank her tight ass and grab her cheek hard.

She gasps for air as her pussy chokes my cock. "Yes, yes, I want to come all over you," she cries.

She rocks back and forth in a desperate attempt to find relief. I reach out and cup her gorgeous tits, pinching her nipples and groaning as her body shivers on top of me. I keep one hand kneading and massaging her breasts while the other reaches between us and rubs her clit, causing her to tense and shout my name.

"I feel you, Thalia. I know you want to come for me," I growl.

Her thighs tighten around my hips, her pussy pulsing wildly as more of her sweet honey pours over my dick. She takes in a huge breath of air and goes completely still…

…and she shatters all around me. Thalia squeezes my cock so fucking tightly it almost hurts as her orgasm ravages her curvy body.

She collapses on my chest and buries her head in my neck, kissing and nipping at me as her hips continue to roll and stutter. I grab her ass and help her grind down on top of me until she spasms again. I feel her orgasm spread throughout her body as I slide one hand up her back to tangle my fingers in her hair and pull her lips up to meet mine.

Thalia moans into the kiss, driving me crazy with the way her tongue slides against mine. I flip us over and pound that pink little pussy with everything I have, swallowing her cries of ecstasy.

Leaning back, I throw one leg over my shoulder and then the other, grabbing onto the headboard as I slam in and out of her. "Mine, fucking *mine*," I growl, looking into her eyes, branding her with my stare, my cock, and soon, my baby in her belly. "Fuck!" I roar, feeling my dick swell up inside her.

"Romeo, oh god, I'm..." Thalia whimpers and claws at the sheets, thrashing her head back and forth.

"Come for me, Thalia. Come for me like a good girl."

Thalia screams and lets go of every goddamn thing, snapping her pussy around me again and again as she's hit with never-ending waves of bliss. She's shivering and sweating and moaning uncontrollably.

With one last thrust, I burst, coming in long, powerful ropes, emptying every last drop deep inside her. Goddamn, the vision of Thalia round with our kid, her breasts full and sensitive... I release another round of hot cum before rolling off to the side and dragging her limp, sated body on top of mine.

Thalia snuggles up next to me and kisses my chest, my neck, my jaw, and finally, my lips.

"That's my new favorite way to wake up," Thalia muses when she's somewhat caught her breath.

I grin as I trace invisible patterns over her shoulder and back. It's on the tip of my tongue to tell her I love her and need her to be tied to me in every way possible, but then the alarm on my phone goes off.

Growling, I turn and grab my phone from the table, shutting off the alarm and tossing the damn thing on the floor. Thalia giggles at my grumpiness, and I roll over, fusing our lips so I can taste her laughter.

When we break apart, Thalia sighs contentedly and closes her eyes as she rests against the pillows. I take one more moment to appreciate her delicate beauty, as well as her sinful curves. She's incredible, and I can't wait to come back here this evening and show her exactly how irresistible I find her.

"If you keep looking at me like that, you might not make it out of bed today," she teases, peeking one eye open.

I groan as I lunge forward, intending to get lost in her body all over again, but Thalia rolls away, laughing when I growl at her.

"What if I don't want to leave the bed?" I say with a considerable amount of whining in my voice.

"You're the boss," Thalia quips, her green eyes sparkling with mischief. "No one would call you out for skipping work."

I'm about to text Dante and tell him to cancel all my meetings and plans for the day, but he texts me first.

Dante: *Two warehouses were hit last night. No casualties, but missing product. Missing funds. Colombos want a meeting to discuss a trade.*

"Shit," I mutter, knowing my plans for the day can't be postponed. Typing away on my phone, I tell Dante to gather the details and the men necessary for a briefing and schedule a meeting with the fucking Colombos. I don't have to ask what they want in return for what they stole. Or, rather, *who* they want.

I will kill any and every man who tries to take my Thalia away from me. I'll scorch the whole fucking world to ensure her safety.

"Duty calls?" Thalia asks from her mountain of blankets and pillows. She doesn't sound sad or disappointed, simply understanding of my demanding schedule.

I'm sad and disappointed, however. Livid, too. When this is all over with the goddamn Colombos, I'm taking a vacation. Somewhere far away where I can spend an entire week wrapped up in Thalia and show her how much I love her.

Putting my phone down, I turn to Thalia, smiling when I see how snuggled up she is. I can't imagine not waking up to this every day, and truthfully, I'm not sure how I managed without her for so long.

"Heavy is the head that wears the crown," I mutter.

"Go out there and kick some ass, then come back to me, and I'll make it better," Thalia offers, crawling out of her blanket cocoon and sitting next to me on the edge of the bed. My girl kisses my shoulder, then rests her head there in the sweetest gesture.

"I promise I'll always come back to you," I murmur, pressing my lips to the top of her head.

Reluctantly, I untangle myself from my woman and quickly shower before getting dressed. This is the last thing I want to deal with today, but it's a matter of Thalia's safety, so it's of the utmost importance.

Hours later, Armando, Valentino, a few other trusted men, and I are scouring the docks and empty shipping containers for the representatives from the Colombo family. They were supposed to be here, in neutral territory, an hour ago. Being late could be a power play, but something tells me it's more. I just haven't figured out exactly what the endgame is yet.

"They were the ones who called this meeting in the first place," Valentino grumbles. "Was it to mess with us?"

"A stupid, pointless joke if that was their goal," Armando replies, crossing his arms over his chest.

"It has to be more than that," I say, mostly to myself. My men fall silent, giving me space to figure out our next move. "They can't be baiting us. Otherwise, they would have ambushed us by now." I pace back and forth, my mind whirling with the possibilities. "The Colombos might be arrogant and sloppy, but they wouldn't plan another attack on our territory so soon after the first one. What am I missing?"

There has to be something else. Something I'm not seeing. A weakness I've overlooked.

My phone rings, and I sigh when I see Dante's name pop up.

"What now?" I say flatly.

"She's gone," is all he says. It's all he needs to say.

My stomach drops to the ground, and my heart slams against my ribcage as I struggle to take in air. I don't realize I'm crushing my phone until the case starts to crack. I ease up, but only to keep a line of communication open.

"Thalia... left?" I choke out.

Did I hurt her this morning? I thought we were on the same page, but I was rough with her. Jesus, if I made her uncomfortable in any way... I can't even finish the thought. It's incomprehensible. Or maybe she realized I'm no good for her. My life, my world, everything I touch is evil. Except for Thalia. She's the one pure, good thing I allowed myself to enjoy, and now...

"I'm not sure," Dante replies, breaking into my racing thoughts. "All of her things are here, but there's no sign of a struggle. No one was in your house except for the usual staff. I checked with the guards and those working the compound, but there were no reports of strange activity, no visits, and no one even came up to the gate all day. I'm not sure what to make of it."

I'm already sliding into the back seat of my BMW and motioning for my driver to head home. "I'm on my way," I clip out before hanging up.

I don't know how they did it, but the Colombos have her. The meeting today wasn't to discuss a trade. It wasn't a power play or a joke. It was a fucking distraction so they could get to Thalia.

Little do they know, they are living on borrowed time. I will tear off every finger that touched my sweet Thalia, then pluck out the eyes of every man who dared look at her.

"I'll always come back to you," I promise Thalia, repeating the words I told her this morning. After today, I'll never let her out of my sight again.

CHAPTER ELEVEN

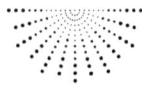

THALIA

"*S*he awake yet?" an unfamiliar voice grunts.

"Aye, I see her starting to move," another gruff voice answers.

Awareness slowly trickles through my body, each limb waking up as I blink a few times to adjust to my new environment. Confusion clutters my mind, and I search my fuzzy memory to piece together how I got here.

I was with Romeo this morning, that much I know. After he left, I grabbed my laptop and pulled up my email to check any new orders that came in over the last few days.

The email.

I should have known it was a trap. Part of me was suspicious, but I panicked and made the only choice I could.

The subject was simply "Romeo." It contained an address and time and instructed me to show up if I wanted to spare Romeo's life. The email detailed how Romeo couldn't protect me forever, and if I ignored the opportunity, they'd make me watch while they slaughtered Romeo before doing the same to me.

My first instinct was to tell Romeo, but I knew he would

tell me to stay put. He'd probably have someone hack my email and find out where the message came from, then go there himself to prove a point. I tried not to picture how poorly that would end, but visions of Thomas being shot filled my mind, his face flickering and switching to Romeo's as blood pooled around his body.

No. I couldn't let that happen. I couldn't let him sacrifice himself for me. Not after he took me into his home, offered protection, fed me, clothed me, and gave me the best couple of days of my life. Romeo has shown me more love and care than I've ever experienced, and I can't let him suffer because I'm the loose end he never tied up.

"Theresa!" one of the men shouts, ripping me from my thoughts.

"It's Thalia," the other one says.

"Doesn't matter. She won't be around for long."

The breath drains from my lungs and my eyes water as my heart thunders in my chest. I will myself not to cry, not to sniffle, not to show any sign of weakness, but I'm losing the battle. Fear settles in the pit of my stomach, a deep, animalistic fear that has me resorting to base survival instincts.

I'm aware of every sound and every scrap of light in the cold, dark basement. One of the men near the only door pulls out a lighter and flicks it twice. A bright blue-orange flame illuminates his face. He has a large nose and thick eyebrows, and I can make out the edges of a large skull tattoo on the side of his neck before the flame dies.

I stare at the lit cigar, the end glowing orange in the otherwise dim light of the basement. Smoke curls and swirls in the air, casting a muted cloud over the dank room.

"Tell Antonio to get his ass down here. She's waking up, and I don't want to deal with another brat today," the man with the cigar says.

"What am I, your servant? Tell him yourself, lazy ass."

The men bicker back and forth, and I close my eyes, trying to remember anything else about how I got here. I ended up taking a train and two buses to get to the address in the email, and that was after sneaking out of the Di Salvo compound. Romeo never told me I couldn't leave, but that did little to ease my guilt as I slipped out a side door and hid in the garden until someone else left and opened the gate.

I hate the thought of Romeo discovering me missing. Will he think I left him because I don't want him anymore? Or because he's not good enough? Nothing could be further from the truth. I remember scribbling out a note telling him I loved him, but I couldn't bring myself to leave it behind. I ripped it up and flushed it down the toilet before sneaking out. If he knew how deeply I loved him, he'd never let me go. He'd come after me and get himself killed in the process.

So I had to go alone, and I had to do it without anyone else knowing.

However, when I got to the location, I knew I had made a mistake. The building was an old storage rental place that went out of business years ago. At first, I didn't see anyone, and I almost turned around and ran back to Romeo's, but then someone grabbed me and covered my mouth with a sweet-smelling rag. And then...

Then I woke up here.

"Calm your fuckin' tits, Jerry," a nasal voice calls from down the hall. "Didn't think you'd complain about watching a piece of pussy. I know it's been a while since you've had any."

My stomach flips as I swallow down bile. If any of these men touch me...

"Fuck off, Antonio," the man I assume is Jerry retorts.

"All right, then. I thought you wanted me to come babysit, but if you've changed your mind–"

"Just get in here already. Jesus Christ, this is why I get migraines when I work with you."

The door flies open, hitting the wall with an ear-splitting bang. Or maybe I'm overly sensitive from whatever drug they gave me to knock me out. Either way, I lift my hands to cover my ears, only to realize my right wrist is cuffed and secured to a chain drilled into the cement floor. Wincing at the loud metal clanging, I curl in on myself, wanting to disappear.

My free hand grazes against something in my pocket, and I almost dismiss it before realizing what treasure I just found.

My trusty crochet hook.

Wrapping my fingers around the cool and comforting ergonomic grip, I bide my time for the perfect moment to employ my weapon.

Jerry tosses Antonio a ring of keys, motioning toward the chain I'm cuffed to.

"Ah, there's our star witness," Antonio exclaims, making his way over to me after slipping the keys into his pocket.

"You got things covered down here?" Jerry asks.

Antonio looks at him over his shoulder and nods. "Yeah, I ain't afraid of this little thing. You two go on upstairs and powder your noses," he says mockingly.

"It's not *her* I'm afraid of," Jerry mutters. The other man who was down here grunts, then I hear them shuffle upstairs, the footsteps fading away into silence.

Antonio turns to me, kneeling a few feet away. I scramble backward, scraping the heavy metal chain against the floor. My back hits the wall, which is uncomfortable, damp, and cold, but still a million times better than being near the man currently grinning at me.

Black eyes squint at me. "Now, now, love. Don't be difficult. You remember our deal, right?"

I nod. "Y-you said you'd sp-sp-spare Romeo if I c-came here today."

The man stares blankly, then his lips pull into a hideous smile, oozing with vile thoughts and intentions. "And do you know what that means for you, little girl?"

"I'm not stupid," I say, my voice growing steadier by the second. "I've been on a hit list for a week now, which means someone didn't finish the job."

Antonio's eyes widen in surprise, then narrow into slits. His nostrils flare and his upper lip curls, revealing yellow, jagged teeth more like a monster's than a man's.

It's working.

"If anyone else from the Di Salvo family showed up to get you, I'd have put a bullet in their head before they ever got inside. But it was fucking Romeo himself. I couldn't kill the Don without direct orders."

"Or you were scared," I toss out.

He snarls, rocking forward on his heels as spittle flies from his mouth. I stare him down, concentrating on not bursting into tears. My heart is hammering, my pulse racing in my ears as I struggle to breathe, but I don't back down.

"What did you say?" Antonio's face is bright red, and his eyes bulge in anger. Perfect.

"I said you were too afraid to face Romeo–"

I don't even get the rest of the sentence out before he lunges for me. Gripping my crochet hook, I swing my arm out and stab Antonio in the eye, pushing the metal hook as far as it will go before yanking it out.

A sickening squelch fills the room, followed by a thud as Antonio falls to the ground, both hands covering his right eye socket, trying to stem the flow of crimson blood from his wound.

I can't believe I did that, but I don't have time to process anything right now. Not when I'm in survival mode. As if on autopilot, my body moves toward Antonio, who is thrashing around and trying to muffle his screams of pain.

The keys fell out of his pocket when he rolled over, and I inch toward them, snatching them up with my free hand. Antonio tries kicking at my hand, but I already have the keys and am working on my escape.

"Fucking bitch!" Antonio hollers. "What the fuck? I'm blind! You fucking blinded me!"

My hands are shaking so badly that I drop the keys twice while trying to find the right one. Luckily, there are only three keys on the ring, and it doesn't take too long to get free. I make a spur-of-the-moment decision to secure the cuff around Antonio's leg, feeling pretty damn proud of myself for taking out a mafia goon.

My journey is far from over, however. I need to get out of this basement and figure out where the hell I am and where the hell I'm going. Will Romeo want me back? Will he think I betrayed him?

Only one way to find out.

Taking a moment, I catch my breath and try to come up with some sort of plan. I've got nothing but adrenaline and fight-or-flight mode, so I do the only thing that makes sense. Fucking. Run.

I throw the door open and sprint down the hall until I see the staircase with another door at the top. Taking the crooked stairs two at a time, I throw myself into the door, praying it's not locked.

The heavy slab of wood gives way, but before I can take another step, large arms wrap around me, picking me up off the ground.

"No!" I screech, fighting my way out of my captor's embrace. "Let me go!"

"Thalia," comes Romeo's deep, soothing voice. "Stop fighting me, angel. I'm here. I'm here now."

Everything comes rushing to the surface; the fear, the confusion, the trauma of being kidnapped, the violence I inflicted on a giant, scary monster.

"I've got you, sweet Thalia. I said I'd always come back to you. I'll always find you. Always protect you."

I wrap myself around Romeo as he holds me close and begins walking through the empty and eerily quiet warehouse. It takes me a moment to realize it's so quiet because the floor is littered with dead bodies. I gasp, letting out a pathetic whimper.

"Close your eyes, *bella*," Romeo whispers. He cups a hand around the back of my neck and tucks my head into his shoulder. "You don't need to see any more violence."

I nod, clinging to him as the adrenaline drains from my body, leaving me cold and wrung out.

"I'm sorry," I murmur, though I'm not sure what I'm apologizing for. Being an inconvenience? For thinking I could help, only to screw things up? What if I killed Antonio? Will that trigger some kind of war?

Romeo doesn't say anything, and my stomach twists itself into a million knots. Of course, he's upset. All he ever tried to do was keep me safe, and I left his home and jumped right into a bad situation. Even if I thought I was doing the right thing, that doesn't change the fact that I'm a sobbing, disheveled mess who made Romeo and his men come after me.

Oh, god, what if I got some of his men killed, too? I'm such an idiot.

Romeo shifts my weight slightly to open a car door, then gently sets me down in the back seat before crawling in next to me. "Home," he clips out to the driver before rolling up the partition.

As soon as we're alone, Romeo turns to me, his dark eyes roaming over my body as if checking for damage.

"I'm sorry," I say again softly before coughing several times. My head feels like it's splitting in two, and I bring my hands up to either side, trying to hold my skull together. I didn't realize I had such a debilitating headache until I sat down.

Romeo gently places a water bottle on my lap, then massages the back of my neck and shoulders in light, soothing touches.

"Thalia," comes his quiet voice. "Look at me." Even at such a low volume, I can hear the command in his tone.

I blink my eyes open, turning to face the man I love more than anything or anyone in the world. I don't know if I will survive seeing disappointment in his eyes, but I owe him this much. "Romeo, I–"

"God, Thalia, I was so fucking terrified I'd lost you," he blurts, cutting me off. He's no longer the intense, dark mafia king with vengeance in his heart and violence on his mind. No, this Romeo is unbearably vulnerable, his eyes shining with tears as he shows me his heart.

I don't have any words, so I simply nod as he pulls me into his lap. Curling up against my man, I let him rock me back and forth, soaking up the warmth and love I feel at this moment.

CHAPTER TWELVE

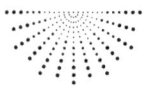

ROMEO

I hold my Thalia, kissing the top of her head as she buries herself further into my embrace. She's shaking, her tears wetting my shirt and breaking my goddamn heart.

What the hell was she thinking? Going by herself to meet up with the fucking Colombos? Of course, it was a set-up.

I have no one but myself to blame. I didn't tell her about this life, didn't prepare her for the traps and pitfalls that come with it. I should have warned her, should have made it clear that she needs to tell me everything, even the scary things. Even the threats. Especially the threats.

Dante was skeptical of me letting Thalia have her laptop in the first place, but I explained to him that she needed it for her job. I wasn't going to take away the one activity that brings her joy. But now I know I should have listened. There's a reason Dante is my second in command.

I didn't hesitate to agree when he suggested breaking into Thalia's computer. I don't give a fuck if that's a violation of privacy. There will be no secrets between us, especially dangerous ones.

It took all of two minutes to find the email and another ten to get to the address. By that point, however, the fucking goons who laid hands on her had moved to a second location. We were able to track them down, and while I'm not sure what my girl went through, it's clear she fought for her freedom as much as I did. I'm so damn proud of her, but I'm still in shock, afraid this is a dream and she's not really here.

"I'm sorry," Thalia says again, her voice cracking.

"Nothing is your fault," I assure her, rubbing calming circles on her back. "Yes, I wish you would have told me about the email, and yes, I need you to promise never to sneak out on me again, but I'm not angry with you. I don't think I'm capable of it."

Thalia leans back slightly, her green eyes peering up at me as they blink away tears. Before she gets a chance to respond, we pull into the compound. I hop out of the car, then scoop up Thalia, cradling her against my chest as I make my way inside, upstairs, and directly into my en suite bathroom.

Setting her down carefully, I reach over and turn on the water, adjusting the temperature so it's nice and warm. Then I peel off her dirty clothes, piece by piece until she's naked.

"Romeo," she whispers, placing her hand over my heart.

"I'm here, sweet girl," I tell her, untucking my shirt and undoing the buttons. "Let's wash the day away. Wash everything away until it's just us. Just you and me, my precious Thalia."

Her bottom lip quivers, but she nods, letting me know she needs this closeness, too. "I just wanted t-to help," she says quietly as she wraps her arms around her torso in a protective hold. I hate that she feels like she needs to shield herself from me. "You've been s-so good to me," she says with a sniffle, "and I couldn't live with myself if you were hurt or killed because of me."

Reaching out, I cup the side of her face, tilting her head so we're eye to eye. Thalia has dirt and grime smudged on her cheeks, along with dried tears and sweat. She's been through so much, and I can tell she's at her breaking point.

"It's my honor to lay down my life for you, my queen," I vow, sealing my promise with a kiss on her forehead. "You don't owe me anything, angel. You give me everything just by breathing, by existing, by finding me worthy of your care."

Tears form and fall from her emerald eyes, and I worry for a moment that I screwed up. But then Thalia gifts me with a small, fragile smile, and I know everything is going to be okay.

I finish stripping down, then join Thalia in the shower, smoothing my hands down her arms as I pull her close. We stand under the hot water, letting it trickle over us and take away every trace of grime from today.

Eventually, I reach behind Thalia and grab the body wash, pouring some into my hands before rubbing it into her soft skin. When I'm done, she does the same to me, her fingertips tracing my tattoos and scars before she combs her fingers through my hair.

"I just have to know why," I say quietly, catching her gaze. "Why did you risk your life, *bella*?"

"Because I love you," she replies easily. "And trading my life for yours was worth it to me."

"You love me," I repeat, my brain stuck on those three little words.

"More than you could ever know," she says, filling my heart with so many overwhelming emotions.

"God, Thalia. I love you with every ounce of my being. You already know I'm obsessed with you, but I don't think you understand quite how much. The thought of losing you... Jesus, it hurts. Don't ever leave me again. I mean it, Thalia. I couldn't survive."

My precious woman wraps her arms around me, squeezing me with all her might. "If you want to keep me, then I'm yours," she says, tipping her chin up to look me in the eye.

"If I want to keep you? Thalia, you are it for me. I know you've spent your whole life feeling abandoned, forgotten, and overlooked, but that's over now. You are my heart. My reason for breathing."

I press a kiss to her forehead, nose, and lips, hoping to convey the truth behind my words. Thalia leans into me, opening up and rubbing her curves against my growing erection.

"Gotta stop," I grunt, reluctantly pulling away. "Don't want to hurt you."

"I'm not hurt. I don't remember much, but I was mostly just scared. Nothing terrible happened."

"Something terrible *did* happen, but I'm glad it wasn't worse," I say, my voice firm.

"Please?" my girl murmurs, standing on her tiptoes to kiss the side of my neck. Her hand trails down my stomach, making my muscles clench at her soft, sensual touch.

I groan when she wraps her fingers around my cock, and the fucker twitches, growing painfully hard as she rubs up and down my shaft.

"Jesus," I grit, tipping my head back and tensing every muscle in my body. She feels too damn good, and I need this connection as much as she does.

First, however, I need to give her a few orgasms.

I look down at my precious Thalia, her eyes filled with lust and longing. I take her lips in a searing kiss as I back her into the shower wall. When she breaks our kiss to suck down air, growl and kiss my way down her body, licking her neck, sucking on her collarbone, biting her nipples, and kissing the soft skin underneath her breasts. I continue nibbling my way down her body, kneeling before her, bowing before my queen.

Grabbing her hips, I guide one leg over my shoulder, inhaling deeply and thanking every god I can think of that she's here with me.

I nip at the inside of one thigh and then the other, loving how her thick curves surround me and tremble each time I find a sensitive spot. Thalia snaps her legs together, but I pry them apart, revealing more of her perfection.

Slowly, so slowly, I drag the tip of my tongue up her slit, barely touching her where she needs it most. Thalia whines, but I continue my excruciatingly slow exploration of her sweetness, pausing briefly to suck on her clit before lapping at the cream dripping from her little hole.

Over and over, I give her just enough to bring her to the edge, then back off and switch, never giving her the relief she needs.

"Romeo," she pleads, bucking her hips. "I need it. I need you."

Unable to hold back any longer, I dive my tongue into her dripping wet pussy, licking up her sweetness and growling for more.

"Ohhhh, oh my *god*, Romeo," she moans.

I dip my tongue in her hole and massage the walls of her tight cunt. Then I flatten my tongue and drag it up her slit until I get to the bundle of nerves that control her pleasure. I swipe over her clit once, twice, three times before kissing her pussy lips.

"You taste so goddamn good. Love your honey on my lips, *bella*."

She spears her fingers in my hair and shoves my face back into her pussy. I chuckle and continue licking and sucking her soaking-wet folds.

She tenses above me. She's close. I lick her up and down,

landing on her clit. Sucking it in my mouth, she begins to shake in my hands. I bite down softly and Thalia erupts, gushing her release, trembling, and screaming my name.

I feel like the king of the fucking world, knowing I gave her that pleasure. I lick her through her orgasm until she pushes my head away, too sensitive from all the attention.

CHAPTER THIRTEEN

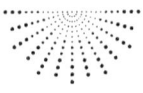

THALIA

he last of my orgasm fades and I slump against Romeo. He stands and kisses me, long and deep, slow and passionate. He slides his hands up to my hips, and I throw my arms around his neck, forcing the kiss to go deeper.

He finally breaks the kiss and nuzzles my neck, kissing my shoulder. "Love watching you come apart in my hands, in my mouth. Fucking beautiful."

He lifts his head and rests it on my forehead. We're both breathing heavily, sharing the same air, the same intensity.

I slide my hands down his neck, over his chest, down his well-defined abs, and grip his hard cock. "Your turn." I grin at him.

He hisses and throws his head back. "Shit, Thalia…"

I kneel before him, and he puts his hands on the wall to steady himself. I stroke him a few more times and then lick the head of his cock like a lollipop.

"Fuck! Ah…" Romeo clenches his jaw, and I see the muscles in his neck strain.

I feel so powerful, commanding the strength of this beast

of a man. Romeo may be the king of the underworld, but right here, right now, he's simply *mine*.

I open my mouth and slowly ease as much of him inside as I can. He squeezes his eyes shut and his throat bobs as he swallows hard. I love knowing I'm giving him this pleasure. Even though I just came, seeing Romeo like this has me so turned on that I'm ready to go again.

"That's it. That's so fucking it…"

When his length hits the back of my throat, I swallow him down. Romeo's eyes flash open and a guttural moan rips out of him.

I continue to suck and swallow, massaging his massive length. He looks down at me with such awe, and I can't wait to taste him exploding in my mouth.

Romeo, however, has other plans.

He pulls out of my mouth with a pop and lifts me into his arms.

"You're incredible, angel, but I want to be inside you. Fuck that. I *need* to be inside you."

Before I can respond, he captures my mouth in a frantic kiss, all teeth and tongue and fire, guiding me backward until my back hits the wall. He breaks the kiss to lift me into his arms. My legs automatically wrap around his hips, and his hard cock rubs along my slit.

"Yes," I moan, grinding against him.

He growls but continues to slide his length through my folds, not penetrating me. His cock slides across my clit, winding that coil deep within tighter and tighter with each stroke.

His mouth roams my neck, chest, nipples, and everywhere in between. The heat of his tongue and the sting of his teeth pepper my skin and set my nerves on fire. My fingers tangle in his hair as I hold on for dear life.

Finally, *finally,* he thrusts his cock deep inside me while biting down on my nipple. The coil snaps and I instantly come, pulsing and shaking in his arms. My scream is caught in my throat, I forget to breathe, and all I can do is drown in wave after wave of pleasure as it washes over me and leaks out from between my thighs.

"Jesus Christ, Thalia. Love when you fall apart for me. So beautiful, baby. You feel so good." Romeo licks my neck and nibbles at my pulse point. His lips brush the shell of my ear. "Breathe, Thalia, take a breath for me,"

I drag air into my lungs, the oxygen pulling pleasure along with it while traveling into my bloodstream and coursing through my body.

I hear Romeo chuckle as he pulls my earlobe through his teeth. "You're so sensitive. I love it. Love seeing you lost in pleasure."

All I can do is moan at this point.

Romeo pulls out and slams back into me, setting a punishing pace. His fingers tighten around my thighs as he holds me in place, pounding into me. It hurts so fucking good as his cock stretches me, his fingers bruise me, and his teeth sink into me.

I tilt my head back, and he covers my mouth with his, swallowing my cries in an all-consuming kiss. He rests his forehead on mine and grunts with each thrust of his hips. I didn't think I had anything left in me, but the pressure builds again in my core and quickly overwhelms me.

Romeo pulls his head back to look me in the eyes. His dark gaze is so intense, and I can't look away. "Let go, Thalia. One more time, beautiful. I need you to come."

I close my eyes as I reach the point of no return.

"Eyes on me, Thalia. I want to watch as your perfect, curvy little body loses control."

I snap my eyes open right as pleasure overtakes my body. Romeo's cock swells inside me and explodes as another wave of pleasure vibrates through me, through him, through us, breathing, pulsing together as one.

"*Fuck*, Thalia, Thalia…" He chants my name as the last of our orgasms slip away, dripping between us.

The moment lasts forever. We never break eye contact, and I see every emotion Romeo is feeling, just like I know he can see all of me at this moment, so raw and unfiltered.

Romeo sets me down, keeping one hand around my waist while his other hand goes behind me, bracing himself on the wall. We're both still shaking, and it seems Romeo is as unsteady as I am on my feet.

He tucks me into his chest, resting his forehead on the wall, covering me with his entire body like he's shielding me from everything outside this moment. I place a gentle kiss on his chest before burying my head there and wrapping my arms around his waist.

Neither one of us says a word as we separate. Romeo grabs the body wash and pours some into his hand before rubbing it all over my body, taking in every curve with such reverence. I do the same to him, soaping up his chest and arms, taking time to memorize the contours of his body.

He turns the water off and dries me with a fluffy towel, then pauses to cup my face in his hands, gently wiping away my tears with his thumbs. I didn't even know I was crying.

I look into his deep brown eyes and see such tenderness there, such depth. I look away, but he turns my face back toward his.

"I felt it too, *bella*. I love you more than I knew I was capable of, and every time we're together, I'm reminded of how perfect you are."

"How do you always know what to say?" I whisper, turning my head to kiss his palm.

Romeo grins at me with a playful look I haven't seen before. I love it. "Maybe my name lent me some romantic charm after all, hm?" he muses before kissing the tip of my nose. "Come, my beautiful Thalia," he says, holding out his hand.

I take it and let him lead me to bed, both of us still naked from our shower. Romeo pulls back the covers for me, then crawls in behind me, turning my body so we're face to face. My ruthless mafia king looks at me with such tenderness and concern, and I love that he's only like this for me.

After a few quiet moments, I muster up the courage to ask the question that has been burning in my mind since Romeo rescued me. "Did I mess everything up for you?" I whisper, fighting the urge to look away from him. I need to see the truth, not just the watered-down version he might try to give me to spare my feelings.

"No, not at all," he's quick to answer. His chocolate eyes never leave mine, letting me see he means every word. "The Colombos fucked with us first, and they already have a world of hurt coming their way."

"But what about…" I trail off, gathering the rest of my strength and pushing through the last question. "What about the guy I killed? Will that, like, bring on a war or something?"

Romeo's lips twitch, and though he's trying to hold back his smile, it's not working. He's pretty adorable, though I don't know if he'd appreciate me telling him that.

"I hate to inform you, my warrior princess, but you didn't end any lives today. The motherfucker you attacked is missing one eyeball and is partially blind in the other but still breathing."

I frown a little, surprised to feel a pang of disappointment.

Romeo chuckles, leaning forward to pepper kisses all over my face. "You're going to make the perfect queen, my love. Very inventive with your weapons. Resourceful. Gorgeous. Sexy. And all mine."

I fake a pout, making my man laugh. "I'll have to go for the nose next time. Maybe I can pull his brains out or something."

Romeo surprises me by rolling me on my back and hovering above me, an arm caging me in on either side. "There's not going to be a next time, Thalia," he says, his tone deep and gravelly. "I have to protect my wife at all costs."

My world freezes and the air drains from my lungs as I stare at Romeo. Did he just say *wife*?

"Yes, wife," Romeo answers. Apparently, I said that last thought out loud.

"Are you going to ask me?"

"What would be the point? I won't accept no for an answer."

This makes me giggle. He's so serious, even when he's being sweet and romantic.

"Well, then, I suppose it's a good thing I love you and can't wait to be your queen."

Romeo's eyes flash with satisfaction and possessiveness. "You're already my queen, *bella*. You own me, body and soul. You alone have the power to destroy me."

I cup his face in my hands, drawing him closer until he's resting his forehead on mine. "Thank you for trusting me," I whisper. "I won't destroy you, Romeo. I only want to love you. Forever."

"For fucking ever, angel," he promises, giving me one last kiss before rolling over and tucking me into his side.

Romeo sighs contentedly, his breaths evening out until he's sleeping soundly. I lie next to him, resting my head on his chest, listening to the steady beat of his heart. Every beat belongs to me. I make a silent promise to cherish it, then close my eyes, drifting off to sleep in the arms of my love.

EPILOGUE

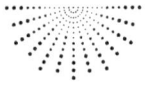

ROMEO

"**C**all back when you have something of substance to tell me," I growl over the phone before hanging up. Resting my elbows on my desk, I hold my head in my hands, hoping to ward off the headache that's been threatening me all morning.

Before I can get too upset, my office door swings open, ushering in my bright, giggly, six-year-old daughter, Bailey.

"Daddy! Look what Mommy made for me!"

The dark cloud hanging over my head dissipates, and the darkness in my soul recedes into the background as I smile at my sweet girl. Her green eyes shine up at me, her laughter contagious.

I didn't know how I would handle being a family man at the same time as being a ruthless mafia king, but from the moment I laid eyes on Thalia, my world and heart expanded to include her, whatever the costs. The same was true when I held Bailey for the first time and again with our three-year-old son, Clayton.

"Is that a new dress?" I ask, pushing away from my desk as she waltzes toward me.

"Yes!" Bailey squeals. "Sparkly!"

She spins, and I smile as I admire the crochet dress made with an array of pastel colors, as well as a strand of sparkly yarn for that added touch. My wife is so talented, and it works out perfectly to have Bailey and Clayton be the guinea pigs for her latest children's clothing line.

Holding out my arms, I prepare for my daughter to launch herself into my lap. When she does, I spin around in my chair, laughing along with her.

"Beautiful, baby girl," I tell her, meaning every word.

"So this one is a keeper, I take it?" Thalia says from the doorway of my office.

I look up, blown away every single time at her beauty. I don't know how my wife has become more radiant in the eight years we've been married, but every time our eyes meet, I'm reminded of how gorgeous and precious she is.

"Yes!" Bailey shouts, making Thalia laugh.

"Sorry she burst in like that," Thalia says as she steps further into the room.

"It's no trouble," I assure her. "I love my girls."

"And me!" Clayton exclaims from under my desk.

"Where did you come from?" I ask in surprise. My son scrambles up from the floor, grinning from ear to ear.

"Secret!" he blurts out before skipping away and circling Thalia.

She bends down and scoops him up, resting him on her hip like it's the most natural thing in the world. For her, it truly is. She's so good with our kids, so kind and attentive. I know she's giving them the love she never had as a child, and I think it's healing some of the pain from her past.

I stand with my little girl in my arms and walk over to my wife, kissing her forehead before planting a kiss on her lips. Our kids groan, and Thalia laughs, her cheeks glowing pink. She's so damn adorable.

"Ready for movie night?" Thalia asks as we head out of my office.

"The pizza is in the oven, and the cupboard is filled with snacks," I confirm.

Bailey gets antsy, so I set her down. Clayton whines and Thalia sets him down as well. Our kids chase each other into the kitchen, leaving my beautiful wife and me alone for a few precious moments of peace.

I guide Thalia so her back is against the wall, then dip my head to whisper into the shell of her ear. "I love you, *bella*. Every time I see you, I fall deeper in love with you."

I feel her smile against my cheek and turn my head to capture her lips. She's sweet and pliable beneath my demanding kiss, her body melting into mine as I slide my tongue against hers.

When we break apart, Thalia rests her forehead on my chest, catching her breath. "What... what was that for?" she asks, peering up at me.

I grin, kissing the tip of her nose before peeling her off the wall. "You should know by now that I'm going to take advantage of every free moment we have," I answer with a smirk.

She pretends to pout, but I know my woman likes the attention I lavish on her. "You're my whole world, Romeo," she whispers, slipping her hand into mine.

I lift it to my lips, pressing them across her knuckles. "And you, my love, are my heart."

* * *

THE END

Want more mafia goodness?
Check out the Moscatelli Crime Family!

DANTE

Blurb:

I haven't seen my old man in years, and I like it that way. Being the second in command of the Di Salvo crime family has kept me plenty busy, not to mention paid for my father's expensive in-home care after he spent his life searching for happiness in the bottom of a bottle.

With the threat of war looming overhead, I don't have time to worry about my father's latest health scare. Until I hear her voice. Cambria.

We've texted in the few months she's been working as my father's nurse, but we've never actually spoken. She tells me it's time for me to come visit before it's too late.

I try brushing her off, but somehow, I find myself on a private jet, heading back home. I wasn't sure what to expect, but it certainly wasn't the stunning, too sweet, too tempting Cambria. She doesn't belong in my world, but I can't stay away.

When my woman becomes a pawn in a much bigger and more dangerous game, I jump into action. I'm going to get my girl back, and then I'm going to do whatever it takes to keep her forever.

CHAPTER ONE

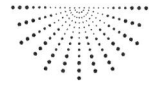

DANTE

*R*omeo leans back in his dark brown leather chair, folding his arms over his chest as he looks around the room at his most trusted men. As the second in command of the Di Salvo crime family, I sit on Romeo's right side during these meetings as a symbol of respect and power. Next to me is Armando, the meat-headed Enforcer, and across from me is Valentino, one of our top Capos.

"After the incident last month, we've beefed up security," Romeo states.

Heads nod around the room, everyone remembering when Romeo's woman, Thalia, was lured away and taken by our rivals, the Colombo family.

The Don goes on to detail the changes around the compound as well as safety precautions for when Thalia goes outside. I try to pay attention, but my goddamn phone has been vibrating in my pocket for the last twenty minutes.

I know who it is without looking. Cambria, my father's nurse. I also know what the text says without even reading it. She wants me to go to Chicago and visit my old man.

Not a fucking chance, sunshine.

I pay for the very best in-home healthcare, the most up-to-date medical technologies, and the top doctors in the area for my father. Isn't that enough? It's not like I'm taking care of him out of love or gratitude for the cold bastard. He chose to deal with life's blows by falling into a bottle of whiskey and not surfacing until he was diagnosed with kidney disease.

No, I don't do it for that bitter, ugly old man. I do it for my mother, may she rest in eternal peace.

A familiar dull ache forms in my chest, and I rub my hand over my heart to break up the tension. I'm a few years shy of forty, and my mother has been gone for most of them. Still, her death is the one weak spot in my otherwise impenetrable walls. The less I interact with my father, the less I have to think about such sad, troubling things.

My phone buzzes again, and Armando shoots me a glare. I don't acknowledge him, which is a general rule of thumb when dealing with the brute. He would rather storm onto a scene and crack skulls without a second thought. On the other hand, I prefer to lay out all of our options, study the eventual end of each of them, and then choose the wisest path accordingly. Needless to say, we don't see eye to eye on much, but Romeo has reminded me over and over not to question who he brings into the inner circle. At the end of the day, I trust Romeo more than I dislike Armando, so it is what it is.

Sliding my phone out of my pocket, I unlock it and stare at the thread of texts from Cambria.

Cambria: *Morning, Mr. Santarossa! Just checking to see if you have any time this week to come to see your father?*

Cambria: *I know you're a busy man, but surely you can spare a few days for family.*

Cambria: *I think you'll be impressed with the progress we've made despite the setbacks this year.*

I don't ask what the setbacks were. I don't care. I pay Cambria and the company she works for a handsome sum to deal with the ups and downs of caring for a cranky old man. Besides, he hasn't kicked the bucket yet. He'll probably outlive us all, fueled only by bitterness and hate.

Cambria: *Yoga has helped with some of the muscle and joint stiffness, and believe it or not, I got your father hooked on meditating in the mornings!*

My eyes roll to the back of my head at the mention of yoga and meditation. If Cambria weren't the best nurse we've had to date, I'd tell her exactly what I think about all that new-age bullshit.

As it is, she's lasted three times as long as any of the previous nurses. Between my father's grumpy ass and my supposedly *unrealistic standards*, the two of us have managed to run off everyone who has applied for that job within a few months. Sometimes a few weeks. One lady quit on her first day.

But Cambria has been with my old man for over a year, so that counts for something. It certainly says a lot about her constitution. From personal experience, I know it's hard to please my dad, and according to the dozen or so nurses who came before, I'm just as impossible to deal with.

Personally, I think the younger generation isn't used to hard work. They want to be coddled, but that's not how the real world works. I don't have time to hold the hand of every caregiver who dares to take up the challenge that is Raul Santarossa, so having Cambria be so competent was a much-needed breath of fresh air.

Until she started in on this whole coming-for-a-visit thing. That shit is getting old real quick.

I stare at the screen, watching those three little dots bounce up and down, indicating she's working on another text. She's persistent, I'll give her that much.

Cambria: *Maybe you could try meditating when you're here. It's a total game-changer!*

For some reason, this is what triggers me to respond. My fingers start typing before my brain has a chance to catch up.

Dante: *I have never, and will never, meditate.*

Cambria: *Raul said the exact same thing!*

I growl at her response, then shove my phone in my pocket again. Romeo turns his attention toward me, giving me a hard glare. I straighten up and nod once, letting him know I'm here and I'm all in. No more distractions.

My phone buzzes again, but I remain resolute, focusing on Romeo's update about the Colombos and our deal with the meat packing plant union. Everything got fucked up last month when the Colombos tried moving in on our territory and taking over our money-laundering operation via the union pension funds. Shit hit the fan, and our contact was shot in the head, along with his goon, who just so happened to be Thalia's brother.

A new head of the UFCW union has been appointed, Brent Carmichael. Valentino is working with him to strike up a similar deal to the one we had with his predecessor. It's all good and necessary information, but my mind keeps wandering back to Cambria and her insistence on me seeing my father.

She's been working for me for nearly a year and a half, but only in the last two months has she started on the father/son reunion kick. Why now? Does my old man want to see me? I'm guessing not since he's not the one texting me. How awkward would it be to show up and have my father kick me out? Once was enough for me, thank you.

"Dante," Romeo says, bringing me back to the present moment.

I blink a few times, suddenly aware that everyone else has exited the room.

"Yes, boss," I answer, standing to meet him face to face.

"Where were you today?"

"I got up at six, my normal time, and made a breakfast of eggs and toast. Then I did some work from my home office before hitting the gym. I had that lunch meeting in Manhattan, then–"

"Not literally," Romeo grunts, cutting me off.

I furrow my brow, wondering what else he could mean. He asked where I was, and I listed the places I'd been.

"What I mean," Romeo continues, "is that your head was somewhere else during our meeting. What has you so distracted? It's not like you, Dante."

Sighing, my shoulders drop slightly as I think of what to tell the Boss. My phone buzzes again, and Romeo gives me a pointed look.

"Go ahead," he says with a nod. "Answer it. Then tell me who it is and why they have more of your attention than I do."

Swallowing thickly, I pull out my phone and glance at the two texts she sent. Then I take time to really look at them, each word sinking into my stomach like a lead weight.

Cambria: *Your father would kill me for telling you this, but he's had several strokes in the last few months. He likes to think he's invincible, and part of me wonders if you think that, too.*

Cambria: *I don't know anything about your relationship, only that it's obviously complicated. I just feel like you need to know the stakes. Raul's health has taken a turn, and I know you don't want to deal with that, but here we are. Please, please consider visiting your father before it's too late.*

"Well?" Romeo asks.

Taking a deep breath, I decide to get it all out there and ask for his advice. I consider Romeo my closest friend, though I'd never tell him that. Neither of us talks about it, but we both know. That's enough for me.

"My father has been ill for quite some time," I start. Romeo nods, encouraging me to continue. "He's back in Chicago being taken care of by the best of the best. But I guess things have… escalated recently. The nurse thinks I should come for a visit."

"Ah, the nurse who does yoga and meditation?"

I roll my eyes. "Yes."

My friend gets a knowing look in his eyes, though I have no idea about what. It's gone before I can decipher it.

"You should go."

My eyebrows shoot up my forehead, and I blink a few times, wondering if Romeo is kidding. The Don never jokes, though, so he must be… serious?

"I… I can't," I stutter. "What about everything I need to do here? Things with the UFCW union are heating up, not to mention the retribution we're sure to get from the Colombos. I can't leave now."

Romeo studies me carefully for a few moments, then clears his throat. "Dante, I'm temporarily relieving you of your duties to the Di Salvo family."

"What? No, I–"

Romeo holds his hand out, palm up, cutting me off.

"*Temporarily*," he emphasizes. "Just long enough for you to fly to Chicago, see your father, and come back."

"What about the–"

"Colombos won't strike back so soon. They need time to regroup, recover, and replan. In the meantime, I have my Capos working on gathering intel."

"And the union–"

"Will be overseen by myself and Valentino. We will keep you in the loop, of course, but you need not be here."

I press my lips together, trying to think of another excuse, but Romeo has me dead to rights. Anything I come up with, he'll counter.

Nodding in defeat, I reluctantly and morosely agree to take the week off to see my father. Romeo dismisses me, and I step out of his office, pausing to lean against the wall outside.

"Fuck," I mutter under my breath. This is the last thing I want to deal with right now, or ever, for that matter.

Reaching into my pocket, I pull out my phone and start typing a text to the persistent and ever-bubbly Cambria. I'm in the middle of delivering the happy news of my arrival when I receive an incoming call from the woman herself.

I stare at the screen in shock, not sure what to do. She's never called before, only texted or emailed. That's my preferred method of communication, and she knows that. However, what little I know about Cambria tells me that she won't stop at one phone call, so I answer it, bracing myself for what's next.

"Mr. Santarossa?" comes the sweetest voice I've ever heard.

I pull the phone away from my ear and double-check that it's the nurse calling. Indeed, it is Cambria Clayton.

"I know you don't like phone calls, but I felt this was important and wanted to speak with you so the meaning doesn't get lost over text."

I blink a few times, trying to figure out why the hell I'm light-headed and tense at the sound of her voice. It does something to me. Something wholly unfamiliar and unsettling.

"I can hear you breathing, you know," Cambria says. "If you don't want to talk, that's fine. I have a feeling I have enough words for both of us."

I snort at that but cover it up with a cough. This woman shouldn't have the ability to make me laugh. Preposterous.

"I know, I know," she continues. "I'm chatty and enthusiastic about pretty much everything, which isn't everyone's cup of tea. But that's not the point."

I grunt at the idea of someone not liking Cambria and then berate myself for giving a fuck. I don't. I can't.

"The point is, your father might not ever say this, but he misses you. In his own way."

This pulls a dark laugh from the pit of my black soul. "The only thing that man misses is having a handle of whiskey permanently attached to his right hand."

"He speaks!" Cambria exclaims. I'd yell at her for disrespecting me, but she's so genuine in her excitement that I don't have it in me to bring her down a peg. Which isn't like me. Not at all.

"You'll be pleased to know I will be in Chicago this week. I'll catch the first flight out in the morning."

"You are correct," Cambria answers, her voice in a lower pitch, presumably in an attempt to match mine. "I am *very* pleased."

What other ways could I pleasure you?

Jesus fuck, where did that come from? Not only is it inappropriate, but I can't remember the last time someone elicited that kind of response from me. I can honestly say I've never reacted to anyone like this, let alone someone I haven't even officially met.

"Good," I manage to choke out. "I'll be there mid-morning tomorrow."

"Thank you, Mr. Santarossa! You won't regret—"

I hang up before she can finish that sentence. Her melodic voice and boisterous laughter are messing with my head. Besides, she's wrong. I'm sure I'll have nothing but regret after visiting my father, but I view this as another mission from Romeo. He told me to deal with my dad and return ready to fight.

That's precisely what I'm going to do. Nothing more.

CHAPTER TWO

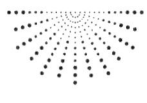

CAMBRIA

"All right, Mr. S, it's about time to get ready for bed," I tell my client, Raul Santarossa.

He narrows his eyes at me. "One more game." His voice is gravelly, worn by decades of drinking and smoking, from what I've gathered.

"That's what you said last time," I point out, raising an eyebrow at the old man.

He tries his hardest to scowl, but a smile is buried deep down there somewhere. He even lets me see it sometimes.

"But fine, one more. Then you get ready for bed while I get your meds."

A spark of triumph lights up Raul's brown eyes, making him look like a mischievous little kid as he gathers the Connect Four pieces and separates them into colors. How can anyone not find him adorable?

When I first took the job, Raul was a little rough around the edges. We had some hard days where he was a stubborn jerk, but I showed him I'm equally as stubborn when it comes to taking care of people. It's my job as an in-home nurse and caregiver, and truly an act of love for each of my clients.

I know all too well what it's like having gruff, jaded healthcare workers mishandling the most important person in my life. I want to make sure I treat everyone with the kindness and grace I wish had been afforded to my mother.

"Ready?" I ask, pushing away the painful memories of those last few months of her life.

"Born ready," Raul replies, his eyes focused on the slotted game board positioned between us.

I smile at his seriousness over a simple children's game. The second week I worked for the Santarossas, I picked up a few board and card games from a local thrift shop and brought them over. I wasn't sure if Raul would go for it, and for a while, he didn't. The games sat in the corner of the living room, unopened.

Then one morning, I arrived early and set up the Connect Four game on the kitchen table, along with a deck of Uno cards. Raul wanted nothing to do with the cards, but he quickly became fascinated with the strategy behind Connect Four. We played a few rounds that morning, and he tried to act disinterested. However, when I moved to put it away, he stopped me and asked for one more game.

Now, we play Connect Four almost every evening before bed.

I drop one of my red chips into a slot on the board and watch in amusement as Raul furrows his brow. He glances at his black chips, then back to the rows and columns on the board.

Everyone at the in-home nursing agency I work for warned me away from taking the Santarossa job, saying the old man's bad attitude was only rivaled by his son's. After one conversation with Raul, I knew he was a softie at heart.

He has a prickly exterior to scare people off and a lot of shame about his past that keeps him isolated.

He just needed someone to be kind and patient and give him the benefit of the doubt. Raul also needed someone to stand up to him and let him know when he was being an asshole. So far, I've managed the perfect balance of each.

I wish those tactics worked on his son.

Dropping another red chip onto the board, I laugh when Raul curses under his breath.

I may have cracked the code on Mr. Santarossa, but Dante is a different story. He's gruff like his father but more detached. Very professional, yet cold and stiff. Stuck-up. A smirk spreads across my face as I remember his response to trying meditation.

I have never, and will never, meditate.

Speaking of Dante, it's probably time I tell Raul about his visit. Truthfully, I wasn't expecting Dante to give in. I've been needling him about coming to Chicago for weeks, if not months. Now that he's booking a flight and headed this way, I need to figure out how to break the news to Raul.

I put my last red chip into one of the remaining slots and watch Raul grin from ear to ear as he plays his last chip, getting a connect four. This is as good a time as any since this is the only time he allows himself to feel happiness.

"I've got some good news," I start, plastering on an enthusiastic smile.

"Is it that I won for the fifth time in a row?" he gloats.

I roll my eyes and start to put the game away. "It's about your son."

Raul drops the chips he's holding and blinks a few times before looking up at me.

I'm on a roll now, so I keep going. "He's coming for a visit. Isn't that great?"

Dark brown eyes fix on mine, and while he's trying to be angry, I see his true emotion. Fear.

"Why?"

"To see you, of course," I answer lightly.

Raul snorts. "When?"

"Tomorrow."

"What the fuck? When were you going to tell me?"

"Right now," I say firmly, letting him know I won't tolerate his raised voice. "It's a bit last minute, but–"

"A bit? Give an old man time to prepare," he grumbles.

"And what do you have to prepare? Last time I checked, I do the prep work around here."

"Cambria…"

"Mr. S…"

He sighs heavily, resting his head in his hands. "It's complicated between my son and me," he says softly.

I pick up the game and put it away before sitting next to Raul. "I know," I tell him just as softly. "I'm not sure what happened between you two, but don't you think it's time to reconnect?"

"I'm not the only one who hasn't picked up the phone in twenty-five years," he grouses.

"True, but you're the parent. Whether you or your son admit it, you hold a place of power in his life—for better or worse. Don't you want it to be for the better? Lead by example and all that?"

"You don't have a kid. You don't know what it's like when you've fucked up as badly and often as I have."

"That's not fair, and you know it. It's not fair to keep punishing yourself, and it's certainly not fair to your son to let your pride get in the way of having a relationship."

I know I'm being harsh, but I want this reunion to go well. Raul is a tough old man who has weathered a lot in his life, but his health has been fragile for quite some time. The numerous strokes this year took longer and longer to recover from, and this last one cost him quite a bit of mobility. It breaks my heart to think about Raul and Dante not seeing each other at least one last time.

That kind of guilt eats away at your soul, and I wouldn't wish it on my worst enemy—even the cold-hearted, aloof Dante.

I have one last card to play, though I feel bad about bringing it up. Still, I'm doing this for the right reason.

"I know it's hard to talk about, but wouldn't Diane want you and your son to have a relationship?" Bringing up his deceased wife was a low blow, but I know I have him when he dips his head. "You have to try. I'm not saying it will be easy, but nothing worthwhile is."

He nods once, then claps his hands on his knees. "I guess I don't have much of a choice, eh?"

"That's the spirit," I joke, standing and helping him with his walker. "Now go get ready for bed. I'll be in with meds in a few minutes."

Raul waves me off before shuffling down the hall.

I let out a breath and deflate against the kitchen counter. The first two hurdles are now over. First, convincing Dante to visit, and second, getting Raul to agree. While he didn't exactly jump for joy, I'll take his defeated acceptance. It's a start.

Twenty minutes later, I'm locking up the back door to the main house and heading to my studio apartment-slash-cottage across the yard. The other nurses complained about that as well. They didn't like the live-in situation that Dante required and didn't understand why they couldn't go home at night.

Walking in the front door, I look around at the little

home I've created. The nurses who managed to work for the Santarossas for a short time told me the cottage was a depressing hole in the wall, and truthfully, it was in pretty bad shape when I moved in. This place looks much more inviting with a good scrub down, some new lights, a few thrift store paintings, and a gorgeous macrame hanging I found in a dumpster. I even hung a beaded curtain to separate the living area from my sleeping area.

I don't mind the simple living conditions. I'm only here in the evenings and don't need much. After my mother passed, I spent the life insurance money on the funeral and medical bills. When that ran out, I sold our home and nearly everything in it to cover the rest.

I started over with nothing and no one, but I got into a good nursing school. Unfortunately, I had to take out a ton of student loans to make ends meet, even working full-time on top of classes. That's a huge reason I took this job. If I stick with it for three years, my debt will be paid off, and I can start looking for a place of my own.

It's a nice thought.

After kicking off my shoes, I beeline to the bathroom and turn the shower on to its hottest setting. Stripping down, I step under the stream and let the warm water ease my tight muscles.

I'd be lying if I said I wasn't anxious about Dante's visit. He's the mysterious benefactor who lives in New York City and has never, not once, been back to see his father. The two haven't spoken in decades, from what little information I could get from the other nurses and Raul himself.

I'm not sure what to expect. Dante is less than thrilled to be pulled away from his busy, successful life, and I get the sense he finds me annoying. It wouldn't be the first time, but with Dante, it feels different. His opinion of me matters, and I don't want to think about why.

Turning the water off, I dry myself with a towel and pull on my sleep shorts and a comfy tank top. I comb through my wet hair and braid it on the side before climbing into bed. Taking a deep breath, I try to calm my nerves and get comfortable. It's going to be a long day of playing peacemaker tomorrow, so I better rest up.

CHAPTER THREE

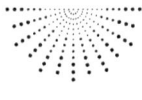

DANTE

I tip the cab driver and gather my shit from the trunk, sighing as I shoulder my bag. Looking at my watch, I groan when I see it's past one in the morning.

I told Cambria I'd be here tomorrow mid-morning, but an earlier flight opened up. I figured the sooner I got here, the sooner I could leave. It seemed like solid logic at the time, but now it's pitch black out, and I don't want to sneak into my old man's house like a thief. Then again, he probably wouldn't expect anything less from me.

Waving the cabbie off, I trudge up the two porch stairs and take a deep breath before opening the door. Only it's locked. Which makes sense. It's the middle of the goddamn night.

Well, this was a stupid idea. What was I thinking? It's not like me to miss an important detail like not announcing my arrival and being locked out. This whole situation has thrown me off my game, and I don't like it. Not one bit.

Looking around the property I bought for my father decades ago, I remember there being a little cottage around back. I'm not sure the last time anyone stayed there, but I've slept in worse places. Besides, it's only for the night. With any luck, I'll upset my father over breakfast and be on my way back to New York before lunch.

I trudge around the side of the house and into the back-yard, frowning when I step in mud.

"Of fucking course," I mutter as I lift my shoe out of the muck. Rationally, I know mud exists in New York City as well. But right now, this is all Chicago's fault.

I eventually find the little structure tucked away in the corner. Finally. I've earned a few hours of shut-eye, however rough they might be.

Gripping the doorknob, I rattle it a few times and shove on the door, stumbling a bit when it gives way. Damn door hardly fits in its frame. I slam it behind me and turn around, only to be assaulted with some sort of net made of beads.

"What the fuck?" I grunt at the same time as a shriek fills the room.

"Stay back!" someone shouts. "I, um, I'm... armed!"

I'd recognize that voice anywhere. As much as I hate to admit it, I heard her voice in my fitful sleep on the plane. I heard it in the cab ride over here. Am I hallucinating it right now?

"Cambria?" I ask as I fight my way out of what appears to be a beaded curtain, not a net.

"No, I'm... Tambria," she says in the most unconvincing voice ever.

"You're a shit liar."

"And you're trespassing."

I manage to untangle myself from the tacky decor, and then I'm face to face with a curvy little ray of sunshine, complete with white-blonde hair that sparkles even in the darkness. Bright blue eyes blink at me, wide and tinged with fear. I'll give her some credit; she may be terrified, but she's standing on her bed, shoulders back, head high, chin out, ready to tackle the monster who woke her. She's clutching something in her right hand, but I don't think it's a gun.

Stupid fucking moron, I berate myself. Of course, the nurse lives here. That's part of her contract. It's not like me to miss these details, and I hate the person I've become, all because of this trip.

Without permission, my eyes wander down the slope of her neck, lower, catching on her generous breasts beneath her barely-there tank top. I can't stop myself from dropping my gaze to her wide hips, my fingers twitching to grab her there and pull her closer, closer, closer until I can feel every single one of her curves pressed against me. Jesus, her thick thighs and shapely calves are on display, those little sleep shorts doing nothing to hide all that skin.

I feel like a feral wolf licking my lips, ready to devour my prey.

"Hey," Cambria spits. "Eyes up here, buddy."

Her forceful tone almost pulls a chuckle out of me. She can't be more than a few inches over five feet, and while Cambria has curves I can't think about, she's petite and no match for me. Still, I respect her spirit, which seems to be about fifteen feet tall.

"I think we got off on the wrong foot," I hedge, stepping toward her with my palms up. I can't say I've ever been in a position of surrender, but something tells me this is the right move. I need a buffer if I want to survive this visit with my dad.

"Yeah, breaking and entering isn't the best first impression," she sasses.

Even though she's encased in shadows, I can see her trembling. Her voice is strong, but it's taking everything for her not to collapse. I can't quite say what that does to me, but I don't think I like her being afraid, and certainly not of me.

"Cambria, I'm not here to hurt you. I'm Dante."

"Dante?" she repeats softly.

Fuck, I like the way she says my name. I like it way too much.

"Dante!" Cambria exclaims, her voice full of warmth and energy.

I don't think anyone has ever been excited to see me, and I'm not sure what to think about it. Everything about this situation is throwing me for a loop.

The curvy little ray of sunshine drops whatever was in her hand, a water bottle, from the looks of it, and hops down off the bed.

"I thought you said you were armed?" I muse, giving the water bottle a pointed look.

"Technically, I *am* armed," she replies, a cheeky grin on her face as she waves her arms in the air.

I can honestly say I'm at a loss for words. Cambria flashes me a bright smile, her light blue eyes sparkling as she grabs a fuzzy robe and wraps it around herself.

She skips into the kitchen area, her braided hair tossed over her shoulder and bouncing behind her.

"I thought you weren't coming until morning," she says over her shoulder as she putters around the kitchen.

I'm frozen in place, watching as this mysterious woman fills up a tea kettle and sets out two mugs, honey, and an assortment of teas.

"Technically, it *is* morning," I answer. Is that my voice? When did it get so deep?

Cambria turns to face me, one hand on her hip as she rolls her eyes. "You know what I mean, smart-ass."

She turns back around and tends to the kettle while I blink a few times and comprehend what the sassy little nurse said to me. She called me a smart-ass. And rolled her eyes at me. No one would dare treat me with such disrespect in New York. If they did, punishment would be swift.

Cambria, however... I want to punish her, too. But my twisted mind and dark, lustful urges don't want to torture her. They want to spank her juicy ass until it's red, then massage her sore skin before starting again, making her count each one.

It takes a moment to realize she's been talking to me. I shake my head at those ridiculous thoughts and try to stay focused. I'm sure it's because I'm tired and out of my element. Nothing more.

"So, yeah. I know there are several empty rooms in the main house, but this works out better for everyone. A little more privacy, but I'm still right here if anything happens. I spruced up the place a little bit when I moved in. Some rugs, a few paintings—"

"Beaded death traps?" I grumble, shooting her a glare.

Cambria smiles and nods. "It worked, didn't it?"

I sigh, wiping a hand down my face. I'm not sure what game we're playing here, but I'm exhausted, and my emotions are all over the place. Strange, because usually, I'm able to shove my feelings down deep and shut the cellar door, never to be heard from again. It's this place. And this woman. Everything will be clearer in the morning.

"Here, it's some sleepy-time tea," Cambria says softly from right beside me.

I startle, not realizing how close she was. "No," I snap, jumping back several steps.

"Relax, I didn't spike it with anything."

"That's not... why would you even say that?"

Cambria shrugs and holds out the drink. "You seem like someone who is always a little suspicious of everyone and everything."

"Well, that's because people and things can't be trusted." I'm not sure why I said that.

Cambria tilts her head slightly, studying me with her

ethereal eyes. I don't like her scrutiny. I'm not sure I measure up, and I can't wrap my head around why I want to.

Finally, she sets the mug on the little breakfast bar in front of me and makes herself a cup of tea. She rests her elbows on the counter, leaning forward slightly as she looks up at me. "Are you going to the main house tonight?"

I find myself shaking my head before I even realize what I'm doing. "I can't," is all I say. I'm not even sure she heard it.

"You're right. It's probably best to get a fresh start in the morning."

I nod, thankful that she doesn't press the issue.

"You finish your tea, and I'll find my sleeping bag. I know I have one around here." Cambria turns to dig through a tiny storage closet behind her. "I'm sure I didn't throw it away," she continues, tossing random things out of the closet as she burrows further inside. "Just in case I need to camp in my car again, you know?"

"You've slept in your car?" I growl, a sudden wave of protectiveness surging through me. It's as confusing as it is fierce.

"Not since getting this job. Thank you, by the way. I never had the chance to thank you in person for hiring me."

I grunt, then tear my eyes away from where the hem of her robe is riding up, giving me a view of those legs and her juicy, round little ass.

"Ah-ha! Gotcha," she says triumphantly. "I'll take the floor, and you take the bed."

A second later, Cambria pulls out a ratty sleeping bag with the liner torn in several places. The thought of her sleeping in her car with that piece of garbage wrapped around her has me feeling some intense emotions I don't recognize.

"You're not sleeping in that," I tell her firmly, walking around the breakfast bar to stand beside her.

"Well, you're certainly not sleeping in it," she counters. "It would barely cover your legs."

"You take the bed, and I'll take the floor. That's final." I reach for the sleeping bag, but Cambria hides it behind her.

"You don't get to barge into my house and make demands, mister." Her blue eyes narrow at me, and goddamn if it's not the most adorable thing I've ever seen. Can't say I've ever used that word to describe anyone before, but it's true.

"You know I'm the one who bought this house, right? And the one who signs your paychecks?"

"Are you trying to bully me, Mr. Santarossa?"

"No, I'm just saying—"

"Let's do rock, paper, scissors for the bed!" Cambria says, cutting me off. "You do know how to play rock, paper, scissors, right?"

"Yes," I say defensively. "Of course."

"Just checking. No offense, but you don't seem the type for schoolyard games."

"What do I seem like?" Why do I keep saying things without thinking them through? It's not like me at all.

Cambria peers up at me, those blue eyes missing nothing as she picks me apart. I feel raw and vulnerable, two things I consider very dangerous.

The curvy goddess smiles softly at me, then shrugs her shoulders. "I guess we'll find out. Now, we're going on three. Ready?" I nod, both of our fists facing off. "One... Two... Three!"

I spread my hand into paper while Cambria keeps her fist balled up for rock.

"Dammit," I curse.

"Yay! You get the bed. It's official."

"Best two out of three?"

"Not a chance," Cambria says with a laugh as she spins away, sleeping bag in hand.

I watch her lay the worn-out piece of shit fabric on the hardwood floor as I take off my shoes, jacket and tie. I packed sweats and a t-shirt, but I don't want to undress in front of her. It feels too personal.

Crawling into the small bed shoved up against the wall, I cover myself with a few blankets and try to get comfortable. All I can think about is Cambria lying on the goddamn ground a few feet away from me. I don't know why I can't let it go. She doesn't care and is willing to give up her bed for the night.

I convince myself everything is fine and it'll only be for the night. Then, for some reason, I open my stupid mouth. "Sleep with me. In the bed. Just sleep. Not… Jesus," I grumble, rubbing my temples.

Cambria giggles, the sound lighter than air. "I'm okay down here."

"I'm not okay with it," I mutter, scooting over in the small bed as far as I can. "Just… just get up here. Don't make it weird."

"If that's not the sweetest invite, I don't know what is," she answers sarcastically.

Despite her sass, Cambria stands, her voluptuous figure silhouetted against the moonlight as she walks toward me. I swear I've had dreams like this.

Before she can see how her presence affects me, I roll onto my side, giving her my back. Jesus, I have to get my raging hard-on under control. Yes, she's undeniably gorgeous and sexy and seductively innocent, but I'm being crazy. It's been a long goddamn day, on top of a long goddamn week, in the midst of a long goddamn month. That's all this is.

The bed dips with Cambria's weight, and she stretches out behind me as she snuggles under the blankets. We're both silent, the cottage filled with just the sound of our combined breaths.

"Want to do a nighttime meditation?" Cambria whispers.

"Hell, no," I grunt.

Cambria giggles again, and dammit, if I don't love every time I can get her to make that sound.

"Just checking. Goodnight, Dante."

"Night, Cambria."

We both lie in the dark stillness, barely touching, as we drift off to sleep. I didn't think I'd be able to get a single wink in, but I already feel more relaxed than I can ever remember. I don't want to think about why.

CHAPTER FOUR

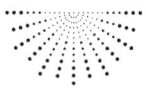

CAMBRIA

*M*y alarm goes off at six-thirty, and I roll over, turning it off without opening my eyes. *Why do I feel like a pile of hot garbage?*

Last night comes back to me in little vignettes. I was startled awake by someone rattling my door and bursting through it. Then a giant beast of a man roared and made an obnoxious commotion, tearing down my beaded curtain like a jerk. I almost squirted him in the eye with my water bottle, but then he introduced himself.

Dante.

God, could he be less perfect? Seriously, it'd be easier to ignore him if he weren't a foot taller than me and rippling with lean muscle beneath his crisp suit. From what I saw of his hands and arms, Dante has tattoos covering his chiseled body. I certainly didn't picture every single place he might have ink on him as I drifted off to sleep last night.

Peering over my shoulder, I'm slightly disappointed to see I'm alone. I'm not sure what I expected. For Dante to wake up and suddenly be a warm and inviting person instead of cold and aloof? I love my sleepy-time tea, but that's a tall order for any beverage.

I climb out of bed and throw on leggings and a sweatshirt before running through my morning yoga stretches. I focus on a posture of open acceptance for whatever the day holds. I have a feeling I'll need all of the mindfulness tools at my disposal to make it through the week.

After stretching, I sit cross-legged on the floor, leaning against the side of my bed. Resting the back of my hands on my knees, I hold my palms open as I silently repeat my intentions for the day; *I release shame, I choose authenticity, and I carry peace within me.*

I'm on my second round of deep breathing when I hear Dante pacing around. Peeking one eye open, my attention is drawn to the kitchen window, where he's stomping in one direction, pausing, spinning on his heel, then stomping in the opposite direction.

"If you need me to come back... No, I haven't seen him yet, but... Yes, Boss. I understand. But you'll still call me if–"

He pulls the phone away from his ear and stares at it. I can't quite see his facial expression from here, but I assume he's trying to melt his phone with laser vision.

"He hung up on me," Dante growls, staring at the cell phone in his hand.

I watch as he shoves it back into his pocket and wipes a hand down his face. Dante's shoulders drop as he lets out a defeated sigh. My heart hurts for whatever weight he's carrying. I don't know what Dante's job is, but I've been told it's very demanding. If he'd let me, I'd give him a shoulder massage and work through a relaxing meditation before showing him some stretches to ease back tension and realign his neck.

As it is, Dante seems to think that if he tried meditating,

he'd burst into flames. That's partially why I'm so determined to get him to do it at least once. The other part of me genuinely believes in the practice of mindfulness, and I think everyone could benefit from a few moments of inner peace.

I close my eyes and get back to my intentions, trying to push thoughts of Dante out of my head. I definitely don't focus on how his taut muscles would feel beneath my hands as I rub the tension from them.

The front door swings open, and in steps Dante. His eyes find mine instantly, and a shiver runs down my spine. I didn't get a good look at his features last night in the dark, but in the cold, hard light of day, I see he's even more handsome than I thought. Damn it.

Deep brown eyes lock onto mine, and I find it impossible to break the connection. He's sharing something with me, but before I can figure it out, he blinks and shakes his head.

"Are you done with your new age nonsense?" he grumbles, waving a hand in my direction.

I smile at the grumpy Dante as he shuts the door and leans against it. "For now," I answer cheerfully, hopping up from the floor. "One of these days, I'll get you to join me. It's not as crazy as you might think."

Dante raises an eyebrow, letting me know he doesn't believe me one bit.

I grab my phone and toss it into my bag, along with a few other things I usually take to the main house.

"Seriously. Most days, it's just stretching and taking a few moments to ground yourself and prepare for the day. Your breath is a powerful tool once you know how to use it. I also paint my face with rabbit's blood and dance naked in the full moon once a month to rejuvenate the crystals I use in my spells, but other than that, it's totally normal."

I wish I could snap a picture of Dante's face right now. It's exactly what I was hoping his reaction would be. His dark eyebrows are hidden somewhere in his hairline, and his eyes are wide as dinner plates as he stares at me. A mixture of disbelief, panic, and what-the-fuck energy pours from him, and I can only hold in my laughter for so long.

"Oh my god, I'm kidding!" I say before breaking down into laughter. Dante's eyes narrow into suspicious little slits, which only makes me laugh harder. "I would never kill a rabbit."

Dante opens his mouth, but I hold my hand up, stopping him. He looks equally as taken aback by that action as he was by my naked moonlight dance, and I won't lie, I love it.

"Kidding again," I tell him with a smile. "I'm not into crystals and don't dance naked, in the moonlight or otherwise."

He mutters something that sounds like, "Too bad."

"What?"

"Nothing."

I stare at him for a moment, trying to figure out what he said. Dante gives nothing away, so I drop it for now.

"It's almost seven, so I need to get up to the main house and start on breakfast and morning meds. Are you ready?"

Dante stares out the window at the main house, a look of unbearable vulnerability cracking his usually rough exterior. I have no idea what happened between him and his father, but I'm having a hard time reconciling the harsh, clipped man from the texts we've shared over the months with the lost man standing in front of me.

He looks so fragile, and I have the urge to hug him. I don't, of course. His head might explode.

I do, however, loop my arm in his, catching him off guard. Something tells me this man isn't often surprised by people, and I'm honored to be among the few.

Dante grows rigid, peering down at me with confusion and shock.

I shine my brightest smile at him and tug him toward the door. "Come on, Mr. Santarossa. The only way out is through."

"That's not true," he counters as I drag him outside. "There are many ways out of a situation without going through it. You look at available resources, possible hurdles, and desired outcomes."

"Mm-hm. Well, it seems you've tried all that when it comes to your father, yet here you are." I give him a pointed look, and I swear to God, he pouts. It's freaking adorable and makes me want to pinch his cheeks. I don't, for fear he might snap my fingers off. "Let's try things my way today."

"Why do I feel like those are famous last words?" he mutters, eyeing me up and down.

I shrug and smile, trying to keep up the positive energy. "I guess we'll find out."

We make it into the house, and I get some water going in the electric kettle for Raul's morning tea and oatmeal. Gathering a mug and bowl, I set them on the counter and pull out a packet of English Breakfast tea, along with the container of steel-cut oats.

Next, I grab the locked box of pills on the counter and dial in the code. One by one, I pull out the various medications. Some for pain, others to regulate the input and output of certain organs, and a few to counteract the side effects of all the other meds.

I notice Dante has barely moved, so I look over my shoulder at him and see him standing in the corner, looking completely out of place. He shuffles his weight from side to side, then crosses his arms before uncrossing them and shoving them in his pockets. Anxiety radiating off him, and I'm sure if I could take a peek behind that steel wall he has around his heart, I'd see it hammering away out of fear.

"That's a lot of pills," Dante says, his words tinged with guilt.

"I've had clients who take more," I say with a shrug. Truthfully, it is a lot because Raul is in bad shape. I seem to be the only one around here not in denial about that. Still, I don't want to pile on when Dante is clearly having a rough day. "Come on," I encourage, waving him over. "You can go ahead and make the coffee."

This earns me another puzzled and slightly offended look from the enigmatic Dante.

I laugh at how shocked he is. "Sorry, but I had to see what you'd do if I gave you an order. You did not disappoint."

Dante furrows his brow, but I'm sure I see the corner of his lip twitch. That's almost a quarter of a smile. I'm determined to get him to show me his full smile one of these days.

"Should my father be drinking coffee with all of that?" He nods toward the cup of pills sitting on the counter.

"The coffee is for you," I say as I pour the boiling water from the kettle into the mug of tea and the bowl of oatmeal. "You clearly need it."

Before Dante can reply, I place everything on a tray and set it on the dining room table in front of Raul's chair as I hear the *click-click-drag* sound of the walker coming down the hall. A moment later, Raul enters the kitchen, giving me as much of a smile as he ever does. Then his gaze falls on Dante, and he scowls.

Good lord, this is going to be a pain in the ass.

"Good morning, Mr. Santarossa!" I say in my most energetic voice. "Dante surprised us by showing up early. Isn't that nice?"

"If you say so," he grumbles.

"Good to see you too," Dante scoffs, turning to face the coffee maker. He busies himself with the task, focusing far too long on measuring out the grounds.

"I didn't ask you to come," Raul mutters.

"Okay!" I exclaim, clapping my hands. "Who's ready for breakfast? Yours is on the table," I tell my client. "And Dante and I will have cereal."

"Excuse me?" Dante chimes in. "Cereal? Like… Raisin Bran?" His nose scrunches up, and the look of horror on his face is priceless. You would've thought I offered him a dirty diaper.

"No, like Fruity Pebbles. I'm not a monster."

Raul chuckles while Dante scowls.

"I'll pass."

"Don't be ungrateful, son," Raul snaps. "Cambria works her ass off around here. If she feeds you cereal, you better take it and thank her."

"I can handle myself, Mr. Santarossa," I interrupt. "Thank you for defending me, but I'll deal with Dante. He can go hungry if he doesn't want my sugary cereal."

This seems to satisfy Raul, and he takes a few bites of oatmeal.

Dante is in the kitchen corner, as far as possible from his father without leaving the room. Raul has his back facing his son, and it's painfully obvious these two have zero social grace, especially when it comes to each other.

"I've got the coffee covered," I tell Dante. "You go sit down at the table."

"Thought you gave me an order, boss," he grunts.

"And now I'm giving you a new one."

Dante opens his mouth to fight me, but I bump him out of the way with my hip. He stares at me, mouth half agape, while I simply wink and shoo him on his way. After a few beats of awkward silence, I roll my eyes and fill up the coffee cups, joining the two stubborn men at the table.

"How was your flight, Dante?" I ask since Raul won't.

"Fine."

I give Raul a look and lightly elbow him. He frowns and moves his arm away from me like a little kid.

"And how is work going for you?" I continue.

"Same as it always is."

Oh my god, this is like pulling teeth. Actually, I'd rather pull teeth. At least that's a pretty straightforward task. Navigating this conversation, however, is a different story.

"Your father recently started–"

Dante's phone rings and he jumps to grab it out of his pocket. Staring at the screen, a look of relief washes over him. "I have to take this," he informs us as he stands from his seat.

"Of course, you do," Raul grunts. "Go ahead. They need you more than I do."

"That's rich coming from a man who depends on me for his home and expensive medical treatments."

"We all know you're not doing it out of love for me," Raul snaps.

"Now, Mr. Santarossa," I butt in.

"That might be the one thing we agree on, old man."

"Dante!" I scold him.

He holds his hands up as he backs away, then turns on his heel and books it out the back door, his phone attached to his ear. I watch him pace around the backyard, then turn back to Raul.

"That went well," he says sarcastically.

"You weren't exactly welcoming," I counter, giving him a pointed look. "Finish up breakfast, and I'll put your shows on. And don't think that because your son is here, I'll let you get out of your daily meditation."

"It's going to take more than *self-reflection* to patch things up with Dante," he sneers.

"Well, why don't you try it first, and if it doesn't work, we'll move on to something more ground-breaking, like starting a conversation or not insulting him in the first thirty seconds of seeing him."

Raul grumbles something, but he's smart enough not to argue with me.

As I sip on my now lukewarm coffee, I wonder if this surprise visit was a terrible idea after all.

CHAPTER FIVE

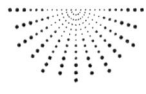

DANTE

"*I* thought Dante was out of town for the week. Why is he calling in for the meeting?" Armando whines.

"I'm gone three days, and you're already looking to take over my position?" I snap.

My eyes wander to the window overlooking the backyard, immediately settling on the little cottage in the corner. I haven't seen Cambria since lunch, and while that shouldn't bother me, I'm unsettled. What is she doing in there? Meditating? Yoga?

I try not to let myself think about her entertaining a man. For some reason, the thought of her having a boyfriend triggers some long-dormant possessiveness way down deep.

"So be careful, okay?"

I realize I've zoned out the last few moments, and Armando is talking to me.

"You be careful," I shoot back automatically. I don't mean to start shit with him; it just comes naturally.

"Dante," Romeo says, his voice firm and commanding. "Armando is trying to say that the Colombos have noticed

146

your absence. Word on the street is they have their men looking for you."

"Caught a guy going through your garbage," Armando adds. "Took him out with an uppercut and a boot to his neck. You're welcome."

"Really?"

"Are you calling me a liar?" Armando growls.

"No, Jesus," I grunt. "I believe you beat the shit out of someone. I meant I was surprised that someone was at my home, digging through my trash." The meat head snorts. "Thank you for doing your job," I eventually say, my words dripping with sarcasm.

Armando sighs heavily, and I feel a flicker of guilt for a moment. I'm hard on him, and we don't see eye to eye on anything, but he did me a solid.

"I'm not your enemy," Armando says, most of the anger drained from his voice.

"I know," I admit, rubbing a hand down my face. "My head is all fucked up from being here."

"Nah, you've always been an ass."

Romeo and Valentino are also on the line, and both are trying not to laugh. For some reason, I don't mind. I know they're messing around and giving me a hard time, like Cambria. It doesn't sting as much when I think of it that way.

Valentino jumps in and updates us on the latest deal with the UFCW union, which appears to be back to normal. We can launder our money through the union pensions for a small fee. We're still working on getting that fee down, but the money is flowing. For now.

Romeo thanks Valentino for his work, then dismisses him and Armando from his office. It's just him and I now, and I have a feeling the Boss wants to share a few words of wisdom.

"How are things going with your father?" he asks.

I can picture him leaning back in his chair, his hands gripping the armrests as he picks me apart with his dark gaze. Fortunately, he doesn't have the advantage of seeing me in person, but I know he's still going to strike to the heart of the matter.

"About as shitty as I expected," I answer truthfully. I'm drawn to the window again, staring at the little cottage and willing Cambria to walk outside. I need to see her and make sure she's okay.

Silence stretches between us, and I wait for Romeo to finish his assessment of me and my situation. I know he has an opinion and won't be shy about sharing it.

"What's the point of this visit?"

"To see my father."

"Don't be obstinate. If that was it, you've already done it. Why are you still there?"

I let out a breath, my shoulders dropping as I squeeze my eyes shut. "Because the nurse insisted–"

"You don't take orders from nurses," he interjects. "So I'll ask you again. Why are you there?"

I don't correct him, but technically, I took orders from the curvy little nurse that very first morning. She bossed me into making coffee and then bossed me into sitting at the table.

"To... fuck, I don't know. Talk to him, I guess. Make amends and whatever end-of-life bullshit kids are supposed to do with ailing parents."

"Is it that bad?"

I shrug, even though I know he can't see me. Truthfully, I don't want to think about it. I never pictured myself caring about my father's passing. Then again, some part of me always thought we'd have time later.

I finally settle on, "It's not great,"

"And have you talked to your father? Made amends and all that bullshit?" he asks, using my words.

"What do you think?" I grumble.

"I think you're a very private person, which I respect. It's your family and your business, but I think you owe it to yourself to have no regrets, not about this, at least. Say your piece, let him say his, and then you'll know where you stand."

"Yes, Boss."

"Dante, I don't tell you this as your boss. I tell you this as a friend."

I pull my phone away from my ear and stare at it. Sure, Romeo is my closest friend and ally, but we don't talk about it. We certainly don't acknowledge it.

"Thalia has given me a new perspective, or maybe I'm getting a little soft, but you deserve to know your place in my life. And as my friend, I want you to make the most of this visit. It sounds like it may be your last."

Something about that finally breaks through. I don't have more time. "Later" isn't guaranteed. This could be it. Am I okay with leaving things this way forever?

"Thanks," I say after swallowing thickly around the lump in my throat.

We hang up a few minutes later, and I slump against the kitchen counter, rubbing my temples. How do I relate to my old man? How do I have a conversation with him when all I can think about is cleaning up his vomit after he passed out on my tenth birthday? Or collecting his drunk ass from bar after bar when he became belligerent? Or his mottled red and purple face yelling at me and kicking me out at seventeen?

The now familiar sound of my dad shuffling around in his walker echoes down the hall, getting closer and closer by the second. I curse under my breath, then straighten, preparing myself for the battle.

"Just wake up from a nap?" I ask as my father makes his appearance.

"What's it to you?" he snaps, making his way into the kitchen and parking in front of a cupboard.

I take a deep breath, holding back my first response of *fuck you too.*

"Just making conversation," I say instead.

My old man opens the cupboard door and tries grabbing a class, but the walker is in the way, and he can't reach it.

"Here, let me help."

"I got it!" he shouts, shooing me away.

"You clearly don't."

"Bah," he grunts, dismissing me.

He presses himself against the walker and stretches up, but he's still a solid six inches away. Stepping up behind him, I grab the glass and set it on the counter in front of him.

"Coulda done it myself," he mumbles.

"Water?" I ask instead of engaging.

"I can do it myself."

Without arguing, I turn on the faucet and fill the glass, setting it on the counter next to him. "Everything doesn't have to be a fight."

My father glares at me, then begrudgingly takes a sip of water. "You've done enough for me," he finally says, breaking eye contact. "I don't need you getting me drinks, too. I'm already enough of a failure without you rubbing it in."

I blink a few times, not expecting that response. "You're not a failure," I start, though I have nothing to back that up.

He grunts out a bitter laugh. "No? Well then, just a cranky old man dealing with the consequences of a lifetime of bad choices."

We're both quiet for a few moments, letting his words sink in. He's not wrong. "The alcohol was always going to catch up to you," I finally say. "Nothing to do about it now but treat what we can."

I stare out the window, but I can feel my father's eyes on me, studying me for the first time in years. I'd like to say I don't give one goddamn fuck about his opinion, but that'd be a lie. He's my dad. I think some part of me will always want his approval.

"It's not just the alcohol, son. I fucked up with you over and over. I know I did."

Keeping my gaze locked on the little cottage, I try not to listen to his words. I don't want to forgive him, even if I know I should. The front door opens, and out walks Cambria, the sunlight kissing her skin and making her curvy figure glow. White-blonde hair glitters in the waning sunlight, and I get the sudden urge to comb my fingers through it.

"After Diane died, I lost myself. I didn't know how to deal with the grief, and–"

I whip my head around and focus the mounting rage on the man who deserves it the most. "Don't you dare say her fucking name," I spit. "Using her as an excuse for your drinking is despicable. I hoped you'd changed, that maybe facing your mortality would realign your priorities, but I see you're the same excuse-seeking piece of shit I knew you to be all along."

"Dante!" Cambria shouts. I didn't realize she was here. She must have slipped in the back door during my rant.

My breath saws in and out of my lungs as I clench my teeth, never taking my eyes off my pathetic father.

"I lost my best friend," my dad says. "My partner. And you were a kid. I had no idea what to do with you!"

"I lost my mother *and* my father that day," I grit.

"Dante, let's take a break," Cambria says from beside me. She rests her hand on my arm, but I yank it away. "Step away and take a few breaths. You're both saying things you don't mean."

"He means every word," my dad spits out. "He's always resented me. He wishes it were me who died instead of his mother."

"You know what, old man? I–"

"Enough!" Cambria yells. She puts her hand on my chest and shoves me back. I stare at her, then look down at her hand. "Back off. I didn't ask you to come here so you could berate your father. I know things are complicated, and believe me, I know what it's like to grieve, but–"

"You don't know anything," I growl, narrowing my eyes at her. "Not a goddamn thing."

As soon as the words leave my mouth, I wish I could yank them back and swallow them down. Cambria curls in on herself, her bright blue eyes filled with tears, though she doesn't let them fall. Her chin trembles, but it's still held high, like the warrior she is. Jesus, I'm an asshole.

"Cambria…"

Before I can say anything else, she pushes past me and runs out the door. I stare after her, not knowing if I should chase her or give her space.

"She didn't deserve that," my father says flatly.

"I know."

I turn on him, ready to blame him for this as well, but when I finally take my father in, I see he's just as broken as I am.

"I did the same thing her first week here. She got too close to all those feelings I've been trying to drown in booze all these years. I snapped and sent her away in tears. She's not the first nurse I made cry, but she was the first one who stuck around after. She was also the first to stand up to me the next day and demand an apology."

This brings an almost-smile to my lips. I can picture the

little five-foot, curvy woman with her hands on her hips, giving my father a harsh talking-to. "What did you do?"

"I realized the same thing you're about to."

I lift an eyebrow at him, unsure what he's getting at.

"That Cambria is special and worth fighting for."

Another few moments of silent contemplation spread between us, and finally, I know what I have to do.

"Shit," I mutter. "I need to apologize, don't I?"

"Sucks, doesn't it?"

This pulls a chuckle from deep in my chest. We're nowhere near patching things up, but I know my father understands the position I'm in. Maybe there's hope for us after all. We both seem to know Cambria is the key to everything.

Now I need to go make it up to her.

CHAPTER SIX

CAMBRIA

*A*s soon as I enter my cottage, I shut the door and collapse against it. The tears I've been holding back rush to the surface, stinging my eyes as they pour out.

After a few deep breaths, I peel myself away from the door and stumble toward the bed, flopping down on it in a pile of pathetic tears. My head is pounding as I try to work through one of my calming exercises, each beat of my heart pulsing painfully in my temples.

Curling up into a ball, I squeeze my eyes shut, attempting to focus on grounding myself instead of berating myself. The old insecurities win out, however, and I replay the entire kitchen scene over and over, feeling like a fool.

What did I think was going to happen? I'd get Dante here for a few days and hope he's willing to bury the hatchet after decades of not talking to his father? Did I expect Raul to flip a switch and suddenly let go of his shame enough to tell his son he loves him?

I sniffle, the unattractive sound making me feel even more like an idiot.

Equally as upsetting is the way Dante snapped.

You don't know anything. Not a goddamn thing.

I must be delusional. I thought Dante and I had some sort of connection, some unspoken bond that had formed over the last few days. Was he annoyed with me the whole time? Am I just a little kid to him? Or maybe I'll never be anything more than the help. I'm good enough to take care of Raul when Dante doesn't want to, but it's not my place to meddle in family affairs.

Some part of me knows it doesn't matter. None of it. Dante will be gone soon, Raul will return to his grumpy ways, and we'll probably never speak of this incident again.

It's for the best.

But then why is my stomach in knots? The thought of never seeing Dante again, of having that be our last interaction, triggers a deep fear. After my mom passed, I promised myself—

My thoughts are cut off by a knock at my door. I tense, not sure I'm ready to face whatever is out there. Am I going to be fired? Is Dante here to yell at me some more? Maybe Raul had a rush of adrenaline from his anger and stormed across the yard to give me a piece of his mind.

"Cambria?"

It's Dante, which isn't surprising. His voice, however, isn't what I expected. Instead of harsh or clipped, he sounds almost… tender.

"I'm sorry. I'm an asshole," he says with a sigh. "I'm sorry for a lot of things in my life, but the way I treated you earlier is at the top of the list."

I sit up in bed, then swing my legs over the side, standing and taking a tentative step toward the door. I hear a muffled thud, and I know Dante is resting his forehead against the scratchy wooden door.

Even though I'm hurt and confused, I can't stand to hear Dante's tortured voice. Closing the distance between us, I turn the knob and open the door, stunned to see the broken man standing before me.

"Jesus," he whispers, his hands automatically coming up to cup my face. "I made you cry." He says it more to himself than to me, and a look of self-loathing and regret fills his face.

Dante wipes my tears away, then gently walks us backward inside the cottage. I'm so stunned and overwhelmed by his tender touch that I don't protest.

"I'm so sorry," Dante says again as he leads me over to the bed. He guides me to sit down, then backs away as if he might hurt me or make me cry again if he's not careful.

He's so broken at this moment, so raw and vulnerable. I've never seen this emotion from him, and I have a feeling he hasn't shown it to anyone in a long time, if ever.

Dante paces in front of me, running his hands through his hair one moment, then shoving them in his pocket the next. He's agitated and angry at himself, flustered that he can't find the words. I watch as he struggles to put his thoughts together, my tears slowly drying the longer I wait.

"My mom," he eventually starts, shaking his head as he tries to get the words out. "She was incredible. This bright, carefree spirit who wanted to bring joy and color to the world around her. Not unlike someone else I know."

He pauses, his brown eyes finding mine. He gives me a tentative smile, and my broken heart starts to mend itself.

"But her light was snuffed out. She was on her way to pick me up from school when she was scraped off the road by an eighteen-wheeler. The driver was over double the legal limit for blood-alcohol levels."

"Oh my god," I murmur, bringing my hand up to cover my mouth. I knew she died when Dante was just a kid, but I didn't know how.

"I was nine," he continues. I get the sense that he needs to get this all out now that he's started. "Imagine my disgust when I found my father passed out with two empty whiskey bottles next to him a few months later. I don't remember him ever touching alcohol before then, but once he had that first drop... I don't know. It took hold of him and never let him go."

Dante shrugs and looks down at his feet. I stand, not realizing I'm moving until I'm right in front of Dante. He lifts his head, those dark eyes latching onto mine and begging me to see his truth.

Resting my hand over his heart, I feel it hammering against my palm. He inhales deeply, then places his hand over mine, the warmth grounding me and tying me to him even more.

"Breathe," I whisper, inhaling deeply as he does the same. I exhale slowly, my eyes never leaving his as we take another deep breath together.

After a moment of silence, Dante continues. "He could have been a workaholic or a hoarder or hell, even done hard drugs, and I would have understood. But poisoning himself with the same shit responsible for my mother's death is extra fucked up."

I nod, validating his experience and hopefully taking on some of his burden.

"The rest of my childhood and teen years consisted of covering for my dad or making excuses for his drinking, dragging him back home when he became too intoxicated to remember where he lived and absorbing his depression and grief while trying to make ends meet. Today, when he used my mother's death as an excuse for his addiction... I lost it. I fucking saw red."

Dante closes his eyes and tilts his head back, his tormented soul on display.

"Breathe," I say softly, pressing my hand against his chest

157

and feeling his heartbeat. "Inhale for a count of four, and exhale for eight." We take another breath together, surrounded by this fragile moment.

When he opens his eyes again, I don't see any trace of the man who yelled at me. In his place is someone filled with genuine regret. He cut himself open and showed me the raw pain he keeps hidden. That means something to me.

"Anyway, I... I guess I wanted you to know. You deserve to hear the whole story, though none of that excuses the way I treated you. Jesus, I know I screwed up, and I–"

"My mom died when I was eighteen," I blurt.

"I'm so sorry, sunshine," he murmurs as he reaches out to cup the side of my neck.

Hearing his endearment for me fills me with warmth. The whispered, almost reverent way he says it ties my heart closer to his. "I knew she was sick. I thought it was a rare but curable immune disease. That's what she told me," I whisper. Dante doesn't say anything, he just rubs his thumb across my jaw in light, calming strokes. "We went through a lot of different in-home care people as well as a few lengthy stays in the hospital, but I guess I just didn't... I don't know. I didn't want to see all the other warning signs."

Dante furrows his brow, and I shake my head, trying to get on track.

"I'm getting ahead of myself. I was inspired to become a nurse because of my mom's struggles. I was away for my first year of college when... when it happened." Swallowing thickly, I blink back a few tears. "She didn't have a rare immune disease," I whisper. "She had Hodgkin's lymphoma. Some people can live five, ten, or even fifteen years after the initial diagnosis. From what I've pieced together, she was waiting to tell me until I graduated. But..."

I close my eyes and whimper against the flood of emotions welling up, still unable to say it out loud.

"But she didn't make it five or ten or fifteen years," Dante finishes for me.

"And I never got a chance to say goodbye," I murmur. I'm not sure he even heard me, but then he freezes. I open my eyes and see that he's completely stricken by my words. "That's why I was so insistent on you coming to visit. I realize now that I just wanted closure for myself. I didn't get to have a last conversation with my parent, but you can. It's not too late."

"Cambria," Dante whispers.

"But I know that was selfish of me. I didn't know the details, and it's none of my business anyway, and-"

"Cambria," he says again, stepping closer as he lets his hands wander down my body. Dante grips my hips and anchors me to him, our bodies pressed together, our hearts beating in time. "You did nothing wrong. You have the purest heart and the sweetest smile, and I'm the monster who made you cry."

"You're not a monster."

"And you're not selfish," he counters. This brings a tiny smile to my face. Dante rests his forehead on mine, his warmth surrounding me and drawing me closer, closer, closer to everything this man is. "Can you forgive me for losing my temper with you? Have I already fucked up everything?"

"I forgive you, Dante," I tell him truthfully, rubbing my nose against his. He gives me a smile, and everything in me clenches and releases. Holy hell, if I thought his scowl was sexy, his smile is on a whole new level.

"Thank God," he murmurs. "If you didn't forgive me, I couldn't do this." He gently tucks a few strands of hair behind my ear, those dark brown eyes filled with vulnerability and unnamed emotions, so different from the man who broke into my cottage a few days ago.

My gaze wanders down the slope of his nose, then rests on his lips, which look soft and welcoming.

"Do what?" I breathe out, swaying closer.

"I'm going to kiss you now, sunshine," he murmurs, his warm breath tickling my skin seconds before his lips claim mine.

Dante teases me with the tip of his tongue, then cups the back of my neck and angles me just right, diving into my mouth with long, passionate strokes. My hands crawl up his torso, slipping under the button-up he's wearing and caressing the dips and curves of his chiseled abs and chest.

"God, your touch..." he groans, his muscles flexing as I run my fingers over them. "You're perfect. So damn perfect."

Dante licks a stripe up my throat, pausing to nip at my pulse point. I let out a surprised squeak, followed by a moan when he sucks on the same spot. My knees tremble when he slides his hands up my body, continuing to leave a trail of kisses up and down my neck. Dante cups my breasts, massaging them and rubbing his thumbs over my tight, sensitive peaks.

"Yes," I whisper desperately, too lost in my pleasure to find my voice.

"You like that, Cambria?" he growls onto my lips, sucking on the bottom one before kissing me properly.

I nod, whimpering into his kiss when he pinches my nipples. Dante hums in approval, nuzzling into the side of my neck as his hand slides down my body and cups my pussy.

I should be embarrassed by how turned on I am, how freaking wet I am for this man, but Dante doesn't mind. It seems to drive him crazy.

This is my first time doing any of this with anyone, but I let my urges take over, chasing the ultimate pleasure I know only Dante can give me. I grind down on his hand, letting him feel all of me.

"Baby, you're killing me," he groans, resting his forehead on mine. "This little pussy is begging to be touched, isn't it?" I nod frantically and wiggle my hips, but Dante just grins. "Need your words."

"I w-want it," I stammer. I barely finish my sentence before Dante backs me into the small kitchen table and lifts me with his hands on my thighs.

I part my legs for him and whimper when he steps in between them and rubs his hard cock over my center.

"Fuck, I feel your heat, baby. Are you wet for me? Do you need this?" He thrusts his hips, hitting my clit through the thin material of my yoga pants and panties.

"Yes, yes, I need you." The words come pouring out of my mouth, almost without my permission.

Dante kisses me again and again, each swipe of his tongue wiping away my fears and doubts until all that's left is his taste, his smell, and his touch.

"Please," I gasp, though I'm not even sure what I'm asking for.

Dante grunts and rubs his fingers against my pussy, over the fabric of my clothes. I grind down on his hand and bury my face in his shoulder to muffle my cries.

"Jesus, you're so damn responsive. I'm hardly even touching you," he grunts.

"So why don't you touch me for real?"

His eyes go dark, and his jaw tenses before he crashes his lips into mine and kisses the breath right out of my lungs. He tears himself away from me, kneeling to press his face into my core, inhaling my scent through the fabric of my clothes.

Dante growls and dips his thumbs into the waistband of my pants. I lift my hips and watch as he peels my yoga pants and panties off in one swift move.

"This okay, Cambria?" he asks, pausing with his hands on my knees, looking me in the eyes to make sure I mean what I say.

I nod. "I want to feel you. I've always wondered what it would be like…" My face burns up at my words, knowing I just gave away my inexperience.

"You've never had anyone taste this juicy cunt, baby?"

His words are so filthy and so…hot. I shake my head no.

"Have you ever had anyone inside of you, Cambria?"

I close my eyes, not wanting to answer his question, and admit just how innocent I am.

"Tell me, sunshine. Tell me I'm the only one. Fucking tell me, Cambria," he demands.

"Only you," I whisper, finally opening my eyes.

"Jesus, you're perfect."

With that, he yanks my legs wide open so I'm spread out before him on the table. Dante flattens his tongue and takes a long, slow lick up the seam of my pussy, stopping to flick my clit and suck on the swollen ball of nerves.

I moan and fall back on the table, allowing Dante to guide one of my legs over his shoulder, followed by the other. I tilt my head and watch as he stares at my pussy. Something about that is inexplicably hot. I clench, and more of my juices leak out of me.

"So wet…" Dante growls before shoving his face between my thighs and making me crazy with need.

He's eating me out in desperate, forceful strokes. His tongue plunges inside my tight little hole, in and out, and then back up to circle my clit. I cry out and claw the table, seeking something to keep me grounded during this hurricane of pleasure.

Dante pulls back for a second, making me whine in frustration. He grabs my hands and puts them on his head. I instantly fist his hair, which causes him to grunt in approval.

"You need to hang on to something, you hang on to *me*."

I nod and shove his head between my legs again, making him chuckle into my soaking-wet folds. I feel the vibrations every-fucking-where, putting me right on the edge.

Dante sucks on my clit and thrusts a finger inside me without warning. I moan at the unexpected invasion and then wiggle my hips to get him to go deeper.

He leans back slightly to watch himself fuck me with his finger. The sloppy wet sounds fill the small room and make me tremble in anticipation. I can't contain the whimper that spills when he adds a second finger. I'm close, so, so close…

Dante's eyes snap to mine. He looks at me like he's going to rip me to shreds with his intense desire. I can't wait to let him. I slam my eyes shut as a delicious wave of ecstasy sweeps through my body and rattles my bones.

"Fuck, that's it, baby," he grunts before leaning down and sucking on my clit in time with the thrusts of his fingers.

I hold my breath as my muscles draw up tight. For a moment, I'm suspended in space, hovering, flying. The hard, merciless rhythm of his tongue is almost painful on my clit, overwhelming in the most glorious way. He twists his fingers and curls them up, breaking the tension over my body as the first wave of my orgasm floods through me.

I bow my back off the table and cry out, my legs slamming shut against his head, trapping him there. Dante slides his hands under my ass and squeezes the soft flesh. Hard. I buck against his mouth as my orgasm drips out of me. The thought of marking him with my release is so filthy and yet such a turn-on. I grind against him again, nearly losing my mind when he growls and bites down on my clit.

The sting of his teeth, followed by his tongue's smooth heat, has aftershocks rippling throughout my body, leaving me breathless and unable to move once I come down.

I'm aware of Dante scooping up my limp body and laying

me down on the bed before crawling in beside me. He guides me to lie across his chest, and I do, snuggling further into his embrace as he wraps me up in his arms.

"Are you okay, sunshine?" he whispers, rubbing calming circles on my back.

"Better than okay," I whisper, my cheeks still flushed from everything we just did.

Dante chuckles, and I prop myself up on his chest, taking in every bit of the sound. "What?" he asks, his eyebrows furrowed adorably.

"Nothing," I say with a smile. "I'm just enjoying your laugh. And smile."

I was trying to be sweet, but Dante's shoulders drop. "You're too good for me," he murmurs, pressing a kiss to my forehead.

"Well, I happen to disagree," I tell him, jutting my chin.

"Is that right?" he says with a smirk, nipping my nose and then my lips.

"Yes. And I want to prove it to you."

Dante stares at me for a few moments, an unreadable expression on his face. Just when I think he's suffering from sudden onset amnesia, Dante blinks and comes back to me.

"I'm ordering pizza tonight," he announces.

I couldn't be more shocked if he told me a saber tooth tiger was outside my window. "I didn't know you ate pizza."

"I'm Italian," he counters, readjusting so he can grab his phone.

I peer over at the screen, then giggle. "That may be true, but I don't think Pizza Barn is winning any authenticity awards."

Dante narrows his eyes at me, and I try suppressing a grin. The next second, he lunges for me, pressing my back against the mattress as he cages me in. "We're having a good old-fashioned movie night. Shitty pizza included."

"At the main house?"

Dante nods, and I cup his cheek, leaning up to give him a quick kiss.

"Thank you," I whisper, blinking back tears. He's trying to connect with his dad. The effort on his part means the world to me.

I'm already falling hard for this man. I just hope he doesn't break my heart when he leaves at the end of the week.

CHAPTER SEVEN

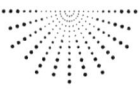

DANTE

I wasn't sure what to expect when I proposed a movie night; I just knew I needed to show Cambria I could do better. I can *be* better— for her.

Looking across the living room at my old man snoring away in his favorite recliner, a sense of peace washes over me. We have a long way to go in mending whatever is left of our relationship, but seeing him at ease settles something deep in my chest.

Hearing Cambria's confession about her mother felt like a punch to the gut. No, that's not accurate. It felt like a searing hot blade being shoved into my chest, cracking it in two. I felt the weight of her guilt with every breath and saw it in every tear that fell from her eyes.

I can't bring her mother back, but I can swallow my pride and try to salvage my relationship with my father. If Cambria found something good in him, maybe there's hope yet. I could say the same for myself. I'm not sure what the bright, sweet, tender-hearted Cambria sees in me, but she found something worth saving.

I just hope she still wants me after discovering what I do

for a living. It never occurred to me to tell her, but now it feels like I'm hiding something.

"What are you thinking about?" Cambria whispers from her spot next to me on the couch.

I peer down at her, smiling at how she's wrapped up in a fuzzy blanket. She has part of it covering her head like a hood, those bright blue eyes shining up at me, and she's so goddamn adorable, I don't know what the fuck to do with myself. I've never had these intense emotions before, never wanted someone so completely, never needed to consume them and make them part of my being.

Jesus, I sound demented.

Instead of admitting all my obsessive thoughts, I rest my arm on the back of the couch, motioning for Cambria to scoot closer. Her cheeks flush pink, which might be my new favorite color. I'm curious how far down that blush goes and what else I can do to bring it out.

"Are you cold, sunshine?" I murmur, sliding a hand into her blanket. Her breath hitches, and she tenses before melting into my side. "I could warm you up."

She nods before I've even finished my sentence, making me smirk.

Carefully, I readjust our positions so Cambria is sitting on my lap, with her back pressed against my chest. She tilts her head back, resting it on my shoulder, and I turn, grazing my lips across her exposed neck.

"That's it, baby," I whisper, covering us with the blanket. "Let me take care of you."

I slide one hand inside her shirt, caressing the soft skin of her stomach as my other hand gently rubs against her core, pressing the fabric of her leggings right up against her heat. She bucks her hips, but I hold her down, soothing her with calming strokes.

"What about Raul?" she asks, suddenly remembering we're not alone.

"You'll just have to be quiet," I tell her, raising an eyebrow in challenge.

She grins and wiggles her ass, making me groan. My dick is hard as a fuckin' fence post, and she's squirming around on my lap in the sweetest torture.

"Shh," she teases, grinding down my thickness.

I grip her hips, freezing her in place while I suck on her neck. "You drive me crazy," I grunt into her skin. Slowly, slowly, I drag a hand from her hip to the waistband of her leggings, flirting with the elastic as she trembles.

"Please," Cambria breathes.

Sliding a finger into her panties, I bite back a growl at how fucking wet she is. Her thighs tighten and snap around my hand, trapping it there. I massage her creamy folds, teasing her and touching her everywhere except where she needs me most.

My woman arches her back, trying to get me to touch her most sensitive spot. "Love how responsive you are," I rasp, circling, circling, circling her clit, feeling it swell but never quite giving in.

Cambria gasps and jerks her hips, and I swear to fucking God, I almost burst. It's like I can feel her excruciating need, her desperate lust, and it only fuels my own.

"Please," she whimpers again, her jagged breaths sawing in and out of her lungs as sweat beads on her forehead.

Unable to hold back any longer, I pinch her clit between my fingers and massage it, holding her down with my other arm across her hips, riding out her pleasure with her.

Right as she's about to hit the point of no return, Raul lets out a huge snore, then snorts himself awake, startling everyone in the room.

Cambria scrambles off me, taking the blanket with her. I

grab the nearest throw pillow and set it on my lap, hoping to hide my massive erection.

"Mr. S-Santa-Santarossa," Cambria stutters, trying to catch her breath. "Is everything all right?"

My father looks confused. His eyes dart from the TV, where the last few minutes of the movie are playing, to me in the corner of the couch and then to Cambria, who's starting to stand.

"Everything is fine," he says, taking a second to clear his throat. "I guess it's time for me to go to bed, eh? Can't keep up with the youths these days."

"Youth?" I ask with a chuckle. "I'm nearly forty."

"And I'm your old man, so don't remind me," he grouses.

Raul's brown eyes glimmer with something close to a smile. I never thought I'd see it again. Never thought I wanted to. But Cambria is changing everything about me.

"I'll bring your meds in," Cambria offers.

"I already set him up with everything in his room," I tell her. "Meds, water, and compression socks. I even turned down the sheets," I say, wagging my eyebrows at her.

She grins, her smile equal parts pride and gratitude. I want her to always look at me like that. I'd do anything to have this woman as mine and for her to be proud of me.

"That's my cue," Raul says as he sits up.

Cambria brings his walker over and helps him stand. He whispers something to her, and she nods, hugging him before sending him to bed.

As soon as my father is out of sight, I tug Cambria into my arms, wrapping them around her as I fuse my lips to hers. She kisses me back with the same intensity, her hands wandering up my chest, desperately clawing at my muscles.

Finally, I step back, chuckling when Cambria sways toward me. "What did he say to you?"

Cambria's lips pull into a soft smile as she looks up at me. "He thanked me for arranging your visit."

"Really?" I wasn't expecting that at all, and I'm not sure what to do with that information.

Cambria nods then takes my hand and laces her fingers through mine. "Want to walk me home?" she asks, her cheeks flushed a deep pink.

"I want to do many things with you tonight, sunshine. If you'll let me." She looks at me with an excited grin, nodding as she tugs me outside.

I storm out the back door, Cambria in tow, ready to claim this woman once and for all. I don't realize I'm sprinting until Cambria pulls on my arm, signaling me to slow down. Instead of changing my pace, I scoop her up and continue running to the little cottage, eager to feast on my woman again.

After shuffling my way inside, I untangle Cambria and set her on the ground, though I don't let her get very far. My hands slide up and down her curves while I kiss her soft, already-swollen lips. She melts against me, her body becoming pliant as I kiss and touch and feel all of her, everything she is.

Cambria runs her hands up my torso and loops her arms around my neck, pulling me back down for a punishing kiss. I open up and take what she's offering, meeting each frantic stroke of her tongue with as much passion and need as she's giving me.

After an hour of teasing and foreplay on the couch, I need this woman more than air. Need every inch of her, need to feel her wrapped around me, moaning my name as I sink deeper and deeper, marking her as mine.

She closes her eyes and tilts her head back, breaking our kiss so she can gulp down air. Her hands drift down to my biceps, where she grips me tightly, keeping me in place. I'm sure as fuck not going anywhere.

I can't keep my lips off her for one goddamn second. I kiss down her neck and lick the hollow of her throat before nipping the sensitive skin there. Cambria moans and digs her nails into my flesh, making me growl and grind my thickness into her heat.

"Gonna lick every inch of your sexy fucking body, Cambria. Then I'm gonna show you how amazing you are. How amazing I can make you feel."

Her eyes pop open, glowing with lust and hunger. Good. I plan to satisfy my woman on every level—carnal, physical, emotional; whatever the fuck she needs, she'll get it from *me* now.

She leans in as I do, our lips crashing together as our need amplifies. Her desperate kiss mirrors my own, her eager hands clawing at my clothes and begging me to give us what we both want. More.

I tear my mouth away from hers long enough to peel her shirt off, and then my lips are back on her skin, trailing down her neck. "Need to be inside you," I murmur into the shell of her ear.

Cambria lets out a sexy, needy whimper as I slip my hand into her tight little yoga pants that have been teasing me all night.

My fingers part her folds and find her clit, massaging circles over the bundle of nerves. "Damn, you need it too, don't you?"

"God, yes, Dante. I need you. Please, please, don't make me wait."

Hearing her beg for me is sweeter than anything I've ever experienced. A wave of pleasure rushes down my spine, drawing my balls up tight and making precum leak out of me like a damn faucet. This woman is my undoing.

I rid her of the last scraps of clothing and lift her into my arms, carrying my incredible woman to bed. I toss her on the mattress and strip down, adrenaline pumping in my veins and urging me to claim her right the fuck now.

Cambria is spread out for me on the bed, her white-blonde hair a tangled mess, her swollen lips slightly parted, her chest heaving with shallow breaths. Goddamn, she's gorgeous. And *mine.* She's all mine.

I climb on the bed and crawl up her body, kissing her thighs, torso, breasts, neck, and finally, her sweet lips. I rub my body against hers, needing that friction, needing to feel her skin against mine.

Cambria captures my lips, her tongue seeking entrance. I give my girl everything she wants, opening my mouth to welcome her kiss. It starts slow, with tentative licks. I groan at her innocence but manage not to take control. Yet.

Cambria explores my mouth, then pulls my bottom lip through her teeth, making me growl. She grins mischievously at me, and fuck, it physically pains me to hold back my orgasm.

"You like knowing you have control over me, sunshine?"

"Mmhm." She nods, her lips twisting into a flirty smile.

Cambria gasps and then giggles as I flip our positions so she's on top. "Then take it, baby. Take control."

She braces herself on my chest, pushing herself up and adjusting to our new position. For a second, Cambria looks unsure of herself, but all of that vanishes when she sees my angry cock trapped between our bodies.

Cambria grabs the fucker and squeezes *hard.* "Jesus Christ," I growl as I clench my fists.

She grins again, knowing exactly the kind of power she has over me. I slide my hands up her thighs and squeeze, helping her rock against me. Cambria licks her damn lips as she rolls her hips, rubbing her pussy up and down my shaft.

The head of my cock taps her clit, and she shivers, repeating the motion.

I cup her tits, weighing them in my hands and brushing my thumbs over her nipples.

"Yes," she hisses, her movements stuttering as she leans into my touch.

I play with her hardened peaks, twisting and plucking them while Cambria claws at my chest and rubs against me, getting herself off without me even entering her. Fuck, it's so damn hot watching her get all worked up, knowing I have so much more in store for her.

Cambria's movements grow frantic as she writhes on top of me. I feel her cream dripping from her pussy, so close to coming already. A shiver runs down her spine, and she holds her breath, preparing for her orgasm. I feel it pushing forward, demanding to be felt, making her whimper with each breath.

Right before it takes her under, I grip her hips and hold her still. Cambria looks down at me with confusion and frustration, but then understanding dawns when I line myself up with her entrance. I groan when I feel her tight little channel pulse around the head of my cock. Goddamn, her greedy little pussy is trying to suck me inside.

"Ready for me, Cambria? Ready to be mine?"

She nods, her hazel eyes glossed over with lust as she circles her hips, trying to get me where she wants me.

I hold her in place above me, not giving in yet. "I need your words, baby. Tell me how much you want this."

"I want you, Dante. I want everything with you. And I want it *now*."

The determined look on her face and the lust crackling between us have me growling like a beast. Cambria eases down the first few inches of my painfully hard shaft, then drops down, swallowing my dick in her tight, wet pussy.

"Jesus, fuck!" I roar, holding her still when she's fully seated. Cambria whimpers, and I lean up to kiss her pain away. "You did so good," I say, trying to make my voice soothing even though the most intense pressure is building inside me, ready to take over and fuck my woman properly. "Take it slow."

She nods and kisses me again, her tense body relaxing as I run my hands up and down her thighs and back. I grip her ass, helping her rock and circle her hips to find what feels good.

"Yes!" Cambria cries out, wiggling her hips and hitting her G-spot against my thick dick. She shudders and moans, rolling her sexy fucking body on top of mine, taking control of her pleasure.

She leans back, resting her hands on my thighs and baring her beautiful body while she rides my cock. I slide one hand up her torso while the other squeezes her ass and opens her up even more for me.

I cup her breast and pinch her nipple, groaning when more of her cream spills out. Jesus, I barely manage to keep it together when I look down and see where we're connected. Watching her soaking wet little cunt stretch obscenely wide to take in my many inches is something I'll remember for the rest of my life.

"That's it, Cambria. That's so fucking it," I growl, moving my hands to her hips, jerking her up and down as I meet her thrust for thrust.

Her pussy flutters around me as her muscles lock up tight. She falls forward, resting her hands on either side of my head. Her lips find mine, and we kiss and fuck like the world is burning down around us, and this is our last chance to find love and passion.

She buries her face into my neck and sobs as her body shakes and tightens around me. My beautiful woman bites my neck and creams all over my cock as she reaches her climax.

Feeling her orgasm devastate her snaps something inside me.

I roll over, changing our position and fucking into that little pussy, unable to control myself. Her back bows off the bed and her legs wrap around me, holding me close. She digs her heels into my ass and claws my back, leaving her mark on me as another orgasm rattles through her.

"So good, baby," I growl, claiming her lips as my own.

I devour her, biting at her lips and spearing my tongue inside her eager mouth, licking up every inch and then sucking on her tongue. It's a wild, messy kiss, one that matches the way I'm fucking her like a goddamn animal.

I slide one hand down her body and grip her ass cheek, changing the angle of her hips and helping her meet me thrust for thrust. My cock scrapes against her most sensitive spot with each fierce stroke.

She's breaking apart for me; I can feel it. Every time I hit the end of her, she cracks a little more, the pressure of her orgasm building and pulsing and pushing her boundaries.

My balls draw up tight as my orgasm gathers in the base of my spine. My rhythm falters slightly as I try to hold on, needing her to come with me. "Get there, baby, fuck, please get there. Need one more from you."

"I don't think I can…"

"I've got you, Cambria. Let go for me. I'm right here. Let go, love. Come for me."

She sucks in a huge breath and holds it, her whole body trembling and then freezing. Every damn muscle is pulled tight as she clings to me with everything she has. With one last brutal thrust, we both shatter.

Cambria floods my cock with her release, and I give her everything in return, my cum splashing into her throbbing pussy as she sucks down every last drop. We grunt, shake, and sweat as we ride that high together.

Eventually, she goes limp in my arms. I bury my face into her neck and pump into her twice more before collapsing. I roll to the side and drape my freshly fucked little angel over my chest.

"Holy shit," she mumbles into my chest, her voice scratchy as she catches her breath.

"Yeah," I agree, as worn out and awed as she is. I mean...fuck. If I didn't know before, I know now. She's it for me. "Are you okay?" Doubt and worry rush in to take the place of euphoria. "I was so rough with–"

Cambria cuts me off with a kiss. "You were perfect," she whispers into my lips before kissing me again. "Absolutely perfect. I can't wait to do it again."

I curse under my breath and tangle my fingers in her hair, angling her head to deepen our kiss. My cock is sore from how hard I fucked her, but damn if he isn't twitching to life, ready for another round.

Cambria automatically curls against me when we break apart, her head resting over my heart. I comb my fingers through her hair, counting the beats of her heart as they slow and settle into an even rhythm.

"You're perfect," I whisper, though I don't think she can hear me.

Soft snores fall from her lips, and I smile, covering us with a blanket before settling down for the greatest night's sleep I've had in a long damn time.

CHAPTER EIGHT

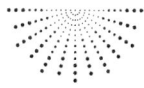

CAMBRIA

I wake to birds chirping outside the window, squinting my eyes against the ray of sunshine peeking through the curtains. Every muscle is deliciously sore, and my entire body flushes with the memory of everything we did last night.

As I slowly become aware of my surroundings. I realize Dante is curled up behind me, his front covering my back in a protective hold. He has one arm tucked under my head as a pillow and the other arm wrapped around my torso, keeping me close.

I carefully turn over in his arms and take in his strong, gorgeous face. I can't help it; I reach out and trace over his thick eyebrows as I watch those long lashes flutter across his cheeks. I let my finger drop down the length of his straight nose before lightly touching the stubble along his jaw.

Dante smiles with his eyes still closed, and I swear I'll remember that look on his face for the rest of my life. His head turns to the side as he kisses my palm. He opens his beautiful brown eyes, and I feel the warmth in them down to my core. I can't help the smile that breaks out on my face.

177

His hair is messy, his eyelids heavy, yet he looks at me with such… love?

Dante leans in and kisses the tip of my nose, making me giggle.

"You're kind of adorable in the morning," I tell him, tracing his lips.

He opens one eye and quirks up an eyebrow while nipping at my finger.

"Hey!" I giggle again.

"I'm not adorable. I'm handsome." He kisses my forehead. "Manly." He kisses my nose. "And extremely sexy." He takes my lips in a scorching kiss that gets me all kinds of riled up.

"Mmm… and adorable," I smirk.

"Call me adorable one more time, woman," he growls, "And see what happens."

"Adorable," I whisper.

In one swift move, Dante flips me on my back and pins my arms above my head, making me squeal. "What am I?" he asks in mock outrage.

"Adorable," I say again, smiling up at him. I like this playful side.

His lips crash into mine, and he sucks my tongue into his mouth, devouring me before releasing me to let me catch my breath.

"Still think I'm adorable?" he asks, his eyes heated.

I nod, too breathless to give him my words. Dante gives me a devilish grin like he can't wait to prove me wrong. I can't wait, either.

He trails his hands over my shoulders, in between my breasts, over my ribcage and stomach, finally resting on my hips. "Fucking beautiful," he murmurs.

Leaning down again, he kisses me slowly and then blazes a trail of open-mouthed kisses down my neck and over my collarbone. He licks one nipple and pulls it through his teeth, making me whimper.

Dante groans, sending vibrations throughout my entire body. "So perfect, sunshine. Every part of you."

He switches sides and gives my other pebbled peak the same attention. He kisses and nips his way down my body, dipping his tongue into my belly button before scraping his teeth over one hip bone and then the other.

Resting his forehead on my lower abdomen, he buries his nose in my soft mound of curls and takes a deep breath. "My new favorite way to wake up," he grunts, prying my legs open and diving into my core.

"Ohmygod!" I cry out. His tongue feels incredible, warm and wet against my clit.

Dante licks me up and down, dipping his tongue into my entrance and then circling my clit. Again and again. He leans back and looks up at me, my juices glistening on his face. It's unbelievably sexy.

"Delicious," he says before lowering his head and licking me from top to bottom.

He swipes a finger through my slit and gathers some of my wetness, offering me a taste. I automatically suck on his finger, eager to please him. He groans as I circle my tongue around and around before nipping the pad of his finger.

Seemingly satisfied, he turns his attention back to my aching pussy. He focuses on my clit, drawing patterns around my sensitive ball of nerves. And then a finger slides inside me.

"So fucking tight, Cambria. God*damn*."

He thrusts his large finger in and out of me while continuing his assault on my clit. I cry out when he adds a second finger, stretching me in the most deliciously painful way. My legs begin to tremble as the now familiar pressure pools in my belly, and my body starts to give up control.

"Ohmygod, oh, Dante!"

He chuckles into my pussy, sending vibrations all over my body. He doesn't let up, though. It feels like I'm on the brink of exploding. My muscles tense, and I make incoherent noises as his tongue and fingers take me higher, higher, higher until...

"Dante!" I scream. My pussy convulses and gushes as my muscles tense to the point of pain, but in the best, most intense way possible.

"I've got you, baby. Give me one more."

He dips his tongue deep inside my hole, lapping up my release, while his thumb circles my clit. The initial powerful wave of pleasure dies down a bit, but my pussy feels swollen and sensitive as Dante continues to work me up with his skillful mouth.

My second orgasm hits me before I'm prepared for it, the force of ecstasy making me forget to breathe. I cry out and jump when his tongue flicks against my clit.

Dante turns his head and bites the inside of my thigh, then licks away the sting. Crawling up my body, he claims my lips like a starving man. Ironic since he just ate me out and pulled two orgasms from me with his sinful mouth.

I taste myself on him, and it's so fucking hot. His hands are everywhere–pulling my hair, squeezing my breasts, grabbing my hips to pull me closer. I break the kiss to get some much-needed air into my oxygen-deprived lungs. He takes the opportunity to kiss down my neck before resting his head on my shoulder.

"Fuck, sunshine. You come apart so beautifully for me. Love seeing you lose control like that," he says before kissing my neck again. He pulls my earlobe through his teeth, making me moan. "Still think I'm adorable?" he whispers into my ear.

"If I say yes, will you do that again?" I ask, still catching my breath.

Dante chuckles darkly and flips me over on my stomach. I love that he can do whatever he wants with me. Like I'm his. His hands reach under my hips and pull me up so I'm on my hands and knees. Then he leans over, his front covering my back, his hard cock pressing between my ass cheeks.

"I might just spank you, baby," he whispers.

Dante leans back, and I hear a slap before I register the sharp sting on my ass.

"Hey!"

He does it again on the other side. My head falls forward as I try to catch my breath. Why does this feel so fucking *good*? Two fingers plunge into my throbbing core once, twice, three times, and then circle my clit.

Dante pulls his hand away and spanks me four times in a row, alternating sides.

"Dante!" I cry out.

He circles my clit again with one hand as his other hand grabs my hair and twists my head so he can kiss me roughly.

"You like that? My dirty girl likes being spanked?" he whispers against my lips.

Dante doesn't wait for my response before straightening up and smacking my ass again. I feel the sharp sting spike through my blood, setting every nerve ending on fire, which only makes his fingers on my clit feel that much more intense. Dante massages my deliciously sore cheeks. I'm so on edge, he could set me off with a single breath.

As if reading my thoughts, Dante lines up with my entrance and thrusts inside me, hitting me deeper than ever before. I come instantly, crying out his name as my body pulses with pleasure.

He fucks me right through my orgasm, his fingers digging into my hips. "That's it, baby. Let go for me."

He grips my hair again, tugging my head to the side to kiss me while he strokes in and out of my swollen cunt.

Dante sits back up and pulls my cheeks apart, spreading me wide open for him. "Love watching you take my big dick."

He speeds up, fucking me hard and so, so deep. I push back into him, meeting him thrust for thrust. Dante grunts and angles his hips, hitting my most sensitive spot each time he fucks into me.

"Oh god… I'm… I'm going to…"

"Take all of me, baby. Come with my name on your lips."

God, his words are so damn dirty.

Dante spanks me one more time, and I lose control, letting go of everything. Pleasure erupts from my core, rippling outward through every square inch of my body, prickling my skin, and gushing out between my legs. He pistons in and out of me, our skin slapping together, making obscene noises as one orgasm rolls into another.

"Jesus, fuck. So. Damn. Good. *Cambria*!" He roars his release as I shudder out the last of my orgasm.

Dante rolls to the side and wraps me in his arms, my back to his front. We're covered in sweat and panting, but neither of us has the strength to move.

"Is it always that good?" I eventually ask as our breathing slows.

Dante hums and kisses the back of my neck. "I don't remember anyone before you, sunshine," he whispers into the shell of my ear. "But I promise you, it will always be this good for us. You know why?"

I look at him over my shoulder, hanging on his every word. It almost sounds like he's going to profess his love to me, but I know that would be preposterous.

"Why?" I ask, nibbling my bottom lip.

Dante leans in, his lips barely brushing mine when his

phone rings. "Shit," he groans, nipping my lip before rolling over to grab his phone. Frowning at the screen, Dante jumps up and silences the call, then gives me an apologetic look. "I have to take this. It's my boss. Might be a little while."

Though I'm a little disappointed, I nod and give an understanding smile. Dante sees right through me, throwing on his pants and a shirt before kneeling beside me on the bed. His phone rings again, but he silences it. I get the feeling Dante is always on call for work and never lets something go unanswered, so I appreciate his attention and knowing he chose me over answering right away.

"I'll make it up to you later," he murmurs, pressing a kiss to the side of my neck.

"It's not that. I just..." I sigh and look away, but my man isn't having any of that. He cups my chin and draws my face back toward his. "We've slept together twice now, and I don't even know what you do."

Dante's eyes flash with something fierce, but it's gone before I'm even sure what I saw. He dips his head, shielding his face from me as he kisses my cheek. "I'll tell you everything soon," he vows.

"When?"

Dante gives me one last kiss on the nose, then stands up, searching for his shoes. "Tonight. I'll pick up groceries while I'm out and make us my mother's *rigatoni alla carbonara* for dinner at the main house with Raul."

"You cook?"

I never thought I'd see Dante blush, but here he is, cheeks flushed all the way to the tips of his ears. "I haven't had a reason to cook in years, but yes, sunshine. My mother taught me everything she knew before..."

I'm out of bed in the next instant, throwing my arms around him. He catches me and stumbles back a bit, looking down at me with confusion and amusement. "Thank you," I whisper. "Thank you for making an effort. Thank you for showing me more of who you are. Just... thank you."

He gives me that same look from the other day like he can't believe I'm saying these things to him. It hurts my heart, but I'm determined to keep filling his head with positive things until he sees himself the way I see him; worthy of love.

"Never thank me, Cambria. You're the one working your magic. I'm happy to be along for the ride."

I smile and lean in for a kiss, but Dante's phone rings for a third time. He gives me a peck on the lips, then untangles himself from my embrace and answers the phone.

"Yes, Boss, everything is fine. Trouble getting out of bed this morning."

Dante is almost out the door when he turns to me and winks, mouthing the words *totally worth it,* and *I'll see you for dinner* before stepping outside.

I take my time in the shower, lounging in my robe with a cup of tea before getting dressed for the day. It's Saturday, so Raul and I have a more relaxed schedule. During the week, I like to keep him to a routine, but everyone deserves to relax on the weekends. Except for Dante, apparently.

As I make my way up to the main house, I try not to obsess over why he wouldn't tell me what he does for a living. But how hard is it to say *I'm a lawyer* or *I don't have a traditional job? People pay me to take my clothes off so they can stare at my glorious body.*

Okay, so that second one probably isn't the case, but good lord, the man could make a living as a nude model. Not that I want to share him with anyone else. He's all mine and finally trusting me with all the little pieces of his story. I have to be patient while I wait for him to tell me everything.

Raul and I have an easy breakfast of toast and fresh fruit, followed by a few rounds of Connect Four and reruns of

Matlock. It's a pretty typical Saturday, but something feels off.

At first, I think I'm just missing Dante. It's crazy, but the enigmatic man has become essential to my being in the five days he's been here.

While I do wish Dante were here, this is something else. Dante makes me feel on edge, but in a thrilling way. I always feel safe with him, so I'm excited about whatever his dark looks and sinful smirks mean.

This nagging feeling in the back of my mind isn't safe. Not at all. It has the hairs on my neck standing up, making me jump at every slight noise.

Still, I go about my daily chores, picking up clutter here and there, gathering trash bags and replacing the lining, and washing the sheets. The sense of unease grows with each new task, and my stomach is twisted into knots by the time I'm ready to take the garbage out.

"I'll be right back!" I call to Raul as I hoist a trash bag over my shoulder. He doesn't answer, and I assume he's passed out in front of the TV. Nothing puts him to sleep like Matlock, but I learned my lesson not to change the channel, even if he's snoring. Somehow, Raul knows when Andy Griffith isn't on the screen.

I head outside, walking faster than usual to the bins on the other side of the garage. I get a whiff of cigarette smoke, which is odd. According to his medical history, Raul quit smoking a decade ago, and I haven't seen him light up once since I've been here. Plus, it's not like he can hop in a car and buy himself a carton of Marlboros.

By the time I walk back inside, I've convinced myself I'm being paranoid. Probably the lack of sleep last night, with all the times Dante and I gave into our pleasure.

"Ready for lunch?" I ask as soon as I step inside. "How do grilled cheese and tomato soup sound?"

"A little plain for my taste," a raspy voice answers.

I barely have time to register the large man dressed in all black coming toward me before his fingers wrap around my bicep, digging in deep as he grips my arm and drags me into the living room.

"Mr. Santarossa!" I exclaim, trying to break free of the intruder's hold, when I see Raul lying on the ground, his walker tipped over as if they pushed him down.

"Ah-ah, little miss," the man tsks, spinning me around to face him. "So this is the woman who made Dante lose his edge," he says. The man licks his lips and gives me a menacing smile, his yellow teeth and rancid breath making my stomach churn. "A little too big for me, but I guess some people have fetishes."

Rage and terror flood my system, the conflicting emotions tangling in my lungs and making breathing hard.

Who the hell is this guy? Why is he here? What does this have to do with Dante?

"Wh-what are y-you–"

His hand smacks against my cheek before I register the burning pain. My head jerks to the side at the force of his slap, and before I can make a sound, his meaty hand covers my mouth in a punishing hold.

"Shut up, bitch," he snaps, his nearly black eyes narrowing on me. "You're good for one thing; being a bargaining chip."

I dart my gaze from side to side, my breaths growing choppy against the stranger's palm. Something shifts in the corner of my vision, and I hear a roar as Raul drags himself into a standing position and charges the man with his walker, hurling it at him and knocking him off balance.

His grip loosens on my face, and he lets go of my arm to fend off the attack. I spin out of his reach and run to Raul, catching him before he falls again.

"Come on," I hiss, dragging his frail body through the living room. "We have to–"

The front door bursts open, and three more men dressed in all black file inside, stopping us in our tracks. Without a word, one man grabs Raul while another grabs me, forcing us face-down to the ground.

I turn my head to the side, my cheek resting on the carpet as my attacker presses his knee into my back and ties my wrists together. Raul is facing me, his brown eyes filled with anger. He no longer looks like a fragile seventy-five-year-old with a life-threatening disease. No, this Raul is fierce and protective, though his body isn't allowing him to fight back.

"We'll be okay," I tell him, blinking back tears when his arms are yanked backward so they can be tied at the wrists. "Dante will come for us."

"I know," Raul says, nodding as much as he can from that angle. "My son is a good man. He will do what's right."

Those words ease the aches and pains in my body. I never thought I'd hear them from Raul, and I'm terrified he won't get the chance to say them to Dante.

"Aye!" shouts the original intruder, stomping over to us. "Thought I told you to shut the fuck up. Guess I'll have to make you." He kneels in front of me and pulls a syringe out of his pocket.

"No! No, I–"

A needle pricks the side of my neck, and I hear a faint scream, though I'm not sure if it's coming from Raul or me. The world fades, and my vision grows blurry before fizzling out altogether.

Hurry, Dante. We need you...

CHAPTER NINE

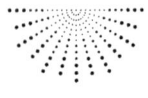

DANTE

*A*fter getting off the phone with Romeo, I took a cab downtown to do some shopping for tonight. Everything has to be perfect. Not just the meal but my words. My actions. I have a chance at happiness, at a future I never knew I wanted. I just need to find the right way to tell Cambria and my father that I'm in the mafia. And convince them to relocate to New York.

No pressure.

As I stroll down Michigan Avenue, I reach into my pocket, my fingers brushing over the little velvet box I purchased from Tiffany & Co. I'm hoping the five-carat diamond ring surrounded by sapphires in a vintage setting will help seal the deal.

Crazy? Obsessive? Over the top? Absolutely. Ask me if I give a single fuck. Cambria is *mine*, and it's time the entire world knows.

I'm about to hail another cab to take me to a market for groceries when my phone buzzes with a text. Probably Romeo with an update on the contract with the meatpacking union, aka the UFCW. Valentino was supposed to settle on a lower fee for their services laundering dirty Di Salvo money earlier today, which is what the call was about this morning.

Looking at the screen, however, I see it's from an unknown number. That's a huge red flag. No one has access to this phone number except those in the inner circle.

I debate what to do for a few moments. If I were in New York, I'd track Romeo down before opening the text. As it is, I'm nearly a thousand miles away with no backup. I didn't think I'd need any for this trip, especially since I only planned to be here for a few days before giving up and flying home.

Another text comes in while I'm making up my mind, this one with an image attachment. I give in and open both texts, my blood pressure spiking when I see what they contain.

I concentrate on not snapping my goddamn phone in half while reading the first text.

Lovely family you have. If you want to see them again, convince Romeo to back off the UFCW.

Unimaginable rage boils up from the depths of my soul when my eyes land on the image attachment. It surges through my veins, pumping adrenaline into every cell and making my muscles scream with the need to pulverize every motherfucker who dared to look at my Cambria, let alone touch her.

My phone shakes as I tighten my grip, my gaze never leaving the screen. Cambria is tied up and slumped against the wall, a piece of Duct tape covering her mouth. Her white-blonde hair is tangled around her face, a mix of dirt and blood woven through the strands. Cambria's head is lolled to the side, her eyes closed. I see a fucking needle mark on her neck, along with bruises, scrapes, and a few open wounds.

Jesus fucking Christ, I can't breathe. My heart comes to a stuttering halt, pain searing through my chest the longer I take in the suffering they put my woman through.

Raul is next to her, his arms also tied behind his back with a piece of tape over his mouth, but it seems they were gentler with him. He's awake, at least, and the rage in his eyes nearly matches mine. I know he doesn't give a shit about himself, but he's ready to murder these men for touching Cambria.

The last thirty years of bitterness and apathy toward my father evaporate instantly, and his words from earlier in the week come back to me.

I realized the same thing you're about to. That Cambria is special and worth fighting for.

"You're goddamn right," I growl, finally tearing my eyes from my phone. The longer I stare at it, the less rational my thoughts are. I've never had a problem focusing my anger into productivity or reining it in enough to come up with a plan, but right now, all I want to do is find those fuckin' Colombos and rip their throats out.

In my hazy rage, I think clearly enough to call Romeo. It goes to voicemail, and I immediately call again. Cursing loudly, I get a few looks from strangers on the sidewalk, but I shoot them a glare that sends them running.

I dial Romeo's office number, hoping desperately that he's there, and left his cell somewhere else. He picks up on the second ring, and I don't let him get a word out before I jump in and tell him the issue.

"They have her. And my father. They… they… they fuckin' got 'em while I was out, tied them up, and, and, and, fuck! Fuck, Romeo, what do I do? Goddamn Colombos have my woman and my dad. They want us to back off the union or else…"

"Dante," comes Armando's voice. Everything in me recoils.

"What the hell—"

"Romeo is, uh, indisposed at the moment."

"Go. Fucking. Get. Him."

"No way, man. If I walked in on him and Thalia, he would pluck my eyes out and chop my dick off before throwing me into the Hudson with a cement brick tied to my neck."

I know he's right, but I don't care. Nothing else matters.

"This is life or death," I grit out.

"Talk to me," Armando says. "I can help."

I scoff, but it's not like I have a choice. "They were digging through my garbage," I say, more to myself than to Armando.

"Yeah, we went over that a few days ago. I didn't know they had tracked you down."

"I didn't either. I didn't think it was a real threat. I just... I wasn't in the right headspace. Fuck, I fucked up, and now they're in danger, and I just found her, and..."

"Calm down, man," Armando interjects.

"Fuck off," I growl.

"I'm serious, Dante. You're no good worked up like this. Trust me. I know you think I'm some idiot who likes to punch things, but I've come a long way since Romeo first found me. It all started with controlling the rage instead of letting it control me. You get what I'm saying?"

"No. I need answers, Armando. I need my hands around their throats. I need to see the life drain from their eyes. I need–"

"To breathe," he finishes for me. "Even if you figure out where they took your father and..."

"Cambria."

"Right. Even if you figure out where they took your father and Cambria, what are you going to do? Barge in by your-self? You'll get them and yourself killed."

I snarl at the thought, but Armando continues.

"And do we know who exactly took her? Was this a

strategic move on the Colombo's part, or did a handful of wannabe's see an opportunity?"

"I don't know. I don't fucking know, but I need to find out."

"Who do we know in Chicago?" Armando asks. "I know you keep up relationships and communications between other families. Never put much stock in that part of your job, but I can see how it's helpful now."

"Right," I breathe out, going through my mental list of contacts in this area. "Chicago is Moscatelli territory."

"Rocco is one of their enforcers," Armando surprises me by adding.

"Yeah, I think that's right. How did you know?"

"Us dumb jocks stick together," he jokes. I don't have it in me to yell at him, and truthfully, I appreciate his level-headedness in this situation. I can't believe I just had that thought about Armando, but this day is fucking with everything I've ever known.

"You get a hold of Rocco, and I'll see if I have Matteo or Luca's number. I have a picture and a number from the kidnappers I'll forward to you."

"I'll get Valentino to run the number and see if we can track it," he offers. "Romeo will be informed of the situation as soon as it's safe to approach him."

I nod, even though I know he can't see me. "Thanks, Armando," I choke, clearing my throat of emotion. Never thought I'd say that, but I don't regret it.

"I've got your back, Dante. We'll find your woman and your father."

A moment after we hang up, an address pops up in the form of a text from Armando. It's an old-school Italian bistro a few blocks away, and I'm sure the Moscatelli family operates it.

Sure enough, as soon as I reach the front door, I'm

ushered inside and led to the back of the restaurant. There, in a separate dining area with dimmed lights and an extravagant bar taking up an entire wall, sit three men in a booth.

"Dante Santarossa," the middle one says, tilting his head toward the light. I can barely make out the strong jawline and furrowed brows in the low lighting, but that voice is one I'd recognize anywhere.

"Matteo Moscatelli," I respond, holding my hand out to shake his.

The man grasps my hand, giving it one good squeeze before dropping it. "I hear you need assistance."

"Yes, I, I mean, my Cambria, uh, well, the nurse who takes care of my father, she…" I clear my throat, trying to get my shit together.

"This is about a woman you love?" Matteo snaps.

I'm not sure if he's about to yell at me, shoot me, or laugh in my face, but I tell him the truth. "Yes. The Colombos followed me here from New York and have my Cambria and my father tied up in a goddamn warehouse somewhere."

Matteo leans forward, resting his elbows on the table as he steeples his hands in front of him. "Why did they follow you here? Are you bringing war to us?"

"No," I'm quick to reply. "The Colombos tried getting in on our territory, taking over one of our businesses. They started this, and they deserve whatever is coming to them. Truthfully, I suspect these fools are acting independently without direct orders from their boss. Either way, they want to use my family as a bargaining chip to scare us away."

"Is it working?"

I growl at the revered mafia boss, who remains stoic as ever. "The Di Salvos will never back down. We are not afraid of anything."

"But you, Dante. Are *you* afraid?"

His dark eyes find mine, and I know we're not high-ranking members from different mafia families at this moment. We're two men who know what it's like to have something precious stolen from them.

Everyone has heard the legend of Matteo and Darlene. When a rival family took Darlene, Matteo went to war for her. It turns out that Darlene was a queen in her own right and handled her shit better than anyone could have imagined.

So, when I answer Matteo, I know I'm talking to a man who understands the stakes.

"I'm fucking terrified to live on a planet where Cambria doesn't exist. I will stop at nothing to bring her back and to keep her safe, with or without your men or your help."

Matteo holds my gaze, his jaw clenched as he assesses me. Finally, with a single nod, I know I have backup.

The back room lights up with a flurry of activity as if everyone was awaiting the signal to spring into action. I suppose they were.

"Did you respond to the text?" Matteo asks.

"Not yet; I didn't know what to do."

"Tell them you'll meet with them to negotiate. I already have my captains searching the area with foot soldiers for any place matching the background of the photo that was sent."

"And we're working on tracing the number of the person who sent you those texts," says the man sitting to the right of Matteo. Luca, his second in command, I assume. We've talked over the phone but never in person.

"Thank you," I say softly, humbled by the work they have already put into place.

I shoot off a text, staring at the screen and willing for a reply with an address. *Give me a goddamn address, and I'll be there.*

Another text comes through at the same time, this one

from Romeo. *Armando filled me in on the situation. The Moscatellis will get you anything you need, and we'll repay them double their efforts. Get your girl and your father and come back to New York.*

I shoot back a text thanking him for his generosity. I should have run this past Romeo before even talking to Matteo, but thankfully, the Boss seems to understand my frantic state of mind. I know he can relate to the safety of the woman he loves being on the line.

"We'll get your family back," Matteo says firmly, bringing me back into the present. His phone rings, and he answers it right away. "Bosco, any news? Southside? Yes. Yes. We'll be there in five."

Guns click and shuffle underneath the table as the men step out of the booth and tuck their pieces away. Matteo lifts the seat of the booth they were just in, revealing a safe. He punches in a code, then opens the top to reveal a stock of weapons.

Luca grabs another gun, along with Matteo. The third man reaches in and then tosses me a pistol. "Just in case," he says. I nod. "Dante, right? Armando told me to watch out for you."

"I don't need a babysitter," I mumble as I check the gun and load the first bullet in the chamber.

He chuckles. "Yeah, he said you'd say that."

I glare at him. "Rocco, I assume?"

"At your service." He holds out his hand, and I take it. "I won't fuck around on this mission," he tells me seriously. "We all know what it's like to have the one person you care about in danger. I promise we'll do everything we can for her."

I swallow past the lump in my throat and nod. "Thank you."

"Let's go, men," Matteo announces.

"Should I wait for them to respond?" I ask.

"If they give us the address, great. If not, we know where they're at. Might as well surprise them."

It makes sense, and I feel foolish for not thinking of it myself. I'm always in control of the situation. I know where everything and everyone is at all times. I've planned for the worst-case and best-case scenarios and have an appropriate weapon for each.

But right now, my mind is flashing hazard lights and shooting daggers into my temples. Fuckin' tension headache won't let up, and I know it won't go away until I have Cambria safe in my arms again.

A handful of minutes later, we pull into what appears to be shipping docks and a crumbling storage facility that have long been abandoned.

"You're sure this is where they're at?" I ask from the back seat. My leg hasn't stopped tapping up and down the entire car ride. I'm crawling out of my skin being cooped up back here.

"One way to find out," Rocco says from beside me.

He reminds me a lot of Armando, and I can see why they would get along. Instead of being annoyed, I find it oddly comforting.

As we climb out of the car, Matteo motions for us to get down. He signals for Luca and Rocco to head around the back of the condemned building, then joins me and points toward the front.

My phone buzzes in my pocket, and I pull it out, showing Matteo a text with the address to the building we're currently standing in front of.

He gives me a satisfied grin, proud of his men for figuring it out. "Perfect timing. They won't be expecting you so soon. Go in, keep them talking, and my men will do the rest. When the bullets start flying, grab your girl. Rocco will get your dad."

I nod, committing the plan to memory. It's not complicated; it's just taking that much mental energy to focus on the next thing. I'm going out of my fucking mind.

"Dante," Matteo grits. His tone is forceful and cannot be ignored. I snap my eyes to his, giving him my full attention. "You can do this. Now, go."

He fades into the shadows around the side of the structure, and I take a deep breath, remembering what Cambria told me all those mornings ago.

It's all about grounding yourself in the moment. Inhale for a count of four, and exhale for eight.

Closing my eyes, I inhale deeply, breathing in her essence, her light, her sunshine, letting everything about my Cambria fill me with purpose. Then I exhale the negativity and bullshit, focusing on the most important thing in my life. When I open my eyes, I'm ready to burn this fucking building to the ground to get my woman.

I bang on the door and kick it open, not flinching when I'm met with two guns pointing at me. "Where the fuck are they?" I shout, drawing the attention of two other men in the back.

Taking stock of my surroundings, I see four Colombos. With Matteo, Luca, Rocco, and myself, we also have four. I happen to know, however, that Matteo has three dozen men surrounding this building, ready to jump in if necessary.

"Let him in," comes the scratchy voice of one of the men further inside. "Wasn't expecting you so soon."

I squint as I adjust to the much darker lighting in the building. I don't see anything at first, but movement in the corner of the room catches my eye.

"Cambria," I growl, taking a step in her direction.

Her face is swollen where one of these degenerates hit

her. A few blood streaks on her face and clothes hint at other wounds. Jesus, seeing her like this...

She rolls her head to the other side as if it takes every last bit of energy. When she sees me, a heart-shattering whimper falls from her lips. Every muscle tenses, and I'm a coil ready to fucking snap.

"Not so fast," one of the men rasps. "Do we have a deal?"

I stare at him, getting a good look at the stupidest mother fucker to ever walk the planet. He's a few inches over five and a half feet and looks like he's spent his entire life trying to be bigger than he is. I don't recognize him, which only confirms my earlier suspicions. I know all the top-ranking members of the Colombo family, as well as a handful of the Don's favorite Capos. This guy? He's some lackey. Some foot soldier. Some dumb fuck on an ego trip trying to prove himself to his Boss. Pathetic.

"What exactly is your plan here?" I ask the inexperienced thug playing dress up.

The more my eyes adjust to the light, the more I see of his outfit. He's wearing dress slacks, a long trench coat, and a bowler hat. He looks like a goon from the 1940s, and if I weren't two seconds away from blowing his goddamn brains out, I'd laugh at his cartoonish appearance.

"Thought I made that clear," he spits, puffing up his chest.

"Oh, it's clear, all right," I counter, taking a few steps in his direction. All eyes are on me, which is perfect. No one will notice Luca slipping in the back, followed by Rocco. "It's clear you're in way over your head. How many of you are here? Four? Did you convince your BFFs to join you on this suicide mission to impress your Boss?"

"Hey, I–"

"Because that's exactly what this is. Does he even know you're here? Are you working on his behalf, or did you go behind his back and piss off the second in command of the most powerful family in New York fucking City?"

"Well, that's not exactly–"

"From where I'm standing," I continue, towering over him as I draw closer, "this is an amateur job done by kiss-assess who are about to get themselves killed."

"Who do you think you are to come in here like this?" he shouts. "I have all the cards here! I have your girl, your dad, and you have *nothing*."

The short man is shaking, his face a mottled red as he heaves out uneven breaths. I look over his head just in time to catch Matteo's signal. Three shots are fired at once, and I lunge forward, grabbing this fucker's neck and throttling him to the ground before stomping on his ugly as-sin face.

He wails, but I ignore him, leaping over his crumpled body to get to Cambria. Her eyes are filled with tears, and her little nose is red from crying.

"Keep your eyes on me," I tell her as I close the distance between us.

A few more shots are fired, and I see Rocco throw a punch at one of the other men before nodding at me and making his way to my father.

Kneeling in front of my precious woman, I carefully peel the tape off her mouth, cupping her face in one hand and holding her gaze while I cut away the ties around her wrists.

"I'm so sorry, sunshine," I whisper as I tuck a few pieces of her matted hair behind her ear.

Blue eyes sparkle up at me, and *fuck*, I don't deserve the look of gratitude in her eyes. I'm the reason she's roughed up in the first place.

"I knew you'd come for us."

"Always," I vow, pressing a kiss to her forehead. "Now, let's get the fuck out of here."

I scoop Cambria up, thanking every god I can think of

that she's in my arms. She curls up against my chest, and I tuck her head into my shoulder, not wanting her to see any more blood or violence. Never again.

Looking back at my father, he gives me a nod of approval as Rocco helps him up and half-drags him out of the building behind us.

We make it outside, and I run to one of the Moscatelli's vehicles, opening the back door and gently placing Cambria inside. Rocco is close behind me, and he helps my dad into the passenger's seat before hopping into the driver's seat.

I join my woman in the back, pulling her onto my lap and cradling her against me as we wind our way through Chicago.

By the time we pull up to my father's house, Cambria is shaking and nearly hyperventilating. "I've got you, sunshine," I whisper, stroking her cheek. "You're safe now."

She nods, her eyes fluttering closed as she relaxes against me. I can feel the adrenaline leaving her body, and each breath feels like it's draining her of energy.

"I love you, Cambria," I murmur, brushing my lips against hers. "And I'm going to prove it to you somehow."

"You already did," she surprises me by answering. "Now get me inside so I can tell you the same thing without an audience."

My father snorts from the front seat.

Rocco chuckles. "Looks like my job here is done."

I thank him, and we plan to visit before I fly back to New York. Right now, I have more important things on my mind. Like getting my dad tucked into bed, then pampering my woman, and taking care of her every need.

CHAPTER TEN

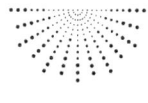

CAMBRIA

"*S*he's resting now, but we'll visit soon. Yes, she's had breakfast. Yes, Dad, I made sure she has plenty of her favorite sleepy-time tea for later. There's no need for you to come over again. You need rest too, old man!"

I can't help the giggle that falls from my lips as I listen to Dante talk to his dad over the phone. They've been suffocating me with attention last night and this morning, ensuring I have water, food, tea, blankets, pillows, and everything else under the sun. I'm not sure who has bossed whom around the most since we got home yesterday, Dante or Raul.

I reminded them that, technically, I was the only person with medical training, but that argument didn't hold any weight. Both men told me to rest and refused to let me help clean up the living room from the intruders or cook dinner. The two of them have been tripping all over themselves to wait on me hand and foot, and it may be the most loved and cherished I've ever felt.

Dante spins around, his brown eyes meeting mine. A

warm sparkle shines from the depths of his soul, and it makes me blush. We still have some things to discuss, like who exactly the Colombos, Moscatellis, and Di Salvos are, but I'm just content to be near my Dante and to have him look at me like this.

"Gotta go, Dad. The patient is up."

I roll my eyes at Dante as he hangs up the phone and strides over to where I'm lying on my little couch. I sit up and pat the spot next to me, smiling when he curls his large frame to fit in the seat.

"How are you feeling after your nap, sunshine?" he asks softly as he cups my chin. "Can I get you anything?" Dante gently turns my head to the left, inspecting a wound on my cheek, then turns it to the right, frowning at a cut on my temple.

"I'm a lot better today," I promise, looping my fingers around his wrist and pulling his hand away from my face. I kiss his fingertips, then nibble on one, making him growl.

"Careful," he warns, those brown eyes flashing dark with lust.

"I don't want to be careful," I say with a pout, scooting closer to Dante. "I just want you," I tell him honestly.

"Cambria, baby, I want you too. Always. But if I hurt you…"

"You won't. You're not capable of it."

"That's where you're wrong," he murmurs, looking away from me. "I'm capable of a lot of horrible things. And I already hurt you by dragging you into my mess. God, Cambria, I'm so fucking sorry. Look what they did to you. Jesus, I'm a monster."

I lean into Dante, placing a hand over his heart. He still refuses to look at me, so I nuzzle into his neck, burrowing ever closer so he knows I'm not going anywhere. "I forgive you, Dante," I whisper. His entire body stills, his muscles growing rigid at my words. "Though not for what you might think. You're not responsible for the actions of others, but you are responsible for telling the truth. So tell me the truth. Who were they? Who are you? What do you do for a living?"

He's quiet for long moments while I hold him, absorbing the doubt and fear radiating off him in waves.

"Whatever it is," I continue softly, "I just want to know who you are. I want to love you. All of you. Please, please let me." Dante's eyes finally meet mine, his brown gaze filled with vulnerability and brokenness. "Don't you know I'll keep you safe too? All the parts you're afraid to show the world, I'll hold them close. I'll protect them."

"Cambria," he murmurs, tilting his head down to rest on mine. "I'm in the mafia," he finally confesses.

My heart thuds against my ribcage as everything clicks into place. That makes sense. The secrecy, the wealth, the demanding schedule, and the Italian family names thrown around like weapons.

"Are you scared of me?" he asks after a beat of silence.

"No," I answer right away. "I trust you, Dante. I trusted you with all of me before I knew, and now that it's out there... I'm just happy we can be honest. That's all I want."

"Maybe you don't understand," Dante protests. "I'm not some foot soldier. I'm the Underboss. The second in command."

He's so serious, and his dark gaze warns me not to push it. But I have to tease him. Just a little. "Brag."

Dante blinks at me, a look of bewilderment on his face. It's priceless. My second favorite look of his. "You really don't care?" he asks slowly.

"I'm proud of you for reaching so close to the top and all, don't get me wrong."

"That's not what I mean." He sighs.

I giggle and readjust on the couch, throwing a leg over his

lap to get properly seated on top of him. Dante's eyes widen, and his hands automatically rest on my hips. I press my forehead against his, needing this closeness.

"I love *you*, Dante. Nothing else matters. Life is complicated, but I know you're a good man. I'd like you to shut up and let me love you forever."

This pulls a chuckle from him, and I smile brightly, enjoying the sound.

"Why are you so good to me, baby?" he murmurs, nibbling down my neck. I tilt my head, giving him better access. "I don't deserve you."

"I can't wait to prove you wrong," I reply before fusing our lips.

I wrap my arms around his neck and hold him close as I grind on his lap. Dante groans and breaks our kiss, only to lick down my neck. I shiver and squeeze my thighs around his hips, needing more.

Dante leans back and cups my face, resting his forehead on mine. We're both breathing heavily, the air thick with what we both crave. He slides his hands down my neck, shoulders, and torso until he grips the hem of my shirt and gently lifts it off my body.

"Are you sure?" he asks, his brown gaze searching mine. "You went through a lot yesterday, and if I hurt you–"

"I love how sweet you are with me," I whisper, cutting him off with a kiss. "And I love that you want to take care of me. Right now, I need to feel you, Dante. Need to be with you like this. Will you give that to me?"

I'm bare before him in more ways than one. I feel vulnerable yet bold. Exposed, yet covered in the safety that is my Dante. My home. My love. His fingertips trail up my sides in featherlight touches as he looks at me with awe and reverence.

"I'll give you anything, love. I need you too."

Leaning forward, Dante captures my nipple in his mouth, gently sucking as his hands slide around to my back, pressing me closer to him. I tip my head back and rock my hips against his, savoring every swipe of his tongue and stroke of his fingers.

Dante hums in approval as he switches breasts, lavishing the other with the same attention. I feel the vibrations deep down in my core, making more of my arousal drip and coat the thin layer of fabric covering his throbbing dick. I feel it swell even more as a soft growl rumbles up from his chest.

I slide my hands down his chiseled chest, pushing him back. He grunts in frustration like I took away his favorite toy. It makes me giggle knowing he wants me that much.

Dante looks up at me with the softest, sweetest smile, making me melt for him even as I'm so turned on that I'm ready to burst.

"Love that sound, sunshine. Love every single time I can get you to laugh."

God, how is this man so freaking perfect? I don't know how to respond to him with words, so I kiss him again as my hands trail lower, lower, lower until my fingers graze the waistband of his boxer briefs.

He tilts his head back, breaking our kiss to growl softly. I scoot back enough to reach inside and pull him out, stroking him and rubbing his precum up and down his thickness.

"Jesus," he grunts, his muscles tensing and flexing as I pick up my pace.

Dante grips my hips and lifts me, positioning me so the head of his cock is right at my entrance. My pussy clenches and releases more of my wetness, helping him to slide in easily.

"This what you need, baby? Need me to fill you up?"

"Yes. God, Dante…" I breathe, moaning as my tight channel stretches to accommodate him.

I feel every vein and ridge of his dick as he enters me. It's so good to be connected like this, to be completed in a way only Dante can provide.

My hands move on their own, tangling in my hair as I stretch my body out for his pleasure. He groans and sucks on my neck as his hands slide up my back and grip my shoulders. He presses my body down on his as he grinds his thick cock against me, hitting my clit just right.

I jerk and tremble in his embrace, gasping for air when he pushes me right to the edge. Dante trails his fingers down my spine, gripping my ass and spreading my cheeks apart as he starts to fuck up into my pulsing cunt.

"Love feeling you, Cambria. Love your sexy fucking body," he murmurs, nipping at my earlobe and causing me to shudder in his arms.

"Mmhm," is all I can manage to say, too lost in the sensation of his cock scraping along my walls and hitting every pleasure point inside of me.

My orgasm blooms deep in my core, throbbing outward and seizing my muscles. My joints lock, and I suck in a breath, bracing myself for what's to come. I squeeze my pussy around him and roll my hips in jerky motions, needing to come so bad it hurts.

Dante senses my urgency, cupping the back of my neck and drawing me down for a heated kiss. He pulls my bottom lip through his teeth before diving in, tangling his tongue with mine as he bounces me off his cock. He tilts his hips and hits that one spot that drives me crazy. Over and over, he hammers into me until the coil snaps, and I cry out my orgasm. Pure pleasure slams into me, overwhelming my senses as I writhe and whimper and get completely swept away by my release.

When I open my eyes, I'm lying on my back, Dante hovering over me and staring at me with a hunger so fierce it makes my cunt contract again, despite my intense orgasm. He growls and begins moving again, his dick still buried deep inside me.

He builds us both up with slow, measured rolls of his hips. His need is palpable, but he's being so gentle with me, sliding in and out, again and again, never breaking eye contact.

Dante cups my face with one hand, wiping away a tear I didn't know was there. He kisses the spot before burying his face into my neck.

"I love you," he murmurs, nuzzling into me as we make love. That's exactly what this is. It's intense, but in a different way than previously. Everything is heightened, our souls tangling together as perfectly as our bodies.

"Dante," I whisper. "I love you so much."

His dick twitches at my words, making me moan. He slides one hand between my back and the couch cushion, pressing me closer to him, needing as much of me as possible. His touch leaves a trail of fire and awareness as he grazes his fingertips over my ass and then grips my thigh. He spreads me open even wider and hooks his hand behind my knee, lifting it and changing the angle.

I gasp and whimper as he hits me so damn deep. My nails dig into his biceps as he slowly pulls out and pushes back in, going deeper with every thrust. Each time he reaches the end of me, I jerk and spasm, electricity flowing through my veins and sparking a fire deep in my core. Flames lick at my nerves as my moans become cries of pleasure, torture, bliss, and an almost painful need for release.

"That's it," he grunts, his hips stuttering as he picks up his pace. "Fuck, I feel you, baby. Are you going to come for me?"

I nod and whimper, my body trembling as I take everything he's giving me. Liquid heat erupts from my core, spilling out of me, making me convulse in his arms as I come around his cock.

Dante grunts and snaps his hips against mine, fucking me roughly as I fall apart. I can't *breathe*. He's so deep, thick, and mind-numbingly incredible. I thought my pleasure had peaked, but I spasm around him again when he unleashes his cum inside me. He grunts his orgasm, grinding his dick down as it jerks and throbs, coating my pussy with his release.

His lips find mine, and he thrusts his tongue inside my mouth, swallowing down my moans and sucking the air out of my lungs. He breaks the kiss, only to scrape his teeth down the side of my neck, across my collarbone, over my breast, and down my torso.

"Wh-what are you…?"

My question is cut off when he settles between my thighs and licks my pussy. I gasp and moan loudly, my body moving on its own to grind against his face. My pussy feels raw and swollen and so damn sensitive from the orgasms I've already had, yet each stroke of his tongue brings me closer, closer, closer to another release.

He growls as he licks up our combined juices. It's so dirty, so fucking filthy. And that only turns me on more. Dante spears his tongue into my entrance, massaging my walls and driving me insane.

My thighs snap around his head when he turns his attention to my clit, sucking on the oversensitized bundle of nerves. I twist in his grip and bow my back off the couch, only to have him spread his hand out over my lower belly and gently press me back down onto the cushions. He keeps his hand there, creating a delicious pressure that radiates from my core.

I claw at the couch as my orgasm fights to the surface, tearing its way out and wringing pleasure from every cell in my body. Dante growls into my pussy, never letting up, using his tongue and teeth expertly to keep me at my peak for so damn long.

I shake and sweat and whimper his name, unable to escape the brutal bliss overwhelming me. An intense, all-consuming pressure tugs at my lower belly. It's unlike anything I've ever experienced, and I'm almost afraid of what's happening to me. My hands tangle in Dante's hair, gripping and twisting the strands, needing him to anchor me here on earth.

Another stronger, wilder orgasm threatens to end me, even as my body reels from my first one. Every muscle draws up tight, my joints locking, my breath frozen in my lungs. Time stands still, waiting, watching as I surrender to the pleasure Dante is bringing me.

All at once, everything inside me unravels. I gush for him, an embarrassing amount of wetness leaving me as I scream and thrash around almost violently.

I can't do anything except whimper and melt, all the strength draining from my body. I'm vaguely aware of Dante scooping me up and carrying me over to the bed, hardly registering when he cleans me up with a damp washcloth.

The bed dips with his weight, though I still can't open my eyes. He drapes my limp body over his, and I automatically curl into his chest. Dante presses a kiss to the top of my head and tucks a blanket around us.

"Sleep now, sunshine," he whispers as he strokes my back in a feather-light touch. "I'll be here when you wake up."

CHAPTER ELEVEN

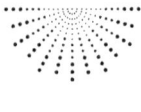

DANTE

I breathe in the warmth and sweetness of my Cambria, her scent lingering on the sheets in the morning light. Today is the day I finally set my plan in motion.

It was supposed to happen several days ago, but the fuckin' Colombos ruined everything. Not this time. I have my woman safe and sound, my father is stable and resting at the main house, the meal is planned and shopped for, and I have a ring burning a hole in my pocket. It's time to claim what's mine.

Rolling over, I'm ready to gather Cambria in my arms and wake her up with a million kisses all over her face, only... she's not here.

I shoot out of bed, hoping my sunshine didn't step out on me. Then I hear the shower running and get all sorts of dirty ideas. Ones that I plan on pursuing very soon.

I'm still naked from the night before, so I walk into the bathroom and marvel at the silhouette of Cambria through the shower curtain. She's so fucking beautiful that it sometimes hurts to look at her.

Pulling the shower curtain back, I'm greeted with the most perfect sight in the world. My woman, dripping wet, with a sexy as fuck grin on her face. I step in and slide my hands all over her body, memorizing every dip and curve before pulling her in for a kiss. God, I missed the taste of her mouth, and it's barely been eight hours.

"I was wondering when you'd join me," she purrs.

I groan into the side of her neck as I suck and nibble her skin the way she likes. She trembles as my mouth works up and down the slender column. Her hand slides down my abs and grips my cock, already hard for her.

"Fuck me," I grunt as I buck my hips into her hand.

She works me over, sliding up and down. "Yeah, that's the idea," she whispers.

I growl and kiss my way down to her perfect breasts, sucking one in my mouth. Cambria inhales sharply and gives me a soft moan that spurs me on as I lick her nipple and scrape my teeth over the hard peak.

I slide a finger up her slit and circle her clit. Cambria's knees shake, and I hold her up, chuckling into her skin. "Love how responsive you are. Are you ready for me?"

"Y-yes, pl-please...oh!" She cries out as I dip a finger into her entrance, still so tight for me.

"You're not too sore?"

"No, ah...I'm ready, oh god, oh my god," her voice cracks as I finger her slowly, building her up and then backing down when she's close to the edge.

Her hand has stopped stroking my dick because she's so caught up in what I'm doing to her. It's probably for the best because I could come just from watching her writhe and melt in my hands, and I want this to last longer.

Cambria grips my biceps and rests her head on my chest, trembling and gasping for air. I love seeing her like this, so lost in lust, in pleasure.

I withdraw my hand, and she whines in protest, giving me the cutest little angry face. I can't help but kiss her as I guide her back to the wall. My hands slide down her curvy frame and grip her ass, lifting her and pinning her to the wall. Her legs automatically go around me, and her arms loop my neck.

Cambria moans so perfectly for me when my cock rubs up and down her slit, the head hitting her clit every time.

"Please, Dante, I can't take any more. Just, please…"

"Please, what, sunshine? Tell me what you want." I thrust harder, faster, growling when her pussy lips try to suck me in. "Tell me what this greedy little cunt needs."

She gets impossibly wetter, her pussy releasing more of her sweet juices as I talk dirty to her. I love that my baby gets off on my filthy words.

"I need… Please… Oh God, fuck me, Dante, fuck me so hard…"

I don't waste another second. I find her entrance and shove my dick inside, hitting her deep and making us both cry out.

"Shit, Cambria." I hold still inside her, relishing how her pussy squeezes me and pulses around my hard shaft.

"You're so big. God, you feel so good." Cambria wriggles in my hands, her body telling me what it needs.

Pulling almost all the way out, I slam back inside, my dick not wanting to be away from his new home any longer than necessary.

"Dante! Yes, oh god…"

Her fingernails dig into my nape as she pulls me down for a heated kiss. Cambria bites my bottom lip as I thrust into her, fucking her good and hard like she asked. I grind my cock deep inside her sweet cunt before pulling out and thrusting back in.

She sucks my tongue inside her mouth and moans

around me, jerking her hips to meet me thrust for thrust. My hands grip her ass tightly, helping her slide up and down my cock.

"Dante, you're so deep like this. So good..."

I grunt in response, unable to say anything else. I'm so lost inside her that words fail me. My spine tingles, my balls draw up tight, and I need her to get there with me.

As if sensing my impending orgasm, Cambria starts shaking, her pussy pulsing, throbbing, begging me to fuck her harder. Our bodies are in perfect sync as I piston in and out. She cries out, a desperate, aching sound escaping her throat. Or maybe that's me. I can't tell anymore.

We grunt, fuck, and kiss with wild abandon. My orgasm rips through me right as her pussy snaps. We come together, scream together, tense and release together. It's intense, primal, and so fucking perfect.

My legs give out as the last of my cum shoots inside her. Gently, I guide us to the shower floor, feeling our combined juices dribble out of Cambria's pussy. It makes me leak more cum inside her, knowing I filled her to the brim. Some part of my brain takes note that we haven't used a condom once, but I can't seem to give a fuck.

Leaning against the shower wall, I hug Cambria into my chest. She buries her head in my neck, her body limp and sated.

"You okay, baby?"

She nods. "So good." It comes out as a sigh, making me smile.

Eventually, I untangle us and help rewash every inch of Cambria before she does the same to me. We dry off and get dressed, and Cambria loops her arm in mine as we walk out of the cottage and up to the main house.

"You okay?" Cambria asks when we get inside. "You're awfully close to brooding."

I chuckle and throw her a wink. "Not brooding," I promise. "Just hoping everything works out this morning."

"Oh? And what do you have planned for this morning, Mr. Santarossa?" she sing-songs as she waltzes in front of me.

I stop her with my hands on her hips, grinning when she lifts on her tip-toes. Her shimmering eyes and radiant warmth make me feel safe, seen, and truly understood for the first time in my life. I planned on doing this differently, but the moment feels right.

I kiss my woman on her pouty lips, cheek, chin, and collarbone before kneeling in front of her. Cambria gasps softly, her hands covering her mouth as she stares down at me.

"I'm planning to make you mine, Mrs. Santarossa," I tell her, my gaze locking on hers as I pull the ring out of my pocket. I gently take her left hand in mine, pulling it away from her mouth to slip on the ring. "I'm planning on making you the happiest, most cherished woman in the world."

"Dante…"

"I love you," I rush to say, needing to get it all out before she can turn me down. "I love you in this terrifying, all-consuming, thrilling way that I'll never get enough of. You're… fuck, sunshine. You're incredible, inside and out, and I need to know you're mine. Forever."

"Are you going to ask me?" she finally squeaks through tears.

"Are you going to say no?" I counter, half joking and half out of my damn mind with nerves. Cambria shakes her head, a smile peeking through her tears. "Cambria, will you–"

"Yes!" she shouts, throwing her arms around me and tackling me to the ground.

I catch her, just like I always will, and wrap myself around her, clinging to the most precious, perfect woman in the world.

"You didn't let me ask," I point out as I brush her hair out of her eyes.

Cambria smiles and leans forward, giving me a peck on the lips. "I got impatient," she says with a shrug. "Plus, I like catching you off guard."

I nip at her lips, making Cambria laugh. "Something tells me you'll be doing plenty of that, my love."

She nods, a mischievous glint in her eyes. Before she can say anything, our moment is uninterrupted by Raul.

"Is everyone decent?" he hollers from the hallway. "I love you kids, but if I see anyone's butt, I'm moving across the country."

Cambria belly laughs while I roll my eyes.

"Mr. Santarossa, did you hear the good news?" Cambria asks excitedly as she jumps up from our position on the floor.

"I did. It seems more appropriate for you to call me dad, doesn't it? None of this Mr. Santarossa bullshit."

My girl beams at the old man, hugging him before helping him sit at the table. I start coffee and water for tea, and Cambria joins me in the kitchen to help with breakfast.

A few minutes later, we're sitting at the table, and I know now is as good a time as any to discuss my plans. Clearing my throat, I fold my napkin and set it down on the table, looking over at my father and Cambria.

"I was thinking," I begin, swallowing thickly. Why is this so difficult? This is what I do. I plan things and execute them. I guess I've never cared about anything the way I do about this. "I could relocate both of you to New York. I'll set you up in whatever situation is best. Cambria and I in one house and Raul in a place next door, or we can shop for a bigger place and have separate wings of the estate. Cambria, you can go back to school, find a new job, or never work again as long as you're happy. And Dad, of course, you'll have the best of the best for healthcare. I know it's a lot to ask, but if you would consider the move–"

"Damn, I owe you twenty bucks," my dad grumbles.

"What?" I ask in confusion. I look over at Cambria, who's grinning from ear to ear. "Is someone going to tell me what's going on?"

My woman stands and walks over to where I'm sitting. I push my chair out, and she plops down on my lap, wrapping her arms around my neck. I'll never get tired of holding her.

"We figured you were going to offer to move us to New York with you. I said you'd buy a mansion and give Raul his own wing. He said there's no way you'd offer to move him in with you."

I stare at her for a few seconds, blinking as I absorb this information. "So, you... want to come with me?"

"Duh," she responds with an eye roll.

I spank her thigh and cup the back of her neck, pulling her down for a punishing kiss. "Still so sassy," I whisper onto her lips.

"Still so fun to sass," she whispers back.

"Okay, okay, kiddos. Enough lovey-dovey shit. Let an old man watch his shows in peace while you go house shopping online."

I chuckle at my father, who's trying to be grumpy, but failing miserably. His brown eyes shine with life, and he can't keep the grin off his face.

Cambria hops off my lap and gets Raul settled in front of the TV while I clear the dishes. When my woman comes skipping back to me, I pull her into my arms and hold her, feeling her soft, curvy body melt into me.

"Go on, lovebirds," my father calls out, waving his hand

above his head to shoo us away. "And try to find me a place with a hot tub. This dump doesn't have one."

I laugh while Cambria gapes at him.

"Come on, love," I whisper into the shell of her ear as I lead her out the back door. "Let's go plan the rest of our lives."

EPILOGUE

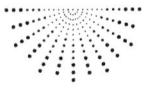

CAMBRIA

"There you guys are!" Thalia shouts, her smile infectious as she skips across the backyard to greet us.

"Auntie T!" our three-year-old, Tanya, exclaims. She lifts her little hands and wiggles her fingers until Thalia scoops her up.

Dante steps up behind me, wrapping his arms around my waist and pulling my back into his front. I sigh and rest my head on his shoulder, loving how he holds me. Whenever we're in the same room, he gravitates toward me, needing to touch me somehow. I don't mind. I love having his hands on me.

"Can I play, Daddy?" Ethan, our five-year-old, asks from beside Dante.

"Go find Cousin Bailey and have her show you her new playground," he suggests, tousling Ethan's messy brown hair.

The energetic toddler makes a revving sound like a race car, and takes off, nearly colliding into Bailey in a fit of giggles.

"Come on and grab some food," Thalia says, carrying

Tanya on her hip. "I'm going to go check on Romeo. He told me he'd be done with work by now." She rolls her eyes, and I nod sympathetically.

"Guess you'll have to remind him who the real boss is," I tease.

"Way ahead of you," she says, wagging her eyebrows.

Dante clears his throat while we laugh, and Thalia spins away to go seduce her man.

"Don't get any ideas about showing me who's boss, sunshine," he whispers into the shell of my ear. His arms tighten around my waist, and I grind against him, giggling when he groans.

"I thought we already established who's boss," I answer, looking at him over my shoulder.

His brown eyes are nearly black, and he narrows his gaze at me, doing nothing to hide his lustful thoughts.

"I seem to remember you following orders from day one, in fact."

Dante pinches my hip, making me squeak. He nuzzles into the side of my neck, sending prickles up and down my spine as his slight stubble scrapes against my skin. He peppers kisses over my soft flesh, then tugs my earlobe through his teeth.

"Love when you sass me, baby," he rasps. "I'm gonna love your punishment even more."

I hold back a moan, reminding myself we're at a family grill out. This man knows how to turn me on with nothing more than a few wandering touches and whispered words.

"This is why I moved out, you know," Raul says from close by. "The public displays of affection were starting to ruin my appetite."

I snap my eyes open, a blush creeping over my cheeks. The old man is frowning, but his eyes shine with pride and love.

"Funny," says Dante. "I thought you moved out because our hot tub didn't have the proper jet system."

Raul chuckles and claps Dante on the back. "You know I'm messing with you, son. I'm grateful for everything you've provided, but mostly, I'm happy to be part of the family."

"Raul," I whisper, resting a hand on his shoulder. "You're going to make me cry."

"And if you make her cry, I'll have to knock you out. Sorry, Pops, those are the rules."

He grins and takes my hand, kissing it before winking. "I better get going then. Wouldn't want to embarrass you in front of your friends."

Dante laughs, and I spin in his arms, wanting to capture his smile. "Thank you," I whisper, kissing him on the cheek.

"For what, sunshine?" he murmurs.

"For loving me. For working through the hard stuff with your dad. For being the best father and most supportive husband. I'm just…" I sniffle, trying to hold back the emotion. Dante's face falls, and even though they are good tears, I know he hates seeing them. "Sorry, I'm so emotional."

"Did I do something? How can I help? What's wrong?"

I place my hand over his heart, stopping him from spiraling. It's one of our favorite calming tools for each other, along with deep breathing and morning meditations. Yes, I *finally* got the brooding, skeptical Dante Santarossa to sit down, shut up, and open himself up to mindfulness.

"Nothing's wrong," I assure my husband. "In fact, I'm hoping it's amazing news." I wasn't sure when I was going to tell Dante, but this feels like the right moment. "I'm such an emotional mess because I found out this morning… we're pregnant."

Dante's eyes widen, and it takes a second for my words to sink in. When they do, his face lights up with a smile, and he lifts me in his arms, spinning me around.

"That's incredible, baby," he croons in between peppering kisses over my face. "Can't wait to get home and show you how excited I am."

I grin and smack his chest playfully. He grabs my hand and kisses each of my fingers.

"I love you, Dante," I breathe.

"I love you so much, Cambria. I never thought I deserved happiness or a family, but these last six years with you have changed everything. I can't wait for what the future holds."

"As long as you're in it, I know it will be incredible."

His lips find mine, and we sway to the pop song playing in the background as we melt into each other. The world fades away until it's just us, sealing our promises with a kiss.

* * *

THE END

ARMANDO

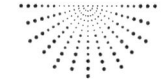

Blurb:

I was obsessed with the blue-eyed pixie from the second she jumped into my arms. Allegra. She clung to me and prayed for me to keep her safe, just for a little while. Allegra had just escaped from her degenerate uncle, and she had no idea she ran straight into a mafia enforcer.

I've always been proud of my position within the Di Salvo family, but I'm not sure someone as sweet and innocent as Allegra will understand. For the first time, I wonder if my profession will keep me from the one thing I want most in life.

With threats both old and new, and everyone in the Di Salvo family on edge, it's only a matter of time before the truth comes out. Will my sweet girl be able to forgive me?

CHAPTER ONE

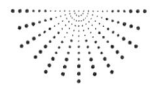

ARMANDO

"Good morning, what can I get for... Oh."

I give the barista my most charming smile, but the hesitancy in her eyes doesn't dim. I get it. I'm six foot eight, nearly three hundred pounds of pure muscle, with ink crawling up and down my arms. I stand out anywhere, but especially in this dainty little coffee shop.

"Morning, miss," I greet her, hoping to put the little lady at ease. I might make a living off of my intimidating size and looks, but I don't enjoy frightening civilians unnecessarily. Strange, I know, considering I'm an enforcer for the most powerful mafia family in New York, the Di Salvos.

"Uh, right. Yes. What can I get for you?" the woman asks, avoiding eye contact.

"Double shot, please. I need it this morning."

She types out my order and takes my money, thanking me when I hand her a twenty and tell her to keep the change. I walk to the other side of the counter to wait for my drink, taking a spot in the back so as not to block the way of the other patrons. They all part for me like the Red Sea, shuffling out of the way to clear a path.

I've gotten used to people staring at me or making a point *not* to stare at me. I hit the six-foot mark by the time I was fourteen, which helped me out in a lot of ways since I looked much older than I was. Specifically, when I was looking for an escape from the torture that is the American foster care system.

I hit the streets shortly after my fourteenth birthday with nothing except for my best friend and what I could fit in a backpack. Leif and I looked after each other, and even though our lives took drastically different turns, he's still my oldest and closest friend.

As soon as Leif turned eighteen, he enlisted in the military. They gave him food, shelter, training, and a purpose— all things we lacked in our lives. I went in a different direction. When I turned eighteen, I also had an opportunity to join something bigger than myself—the Mafia.

Leif still doesn't understand, but I don't expect him to. Especially now that the bastard has found himself a woman after all these years. Never thought I'd see the day, but Maribell is just what he needs. After he was wounded overseas, there were some dark times. I was there during the surgeries and most of the healing process, but his wounds were far more than skin deep.

I couldn't help my friend out of his depression or even begin to understand what living with PTSD must have been like for him. But Maribell waltzed into his life and eased his pain.

I'm happy for him. Truly, no one deserves a happily ever after more than Leif, especially after everything he's been through. I'd be lying if I said I wasn't a little jealous. Not of Maribell, specifically, but just having someone. Caring for someone. Being the most important person in someone's life and doing whatever it takes to keep them safe and happy.

"Double shot for Armando," the lady calls from behind the counter, startling me from my thoughts.

Jesus, I'm losing it. When did I become a sappy fool? Maybe something is in the water. Not only did Leif settle down with a woman, but the big Boss himself, Romeo, found the love of his life. And even more shockingly, the cold, aloof underboss of the family, Dante, also fell ass over heels for a woman last week.

It's a lot of change all at once. Staring down the barrel of my fortieth birthday has me feeling some kind of way about the life I've built. Don't get me wrong, I'm proud of my rank within the Di Salvos, and I've worked my ass off to get to where I am today. I went from sleeping in a cardboard box under an overpass in the South Bronx to living in a three-story, five-bedroom, three-bathroom house with a gym and home theater in the basement. By all accounts, I've made it to the top.

There's just one thing missing—someone to share it with.

Clearing my throat, I rub the heel of my hand over my chest to ease the tension there. I step up to the counter and grab my drink, downing it in ten seconds. The liquid burns my throat, both from the temperature and the acidity. That's how I know it's good espresso.

I set the tiny mug in the dirty dish tub before making my way to the exit. It's just past ten in the morning, and that was just the pick-me-up I needed to get me through the rest of the day. This afternoon, I have meetings with the Boss and Dante, his number two, which isn't my favorite activity. I'd rather be out on a mission, using my strength for the good of the family.

Still, Romeo is constantly reminding me that this job is more than just throwing our weight around. It's about strategy too. That's always been more of Dante's wheelhouse than mine, but I'm trying to be more open. It might just kill me.

I open the door of the coffee shop, holding it for an older couple on their way inside. As soon as I step onto the sidewalk, a flash of light red catches my eye, and I turn my head to see a petite woman sprinting toward me, her long, strawberry-blonde hair flowing behind her as she picks up speed. I swear she's about to run right into…

The woman's bright blue eyes latch onto mine, a look of fear and desperation emanating from them. The next second, she collides into my chest, wrapping her arms around my neck and clinging to me with every ounce of strength she has.

"I'm sorry," she murmurs, her voice scratchy and broken. "Please," the woman whispers, tears clogging her throat as she buries her head between my neck and shoulder. "Please just… I just… I'm sorry." My chest caves in at her words, and I hold her close, not sure what drove her into my arms, but knowing with absolute certainty I will destroy whatever and whoever made her feel like this.

"Are you in danger?" I ask, though I already know the answer. The woman sniffles and nods against my shoulder. "Running from a bad man?" Again, she nods, a shiver wracking her body, which I'm trying not to ogle. It's nearly impossible when her curves are pressed against me, her softness melting into the hard slats of my muscles.

I carry the trembling, terrified woman back inside the coffee shop, hoping to hide her from whoever is chasing her down. Ignoring the curious and shocked glances, I stride through the seating area until I find a booth along the back wall. It will give us some privacy while I figure out who this gorgeous, frightened woman is and how I can help her.

Setting her down on her feet, I guide the woman to sit in the booth. She nearly collapses, but I keep her hand in mine, easing her into the seat. I'm about to grab some napkins from the counter to dry her tears, but as soon as I try to withdraw my hand, she grips it tighter, a heart-shattering whimper falling from her lips.

Kneeling in front of her, I look up into her clear blue eyes, rimmed in red and watery from crying. She sears me with a look of pure sorrow mixed with helplessness. Without knowing a single thing about this woman, I understand her more than she could possibly imagine.

"S-sorry," she stutters out, blinking away more tears. "I don't… I don't… I didn't know what to do."

"It's okay," I say softly, rubbing the pad of my thumb over her knuckles in what I hope is a soothing gesture.

She's silent for a few moments, and I encourage her to take a few deep breaths. She's shivering from head to toe, and I notice for the first time that her shirt is ripped. It's a V-neck with some logo I don't recognize, and it's far too tight for her ample chest. It looks like someone grabbed the hem to keep her from escaping, resulting in a good-sized tear up one side.

My gaze wanders up her arms, pausing to examine the dark bruises on her wrists and biceps. *What the fuck has she been through?* Rage rolls over me in waves, my adrenaline spiking once more at the thought of some motherfucker's grubby hands on this precious woman.

"I just s-saw you and knew you were big enough to p-protect me."

"I am. I will," I vow. I've never meant anything more in my entire life. She's tied to me now. I can't explain it, and I don't want to. I need to get her to safety. We'll figure everything else out from there. "What's your name?"

Her cheeks flush a light shade of pink, making her glow even as she's falling apart in front of me. "Allegra," she murmurs, tucking some of her hair behind her ear. She gives me the smallest of smiles, and Jesus Christ, I can hardly breathe when she looks at me like that.

"Allegra," I repeat, committing each syllable to memory. I like the way it rolls off my tongue. "I'm Armando," I tell her, lifting her hand already clasped in mine and shaking it.

Another hint of a smile lights up her face, but it's soon replaced by a nervous, desperate anxiousness.

"Can I get you some tea? Something to calm your nerves? Or maybe a muffin? They have great coffee cake here too."

Allegra shakes her head no, then drops her gaze. "I don't have any money," she whispers. "I don't have... anything. I don't have *anything*." She blinks a few times as if the reality of her situation is dawning on her. "I don't have anything," she repeats, her bottom lip quivering.

"Hey now," I say in what I hope is a calming voice. "That's not true. You have me."

I hoped to make her feel safe and protected like she asked, but the terrified woman muffles a sob as tears stream down her cheeks. Seeing her in this kind of agony is excruciating, and without thinking, I pull her into my lap.

Allegra curls up against me, burying her head into my neck. I cup her head, keeping her close as I wrap my other arm around her back, pressing her further into my embrace.

"I've got you," I murmur, running the tips of my fingers up and down her spine in soothing strokes. "I don't know what you're running from, but you picked the right person to protect you."

Allegra nods, settling something deep in my soul. On some level, she knows she's safe with me. It's a start.

I push down the crazy, possessive thoughts of her going to someone else for help. They could have taken advantage of her situation. They could have hurt her worse than she already is.

"Everyone is staring at us," she whispers, her body growing stiff in my arms. "I'm making a scene."

"I'll pluck their eyes out if it will make you feel better," I half-joke. She has no idea what lengths I'd go to in order to keep her comfortable. I'm already obsessed with her, and I'm not sure what to do about it.

A soft giggle falls from her lips. God, I'm already addicted to it. This woman is going to destroy me.

I can't wait.

CHAPTER TWO

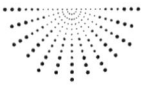

ALLEGRA

I don't know what comes over me, but hearing the handsome man grunt about plucking eyeballs out is hilarious. A laugh bubbles up from some hidden reservoir as this stranger holds me in his arms.

A million thoughts race through my mind as my laughter turns into something else. Something manic. Unhinged, almost. I hear myself laugh and then choke on a sob, but it doesn't feel real. It doesn't feel like my body or my voice.

"I've got you," Armando whispers again, cupping my face. "You're safe now. Look at me." He wipes away my tears with the pad of his thumb, guiding me to face him. "That's it, sweetheart," he says softly. "I'm right here, and I'm going to get you through this."

I want to protest, to tell him he shouldn't get involved with me and that I'm not worth the trouble, but the words die on my tongue when his hazel eyes meet mine. They're filled with understanding and surprising tenderness, and the longer I stare into their depths, the warmer I feel.

He's surrounding me with his strength and presence, but it's not suffocating like so many other men in my life.

Armando may be nearly double my size, but he's treating me gently like I'm some treasure. Truthfully, I'm the furthest thing from precious. I'm a disaster, and a dangerous one at that. Still, I want to soak up every ounce of peace and safety from Armando while I can.

Armando gives me a small smile, his thumb still stroking my cheek soothingly. What is it about this man? Why did I jump into his arms? After what I've been through, throwing myself at a giant muscular beast probably wasn't my best move. Maybe my self-preservation instincts are broken, which makes a lot of sense.

"I, um…" I trail off, not knowing what I was going to say.

God, I'm such a mess. How did I end up here? *My uncle…*

I slam my eyes shut, unable to even think the words. Shit. I need to get out of here. I need to move far, far away, and disappear. Go off the grid. He has connections all over the city, and the longer I stay here, the more time I'm giving him to track me.

Fuck. *Fuck.*

I attempt to scramble off the kind stranger's lap, but he draws me further into his comforting embrace.

"Are you okay?" he whispers.

"Yes," I answer automatically. I'm always okay. What other choice do I have? It's not like anyone cares.

"You should wait a few seconds next time someone asks you that," he says. I lean back enough to give him a questioning look. "If you answer too quickly, they'll know you're lying. Give it a moment or two before settling on an answer. Take it from someone who faked being *okay* for a long time."

I blink at the man before me, unsure what to do with that information. He clears his throat and averts his gaze as if embarrassed at his confession. It endears him to me, knowing he put himself out there to make me feel better.

"Thank you," I murmur, nibbling on my bottom lip. "I…

I'm not okay, truthfully," I add. "But it's not something for you to worry about. It's no one's problem but my own."

This time, when I untangle myself from Armando, he lets me. I know it's irrational, but a pang of disappointment echoes in my chest. I thought maybe this man would fight to keep me pressed against him, but that's absurd.

As soon as I stand, Armando joins me. "Where are we going, angel?" he asks, a smile curling up the corner of his lips.

I didn't get a good look at him before jumping into his arms. I knew he was tall, but holy crap. Armando has to be over a foot taller than me. His shoulders are so wide and muscular that I'm surprised he can fit through doorways. Coupled with sharp features and a perpetual five-o'clock shadow, he's the kind of man I should be afraid of, the kind of man I *am* afraid of, but with Armando...

It's his eyes—golden brown with a hint of green. Buried underneath layers of beautiful colors, his eyes hold something gentle. Something fragile that I want to protect.

Crazy, I know. I'm not making any sense, but then again, this whole day isn't making one bit of goddamn sense. Who can I trust? Not my family, not my friends, not my co-workers, so why not this man? He's done more for me in the last ten minutes than anyone else has in the previous twenty-one years of my life.

"Allegra?" he prompts softly when I still haven't answered. "Do you have anywhere to stay?"

"Yeah, of course," I lie. Armando raises an eyebrow, calling me out. "I mean, I will. As soon as I call a shelter." Looking away from his golden-brown gaze, shame creeps up my spine and winds around my lungs until it's hard to breathe.

Here he is, tall, chiseled, handsome, and kind, wearing an expensive suit, shiny shoes, and what looks to be a very pricey watch. I'm homeless, jobless, and truly alone in this world. I have nothing and no one. How pathetic is that?

"Breathe for me, sweetheart," Armando whispers, gathering my hand up and placing it on his chest. He inhales deeply, nodding as I do the same. I didn't realize how shallow my breathing had become. We exhale slowly, and his heart beats reassuringly beneath my palm. It grounds me in a way I don't understand. "Good. Again," he murmurs.

Hazel eyes meet mine, pulling me closer, tethering my soul to his. The crashing waves of anxiety slowly recede, and I'm no longer drowning in terror.

"Now," Armando continues, his gaze never leaving mine. "How about I take you back to my place? You can wash up, get some food and water, and take a nap."

"No, that's too much," I deflect, stepping back. "I need to get away from here. Can you drop me off at a bus station?" My mind starts spinning again when I remember I don't have anything with me. No cash, no phone, no ID, nothing. "I'll pay you back for the ticket once I get set up…" I trail off, knowing I have no future and no way to make money.

"We'll take it one step at a time. You don't have to plan everything out right now. Just take the next step."

"I don't even know what the next step is," I admit softly, dipping my head.

Armando lifts my chin with the crook of his finger and tucks a lock of hair behind my ear. "Do you trust me, Allegra?"

My instant reaction is *yes*, though that's quickly followed by, *oh, fuck no.*

"I… I want to," I answer honestly.

"I can work with that," he says with a soft smile. "Step one is letting me take care of you, just for tonight. We can reassess in the morning."

"But…"

"I have more than enough room. You'll have a room with an en suite bathroom. Locks on both doors, and I'll understand if you want to go straight to your room and lock me out. It will be your safe space, and I'll only enter if you give me permission."

"But…"

"And I have a giant lasagna made by my friend's fiancée yesterday, so you'd be helping me by emptying my fridge."

"But…"

"Clothes! I can get you clothes. Girly shit. Whatever you need."

Armando looks frazzled, like he's trying to come up with a way to provide everything for me right here and now. The only question I have is…

"Why?"

Armando stares at me for a moment, studying the very depths of my being. I feel raw and vulnerable, yet seen and understood.

"Because someone did the same for me when I was in a similar situation," he whispers, cupping my cheek. "You don't know this yet, Allegra, but life isn't supposed to be this hard. I don't know your story, but I've seen enough to know you were dealt a bad hand. Let me help. Let me make up for how you've been treated for so long."

I blink back tears, not comprehending the man standing before me. Is he really this kind? This caring of a stranger who jumped into his arms and begged for protection?

"Okay," I hear myself say.

"Okay?" he repeats, sounding shocked and excited at the same time. It's kind of adorable.

I nod, slipping my hand into his. Armando wraps his fingers around my hand, tucking me into his side as we walk to the back of the coffee shop.

"I texted my driver to pull around to the alley. More coverage that way. I can keep you safe."

I want to ask what he does for a living. He clearly has a lot of money, and now I find out he has a personal driver. We'll have time to talk about that stuff later. Right now, I'm having a hard time putting one foot in front of the other.

"I've got you," Armando murmurs, scooping me into his arms once we're outside.

"I can walk," I protest weakly.

"And I can carry you," he counters, looking at me with that grin I'm starting to love.

He sets me down in front of the car, opens the back door, and crawls in behind me. Armando gives the driver a quick nod before focusing on me. His arm rests on the back of the seat, and I automatically scoot closer, sighing with relief when he bundles me further into his side.

Resting my head on his shoulder, I breathe in his cedar and spice scent as my heavy eyelids close.

The last thing I remember is Armando whispering that I'm safe.

CHAPTER THREE

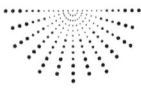

ARMANDO

$\mathcal{T}$he angel in my arms stirs as the driver stops outside my home. He moves to get out and open the door for us, but I shake my head, silently letting him know I'll handle it from here.

I look down at my precious cargo, her eyelashes fluttering against her porcelain cheeks the more she wakes up. "You're safe, Allegra," I whisper, knowing she might be disoriented.

"Armando?" she whispers, peeking one eye open.

"Right here," I assure her, giving her a small smile. She relaxes at the sound of my voice, making me feel like the king of the fucking world. My girl trusts me. "Let's get you inside, yeah?"

Allegra nods, regrettably untangling herself from my embrace. I hop out of the car, peering around the front drive and yard for any sign of disturbance. I don't know what the beautiful angel is running from, but I have some powerful enemies of my own to watch out for. Good thing my home is a fortress, and once we're inside, nothing will be able to reach us.

I hold out my hand, and Allegra takes it, clinging to me as I guide her to the front door, which only unlocks with my thumbprint. I make a note to add Allegra's print to the registry. This is her place, too, after all.

Stepping inside, my eyes quickly adjust to the dimmer lighting, and I cringe when I see the dirty dishes from breakfast on the table and counter. I have a few books scattered about and wraps for my knuckles that I use in the gym downstairs. Does it smell funky in here? When was the last time I vacuumed?

I release Allegra's hand and gather the dishes and books, dumping everything onto the counter next to the stove, where they will be mostly hidden until I can clean. Shit. I'll need to grab some cleaning supplies later today. And throw pillows. Women like throw pillows, right? And fuzzy blankets? Candles? I can get that stuff.

After a few moments of tidying up junk mail and dishes, I realize Allegra hasn't spoken a single word. I look through the open kitchen and living room to see her standing inside the door. She hasn't moved an inch, and her arms are wrapped around her torso in a protective hold.

She looks heart-achingly vulnerable as she folds in on herself, her eyes wandering from her dirty clothes and scuffed shoes to my carpet and couch. Allegra stays huddled in the doorway as I take slow steps in her direction so as not to startle her.

"Hey," I say softly. "Sorry about the mess. Please, make yourself at home."

"I'm… I'm gross. I'll make everything gross," she whispers.

Jesus, this girl. She's ripping my heart out with every word. I need to find whoever has her so scared, filled her head with lies, and put their hands on her. Once I have a name, I'll make it my mission to erase them from the face of the earth.

However, Allegra doesn't need that energy from me right now, so I rein it in and focus on the angel before me.

"You're not gross, Allegra. But I understand if you want to rinse the day off. Can I show you your room? It has a bathroom."

She nods, looking up at me with wide, blue eyes. I hold out my hand, loving how Allegra automatically takes it, wrapping her soft fingers around mine.

"You saw the kitchen already," I tell her, nodding in that direction as we stride past the couch and fireplace. "And the living room," I gesture around us. "There's a gym downstairs and a theater if you're into movies."

"You have a theater?" she whispers in bewilderment.

I pause the tour, grinning down at her. "I may have gone a little overboard when I moved in," I admit sheepishly. "I missed out on movies and TV when I was growing up, so I promised myself that when I made it to the top, I'd build a home theater where I could watch anything I wanted. I even have a legit popcorn machine with the butter sauce and everything."

"Really?" Allegra's eyes sparkle with excitement, and I swear to Christ, my heart stops beating in my chest. She's exquisite. Breathtaking. And when she smiles at me, I'm ready to drop to one knee and demand she be mine forever.

I'm out of my damn mind. I know this. But when it comes to Allegra, I don't seem to give a single fuck. I'll need to take it slow with her. She's fragile right now, and the last thing I want is for her to think I'm a creep who only wants one thing from her.

That couldn't be further from the truth. I want *everything* from this girl, and I'll give her all of me in return.

"Really," I finally answer. "I also have connections with

movie studios and can get almost any film sent to me. Even ones not in theaters yet." Am I bragging? A little. I found something my girl is interested in, so hell, yeah, I'm going to go all in.

"What do you do for a living?" she asks. "I mean, you have a beautiful home, a driver, and a theater. You must do well for yourself."

"I, uh…" *Shit*. How can I tell the traumatized angel I beat people up for a living? For the Mafia, no less. She'll think I'm a monster. Hell, I *am* a monster, but I would never hurt her. The thought of harming her makes my stomach churn and acid crawl up my throat.

"Never mind. It's none of my business. I'm sorry. God, that was so rude of me…" Allegra trails off, pulling her hand from mine so she can wrap her arms around her torso.

I hate seeing her like this, and I hate even more that I caused her discomfort. "There's nothing to apologize for," I assure her. "It's true I do well for myself. And I don't mind sharing the spoils."

I give her a wink, which earns me the tiniest smile. I'll take it. I know I need to tell her about my profession eventually, but I hope to have more time to show her I'm more than my job.

I take Allegra's hand again and guide her upstairs to the second room on the right. Opening the door, I step aside to let Allegra look around. She's immediately drawn to the bed, her fingers sliding over the sheets and pillow as if they are the softest things she's ever felt.

My heart clenches in my chest, thinking about where she came from. Did she not have a bed? Blankets? Pillows?

Taking a deep breath, I make a concerted effort to unclench my fists. There will be time to ask questions later. Right now, my woman needs a warm shower, a warm meal, and a warm bed.

"The bathroom is straight through there," I say, pointing to the open door on the east side of the room. "I'll set some clean clothes right outside your door. Take as much time as you need, angel."

Her cheeks flush a gorgeous shade of pink, and it takes everything in me not to pull her into my arms and kiss her. I've never had these intense feelings about anyone before, but I'm not afraid of them. Everything in my life is all or nothing, so it makes sense that love would be the same way.

Holy shit. *Love.*

"Thank you," Allegra murmurs. "For everything. I still don't know why you're being so kind to me. I'm not worth it."

"It kills me to hear you say that. One day you'll see what I see."

Blue eyes latch onto mine, filled with questions. "What do you see?"

"A warrior who has been through hell and back, yet wakes up every day ready to do battle again. That's strength, Allegra. Resilience. I see a woman who has fought for every breath in her lungs and still manages a sweet smile. That's character. Kindness. Selflessness."

"Armando…"

"I know, I know, I'm coming on way too strong. I just–"

"Thank you," she cuts me off, wiping away a tear. "I didn't… I didn't know I needed to hear that. I don't believe everything you said, but I want to live up to that person you described. She sounds incredible."

"*You*, Allegra. You are incredible. I want to help you see that."

Clear blue eyes blink at me before Allegra dips her head, breaking our connection. I need to back off and let her have her space, but it's nearly impossible. Still, I know I gave her a lot to think about. If I want her to trust me, I can't hover over her every second of every day, even if that's exactly what I want to do.

"Come out to the kitchen whenever you're ready. I'll have some food for you."

Allegra nods, and I stand in front of her, unsure if I can leave. Like a dork, I wave at her, then spin on my heel, shaking my head as I make my way to my room.

Once there, I close the door and lean against it, rubbing my hands down my face. My heart is jackhammering against my ribcage, my palms are sweaty, and my mind is racing with a million thoughts and plans.

Right now, I need to focus on one thing at a time. I may be ready to spend the rest of my life with the woman I've only known for half an hour, but she needs time. I'll need to ease her into the idea of forever with a big brute like me.

Filled with a renewed sense of purpose, I dig through my dresser and find a T-shirt, socks, and sweatpants for Allegra. I debate whether to grab a pair of my boxers and ultimately decide to provide everything.

After stacking the neatly folded pile of clothes outside her door, I head to the kitchen and remove the lasagna from the fridge. It's only a few minutes past eleven in the morning, but my girl needs a good home-cooked meal before getting some sleep. I'm not much of a chef, so besides this lasagna Thalia made for me, I only have frozen dinners.

I spend several minutes tidying everything up, frowning at my empty mantle and blank walls. I never realized how lifeless this place is. Even the furniture is generic—I bought the whole set from some fancy store in the Upper East Side after the sales clerk said it was a timeless classic. It was good enough for me at the time, but now I wish I'd gone with something more personal.

It doesn't matter now. Allegra can go on a shopping spree to redecorate. Or, if she doesn't like doing that stuff, I'll give her free rein to hire an interior designer to do it for her. As long as she's happy.

The water from the shower shuts off, snapping me from my thoughts. I try not to picture Allegra stepping out of the shower completely naked, droplets of water cascading down her dips and curves…

Stop it, I scold myself.

Returning to the kitchen, I cut out an enormous slice of lasagna and put it on a plate to warm up in the microwave. I can't stop my foot from tap-tapping nervously against the tiled floor in anticipation of Allegra's presence.

As if conjuring her up, Allegra pads down the hall and appears in the kitchen doorway. She pauses, leaning against the wall as if uncertain of her next steps. I want to pull her into my arms but stay back, letting her come to me.

"Hey," I say softly. "How was the shower?"

"Amazing. Thank you," she whispers.

Allegra takes a few tentative steps into the kitchen, and I register what she's wearing. Goddamn, I like seeing her in my T-shirt, which hangs down to her knees. She doesn't have the sweatpants on, and I'm guessing it's because she was drowning in them. I don't mind. Allegra has my socks pulled halfway up her shins, and she's so fucking adorable I don't know what to do with myself.

I hold out my hand, watching as the tension drains from her shoulders. She gives me a smile and closes the distance between us, taking my hand. I study her face, noticing the freckles on her nose and cheeks for the first time. I notice something else for the first time, too. A deep horizontal scar on the right side of her neck. It's nearly an inch thick and four inches long.

Allegra gasps softly and drops my hand, immediately covering up the scar. "Sorry," she murmurs.

"Stop apologizing for everything, sweetheart."

Allegra nods, but her shoulders curl in, and she's doing her best to hide from me.

"Look at me, Allegra."

She takes a cleansing breath and raises her head, meeting my gaze again.

"Good girl."

Shit, where did that come from?

I'm about to apologize, but then I see something flash in her eyes. Fuck me. She likes it. I can't think about that right now. I have more important things to deal with.

"Don't hide from me," I murmur. "Scars are nothing to be ashamed of. They prove you survived."

Keeping my eyes locked on hers, I lift the hem of my shirt to reveal a similar-sized scar crawling up my left side.

Allegra's eyes widen, and she reaches out to place her hand over my skin, stopping when she's a millimeter away. "Does it hurt?"

"Not anymore."

Allegra presses her hand against the raised skin as if her touch alone could heal me. She has no idea that's exactly what she's doing. I rest my hand over hers, leaning down and brushing my lips against the shell of her ear.

"You're beautiful," I breathe. "You survived. You're here. And you're safe."

She surprises me by throwing her arms around my waist and burying her head in my chest. "This has to be a dream," I hear her say. "You can't be real."

I hold her close, resting one hand on her lower back while the other strokes up and down her spine.

"I thought the same thing about you," I tell her truthfully.

Allegra loosens her hold and leans back slightly to give me a questioning look. Before I can respond, my phone rings. Allegra squeaks and jumps back while I curse.

"Sorry, sweetheart," I apologize, hating how jumpy she is.

It's a testament to everything she's been through. Romeo's name flashes across the screen, and I know I need to check in for the day. "I have to take this. There's a huge slice of lasagna in the microwave. Just heat it up for a few minutes, and you should be good to go."

Reluctantly, I step away from the beautiful, broken angel and silence my phone before it rings again. "Make yourself at home," I tell her as I gather my things. "I'll be back in a few hours."

Allegra nods and waves from the kitchen as I open the front door. I want to kiss her, promise her ridiculous things, and proclaim my love for her, but it's all too fast.

Instead of doing any of those crazy things, I wave back and smile, counting down the minutes until I can return home to my woman.

CHAPTER FOUR

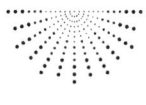

ALLEGRA

I roll over and snuggle into the softest, warmest bed I've ever slept in.

And then it hits me.

I don't own a bed.

Panic punctures my lungs, and I struggle to breathe as I try to remember how I got here. *Did someone drug me? Knock me out? Did my uncle sell me off to the highest bidder like he's always threatening?*

My stomach churns violently at the thought, and I sit up, hoping to get a better idea of the threat I'm dealing with. Swinging my legs over the side of the bed, bits and pieces of the last few hours filter into my mind.

I was running, running, running, looking for somewhere safe to hide, and then...

Armando.

He held me in his arms, his warmth and strength radiating from him as he carried me inside. Closing my eyes, I remember his gentle touch and kind words as he talked me through the most traumatic moments of my life.

More of the day plays out in my head. Armando convinced me to stay with him. I took a hot shower, and then he fed me. We shared a moment in the kitchen. I lift my hand to my neck and run my fingers over the marred skin.

Armando saw my brutal scar and showed me his. He'll never understand how much that meant to me. He looked at the ugliest part of me and didn't back down. The man doesn't even know me, yet he revealed a vulnerable part of himself to comfort me.

I have no idea why Armando is being so patient and kind. I leaped into his arms and clung to him like a spider monkey, but he can't be doing all of this out of some misplaced obligation, right? Most people would have shrugged me off or, if they were half-decent, given me a ride to the nearest shelter.

Wiping away my tears, though? Offering a room in their home? Providing a hot shower and an amazing meal? That's too much. Too good to be true.

What if he's working for my uncle?

Fear spikes through my veins, causing me to jump off the bed. I stand, frozen in place, listening to everything around me. My skin prickles with awareness as I catalog every sound, from the clock ticking to the dishwasher running downstairs.

Could the kind, understanding man from the coffee shop be fooling me? Could he be trying to make me comfortable enough to let my guard down, only to toss me in the back of his car and drop me off with my uncle?

But he's already had the opportunity if that's what he wanted. I fell asleep on the ride to Armando's house, so wouldn't it have made more sense to get rid of me then?

My head spins with possibilities and doubts. There's one sure way to know if I can trust Armando.

I slowly make my way to the door, resting my hand on

the knob. I remember Armando telling me I could lock him out. In my experience, doors lock from the *outside*, keeping whoever is inside trapped. Namely, me. Is this just another cage I've walked into?

Taking a deep breath, I turn the knob, pushing the door open to reveal an empty hallway. Huh. I guess that's one point in Armando's favor.

I peek out, looking left and right, but no one is in sight. Shoring up what little courage I have, I step into the hallway and head for the warm light coming from downstairs.

I'm unsure what I expected to find, but it certainly wasn't Armando reclining on the couch with a book. He looks uncomfortable with his foot tapping up and down and his shoulders hunched up to his ears. As I reach the bottom of the stairs, I see he's holding the book upside down.

Weird.

Armando peers over the top of the book, and his eyes meet mine. A smile takes over his features, and his shoulders drop as if all his tension drains away when he sees me. He's genuinely excited and relieved, and I blink back tears. I don't think anyone has ever been this happy to see me. The doubts from earlier vanish the longer I look at him.

"Hey, sweetheart," Armando greets me, his smile growing bigger as I clear the last stair and walk into the living room. Hazel eyes catch mine, and the emotion there is over-whelming and unfamiliar.

"Good book?" I ask, eyeing the well-worn paperback.

Armando flips through the pages and then realizes it's upside down. The tips of his ears turn red, and oh my god, is he blushing? How is it possible for the hulking giant of a man to be this adorable?

"You caught me," he says sheepishly, closing the book and setting it on the coffee table. "I was worried about you and couldn't figure out what to do with myself. After nearly wearing a hole in my hardwood floors from pacing, I thought I'd try to get some reading in." Armando rubs the back of his neck and looks at the book before returning his magical eyes to mine. "As you can see, it didn't go very well."

He was worried about me? My heart flips in my chest, but I try not to let it mean anything. He's being nice for reasons I still can't comprehend.

I'm drawn to Armando, my feet padding forward without my permission. I can't explain it, but I need to be near him. I need his calming touch, grounding scent, and deep, comforting voice that sends tingles racing up and down my spine.

"Can I get you anything?" he asks. "Water? Food?"

"Oh, that's okay. I ate before my nap."

"I'm guessing that was shortly after I left for work?"

I nod and look out the front window, noticing for the first time that it's dark out.

"I figured. That was nearly seven hours ago."

My eyes widen when I realize how long I've slept. "Sorry, I'm a terrible guest," I mumble, automatically wrapping my arms around my middle for protection.

"Allegra," Armando whispers, standing in front of me. "No more apologies, remember?" He crooks his pointer finger and tips my chin so we're eye to eye. "You needed sleep, and I'm happy I could provide that for you. I was concerned you were sick."

I shake my head and am immediately rewarded with a dazzling grin. Good lord, this man is devastating in the best possible way. I could get addicted to a smile like that.

"I'm feeling a lot better than this morning," I tell him truthfully. "Thank you. For everything. I don't know what I would've done if…" I trail off, not wanting to think about it.

"Good thing we don't have to worry about that," Armando says softly. "I'm here, and you're safe."

"Safe," I repeat in a whisper. He keeps telling me that, like he knows I don't believe it yet.

"That's right, Allegra." Armando cups the side of my face, holding me still as he leans down and presses the lightest kiss to my forehead. He immediately drops his hand and steps back, leaving me cold and swaying on my feet. "I'm sorry, that was too much," he rushes to say, taking another step back.

I grab his hand and keep him anchored to me, pulling his muscled frame closer. "Not too much," I murmur. "I… I like being near you," I admit.

A second later, his arms are around me. "Good," he grunts, pressing our bodies together. "I like it, too."

After a few moments of being engulfed in Armando's embrace, he loosens his grip and guides us to sit on the couch. I try sitting next to him, but Armando isn't having any of that. His hands slide down my waist until he's circling my hips and pulling me down on his lap.

"Still okay?" he asks, his lips brushing the shell of my ear.

I nod, leaning against his solid chest. Armando hums in approval, and the vibrations of his voice echo through my veins until they reach my throbbing core.

It's inappropriate, and I have zero experience in this department, but tell that to the ache blooming between my thighs. I wiggle a bit to get comfortable, and Armando groans. His fingers dig into my hips, creating a sense of urgency.

"Careful, angel. You have no idea what you do to me. I'm trying to be a good man when it comes to you."

"You are a good man," I tell him firmly, looking at him over my shoulder. "You've done more for me in the short time I've known you than anyone in my family…"

My voice cracks, and I close my eyes, curling in on myself at the thought of my family.

"You don't have to tell me everything," Armando whispers. "But I need to ask some questions, okay? I need to know how I can keep you safe."

I freeze, not wanting to relive everything that brought me to this point. Armando leans back on the couch and readjusts my position so I'm sitting sideways on his lap. On instinct, I relax against his chest and tuck my head into his neck. My gentle giant cradles me in his arms, combing his fingers through my hair.

"I know, sweet girl," he coos. "I know it hurts. Do you trust me?"

"Yes," I whisper into his skin.

"Let me in. Just a little, Allegra. I promise to protect all the pieces of your heart."

"You don't even know me," I remind him. My voice is so quiet I don't know if he heard me.

"That's not true," he counters, his tone matching mine. "I know you're brave as hell to get out of whatever situation you were in. And we've established how strong and selfless you are. We've also been over how beautiful you are, inside and out."

God, his words pour over me like a calming salve to my broken, battered heart.

"Okay," I finally murmur, nodding once. "I'll answer some questions."

"Good girl," he rasps, pressing his lips to my temple.

My skin sizzles whenever he calls me that, but I try pushing those thoughts aside and focusing on the questions.

"You told me earlier you were running from a bad man."

I nod, bracing myself for the next part.

"Who hurt you, Allegra? Who was chasing you?"

"My uncle," I whisper.

"Was he the one who left bruises on your skin?"

I nod, folding in on myself to be as small as possible.

"Jesus," he grunts. "And he's still looking for you?"

"He'll never stop," I admit, my voice barely more than a whimper.

"I've got you," Armando reminds me, smoothing his hand up and down my back while holding me close. "He'll never hurt you again, angel. I promise."

We sit in silence for a few moments while Armando absorbs the little information I've given him. Eventually, he peels me off his chest so we're face to face.

"Can you tell me what happened this morning? What sent you running?"

I take a deep breath and look up at the ceiling, willing the tears to recede until later when I'm alone in bed. Armando has already wiped away too many of my tears to count.

"He was always angry," I whisper, still unable to look Armando in the eye. "He became my guardian when I was eleven. I never knew my dad, and my mom struggled with numerous addictions until she finally succumbed to an overdose. I almost ended up in a group home, but a lawyer found a will my mom drew up after I was born and named my uncle, Tommy, my legal guardian. He's hated me ever since."

"I'm so sorry," Armando says, his breath tickling my lips. "Was it your uncle who gave you that scar, sweetheart?"

The question surprises me, but what shocks me more is that I want to tell him. I finally look into Armando's multi-colored eyes, finding deep sympathy and understanding in their depths. It gives me the courage to continue.

"We had a fight," I whisper, swallowing down the emotion clogging my throat. "I was thirteen, and he forgot to pick me up from middle school. I walked home and interrupted him with a woman, and... it wasn't pretty. She left, which sent my uncle into a rage. He pulled a knife on me, and I thought... I thought he was going to kill me," I say in a rush before my voice cracks.

"Jesus Christ," Armando growls, tension coursing through his muscles.

"I got out of his hold and ran to my room, where I shoved my dresser and anything I could find in front of my door. My uncle never tried to open it. He didn't say anything the next day, even when I had a huge bandage on. When he got home from work that night, he tossed me a bottle of super glue and said, *go patch yourself up.*"

"Allegra, fuck," he mutters in disbelief. The tips of his fingers find my scar, stroking the raised skin. Instead of feeling ashamed, I feel seen and understood.

"Things got better for a while when I started waitressing at his... business establishment." I stumble over the last two words, not wanting to admit what it was. A sketchy strip club offering anything for those willing to pay the right price. "I thought maybe we had turned a new leaf, and he needed proof I wasn't going to mooch off him forever. I wanted to show him I could earn my keep, you know?"

"You shouldn't have had to prove yourself, sweet girl. It was his responsibility to care for you."

I shrug, dismissing his words. The concept of getting something for nothing is absurd, but I don't tell him that. I have a feeling Armando is going to prove me wrong.

"After I graduated high school, I worked more hours, but it wasn't enough to pay the rent he started charging me. I ended up staying at... Well, it doesn't matter. I survived. I was working on saving up and getting out of here for good, but then..."

I break eye contact as every muscle in my body tenses. I can still feel his hand wrapped around my bicep, his fingers digging into my skin as he dragged me out of my makeshift bed in the closet. I can still smell his alcohol-soaked breath as he told me I had been promoted to serve exclusively in the VIP lounge.

"Breathe for me, baby," Armando murmurs, cupping my cheek and tilting my head. I do as he says, inhaling deeply and exhaling, my eyes never leaving his. "Good girl."

I sit up a little straighter, loving his praise even in the midst of telling him my whole fucked up situation. "This morning, my uncle informed me I would be working in the VIP lounge," I continue, my voice shaky but still there. "It's, um, a lounge for... uh, men who have lots of money and want to spend it on treating women like objects."

"Goddammit," Armando growls, his features turning hard as stone while he listens. "Did anyone touch you? Like that? Fuck, angel, please tell me they didn't..."

"No," I rush to say. "I refused. I fought him off. I knew I wouldn't survive if I went through something like that. I somehow got out of his hold and bolted outside. I had no idea where to go or what to do. I just had to keep going, putting one foot in front of the other until... until..."

"Until you found your safe space," Armando finishes. "Until you found me."

I nod, resting my forehead on his. "Until I found you," I repeat softly.

We breathe together, our hearts beating in sync as Armando rubs his nose against mine. It's such a sweet, tender moment, and I can't believe I met this man less than twenty-four hours ago. Still, our connection is undeniable.

"Are you going to kiss me?" I whisper, my cheeks immediately burning with the boldness of my question.

Armando groans, rolling his forehead against mine. "I want to, angel. But you understand why I can't, right? It would kill me if you ever thought I was taking advantage of you, of your vulnerability. You came to me for help."

"I came to you for safety," I correct, staring at his lips. "And you make me feel safe enough to do anything. Safe enough to sleep, safe enough to tell my story, safe enough to ask for what I want."

The hulking man trembles beneath me, his muscles shaking with the effort of holding back. Knowing how much I affect him sends a delicious shiver down my spine.

"What do you want, sweet girl? I'll give you anything." God, his voice is deep and filled with dark desire that slices through my nerves and spikes my awareness.

"I want you to be my first kiss," I whisper.

"Your first..." Armando inhales sharply, his nostrils flaring as his hazel eyes turn dark brown. "I'm going to hell for wanting you the way I do, but Jesus, I can't stop."

His mouth is on mine in the next second, nipping at my lips until I open up for him. I moan as his tongue slides against mine, lapping at me in steady strokes. He tangles his fingers in my hair, angling my head so he can dive deeper and give me everything I've been missing.

I fist his shirt and claw at his chest, grinding on his lap with each toe-curling stroke of his tongue. Armando growls into our kiss, skimming his other hand down my back to grab my ass in a punishing hold. He holds me in place while rubbing his thick erection into my core, causing me to cry out when he hits some super sensitive spot.

"Allegra," he rasps, finally breaking the kiss. We're both gasping for breath, the frantic need for each other hanging in the air. "So sweet. So responsive for me."

He nuzzles into the side of my neck as his arms circle my back, pulling me in for a hug. It's surprisingly tender after the way we just devoured each other, but I need this, too. Need his gentle care after such a mind-blowing first kiss.

I'm not sure how much time has passed when I'm jostled awake. I don't remember falling asleep.

"I've got you," Armando whispers, carrying me through the house. "I'll tuck you into bed, angel. We'll deal with everything else tomorrow."

I nod, snuggling into his chest. It's the safest, most loved I've ever felt.

CHAPTER FIVE

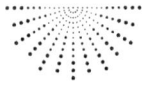

ARMANDO

"*H*ow is Cambria adjusting to life in New York? And your father?" Romeo asks Dante.

The inner circle members are all in Romeo's office for our weekly update and assignments.

"Just fine," Dante answers in a clipped tone. He's not nearly as aloof as he once was, though he would claim otherwise. Still, his voice has more warmth than usual, and I know it's all thanks to his new woman, Cambria.

"And the dumb fucks who kidnaped them have been dealt with, correct?"

"Affirmative," Dante growls. "I took out the leader of their little group of rebels, and the Moscatellis took care of the rest. They didn't appreciate another family on their territory, and they promised to contact me if they found any more Colombos in Chicago."

"They're good allies to have," Romeo says, pacing his office. Whenever the Boss is fidgeting instead of sitting at his desk and brooding, I know it's going to be a busy week. "While the Moscatellis keep tabs on our enemies in Chicago, we'll do the same here. After their attempt to harm my Thalia and the lives we took to get her back, I know they'll retaliate. I can't say for sure how the Colombos feel about the group of thugs who came for Cambria without permission, but we can't rule out their wrath for that incident, either. This game is about pride, and we've damaged theirs."

"What do we need to do, Boss?" I ask.

My foot won't stop tapping up and down, and I know I sound more than a little eager to get going. It's not out of character for me to be impatient while awaiting instructions, but today I'm antsier than usual. I have a beautiful warrior goddess in my home, waiting for me to return. Fuck yeah, I'm itching to get back to her.

"We'll focus on gathering information from our mutual connections. Dante, you and I will invite some of the financial world's bigger players to a black-tie dinner to get a read on where Colombo money is going."

Dante nods, scribbling down notes. What a nerd.

"My specialty isn't tuxedos and champagne, it's back-alley brawling," I mutter under my breath.

Romeo spins on his heel and narrows his eyes at me. "I'm used to you wanting to get out there and crack skulls, but you seem particularly restless today, Armando," he says carefully, assessing every one of my breaths. He's trying to get a read on me, but I don't mind.

"I am, but I'm always ready to give two hundred percent. You know that," I respond.

After a beat of silence, Romeo nods once before continuing. "You and Valentino will handle our contacts on the ground. Known business fronts, strip clubs, the seedier side of our city. They'll likely talk more than the financial hotshots, but their intel can't always be trusted. I know both of you will use your best judgment on what information makes it back inside this office."

Valentino and I share a look, then nod in deference to the Don.

"Yes, Boss," Valentino answers.

"Of course, Boss," I add.

"Good. It's settled. This is our number one priority. We need to strike while they're still scrambling."

Romeo dismisses us a few minutes later, and Valentino follows me into the hallway.

"You, uh, doing okay?" he asks, giving me some side-eye. "You seem ready to bolt out of here. Don't tell me you have some chick waiting for you."

"She's not *some chick*," I snarl, looking Valentino dead in the eye.

Valentino is the youngest member of the Di Salvo family inner circle, but he's proven himself loyal in a short amount of time. Valentino's past is a bit of a mystery, and while Dante has his suspicions, I know better than to question the Boss's decisions. If Romeo says he's legit, then he's legit.

Right now, however, I want to rearrange his face with my fist for disrespecting Allegra.

"Jesus, not you, too," he groans. "First Romeo, then Dante, and now…" Valentino sighs as he gestures vaguely in my direction.

"You have an opinion about the Boss' woman? I'm sure he'd love to hear it."

The tall, tatted-up man raises his palms in mock surrender. "Not trying to start anything. Just saying I don't understand. You all went so long without having these… entanglements, so why start now?"

"First, I'm only eight years older than you. Don't talk to me like I'm elderly," I grunt. "And second, by *entanglements,* you mean…?"

Valentino rolls his eyes, exasperated by my question. "I mean all the complications that come with women and relationships in general. All three of you are at the top of your game, so I don't understand why you're so willing to throw it all away."

"Who says Romeo is throwing anything away? Is he not still the Boss? And is Dante not still his second in command? Why would being in a relationship change that?"

"Hey man, I'm just calling it like I see it. The more attachments a person has, the more there is to lose. I just figured men like us, having the careers we have, would think twice about falling in love."

It's true that Valentino is only eight years younger than my thirty-nine, but right now, he looks like a petulant child with his nose scrunched up. This tempers some of my initial anger. Valentino isn't being an ass; he just has a giant chip on his shoulder. Interesting.

"When it happens to you, you'll understand there's no choice," I tell him, resuming my walk out of the house and over to my parked car. I have a driver for almost everything except for my meetings at the compound.

"When what happens to me?" Valentino asks, trailing along behind me.

"When you fall in love. It's not really falling, in my experience," I muse, remembering the moment I saw Allegra. "It's more like getting clobbered."

Valentino snorts. "And you're advocating this? Getting clobbered by love?"

I unlock my car and slip inside the driver's seat, looking up at my colleague through the open car door. "It's the best goddamn thing that's ever happened to me."

"You're crazy," he scoffs, though I see the hint of a smile.

"A piece of advice, kid?" I say with a smirk. "When it happens to you, don't fight it. You won't win."

"Whatever," Valentino mutters as I close the car door. "I'll call you tomorrow morning, and we'll plan our week," he shouts as I rev the engine.

I nod once, then peel out of the Di Salvo compound with one thought on my mind. *Allegra.*

The normally twenty-minute drive home takes only ten. I try taking a few deep breaths to calm myself, but my heart won't stop racing. I've only been away for three hours, but I miss my angel already.

When I step inside, I'm greeted with the sweetest sight; my Allegra in an oversized t-shirt, humming to herself while wiping down the kitchen counter. Her hips sway to the tune in her head, and the sunlight pouring in through the window catches on her strawberry-blonde hair, making it glitter.

My feet carry me forward as if in a trance, my eyes unable to part from her for a single second. Allegra looks up at me, and her blue eyes light up when they meet mine. God, she's perfection. Sweet, innocent, tempting perfection.

"Welcome home," she says seconds before I scoop her up in my arms.

"Love seeing you in my clothes," I grunt like an animal.

Allegra giggles and I have to capture the sound on my tongue. Our lips meet softly at first and then with more passion. I open my mouth, needing more, needing to consume her and tie her to me in every way. Our tongues tangle, each giving and taking in perfect measure.

Never breaking our kiss, I walk Allegra backward and set her on the counter before stepping between her parted thighs. My girl moans for me, her aching core rubbing against the thick, painful erection trapped in my pants.

I need more. I need her skin under my tongue, need to lap at those perky nipples, need to breathe her in. I need to see her come. I need to smell her release as it drips down my chin.

Reluctantly, I break our kiss so I can fill my lungs with

air. She follows me like our lips are connected by magnets. It pleases me to know she's as addicted to me as I already am to her.

I watch as she catches her breath, her eyes closed, her lips swollen, and her cheeks flushed.

"Beautiful," I whisper into the side of her neck before placing a soft kiss there.

Allegra's pulse beats rapidly, making me groan and lick the same spot. She bucks her hips, grazing her hot little pussy against me.

"Do you like when I kiss you here, Allegra?" I ask as I continue trailing kisses up and down her slender column.

"Yes, sir," she whimpers.

I growl into her skin, my already hard dick turning to granite at her words. Goddamn, I didn't know what a turn-on that would be, but I can't get enough. She arches her neck, baring the soft flesh to me. I'm like a wolf, ready to sink my teeth into my prey.

"Fucking love when you call me that," I growl again, sucking and licking and nipping as she moans for me.

My lips trail lower, grazing her collarbone, where I suck and bite her, just enough to turn her skin pink, not enough to leave a mark. But fuck, I want to mark her. Claim her. Devour her.

"Please," Allegra whimpers as I slowly kiss my way down her chest and over the fabric of her shirt. "I need more. Please, Armando."

"Who?" I ask before rolling her nipple in between my lips.

"Sir! Please, sir…"

I reward her by slipping my fingers under her shirt to explore her silky-smooth skin. My large, rough hands skim her soft tummy, higher, higher, until my thumbs graze the sensitive underside of her breasts.

Allegra lifts her arms, giving me permission to explore

more of her luscious body. I grip the hem of the too-large shirt and slowly slide it up her body, revealing inch after creamy inch of skin to my hungry eyes.

I practically tear the shirt off her, then stand back to admire the most perfect pair of tits I've ever seen.

"Fucking hell," I whisper. I brush the back of my knuckles down the top of one breast and over the pebbled nipple, loving how she trembles at my touch.

Leaning down, I lick over her aching peaks before blowing cold air on them. Allegra gasps, and her thighs tighten around my waist. I suck on her breast *hard*, loving how her body fits perfectly with mine. I caress her thick thighs as I suck and nibble one breast and then the other. She leans back with her hands on the counter, thrusting her chest out for me and pushing her breast deeper into my mouth.

I groan at her offering and pop off her tit, only to repeat the process on the other one. The whole time, my thumbs massage circles on the insides of Allegra's thighs, inching higher and higher.

"Oh, God, ohmygod, I…"

Allegra trembles beneath my touch, and I swear she's going to come from this alone. She cries out as I pull her nipple through my teeth, her legs shaking, her heart pounding in her chest. I feel the heat of her pussy as she grinds down against my throbbing cock, seeking the friction she needs.

"I'm… I think…"

My hands slide around her back, holding her up as her arms give out. Allegra throws her head back in a silent scream as I bite her nipple. I watch in complete awe as this goddess falls apart in my arms. I feel every muscle in her back tense and release as I hold her close and kiss all over her breasts and neck.

Finally, Allegra goes limp in my arms. I gather her up and hold her close to my chest, kissing the top of her head.

"So sensitive," I murmur as I stroke her back. "So damn responsive."

She looks up at me and blushes, burying her head in my chest again. "Sorry," she whispers. "Is that bad?"

"Not at all. I love it. I love that I get to explore your body and show you how good you can feel."

She tries hiding from me, but I peel away one small hand and then the other, placing a kiss on both palms and wrapping them around my neck.

I rest my forehead on hers and breathe her in. "Do you trust me, sweetheart?"

"Yes, sir," she whispers.

I grunt in approval and kiss my way down her neck and chest until I'm nuzzling between her perfect mounds.

And then I kiss lower.

My lips trail over her ribcage and stomach as I gently lay her out on the counter and kneel in front of her.

"Am I going to be the first to lick your dripping pussy? The first to taste you and suck on your needy little clit?"

Allegra moans as I hook my thumbs in the waistband of the boxers she's wearing. I pause until I hear her say it.

"Yes, sir, only you."

I slide the boxers off her and trail kisses up the inside of one thigh and then the other. I stroke my fingers through the soft patch of curls decorating her mound and grin when she shivers and squirms.

"And will I be the first to dip my fingers into your tight little cunt?"

"Yes!"

I smack her pussy, not too hard, and Allegra spasms and gasps in surprise.

"Yes, who?"

She's panting now, her fingers gripping the side of the counter so hard her knuckles are white. "Yes, sir. Please," she whimpers.

"Love when you beg so nicely for me, angel," I growl as I throw her legs over my shoulders.

I part her lips with my thumbs and stare at the most decadent pussy I've ever seen. She's soaking wet, and her clit is engorged and throbbing for me. Precum leaks from my aching cock as her scent washes over me.

Her body shakes in my hands, vibrating with need and anticipation. I blow warm air over her tight cunt, watching it convulse as a wave of wetness gushes from her virgin hole. One drop of honey trickles down to her puckered little asshole, and I lick it up, not stopping until I circle her clit with the tip of my tongue.

"Armando…" Her voice cracks as she gasps for air.

God, her sounds… Fuck, it makes my cock throb and my balls ache. How can she unravel me with just that small thing?

"Say it again," I demand.

"Armando," she moans. "I like how it feels."

"Good," I murmur. "I like the way it makes you say my name."

I lap at her sweet pussy, spearing my tongue inside her entrance and scooping up more of her juices to swirl around her clit. Allegra's hips buck against me, her thighs tighten around my head, and I can tell she's about to let go for me.

But I want to drag it out.

I look up from between her legs and watch her tits rise and fall as she pants for air. Everything about her is captivating.

I slowly lick the seam where her leg meets her hip, first one and then the other. I trace the outside of her pussy lips and dart my tongue into her slit, licking her clit once. She twists, and I move my tongue back to lazy circles around her folds and dips. I repeat this process, torturing her, bringing her closer and closer, one lick at a time.

Sucking her clit into my mouth, I swipe my tongue over the tight bundle of nerves again and again until her muscles pull tight and her breath catches in her throat. And then…

I back away, grinning when I hear her frustrated grunt.

"I need more," she whines, twisting beneath me.

"Trust me, Allegra. I'll make it worth the wait."

I play with my girl some more, swiping a finger up and down her pussy, chuckling when her greedy cunt tries to suck me inside.

"So damn sexy," I tell her before plunging my finger inside her.

"Oh!" Her surprised little yelp turns into a moan as I pump in and out. "More!"

I withdraw my finger and smack her clit, making her gush for me and cry out. I plunge two fingers into her tight channel, in and out, curling them up and rubbing them over her G-spot. I take them out just as quickly and smack her pussy again.

"How do good girls ask for what they want?"

"More, sir, please, please…"

I growl in approval and shove three fingers inside her dripping pussy while biting down on her clit. Allegra bows her back off the kitchen counter, every muscle in her body drawn up tight. Then she jerks her hips up and thrashes underneath me so hard I have to keep my other hand over her stomach to keep her from falling off the damn counter.

I keep fingerfucking her as her pussy squeezes me tightly, my thumb taking the place of my mouth so I can watch her curvy body get overtaken by pleasure. When Allegra gasps for air, I can tell she thinks it's over.

But I keep going. I curl my fingers up again while keeping

267

her pinned to the counter. I feel it. I *feel* her orgasm deep in her core, rising to the surface as I beckon it with my fingers deep inside her.

"Armando, I'm…"

"Let it happen, Allegra. Let go for me."

"Ah, ah, ah, oh fuck, ohmygod, there, right there…"

Allegra screams and shatters so beautifully for me. I withdraw my hand and bury my face between her legs, gripping her ass and bringing her closer to me so I can drink her release. I can't breathe, but I don't give a fuck. She's exquisite.

"Too… much…" She tries to twist out of my grip.

I snarl like the feral beast she makes me, licking her pussy clean until the final tremors of her orgasm leave her in a shuddering breath.

I stand, scooping Allegra's limp body into my arms and sitting us on the couch, with her curled up in my lap. It's a special kind of hell having the sexiest woman I've ever seen naked on my lap. My cock aches and is harder than it's ever been, but this wasn't about me. Her pleasure will always come first.

I cup her head with one hand and tuck her into my chest, stroking her bare back with my other hand, hoping to comfort her after such an intense first sexual experience.

"You did so good. You're so brave, letting me have control of your pleasure like that," I whisper before kissing the top of her head. "Are you okay, sweetheart?"

Allegra takes a stuttering breath, and for a moment, I worry I've pushed her too far.

"I've never felt… I didn't know…" She sighs. "I'm so good, Armando. I mean, sir."

I chuckle and kiss the top of her head again. "You can call me Armando. Sir is for when we play. Do you understand?"

She nods into my chest.

"Need your words, Allegra."

"I understand."

"Good girl. My sweet angel," I praise. "Rest now. I'll be here when you wake up."

No sooner do the words leave my mouth than her eyes flutter closed. I grab a blanket from the back of the couch and drape it over her gorgeous body, needing her to be safe and warm above all else.

CHAPTER SIX

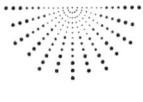

ALLEGRA

*S*omething tickles my chin, then my cheek, slowly moving up, up, up, until I feel the soft tickling on my temple. Slowly blinking one eye open, I'm greeted with hazel eyes and a warm smile.

"There you are," Armando whispers, nuzzling his nose against mine.

"Here I am," I answer sleepily as a yawn escapes. The more I wake up, the more aware I am of my surroundings. Armando is holding me on his lap on the couch, and from the looks of the orange sunlight streaming through the front window, we've been here for a while. "Sorr–"

Armando cuts me off with a quick kiss. "I hope you weren't about to apologize." He lifts a skeptical eyebrow.

"Who, me? I would *never!*" I bat my eyelashes dramatically, making him grin.

"Love seeing your sassy side," he murmurs before kissing me again, for real this time.

Armando slides his tongue against mine, striking a match with each stroke until my body is on fire for him. One of his hands sneaks under the blanket I'm wrapped up in, his rough fingertips tickling my sensitive flesh. My arms circle his neck as I cling to him, my need growing more urgent with each passing second.

"Gotta stop," he grits, breaking our kiss to trail his lips down my neck. "I don't want to pressure you or make you uncomfortable."

"I'm comfortable," I breathe, leaning forward and stealing a kiss. "I could be more comfortable, though," I pant. The blanket falls from my body, leaving me naked in his arms. Rolling my hips forward, I gasp when I feel his thick dick harden even more beneath me.

"Jesus, Allegra. Need you to tell me exactly what you mean." Armando grips my hips, holding me in place while grinding against my soaking-wet center. "Fuck me, angel. I'm trying to be good…"

"Be bad with me," I whisper, brushing my lips over the shell of his ear.

Who is this bold woman speaking through me right now?

I don't have time to question my newfound sense of confidence. Not when Armando is looking at me like I hold his life in my hands. A pained sound rumbles up from his chest as his hips jerk, grinding his massive cock against my swollen pussy.

"Please, sir," I moan, loving how it's working him up. "Please… *fuck* me."

Armando lets out a savage snarl as he leaps to his feet, tossing me over his shoulder as he bounds up the stairs.

"Hey!" I shout, though I'm mostly laughing.

My man palms my ass, giving it a squeeze before smacking it. "You're killing me," he groans. "This sexy fucking body…"

The next thing I know, I'm falling through the air before my back hits the soft mattress. Armando falls on top of me, pinning me down with his weight, blanketing me in his strength. His lips are on mine, picking up where we left off in the living room.

Armando holds himself up with one hand at the side of my head while his other slides down my body, cupping my breast. He squeezes lightly, groaning into my mouth. Then his hand moves lower, gripping my hip, sliding down my thigh, and tickling my bare skin. He squeezes me there and groans again, pulling my leg to the side so he can settle between my thighs.

"Need to get naked, but I can't stop kissing these lips," he whispers, grinding himself against my core as he kisses me again.

I make some desperate sound in the back of my throat, then tear my mouth from his, breathing fresh air into my burning lungs. Armando rests his forehead on mine, taking deep, ragged breaths. Knowing he's this wound up because of me is even more of a confidence booster.

I push on his chest, giving him a devious grin as he sits up. I follow him, standing right in front of the ripped demigod of a man. I tug at his shirt, silently demanding that he take it off. His eyes flash with wicked intentions that match mine as he pulls his shirt off.

My hands find his chest, my fingers teasing his skin in featherlight touches. Lower, lower, lower my exploration goes, learning the dips in his defined chest and abs. A shiver runs through his body and into mine, drawing us closer together.

I still can't believe he wants me. I'm a mess, inside and out. My life is falling apart, and I have zero experience. Not to mention, Armando is like a twenty on a scale of one to ten, and I'm hovering at about a three. In no world does this strong, sexy, surprisingly sweet man choose me.

Armando tips my chin and kisses me soundly as his fingers tangle in my hair and tug at the strands. I let go of every thought, moaning softly when his other hand slides up my spine, caressing my skin in barely there touches, despite his obvious need for me.

I'm so lost in his touch, it takes me a second to realize he's trailing kisses over the ugly scar on my neck. Instinctively, I pull back, turning my head to hide the mark.

"Allegra," he says softly. "What did I tell you about your scars?"

"They prove I'm a survivor," I whisper, my eyes locking onto his.

"Good girl. That's right. Every part of you is perfect. Every inch. Can I show you?"

Armando doesn't push me for an answer, he simply offers me his hand. *How does he know exactly what I need?*

I slip my hand in his, letting him pull me closer as his eyes roam up and down my chest, torso, and legs before reversing their path. When Armando finally meets my gaze again, he gives me a gentle, reverent look. He's letting me know he wants to cherish me as much as he wants to devour me. I feel the same.

"You're so beautiful, angel," he murmurs. "I'm going to ravish every inch of you, Allegra. I hope you're ready for that."

My core clenches and releases, making more of my arousal drip down my thighs. I can't keep my eyes off his hands, which are working furiously to rid himself of his clothing. As soon as he's naked in all of his glory, he grips my hips and walks me backward until my knees hit the edge of the mattress.

Armando cups my face in his hands and brushes his nose up and down mine in the lightest touch. "Do you trust me?"

"Yes, sir. With all of me," I don't hesitate to answer.

We share a tender moment, so many unspoken words passed back and forth with just one look. Then his hard length grazes against my center, and just like that, I'm aching for his touch.

Armando tips his head back and groans when I grab his cock and rub the tip with my thumb, spreading his precum around. "Fuck, you feel so good. I'm clean, Allegra. I haven't been with anyone in years. A decade or more. I want inside your tight, wet heat with nothing between us, but I'll put a condom on if you want."

"I want to feel you, too," I whisper, my cheeks heating at my words. I should feel embarrassed, but there's no room for shame when Armando is looking at me like that. He wants me as much as I want him, and I'm not about to ruin this moment for anything.

"Goddamn," he growls, pushing me down on the bed.

I'm expecting him to join me, but he sinks to his knees instead. He grips my thighs in his large hands and pries my legs apart. I cry out and bow my back off the bed when he presses his thumb over my clit. A sudden powerful burst of pleasure slices through me and rattles me to my core.

My pleasure grows more intense when his tongue slides through my dripping folds, licking me and nipping at my sensitive flesh. He nudges my clit with his nose and spears his tongue into my little hole, scooping out my juices and drinking them.

Armando drags his tongue lower, lower, lower, until it's teasing my back entrance. I gasp at the filthiness of it all, but the forbidden nature makes me even wetter. He licks around the tight ring of muscle and growls.

"Oh god," I whisper. "Ohmygod, Armando, oh fuck." My whisper becomes a loud moan when the very tip of his tongue pushes inside. He rubs my clit in furious circles, and I grip the sheets, twisting them in my fists as my body expands and contracts. "I'm…"

I shatter before I even finish my sentence. My orgasm

rushes through me with such intensity, I shoot up off the bed, trying to escape the overwhelming pleasure. Armando shoves me back down with a hand spread over my stomach. He holds me there, making me feel all of it, every last drop of bliss.

He grunts in satisfaction, crawling up my body and crashing his mouth down on mine in a passionate kiss. "Needed your taste on my tongue before I fuck this tight little pussy for the first time."

Leaning back slightly, Armando gathers my hands and guides them over my head. Pinning my wrists down, he drags his thickness through my folds, coating himself in my cream before lining up with my entrance.

"Ready, Allegra?"

"Yes. God. Yes, sir," I breathe.

He kisses me as he thrusts all the way inside, tearing through the last barrier between us. I tense up at the slight pinch deep in my core, holding my breath until it passes.

"I'm sorry," he whispers. "It won't hurt after this. I'll make you feel so good, angel. So fucking good."

"I'm okay," I promise him. "I want you so bad. Please don't stop."

"I'll take care of you, Allegra. My good girl. Always."

I nod and clench around his hard length, making him groan. I'm so full, stretched to the point of pain, but in the best way possible. It heightens my pleasure, sparks my nerves, and makes me thrust my hips, taking him deeper.

"Then do it, already," I practically growl at him.

Armando chuckles, and I feel the vibrations with every inch of me, inside and out.

He leans down and kisses the side of my neck, biting down gently on my pulse point. I writhe beneath him, pleasure taking over the pain. Armando pulls out almost all the way, hovering above me and driving me crazy.

Armando gives me a dark, delicious look before thrusting back inside me. His thickness scrapes along my walls, the friction like striking a match as instant, overwhelming heat engulfs me. I bow my back and push against his hand still holding my wrists, grateful for an anchor in the raging storm of sensations.

He pulls my leg higher on his hip, changing the angle. I whimper as his cock slides against some magical place inside me that has me sobbing his name louder with each thrust. He snaps his hips, grinding his pelvis against my clit while hitting that spot over and over.

Armando grunts my name every time his balls slap my ass. I can feel him losing control, his strokes becoming deeper, harder, so damn rough. I love it. I convulse as he thrusts into me relentlessly. The exquisite pleasure bordering on pain builds and builds, higher and higher, one more, one more, again, again... until I break. Shards of pleasure cut and heal me as I cry out for him repeatedly.

My orgasm rips through me, holding my body hostage, forcing me to feel every wave of bliss until tears drip down my face and I'm a sweaty, soaking mess beneath him. Armando stays still, buried deep inside my spasming pussy.

When the last of my pleasure leaves me, Armando growls and slams into me, letting go of my wrists and sliding his hand down my body. He squeezes my breast, leaning down and bringing the nipple to his mouth and lavishing it with attention until I'm shaking beneath him.

"Oh, God, Armando," I choke out. I claw at his back as he rips me apart in the best way possible. Each gut-twisting stroke winds me up higher and higher until I'm right on the precipice, teetering on the edge.

His hips stutter as he loses his rhythm and starts rutting into me. His fingers dig into my hips as my nails bite into his skin, both of us clinging to this tension-filled pleasure. A shiver runs through me, followed by another and another, until I'm shaking violently.

We both cry out as his hot seed spills into me. Wave after wave of his cum splashes into my pulsing channel and then drips out, and still, there's more. My pussy snaps around him as I sob my climax.

I gasp for air as I float back down to earth, the oxygen burning my lungs yet somehow sending jolts of pleasure to my core. Armando buries his face in my neck, and I wrap my arms around his torso, keeping him on top of me while we catch our breath.

"You're perfect," he whispers. "You're all mine."

I nod and pull him closer until most of his weight is resting on top of me.

Armando understands my need better than I do. He surrounds me with his strength, blanketing me in his warmth. "I'm right here, Allegra. I've got you."

We stay attached as long as possible, but I start to shiver from the sweat drying on my body. Armando rolls over and drags me with him, tucking me into his side. My eyelids grow heavy, and my body melts into his. I'm vaguely aware of Armando pulling the covers over us, but I'm too tired, too worn out to look.

"Get some sleep, sweetheart. I'll be right here when you wake up."

I nod, feeling safe, warm, and completely satisfied. As I drift off to sleep, I swear I hear Armando say he loves me. I want to say it back, but sleep takes me before I get a chance.

CHAPTER SEVEN

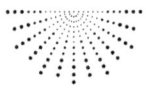

ARMANDO

I lie awake, listening to Allegra's soft snores and counting her breaths. I feel each intake of air as her lungs expand and contract. It's calming in a way I didn't know I needed.

The sun set quite a while ago, but my Allegra and I haven't moved. She passed out when I tucked her into my side, but I don't mind. The girl deserves to rest after what we did.

God, being with her was incredible. More than incredible. It was life-altering. Soul-shattering. Coming deep inside her was indescribable—the most profound moment of my life.

My dick grows hard thinking about her stretched out beneath me. She trusted me with her body, her virginity, and her pleasure. She begged me, and I'll never forget our first time together. I can't wait to be inside her again, but I know my girl has to be sore. Each thrust tore at my sanity until I lost my mind and fucked her so damn hard.

Allegra moans softly in her sleep, then wiggles her hips, trying to get closer to me. I can't stop the deep, hungry growl rising from my chest when she adjusts her leg and grazes my hard as fuck dick. She's still asleep, but her leg hooks around mine, her knee rubbing against my nearly painful erection.

I reach down and wrap my hand around the back of her knee. I mean to push her leg away so I don't come all over myself like a teenager, but instead, I find myself grinding against her. I sink my teeth into my bottom lip as unbelievable pleasure rolls through me. How can I be so close to the edge from just this simple touch?

But I already know the answer. It's her. Everything about her. I'll never get enough. I know I need to stop, but she feels so damn good. Precum leaks out of me, my raging hard-on needing some relief. When Allegra rubs her soaking wet core against my thigh, I groan loudly, unable to contain the sound.

Allegra returns my groan with one of her own, awareness slowly creeping into her movements as she wakes up. Her nails bite into my bare chest, snapping the last thread of my control. Wrapping her long hair around my fist, I tilt her head back, growling when I see her blue eyes ablaze. My lips are on hers in the next second.

I swallow down her cries of pleasure as I devour her. Her hot little body writhes against mine, creating delicious, torturous friction. I need more. Need to feel her from the inside out. Need to consume her, taste her sweat, bite her soft skin, and drink down everything she's offering.

"Armando," she whimpers into my mouth, capturing my lips again. I pull her on top of me so she's straddling my lap. Allegra breaks our kiss, gasping for air. "Armando," she repeats as she rolls her hips.

Allegra's pussy lips wrap around my cock, fluttering around my length and driving me insane. I've never had this overwhelmingly primal need to claim, to possess, to own someone completely. Allegra rests her forehead on mine as a shudder ripples through her soft, curvy body. I know she's as desperate as I am when a pained whimper escapes her mouth.

She sits up, steadying herself with both hands on my chest. I grip her hips and lift her, positioning her dripping wet hole over the head of my cock. I hiss out a breath and squeeze my eyes shut, trying with everything in me not to come like this. Her cunt pulses, massaging my sensitive dick and making me buck my hips involuntarily and slide a few inches inside her.

"Are you sure, angel?" I grit.

Instead of answering, Allegra bites her bottom lip and nods, her big blue eyes telling me everything I need to know. Slowly, so slowly, she sinks down on my length, her pussy stretching obscenely wide around my cock.

I drag my eyes up her body, taking in her pale skin and strawberry-blonde hair. She's practically glowing in the moonlight streaming through the window. I watch in awe as the silver light kisses the side of her face, her breasts, and her thighs. My fingers skim over everywhere the light touches, needing to feel this goddess as she brings me unimaginable pleasure.

Allegra tilts her head back and claws my chest, gasping for air once she's fully seated. I grip her hips, anchoring her to me, keeping her right here. Her core ripples around my cock, making the fucker jerk and leak more precum inside her.

"You feel so good," I whisper, unable to find my voice as I get lost in how our bodies are connected on every level.

I help her find her rhythm, rolling her hips and grinding her down on my swollen dick. Each movement sends sharp pangs of ecstasy shooting through my veins. I know she feels it, too, with each breathy moan that falls from her lips.

Allegra's eyes snap open, locking on mine. I see the moment she recognizes her power. Her strength. Those blue eyes turn fierce, almost feral, as she lifts on her knees and drops down on me, her little hole swallowing my dick completely.

An animalistic growl rumbles through her, wracking her body as she fucks me furiously. Christ, it's all I can do to hold on. I want this for her, need this, need her to take control and understand that I'm hers. She owns me, body and soul.

I cup the back of her neck and pull her down for a kiss, tasting her sweetness as she brings us closer, closer, closer...

"Armando," she whispers. "Armando... Armando... please, sir..." Her whimpers turn into moans, louder, louder, until she's crying out my name, her voice broken as she comes around my cock. Goddamn, she comes with her whole body, every muscle tensing and releasing as her orgasm works its way through her.

I keep her right here with me, her forehead resting on mine as she shakes and releases more of her juices. Her cum drips down my dick and coats my balls... and holy hell, is she coming again? Allegra buries her face in the side of my neck, muffling her scream as an intense orgasm rips through her curvy little body.

Something breaks loose inside me, leaving me unhinged and wild with need. I flip Allegra onto her back and rut into her throbbing pussy, grunting with each thrust. She bows her back and wraps her legs around my hips, digging her heels into my ass.

"That's it," I growl. "Such a good girl for me."

I lean down and suck on her breast, teasing one nipple and then the other, back and forth until her fingernails bite into the back of my head. She pulls my hair and tilts my head before slamming her mouth down on mine.

My greedy girl rocks into me, meeting me frantic thrust for frantic thrust. I break our kiss and inhale sharply as my orgasm barrels through me. With a roar, I let go of every fucking thing and come so damn hard my bones rattle.

Allegra's cries carve through the night air as her channel squeezes and snaps around me, milking me and prolonging our pleasure. We're both shaking and panting as we cling to each other, riding out the last of our climax.

I collapse on top of her, gathering her limp body in my arms. I try rolling to the side to keep from crushing her, but once again, Allegra urges me to stay right where I am. I'll be her safety blanket whenever she needs it. We stay wrapped up like that for long moments, Allegra taking deep breaths while I whisper how much she means to me and that she's safe in my arms.

Eventually, her grip on me loosens, allowing me to roll onto my back and drape her over my chest. After a few moments of silence, I begin to worry I've hurt her. I tore into her like a beast after taking her virginity only a few hours ago.

"Allegra?" I murmur, cupping the back of her neck and guiding her to look up at me. "Are you all right?" She nods, but I can't quite see the look on her face in the darkness of the room. "Need your words, angel. Did I… did I hurt you?"

"Not at all," she assures me.

The pressure in my chest releases, allowing me to breathe again.

"That was…" She nibbles her bottom lip, searching for something to describe what we just shared.

"Yeah, it was," I agree, kissing her forehead and the tip of her nose.

Allegra sighs contentedly before curling up on my chest again. We lie in silence for a few moments, soaking up the love we've found. It's on the tip of my tongue to tell her my intense feelings, but I'm not sure she's ready to hear it. Allegra has been through so much, and even though I'm ready for our forever, it's understandable for her to need more time.

I can be patient. I think. It's never been a particularly strong trait, but I'd do anything for my angel.

"This is seriously the comfiest bed in the world," Allegra sighs, snuggling up closer while pulling the blankets around her.

My chest grows tight at her words, remembering when she first stepped into her room and marveled at the sheets and pillows. I want to know everything about her, but I need to tread carefully.

I gently stroke Allegra's back, the tips of my fingers barely touching her silky-smooth skin as I trail them up and down her spine. She melts against me, letting me soothe every worry and doubt.

"Where were you sleeping before you met me?" I ask softly.

My sweet girl tenses and curls in on herself.

"Don't hide from me," I whisper, kissing the top of her head. "Remember who you are, Allegra. Strong, brave as fuck, kind, and beautiful. Nothing about your past can change that."

"How do you always know what to say?" she murmurs, tipping her head up. Blue eyes lock onto mine, and vulnerability clashes with growing confidence as she braces herself to tell me her truth.

"I'm not usually good with my words," I admit. "But with you… I'm trying so damn hard to be what you need."

"You are," Allegra whispers. She tucks her head into my neck, clinging to me while searching for her words. I'll wait however long she needs. "After my uncle kicked me out for being late on rent, I didn't know where to go. I still had my job as a waitress, and if I could find someplace to live for free, I'd be able to save enough money to get out and start over somewhere new."

I hum softly, resuming my steady, gentle strokes along her spine. I can tell Allegra has never spoken about this with anyone, and knowing she trusts me with her past and her secrets is humbling.

"Where did you end up?" I ask, though I'm sure I won't like the answer.

"I went into work like usual, then hid in the bathroom or out by the dumpsters until everyone else left around two-thirty or three in the morning. I sneaked back inside and made a little nest in a storage closet out of coats from the lost and found. Eventually, I stashed a blanket and pillow in the closet, but my uncle found them after a few weeks and threw them out after yelling at everyone for being lazy pieces of shit. I didn't try anything stupid like that again."

"Allegra," I murmur, cupping the back of her neck and nudging her to look up at me. "Jesus, sweetheart. I'm so sorry you had to live like that." She shrugs and looks away from me, but I don't let her get away with that. "I know what it's like to survive with nothing but the clothes on your back."

This gets her attention. Allegra gasps and her blue eyes grow wide. "What happened?"

"I..." Taking a breath, I let it out and focus on what's important. I can't derail this conversation with my sordid past, but I know we'll need to talk about everything soon. "This isn't about me right now, sweetheart. I need you to know I don't think less of you. It takes courage and persever-ance to push through that shit and wake up every morning. I'm so proud of you."

"Proud of... me?" Her voice is soft and broken, tugging at my heart painfully.

"Yes, sweet girl. You're a survivor."

"I don't deserve this," she whispers.

"Deserve what?"

"This… you, the bed, a fresh start. It's going to be ripped away. I'm going to screw it up, and–"

"Never," I say firmly, cutting her off as I flip her on her back and hover over her, caging in my beautiful angel with an arm on either side of her head. "You're not going to screw up anything, Allegra. Nothing is going to be ripped away. I'm your safe place, remember? And I'm not going anywhere."

My beautiful girl nods, cupping my cheek. I lean into her touch, closing my eyes and breathing in her sweet, honied scent. My lips are drawn to hers, and she opens up for me, accepting my kiss and asking for more.

"Thank you," she breathes against my lips before tangling her tongue with mine.

I groan as Allegra slides her hands into my hair, scratching my scalp and neck to pull me closer. I cover my sweet girl with my large frame, taking long, lazy sips from her addictive mouth.

"Never thank me," I rasp. "You give me everything just by breathing."

I rest my forehead on hers, sharing the same breath as we come back down. Rolling over on my back, I open my arms, smiling when Allegra snuggles into my side.

We still have a lot to talk about, including my career, but right now, I'm content to have the love of my life in my arms. We'll figure everything else out.

CHAPTER EIGHT

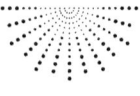

ALLEGRA

"*M*orning, Allegra," someone whispers.

My heart kicks violently, ripping me out of sleep as I pull the blankets over my head like a shield.

Where am I? Who's with me? Am I in danger?

"You're safe," comes the voice I now recognize as Armando's. "Sorry, angel. I didn't mean to scare you."

I lower the blankets and blink, adjusting to the morning light illuminating the room. Kind hazel eyes meet mine, and a soft smile stretches across his handsome features. "I guess I'm still a little jumpy," I murmur, feeling heat crawl into my cheeks.

Armando frowns, but then offers a genuine, heart-stopping smile as he cups my cheek. "I hate that you ever had to wake up in fear. Never again, sweet girl."

I nod, fighting back the tears. I still can't believe this is real, that *he's* real. Last week I was sleeping in a closet, struggling to survive. And now? I'm in a cozy, warm bed with the sexiest man alive, and he's kind and gentle and knows how to speak directly to my soul.

It's too good to be true.

I peer over at Armando, sitting on the bed, fully dressed in a suit and tie. It strikes me how little I know about the man I've been living with. And now sleeping with.

"Going somewhere?" I ask, giving him a smile. I feel dumb for freaking out on him, but I know Armando isn't judging me.

"I have a meeting this morning." The answer rolls off his tongue easily enough, but something is off.

"What do you do? We haven't talked about it much," I hedge, sitting up in bed a bit.

Armando takes a deep breath, running a hand through his close-cropped, dark hair. "I wear a few hats at my job. Security, collections, stuff like that."

"But, like, where do you work? Security for who?"

He's quiet for a concerning amount of time before answering. "It's... complicated."

I frown, studying his face for any hint of why he's being so dodgy. "Okaaaay, well, where is your meeting?"

"Other side of town."

I roll my eyes, growing tired of his non-answers. "We're in New York City. Can you be more specific?"

"Sorry, old habit. Our meetings are private, so we're trained not to disclose that kind of information. Besides, I'll be back soon, so no need to worry." He smiles, but it doesn't reach his eyes.

Trained? Private? Complicated? Who is this man?

"I thought maybe I could come with you? Not to the meeting, but I could look for some work applications. I'm not going back to my uncle, so I figured I should start earning my–"

"No," Armando says forcefully, cutting me off.

I stare at him, blinking a few times to reconcile this man with the one who whispered such sweet, soothing things to me last night.

"I'm sorry. I'm not mad at you, sweetheart. I know that all must sound like bullshit," Armando says with a sigh. "I promise I'll tell you everything."

"Can you at least pick up some applications?"

Armando smiles, a real one this time, making me almost forget his strange reaction to my questions. "There's no need for you to work, angel. I make plenty for us to have anything and everything we need."

And just like that, my suspicions are back. Growing frustrated with this man, I cross my arms over my chest and narrow my eyes. "How am I supposed to trust that you'll provide when you won't even tell me what you do for a living? Plus, what if I want to work? It's not always about the money but about having a purpose. Or are you saying my only job is to wait around for you to come home?"

I'm out of breath by the time I'm done with my rant. My brain finally catches up to what my stupid mouth has been saying, and panic twists with regret in my stomach. In my experience, telling men off usually ends badly. Looking up at Armando, I can't read his expression, so I dip my head and curl my shoulders, bracing myself for his wrath.

"I'm sorry," he says, surprising the hell out of me. "I'm not trying to control or isolate you, Allegra." He reaches out, brushing his fingertips across my temple and cheek, urging me to look up at him. His multi-colored eyes reach deep into my soul, begging me to believe him. "I'll explain everything when I get back, okay? All I want is your safety and happiness."

I nod, letting Armando press his lips to my forehead. He tells me he'll be back soon, and I smile, but inside, I'm numb. Armando says he'll leave his card on the counter next to his iPad and I can order anything I need. Then he promises to bring back lunch. I can barely hear him over the alarm bells ringing in my ears.

My emotions are tied up in a massive knot in my belly, but I ignore them, choosing survival once more. I refuse to be taken advantage of again.

Once he's out of the bedroom, I spring into action, throwing on my old clothes and putting my hair up into a messy bun. Armando thinks I went back to sleep, but I sneak down the stairs and listen while he calls his driver and gives him the address he needs to be dropped off at.

Bingo.

Ten minutes later, I'm in the back of a cab hurtling toward the South Bronx on my first ever recon mission. I'm sure Armando didn't intend for me to order a taxi with his card and iPad, but I had to use the tools available.

I want to believe Armando. A less jaded version of me probably would. But I'll be damned if I'm going to trap myself in another helpless situation like I was with my uncle. If Armando won't tell me what his day job is, I'll have to find out for myself.

"You sure this is the right address, miss?" the cab driver shouts. He's nearly a hundred and fifty years old if I had to guess, and as far as I can tell, he can only hear out of one ear and see out of one eye.

"Yes," I reply, though my stomach churns as he comes to a stop in front of a seedy strip mall with most of the storefronts abandoned.

The old man shrugs, apparently not overly concerned about fighting me on the matter. Fair enough. I don't know what I'd tell him, anyway.

Stepping out of the car, I quietly close the door and take stock of my surroundings. It looks like the only two businesses still open in this decrepit structure are a pizza place and a car repair shop, neither of which seems like an ideal meeting spot.

What the hell is your job, Armando?

"Easy now, we don't want any trouble," someone says from inside the repair shop.

"No trouble? Then why did you bring the muscle?" another man replies, his voice higher pitched and weasely. It sounds familiar, but I can't place it.

"In case you decided to run your mouth again," Armando growls.

I stop dead in my tracks a few feet from the entrance to the shop. *Armando is the muscle? He said he was in security...*

A few other voices overlap, and I creep forward, peering through the glass door to see where the commotion is coming from. No one is in the front lobby, and I look around the door, trying to see if there is a bell or alarm that would trigger if I opened it. I don't see anything, so I take a chance and slip inside, closing the door behind me.

I take a calming breath, willing myself to stop shaking. I need to see who Armando is talking to and why they sound so familiar. The front desk is abandoned, but behind the reception area is a small hallway with a light at the end. The voices get louder the further down the hallway I venture, and I know I'm close.

"...any other customers lately?" the first man asks.

"What are you guys getting at?" the familiar voice whines. *Where have I heard it before?*

I slide along the wall until I reach the office at the end with the bright light on. Gathering up every scrap of courage, I peek through the crack in the door, and the air drains from my lungs when I finally see who's inside.

Aaron Charmicael.

My uncle's business partner.

I can't breathe, can't blink, can't feel my heart thumping in my chest as I absorb what this means. Has Armando known this whole time? Did he strike a deal with my uncle and Aaron? Oh, God, does he work for my uncle? Does he...

"Hey!" Aaron shouts, his brown eyes cutting across the room and landing on mine. "Who is that?"

I stumble backward, falling on my ass and banging my head against the narrow hallway wall. Jumping to my feet, I sway slightly at the sudden movement, then gasp when the office door is wrenched open.

Aaron is standing in front of me, a look of confusion plastered on his ugly mug. "Allegra?"

"Allegra!" Armando shouts at the same time.

"Who the fuck is Allegra?" the other man grumbles.

This can't be happening. It's worse than anything I could have imagined. Why am I so stupid? He said all the right things, and I fell right into his trap.

I back away with my hands up as I stumble out into the reception area. *Shit.* I don't have an escape plan. I didn't bring the iPad with me or the credit card. *What the hell was I thinking?*

"Your uncle has been looking for you everywhere," Aaron continues, following me into the main lobby. "He's pissed as hell, too. Shit, girl, I almost feel bad sending this text."

My eyes snap to his hands, where he hits his phone screen a few times and then shoves it into his pocket. "No, please–"

"You know her uncle?" Armando yells from down the hall.

Wouldn't he know that? Aren't they working together? What the fuck is going on, and how did I misread Armando so badly?

My thoughts spiral out of control as my heart hammers painfully in my chest. I try taking a breath, but it gets caught in my lungs, making me cough and nearly black out from lack of oxygen.

I need to leave. I need to get as far away from this fucking place, from these people, from this goddamn city as possible. I need to disappear and regroup.

Throwing my weight against the front door, I fall outside,

then scramble to my feet, somehow keeping my balance enough to run across the empty parking lot. I don't know where I'm going, only that I'll die if I stop.

"Allegra!" I hear Armando shout. "Allegra, wait! This isn't what you think. You're not safe here!"

No shit, Sherlock, I think bitterly. I'm not safe anywhere.

Despite my better judgment, I look over my shoulder at Armando, my heart splintering into a million pieces when his hazel eyes meet mine. Was anything he said real? Or did I swallow it up, hook, line, and sinker, like the idiot I am?

I'm jolted out of my pity party when I run smack dab into a solid structure. I nearly fall over, but someone grabs my arm, twisting it painfully as they pull me up.

"There you are, you ungrateful bitch." Fear strikes my heart at the sound of my uncle's voice, sending echoes of regret and panic through my body. "Get in the fuckin' car and don't make a sound. I haven't decided if I'm going to let you live or not."

I nod in defeat, letting him know I won't fight. I know I can't win.

He sneers at me, the sadistic sound coiling around my chest and squeezing until it feels like I'm breathing through a straw. Black circles dot the corners of my vision, and the last thing I see before I pass out is my uncle's mottled face, bulbous nose, and yellow-ish brown teeth as he widens his smirk.

CHAPTER NINE

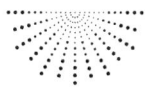

ARMANDO

A feral roar releases from somewhere deep in my chest. I grab the back of Aaron's collar, pulling him backward and slamming that motherfucker to the ground. He coughs and sputters for air, and I kick him in the ribs as I step over his body and sprint out the door.

"Allegra! Allegra, wait! This isn't what you think. You're not safe here!"

My beautiful, broken angel looks at me over her shoulder, searing me with a look I'll never forget. Pure betrayal bleeds from her gaze, a sorrow so deep, so heavy, I nearly collapse underneath its weight.

Still, I press on, needing to get her to safety. She can yell and curse and hit me all she wants as long as I know she's out of harm's way.

I pick up speed when I see a black SUV tear into the parking lot, and my vision grows red when a large man with a round, tomato-red face steps out. I open my mouth to scream at Allegra, but it's too late. The man grabs her and shoves her in the car before I can do anything.

I pump my legs, willing the adrenaline to push me to

superhuman speed as I chase after the vehicle. I'm aware of Valentino shouting my name in the distance, but nothing else matters. Allegra is in danger. I promised her my protection, promised she'd never have to go back to her uncle.

As the SUV turns a corner and gets lost in traffic, the realization finally sinks in. *I failed her.*

Black edges in on my vision as air saws in and out of my lungs. I reluctantly come to a stop before I pass out, doubling over to catch my breath.

"Armando," Valentino says from right next to me. I didn't realize he was so close. "What the fuck, man? Who was that? Why did you attack Aaron? Jesus Christ, are you okay?"

"I… Allegra… danger…" I huff, trying to put my thoughts into order. "No time."

"Breathe, buddy," Valentino says, patting my back. "That's the woman who has you all messed up in the head? She step out on you or something?"

Despite the exhaustion currently overtaking my body, I land a solid punch to his left arm. "Never speak ill of Allegra again," I growl.

Valentino holds up his hands and takes a step back. "I'm trying to figure out what the hell happened. Are we going after her?"

"We?" I ask, finally gaining enough strength to stand up straight. My hands shake as I pull out my phone, and honestly, I'm not sure who I'm going to call.

"Well, yeah," Valentino answers as if it's obvious. "You go, I go."

"I thought women were a *complication.*"

"I'm not saying I understand your relationship, just that I have your back. I don't know that I'll ever love someone the way you obviously love Allegra, but that doesn't mean I don't want you to be happy. And I'm not okay with her being in danger."

"Maybe there's hope for you yet, kid," I grunt.

Valentino smirks, then returns to the task at hand. "What do we know?" he asks, getting right back into business mode.

"Allegra's uncle owns a strip club. Wants to force her to work there doing…" I trail off, not even wanting to think about the atrocious things my precious girl could be subjected to.

"Got it," Valentino pipes in. "And Aaron?"

"Shit." I curse, turn on my heel, and sprint back to the auto shop.

"Give a guy some warning next time," Valentino mutters as he follows close behind.

We burst through the door, and to my relief, Aaron is still squirming on the ground in the hallway. I nod at Valentino, who gathers up the pathetic man and ties his hands and feet. I don't have to tell him we're going to interrogate Aaron. He already knows and has his gun pressed against the fuck's temple, ready for questioning.

"How do you know Allegra?" I rasp, staring into Aaron's wide, terrified eyes. He's sweating profusely and bleeding slightly from a cut on his lip. It's a start, but nowhere near satisfying my appetite for revenge.

"I… Well, uh, I'm…"

Valentino digs the muzzle of his gun into Aaron's temple, prompting him to swallow thickly.

"Want to try that again?" I seethe.

"H-her uncle and I run a strip club. Teasers. Sh-she works there."

"What do you know about her uncle?"

"Tommy Brenshaw," he's quick to answer. "Real piece of shit, but a good eye for talent, if you know what I mean."

I sink my fist into his face, feeling somewhat better when his nose snaps. Blood pours down his face, the river of red matching my clouded vision.

"Jesus!" Aaron wails, wriggling in his restraints. "Is this why you came here? To ask about Allegra?"

"It is now," I answer, landing another blow.

"Armando," Valentino says, getting my attention. "We'll make him pay later. Save your wrath for her uncle."

I growl, not liking him telling me what to do.

"We have the info we need. The most important thing is getting your girl, remember?"

Nodding once, I knock Aaron out with a backhand to the head. Valentino tucks his gun away and motions toward our vehicle parked out back. I follow him, looking up directions for Teasers on the way.

"I've got the address here," I tell him when we get to the car.

"I texted Romeo and let him know what's up. He's sending Dante to meet us at Teasers."

Wrenching the driver's side door open, I startle my chauffeur, who takes one look at me and scrambles out of the way. Good man.

My hands shake as I take the wheel, and Valentino surprises me by clapping a hand over my shoulder. I'd punch him, but this car is too small for me to get enough momentum to do any damage.

"Whatever fear is pressing down on your chest and scrambling your thoughts? Don't give it power. You control this situation. We *will* get Allegra back. Got it?"

I nod, letting his words sink in. The tremble in my hands subsides enough for me to start the engine and peel out of the parking lot, heading north toward Teasers. Valentino is good under pressure, I'll give him that much.

Ignoring traffic laws and speed limits, I weave between lanes of cars at a break-neck pace. To his credit, Valentino doesn't say a single thing about my driving. He knows I'd just as soon unlock his door and shove him out if he tested me right now.

As soon as I see the hot pink sign for Teasers, I turn the wheel, jumping the curb as I pull up next to the decrepit structure with no windows. I'm about to tear the door off its hinges to get to my girl, but once again, Valentino rests his hand on my shoulder. Bold move, seeing as I'm ready to break necks first and ask questions later.

"You're in control," he repeats. "Don't let the anger and fear cloud your judgment."

"When did you become some new age guru?" I snap. "Every second we sit here is more time she's in danger."

"I'm trying to help," Valentino answers calmly. "I've been guided by rage before, and it nearly destroyed me. I don't want the same for you or Allegra."

"Fuck," I sigh, wiping a hand down my face.

"I've got your back. Let's be smart about this. We have the element of surprise. Tommy doesn't know we're associated with Allegra." I bob my head, listening to his plan. "I'll go in and conduct business as usual. We were supposed to talk to our mutual contacts in shitty establishments, and this fits the bill. I'll ask for Tommy. If he's half as smart as Aaron says he is, I'm sure he'll recognize the Di Salvo family when they show up. I'll distract him while you look for Allegra."

"What if they aren't here?"

"Then we'll figure it out. But something tells me Tommy will want to put your girl to work sooner rather than later."

I growl, the rush of adrenaline spiking once more. Valentino catches my eye, and we nod, knowing what needs to be done.

We get out of the car, and Valentino conceals his weapon as he straightens his suit. He heads to the front door while I hang back, sticking to the shadows as I make my way to the side entrance.

The door is propped open with a cracked cement block that doubles as an ashtray. I peer inside, noting the layout. It appears to be a prep room for the dancers and other workers, with lockers on one wall and a row of vanity mirrors on the other.

Luckily, it's early in the day. Hopefully, they'll be operating with a smaller staff until the sun goes down. I've learned from experience that darkness gives people permission to sin.

Keeping a hand on my gun, I step inside the building, ducking so my large frame can fit through the doorway. I'm immediately hit with the smell of cheap perfume and even cheaper alcohol. My angel deserves so much better than this.

"Yo, Tommy!" someone shouts. I freeze, every muscle pulled tight as I wait for the reply. "Tommy, you got some goon here to see you. You owe money again?"

"Stop runnin' your goddamn mouth, boy," the man I assume is Tommy grinds out. "Told you, I'm busy."

"He was very insistent, boss. Said something about the protection offered on this joint is in jeopardy. I thought we already had a couple bouncers, so I'm not sure what he's referring to, but–"

"Jesus H. Christ," Tommy mutters. "Fine."

Smart move on Valentino's part. While this strip club isn't under Di Salvo protection, it's a good bet that one of the local gangs struck up a deal with the business on this block. If Tommy thinks his club is in danger, he might take Valentino a bit more seriously. I just hope the Capo knows what he's doing.

There's a shuffling sound, followed by a gasp, and then Tommy hisses out, "If you move a fuckin' muscle, I'll stop being so nice. Understand?" A brief pause, followed by what sounds like a hand slapping against the wall. I hear a muffled cry that sends fury blazing through my veins.

Allegra.

Instinct takes over, and I reach for my gun, holding it at the ready as I fling open doors trying to find where that fuck put my angel. Valentino's words come back to me, reminding me to stay in control of my rage long enough to ensure Allegra's safety.

The sound of a thick curtain being pulled back gets my attention as I wander through the maze of private rooms presumably used for illegal goods and services. Noise from the front of the strip club grows louder, and I hear Tommy ask someone where the goon is.

It's time.

"Allegra," I call out, running down the hall where I heard her cry. Another muffled whimper stabs at my heart, but it's enough for me to lock onto the room she's in.

I kick down the door, which splinters far too easily, not that I'm complaining. Allegra's eyes widen in fear as she stares down the barrel of my gun, and then she ducks her head and turns away, trying to hide from me.

My heart rips in two at the sight of my sweet girl cowering in fear. The pain is amplified when I realize she's afraid of *me*.

I tuck my gun away and kneel in front of her, unsure where to begin. "I'm so sorry," I whisper, hovering my hands over her body.

She's tied to a chair with a rag covering her mouth to prevent her from speaking. My beautiful girl is trembling, her blue eyes bloodshot and rimmed in red.

I carefully untie and remove the cloth from her mouth, then get to work on her hands. "I'm so sorry," I repeat, rubbing the red, raw marks on her wrists from the rope burns. "I'm not going to hurt you," I whisper, sitting back on my heels to take her in. "I didn't know Aaron was associated with your uncle. I swear, Allegra. I would never…"

I clench my jaw so hard I'm positive I've cracked a tooth, but I can't help it. The thought of knowingly harming my woman, of sending her back to this disgusting establishment, has me ready to tear these walls down with my bare hands. I still might.

"Please trust me," I beg, leaning close enough to take her hand in mine. "I owe you answers, and I'll tell you everything when we get home. Right now, I need you to trust that I would never put you in danger. I would never hand you over to your uncle. I need you to trust me enough to let me get you out of here, okay?"

She hasn't said anything yet, and exhaustion weighs heavily on her shoulders. Tired, mournful eyes stare through me, like she doesn't know who or what to believe anymore.

"I'm so sorry, angel," I repeat. "We don't have much time." Without another word, I scoop her up in my arms.

Allegra curls up against me, burying her head between my neck and shoulder while silent sobs shake her body.

"I've got you," I whisper as I carry her through the hallway, dressing room, and out the side door to my car.

Dante is parked next to me, and his eyes immediately fall on Allegra. I give him a nod, and I know we're on the same page. *This is the most important thing to me. I have to go kill the man who hurt her, and you're going to watch over her.*

I open the back door to Dante's vehicle and gently set my girl down. Taking off my suit coat, I drape it over her body and then smooth her hair behind her ears, revealing more of her face to me. She has a few scrapes and smudges of dirt, but Allegra is still the most gorgeous creature I've ever laid eyes on.

"I'll be right back," I promise. "I'm going to make sure he never hurts you again."

Blue eyes meet mine, and she blinks once, letting me know she understands.

With Allegra safely out of the way, there's no need for subtlety as I rampage toward the front door of Teasers, tearing the fucking door off its hinges and throwing it behind me. Valentino is sitting with Tommy at the bar, and he grabs the man's right arm before he can pull out his gun. Tommy shouts as Valentino forces him into a standing position and twists his arm behind his back, holding him in place as I storm over.

Circling my fingers around his throat, I squeeze Tommy's neck until his eyes bulge and his face turns from red to purple. "I've killed many men, but this will be my most satisfying yet. Hell, putting an end to your pathetic life and the suffering you've caused might just make up for some of the other shit I've done."

Tommy sputters, trying to defend himself. I don't give him a chance.

"Enough. You don't deserve any last words. As much as I want to torture you and draw out your agony, I want to be with my Allegra more, so I'll make this quick."

Valentino steps out of the way as I shove Tommy to the ground with my hand still around his throat. I pull out my gun and rest the muzzle against his forehead, relishing in this man's final moments before pulling the trigger.

"Armando. *Armando!*"

I shake my head, then look up, realizing Valentino has been trying to get my attention.

"It's over. Go get your girl."

I blink a few times, then look down at the gory remains of Tommy, where my hand is still trying to choke him out. Releasing his neck, I stand and take a few steps back, reorienting to my surroundings.

"Hey. I got this," Valentino says as he hands me a damp rag. "We'll take care of the body. You go with Dante, and I'll get your car back to you."

I nod numbly, the words flowing over my head. "Clean up your hands and lose the shirt before going outside. Don't want Allegra seeing any more blood, yeah?"

This jolts me out of my stupor. "Right," I agree, getting to work on washing the blood from my hands. I unbutton my shirt, tossing it aside, along with my tie. Thankfully, my undershirt didn't get much on it, so I decide to leave it on. I'm not sure what Allegra thinks of me, and I don't want to crowd her space while half-naked.

I try taking deep breaths as I make my way back to Dante, but my mind is buzzing with what Allegra is going to say. She has every right to hate me. I'm a violent monster who deceived her about my line of work. It would make sense for her to not want anything to do with me after this.

When I see my angel curled up in the back of Dante's car, every doubt evaporates. I don't care if she never wants to see me again after this, so long as I get to hold her and make sure she gets somewhere safe.

I open the back door and slide in, not sure what to say or how to tell her I need to touch her before I go insane. Allegra shocks the hell out of me by crawling into my lap. I wrap her up in my arms, holding her close while Dante drives us through the city, back to my place.

"You're safe now," I whisper, absorbing her tears as she clings to me.

Allegra doesn't say anything. She simply nods and tries to get herself even closer, like she wants to dissolve into me. I don't mind. After today, I don't know that I'll ever let her out of my sight again.

CHAPTER TEN

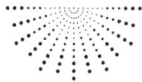

ALLEGRA

I can't let go of Armando. My arms are locked around his neck the entire ride back to his house, and I don't loosen my grip even when he shifts my weight to get out of the car. Armando carries me inside without missing a step, then collapses on the couch.

I immediately tuck my face into his shoulder, feeling raw and exposed. My head is spinning, my body aches, and my temples throb. I'm not sure what to think about anything or anyone. All I know is that Armando makes me feel safe. He rescued me. That has to count for something.

"Did he touch you?" Armando asks, his fingers skimming over my arms and neck, searching for wounds. "Are you hurt? I mean, Jesus, I know you're hurt. Fuck," he mutters. "What can I do? How can I make it better? God, Allegra, I failed you."

His voice cracks along with my heart. I peer up at him, seeing the worry, regret, and self-loathing in his hazel eyes.

"Precious girl, I'm so sorry. Tell me how to fix this."

"The truth," I rasp, my voice scratchy from crying. "I want

to believe you," I add. "You're the only good thing that has ever happened to me."

"I should have been honest with you from the beginning. I see that now," he starts, tucking a few strands of hair behind my ear. "I was afraid I'd scare you off with my profession, and I wanted more time for you to get to know me, to see who I am away from what I do."

I nod slowly, trying to understand. "Do you work for my uncle?" I whisper, not strong enough to ask the question out loud.

"Fuck no," he answers forcefully. "Never."

The tight band squeezing my chest loosens. Armando's eyes burn with conviction, and I know he's telling me the truth.

"I work for the Mafia," he continues. My breath catches in my throat, and I blink at him a few times. "I'm an enforcer for the Di Salvo family."

"Security and collections," I say softly, repeating what he told me this morning.

"That's right. I use my strength to protect the family, secure assets, and take out the garbage." I nod, taking in his words. "We may be criminals, but we have a code. The Boss, Romeo, is very clear on that. No women, no children, no human trafficking."

The longer I stare into the brutally honest eyes of the man I love, the more my heart softens. I can see him breaking apart, crumbling at the thought of losing me.

Armando strokes my cheek, his touch achingly tender. "Remember when you asked me why I took you in and gave you a place to stay?" I nod, furrowing my brow. "I was nothing more than a dirty street rat. I got sick of being shuffled around foster families and group homes, so I ran away with my only friend, Leif. We did what we had to do to survive."

"Oh my god," I murmur, stunned by his confession. I would never have guessed the man with a home theater who always dresses in a suit was homeless as a teen.

"Leif found a way out through the military. I knew I couldn't follow him. Never could picture myself as a soldier, but I guess I needed to find a different leader to follow."

The corner of Armando's lip twitches, and I somehow know it's a joke he must share with his childhood friend. I get the strangest urge to meet him and thank him for having my man's back.

"Romeo caught me stealing from one of the Di Salvo warehouses," Armando goes on. "I thought he was going to shoot me, but instead, he offered me a job and a place to live. I was suspicious as hell, but smart enough to realize I'd never have an opportunity like that again. I know it's a lot to process, Allegra. I understand if you don't want to see me anymore. I'll leave you alone if that's what you−"

"Don't leave me," I whimper, my heart squeezing painfully in my chest. The words come spilling out of my mouth before I can think them through, but I don't regret it.

Armando cups my face, wiping away my tears with the pads of his thumbs. "If you want me, I'm yours, Allegra. But you have to say it. Tell me you can forgive me for failing you."

Leaning forward, I rest my forehead on his. "I forgive you for not being honest, though I understand why you did what you did." The tension drain from Armando's muscles, like he's finally able to breathe for the first time all day. "You didn't fail me, though."

"I did," he counters. "I failed to protect you. I promised your uncle would never harm you again, but…" He shakes his head in disgust, but I stop the motion with a kiss to his forehead. This man is unraveling before me, destroyed at the thought of anything bad happening to me under his watch.

"I followed you," I admit. "I overheard the address you told your driver and ordered a cab with the iPad. It was my fault, Armando. I put myself in danger because I didn't trust you."

"No, sweet girl. None of this is your fault. I didn't give you a reason to trust me."

"You gave me a thousand little reasons. I let my fear take over and jumped to the worst conclusion."

Armando combs his fingers through my hair, letting his fingers trail down my spine. "You have been through a lot of trauma, Allegra. It makes sense that you wouldn't trust easily. I should have known you would see me for me. I should never have given you a reason to doubt me in the first place."

My incredibly gentle yet fierce protector closes the distance between us, kissing me softly, taking his time to taste me and explore my mouth. It's so sweet and tender I feel like I might cry.

"Armando," I breathe, feeling our connection once more.

There's no room for doubt when he's pouring his heart and soul into every touch, every whispered word, every kiss. I need him in the most primal way, need him to take control and show me how perfect we are together.

"Angel," he murmurs, his lips brushing against the shell of my ear. "Do you need something from me?"

"Please…" I whimper, pressing my body against his and trailing my hands up his chest. God, I never thought I'd see him again, let alone touch him. I need more.

"I've got you, sweet girl. I know what you need," he murmurs.

Armando gives me one last kiss and stands from the couch. Before I can protest, he lifts me in his arms and carries me toward the bathroom, kissing me the whole way there.

As soon as he sets me down, he turns on the water in the

shower, testing its warmth. When he's satisfied, he turns, his dark eyes nearly feral as they roam over my body. Slowly, he slides his hands up my torso beneath my shirt. He gently pulls it off, followed by my bra and jeans.

When I'm in just my panties, he growls and cups my pussy, rubbing me through the thin material. "I feel your heat, angel. Feel how much you need this."

I nod, gasping when Armando fists the fabric and rips it off my body. His mouth covers mine, swallowing my breath in a devastating kiss. We break apart only so he can strip down.

He helps me into the shower once we're both naked, his fingertips following the streams of water as they pour over my shoulders, my breasts, my torso, my hips, and finally my throbbing pussy. I moan as his knuckles barely graze my mound before continuing down my inner thighs.

Armando's other hand wraps around the back of my neck, pulling me in for a punishing kiss. I open up for him, needing to taste and touch and feel him everywhere. He tugs my hair, pulling my head back so he can deepen the kiss. Two fingers dip into my slit and circle my little bundle of nerves in slow, steady strokes.

I grip his biceps, digging in my nails as one finger pushes into my entrance, then two. Armando thrusts his large digits in and out of me, slowly at first, and then faster, faster, faster, grinding his heel down on my clit all while devouring my lips.

Breaking the kiss, I bury my face in between his neck and shoulder as I cry out. I'm *right* there, so close to my much-needed release. He keeps pumping his fingers, twisting and curling them up to rub against my G-spot. Again, again, one more time…

Suddenly, his hand is gone. I nearly fall over at the loss of him, but I regain my composure and glare at him. Armando just grins, which makes my pussy clench.

"Not yet. Patience, sweetheart," he rasps.

With that, he spins me around, my back to his front, and starts massaging me everywhere. His large, calloused hands squeeze my breasts, hips, and my soft, round belly I've always been a little self-conscious about. Armando has made it clear he loves every inch of me.

His hands trail lower, teasing my pussy lips. My clit throbs in time with my heartbeat, begging him to do something about the unbearable ache he's created.

"Armando…" I moan, wriggling my hips to get him to touch me where I need him most.

"Not yet," he murmurs again, licking the shell of my ear before trailing kisses down my neck and shoulder.

His hard cock digs into my ass, so I wiggle a bit more until I feel his length nestle between my cheeks. Armando groans and rotates his hips, grinding his thick shaft against my ass.

"God, please, Armando," I beg. My legs shake, and I lean forward to brace myself against the wall.

A low growl rises from deep in Armando's chest, and the sound vibrates through me, nearly making me come on the spot. He grips my left leg under my knee and lifts it so my foot is resting on a bench I didn't notice before in the corner of the shower.

"That's it. Fuck, I love it when you're spread out for me." He continues touching every inch of me, caressing my thighs and widening my stance.

Armando gives me a satisfied grunt, which makes me giggle. My laughter is cut off when his cock slides along my slit. He taps my clit, nearly sending me over the edge. I'm so damn sensitive and ready to come, I think I might die if he doesn't get inside me soon.

"I've got you, Allegra," he murmurs, lining himself up with my entrance.

I'm expecting him to thrust inside me and fuck me hard. I know he's as desperate for me as I am for him. But Armando slowly inches inside, prolonging the sweet pain deep in my core. He grips my hips, holding me in place as he stretches me open. I hold my breath as he slides home, hitting the very end of me.

"You feel so damn good," he murmurs, more to himself than me.

Armando pulls out just as slowly, making me whine. I open my mouth to tell him to fuck me already, but then he slams his thick dick all the way inside, making me come instantly.

He wraps his arms around me, holding me up as I spasm around his cock. He fucks me through it, hammering into me over and over as I continue to convulse and cry out his name. He grips the inner thigh of my leg that's propped up, spreading me wider and angling my hips so he's hitting that special spot with every thrust.

"Y-y-yesss…" I hiss as I pound my fist against the wall and throw my head back against his shoulder.

Armando wraps his hand around my throat, keeping my head tilted back as he splits me open with his dick. "So tight for me, love," he grits.

I whimper as another orgasm rushes to the surface. He must sense it, too. He keeps a firm grip on my neck, which is hot as fuck, and then trails his other hand down my body, circling and pinching my clit.

My orgasm slams into me, hard and fast, ripping a scream from my lips. Armando growls and ruts into me, rubbing furious circles over my swollen, pulsing clit. A painful, delicious pleasure takes over every part of my body as I come again for him, sobbing his name.

Armando pulls out and spins me around, crashing his lips down on mine as he lifts me and spears me with his cock. I wrap my legs around his hips and hang on for dear life as he pins me to the wall and fucks me like a man possessed.

"Mine, mine, fucking *mine*. Say it, Allegra. Tell me."

"Y-yours," I whisper, my voice scratchy from screaming his name.

"Louder," he growls.

"I'm yours!" I cry out, writhing in his arms.

Armando roars and bites my shoulder as he comes, marking me, claiming me, fucking me raw. I gasp and open my mouth in a silent scream, my entire body pulsing, tensing, stretching… and then collapsing in on itself as my orgasm ravishes me from the inside out.

I swear I feel Armando come again, shooting his cum deep inside me in forceful bursts.

I drag air into my lungs in short breaths, trembling in Armando's arms as he keeps me pinned to the wall. I comb my fingers through his hair while he nuzzles into my shoulder, kissing over the spot where he bit me.

Eventually, he sets me on my feet, grabbing the body wash and massaging it all over my skin. I lean against him, letting him hold me up as the water sluices down my back, carrying the soapy suds with it.

"I love you," he murmurs, circling his arms around my back. "I love you so much it hurts. I love every single thing about you, and I've wanted to tell you the moment you leaped into my arms that first day."

My heart bursts with so many emotions as I cling to this incredible man. "I love you too," I squeak.

Armando stills, then peels me off of his chest. "Say it again," he commands, his magical eyes never leaving mine.

"I love you, Armando. You make me feel confident and sexy, and most of all, safe."

"Even after today?" he asks softly.

"Always. I know you'll come for me if I'm ever in danger. I know you'll fight for me when I need it. I know you'll protect me no matter the cost."

Armando nods, cupping my neck and pressing his lips to my forehead. "Love you with my whole goddamn heart, angel."

With one last kiss, Armando shuts off the water and wraps me in a fluffy towel, drying every inch of me before scooping me into his arms. I relax in his embrace, half asleep by the time he tucks me into bed and crawls in behind me, curling his body around mine.

We have more to talk about, but right now, all is right in my world.

CHAPTER ELEVEN

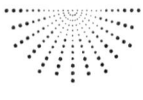

ARMANDO

*I*t was almost impossible to leave Allegra this morning, but Romeo called a meeting. After everything that went down yesterday, including an unsanctioned execution and clean up, I knew I couldn't decline.

My girl said she understood, and even wanted me to pass along her apologies, which of course, I won't. It's entirely too sweet. Then again, that's my angel. Tender-hearted, despite everything she's been through. And she said she loves me. How fucking crazy is that? I still can't believe it.

"Yo, I'm glad you got your girl home safe, but you gotta wipe that dopey look off your face, man. It's freaking me out," Valentino whines.

"He's always been dopey," Dante quips. His smirk isn't nearly as potent as before. Probably because there's less of a bite. After entrusting my Allegra to his care, there's an unspoken bond between us.

"And how is Allegra? Should I send the doctor over?" Romeo asks.

"Thank you, but that won't be necessary. She's recovering fine. Still shaken up, but then again, so am I."

Valentino scoffs, but Romeo nods. "I'm glad she's resting," he says, crossing his arms over his chest the way he does at the end of most meetings. "I know you're even more anxious than usual to get out of here, so I won't keep you much longer. We do, however, have some news about the Colombos."

At this, every man sits up straight, including myself. Valentino and I didn't have much success in gathering intel yesterday, but apparently, Romeo and Dante had better luck.

Romeo cuts a glance to Dante, who stands and takes the lead.

"A large sum of money was recently transferred from one of the Colombo's offshore accounts to a known black-market weapons dealer. A few days later, a shipment of explosives, guns, and ammo was intercepted and redirected to New York City. We don't know where exactly it ended up, but it's no coincidence."

"They're stockpiling," I grunt.

"Enough for a war," Romeo finishes for me. "We have our own reserves, but let's hope it doesn't come to that."

The room is silent, the air still as the realization of war sets in.

"Our number one priority is finding the stockpile of weapons. Without that to fall back on, we might be able to get the upper hand and mitigate lives lost," Dante rattles off. I'm sure he has plans on plans and three backup plans for each additional plan, but I'm not in the headspace to go over the minutia.

"Armando and I will hit the streets again, hopefully with more luck this time," Valentino says.

I nod in agreement, though I'm hoping to see Allegra before going on another assignment. As if reading my thoughts, Romeo stands from his chair and interjects.

"Tomorrow. For today, rest. We have many battles ahead of us, men."

"Yes, Boss."

"Aye, Boss."

"We're with you, Boss," all three of us say in unison.

He dismisses us, and I bolt out of his office, not bothering to say a single word to anyone else. Tensions have been high between the two families for a long time, but now it seems war is imminent. It makes every moment with Allegra that much more precious.

Hopping in my car, I rev the engine and get the fuck out of there, hitting the road at nearly twenty over the speed limit. With the timing of everything, I'm more positive than ever I made the right decision this morning to stop by the jewelry store.

I don't know jack shit about rings, but luckily for me, Leif recently married the love of his life. They were both all too happy to help me pick out the perfect ring for my angel. Now I just need to figure out a way to ask her.

As soon as I step inside my house, my eyes are drawn to Allegra. She's lounging on the couch, scrolling through the iPad.

A smile takes over her delicate features when she sees me. "You're home," she says excitedly, patting the seat next to her.

"So are you," I reply, sitting down and drawing her into my arms.

"Really? I mean, I was hoping, but just in case, I was looking at apartments…"

"I want you here with me," I tell her, capturing her blue eyes and letting her see how much I mean it. "I don't think I'll ever be able to sleep without you by my side."

"Are you sure? Everything happened so fast between us, and if you need space–"

Unable to listen to any more of her doubts, I untangle myself from Allegra and slide off the couch, kneeling on one knee in front of her. She blinks down at me, a look of shock and disbelief written across her face. I hope it's good shock, but I can't be sure.

"I never want space from you," I rush to say. "Knew you were it for me as soon as I held you. It was my mission to protect you, and even though I let you down once, I'd like to apply for the job full-time. Forever."

I take out the little velvet box, opening it to reveal a white-gold ring with a princess-cut diamond in the center, surrounded by light blue sapphires that match her eyes.

"Armando… oh my god," she breathes, her eyes filling with tears.

Shit. "It's too much," I mutter to myself. "I'll take it back. We'll get something else. Whatever you want. One for each finger. We can–"

"Armando," she says again, snapping me out of my spiral. A smile curls up one side of her lips, and the sparkle has returned to her beautiful eyes. "It's beautiful. I can't believe you want to keep me."

I take her left hand and slide the ring on her finger, not giving her a chance to turn me down. "I thought I made that clear," I tell her, standing and caging her in with my body. "You're perfect, Allegra. My sweet girl. Yes, things happened very fast between us, but what we have is real. You feel it too, right?" She nods, easing the tension in my shoulders. "So what do you say?"

"You didn't really ask, you know," she sasses, nibbling on her bottom lip.

"Allegra. My strong, brave, brilliant, precious girl. Will you do me the honor of being my wife?"

A devious spark flashes in her eyes. Christ, I'm going to love bringing more of that out.

"Yes, sir," she purrs, looping her arms around my neck and pulling me down for a kiss. I get lost in everything she has to offer, and my hands wander over her body, massaging her flesh as we devour each other.

Soon, I need more. More access to her creamy skin and tight little pussy. More kisses, more moans, more everything. Unable to wait another second, I lift Allegra in my arms, making her gasp.

"Need to show my fiancée exactly how good I'm going to make her feel every single day," I grunt before blazing a trail of kisses up her neck.

"Yes, please," she pants, tightening her thighs around me as I carry her upstairs and into our bedroom.

As soon as the door clicks shut, I press her back against the wall with the weight of my body and slam my mouth over hers, thrusting my tongue in between her lips so I can have another taste. She moans softly for me, then loudly as I tangle my fingers in her long hair and angle her head to deepen the kiss. A sharp thread of desire slices through me when her teeth sink into my bottom lip.

"God, Allegra," I groan, kissing down her neck and nipping at her pulse point.

Her deft little fingers are already working at my shirt, and soon it's discarded on the floor behind me. Then she attacks my belt, followed by the button and zipper of my pants. She shoves her hand into my boxer briefs and pulls out my throbbing cock, giving it a rough stroke that nearly brings me to my knees.

I cage her in with a hand on the wall beside her head as she pumps my massive erection with both hands. I squeeze my eyes shut and concentrate on how the soft skin of her hands glides up and down my shaft, teasing me with each stroke. I thrust my hips and shove my dick deeper into her tight grip. Again and again, we work together to jerk me off.

I should probably be upset that I'm going to come so soon, but I know I'll be hard for her all fucking night, no matter what.

My balls draw up tight as she swirls the pad of her thumb over the tip of my cock while her other hand squeezes the base. The fucker jumps in her hands and swells up, almost ready to go off…

And then she's not touching me.

My eyes snap open and I look down to see Allegra on her knees for me, tugging my pants and boxer briefs all the way down so they pool at my ankles.

"Jesus," I grunt, unable to stop the first spurts of cum from leaking out of me.

Allegra licks the drops off of the tip of my dick, massaging the little slit there and making my knees shake. I watch in awe as her pink tongue darts out and tickles the underside of my cock from tip to base. I ball my hands into fists on the wall and hold on to my release as long as I can.

She licks me up and down and then presses a kiss to my balls, making me growl. Allegra pulls back and stares up at me, her blue irises practically swallowed whole by her dilated pupils.

"You like that? Like my big fucking cock?"

She nods enthusiastically and bites her bottom lip. "Yes, sir."

"Show me," I grunt, barely hanging on.

Her nostrils flare and her eyes go wide with the challenge. Goddamn, what that does to me. Allegra unhinges her jaw and takes me into her hot, wet little mouth, sucking me down with the same frenzied need building deep inside me.

She sets a relentless pace, bobbing her head up and down my thick dick, taking more of me with each downward stroke. I pound my balled-up fist on the wall when she swirls her tongue over a particularly sensitive vein. The little siren does it again and again, making me tremble.

Her nails rake down the back of my thighs and I almost collapse from the sudden urgent need for release. Not like this, though. It was supposed to be about her.

With an incredible amount of self-restraint I didn't know I had, I peel Allegra off my painfully hard cock and pull her up, tilting her head back with the hand in her hair. My lips claim hers in a wild kiss.

I growl and nip at her lips, her chin, her neck, and then rest my forehead on hers, panting for air. Allegra looks disheveled, her hair sticking out, her cheeks stained red, her lips swollen. She closes her eyes and leans against the wall while I gaze at her.

One word echoes in my head, beats in my heart, and swims in my veins.

More. More. More.

I strip off what little clothes I have left and practically tear Allegra's clothes off her.

"Hey!" she shrieks and giggles.

"Need you," I grunt, biting and kissing her again.

She gasps when I lift her into my arms, automatically wrapping her legs around my waist as I carry her to the bed.

"I ache for you," she whispers against my lips.

It's more than I can take.

I stand in front of the bed with her in my arms and lick my way up and down her slender throat. Fuck, I swear I can feel her skin buzzing underneath my tongue.

Allegra lowers her head and kisses me with fire and fury. Her pussy grinds against my abs, which instinctively flex as she rubs her juices into my skin. Jesus, I don't think I'm going to make it the two steps to the bed.

I lift Allegra and reposition my hips slightly before sinking into her tight, perfect little pussy.

"Oh, god," she moans. "More, sir. Please…"

I cut her off with a kiss, needing to taste her while I fuck her mid-air. My hands wrap around her thighs as I lift and drop her sexy fucking body on my cock again and again.

"Just gotta take the edge off, Allegra. Just a little longer," I grunt.

She whimpers and buries her face into the side of my neck, rocking her hips in rhythm with my thrusts. I feel her tighten around me, her cunt soaking me and pulling me deeper inside her. Right before she reaches her climax, I toss her on the bed and climb on top of her, entering that tight little hole in one hard thrust.

"Armando!" she screams, her back bowing off of the bed.

I hold myself up on one forearm beside her head, while my other hand slides down the dips and curves of her body. I squeeze her breast and massaging her luscious hips before finally gripping her ass and angling her hips so my rough strokes hit her most sensitive spot every time.

I lick the sweat from between her full, tempting breasts, and then suck on her nipples until Allegra comes so perfectly for me, trembling and moaning my name over and over. She's still writhing beneath me as I roll us over, flipping our positions, my dick still deep inside her pussy.

"Fuck," I whisper to myself. Seeing her like this has me on edge.

She pushes herself up on shaky arms and tosses her head back as she groans and adjusts to our new position. Her hips move slightly to the side, which makes her pussy flutter and suck me in. Allegra gasps and does it again, unaware of the exquisite torture she's putting me through.

Then she opens her eyes, searing me with her crystal blue gaze.

"Ride my hard as fuck cock, Allegra. And tell me how much you love it," I growl before smacking her ass.

Her eyes grow dark as she lifts herself on her knees slowly, so fucking slowly, dragging her quivering pussy up my shaft one agonizing inch at a time. When just the tip is inside her, she flashes me a devious smirk and drops down on me, swiveling her hips and grinding that sweet cunt into the base of my cock. I roar as her nails tear into my skin, bucking my hips to meet her thrust for thrust.

"You feel so good, sir," she moans. "You're so deep like this. I love it. I love your cock."

"Goddamn, Allegra," I grunt, flexing my hips as she continues to ride me.

She lets out a throaty moan that has me ready to burst. Then she sits up and grabs her tits, squeezing them hard. Jesus, I feel her pussy walls contract each time she pinches her berry-pink nipples.

My goddess rolls her body and kneads her breasts, giving me the sexiest show of my goddamn life. I hold her hips in place and fuck up into her so hard she falls forward onto my chest, catching herself with a hand on either side of my head. Those delicious tits dangle in front of me, so I take the opportunity to suck on them while gripping her ass, continuing my hard thrusts into her tight, hot cunt.

Allegra lets out sexy little whimpers each time I hit the end of her. Her muscles tighten, her skin dripping with sweat, and her entire body shakes with the effort of holding back her orgasm.

"Don't come yet, angel. Don't you dare come yet," I whisper into her neck before kissing her there.

"Please, sir," she moans. "I n-need it."

I spank her, making us both cry out with the sensation. Another swift smack to the ass has her pussy pulsing around me, almost setting me off.

"Not yet," I warn.

"Oh god, oh my god, please, sir, please, fuck, please..."

I thrust into her, holding her in place and spearing her with my cock. I can feel my orgasm crawling down my spine with each stroke. Allegra gasps for air, her eyes shining with tears as she pushes her climax back, fighting off every instinct in her curvy little body. It's so fucking beautiful, the way she controls herself for me.

I lift her all the way off me and then slam her down one last time. "Come for me, Allegra. Come for me right the fuck now," I grit.

She screams her release as her arms give out. I hold her tightly against me, my ridged cock buried to the hilt as the wild throb of her orgasm travels the length of my shaft. The sensation is incredible, like nothing I've ever felt.

I empty myself inside her as Allegra keeps coming around me, our joined climax wringing out every ounce of pleasure from our bodies. She holds her breath as deep spasms tremor through her muscles, milking me dry.

I kiss her softly as each shudder passes through her, pressing my lips to her chin, cheek, nose, and forehead.

Allegra snuggles deeper into me and tucks her head under my chin. I chuckle softly as she curls up on my chest like a cat. She even purrs like one, too.

I gather her left hand in mine, lifting it to my lips and kissing her ring. It looks perfect on her little finger.

"I love it," she whispers, peering up at me. "I love *you*."

"Love you so fucking much, angel."

She smiles at me, then yawns adorably.

"Get some sleep, love," I say softly. "I'll be right here, always."

"Always," she repeats as she drifts off.

Her confidence in me, even after the last twenty-four hours, is humbling. I'll spend the rest of my life making sure she never regrets trusting me that first day she ran into my arms.

EPILOGUE

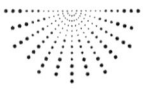

ALLEGRA

"Go set these on the table and then come back for your next assignment," I tell Aaron, our five year old. He beams up at me as he takes the napkins, his eyes the same magical hazel color as his father's. I watch Aaron's chubby little legs carry him into the dining room, where everything is ready for Armando's birthday dinner when he comes home.

Something tugs on the hem of my apron, and I look down to see little Alison, our mischievous three year old, with a marker in one hand and a fistful of my apron fabric in her other hand.

"And what are you doing, little miss?" I ask as I scoop her up into my arms. Little red ringlets bounce in front of her eyes, and I blow them out of her face, making my daughter giggle.

She shows me the marker in her hand, which thankfully still has the cap on, and grins like she just won a prize.

"Yes, I see. Have you been convincing your brother to get things for you that you know you aren't supposed to have?

Alison's eyes grow wide, and even at such a young age,

she's learned to pretend to be innocent. It's a good thing she's a terrible liar. It'll keep her out of trouble for a little bit longer, anyway.

"What now?" Aaron asks as he bounces into the kitchen and stands next to me.

"How about giving me a hug?" Armando says as he strides into the room.

"Dad!" Aaron squeals, racing into his father's arms. "Happy birthday!"

Armando tosses our rowdy boy in the air and catches him, spinning him around the room before setting him back down and turning his attention to me.

"Hey, beautiful," he murmurs, pressing his lips to my temple. "Missed you."

I smile up at my husband, knowing he means every word. Even though Armando has scaled back on the number of assignments he takes, the days he has to go into work are always long. He always makes up for it, though. By the way his hand is lingering on my lower back, I know he's thinking the same thing.

"Missed you, too," I tell him, leaning in for a kiss. My husband slides his hand against the side of my neck, holding me close as his lips claim mine. We've been married for over six years now, but each kiss is just as life-giving as the first one.

"Dad!" Alison shouts right in our faces. I almost forgot she was propped up on my hip.

Armando chuckles, breaking our kiss. "Ali," he says in the same tone, booping her nose. She bursts into a round of giggles, which only intensify when Armando takes her from me and starts tickling her round little belly.

"Alright, kids," I say, looking between Aaron and Alison. "Go wash up for dinner." They do as I say, and Armando turns to head that way as well. I grab him by his sleeve and pull him into me. "Not you," I tell him with a smirk. "I'm not done with you yet."

Armando grins wickedly, circling his arms around me and fusing his lips to mine. I open up for my man, savoring his kiss, the way his tongue glides against mine in steady strokes. I'm vaguely aware of being lifted and set down on the counter, my thighs spreading so my husband can stand between them.

"And how can I be of service, my sexy wife?" he purrs into the side of my neck. "Need me to kiss you some more?" I nod, sighing when Armando licks his way up and down my slender column. "Need me to taste you, angel? Need me inside you?"

"Yes," I hiss, looping my arms around his neck and pulling him down for more.

"God, Allegra," he groans.

Right as he's about to devour me, the kids come back.

"Ew," Aaron states as he walks past us. Armando laughs, tucking my hair behind my ear and placing a kiss on my forehead before helping me off the counter.

"Aaron, why don't you tell your dad what we made for dinner?" I ask, still flushed from that kiss.

"You made dinner?" Armando asks our son. Aaron holds out his hand and leads his dad around the table, showing off the dishes we made for his special birthday meal.

"Mom helped a little," he says, throwing me a bone. I roll my eyes as Armando stifles a laugh. I don't mind.

Aaron has been really into cooking lately, and I love encouraging that in him. It's worth the stacks of dishes in the sink and the disaster zone that is the rest of the kitchen to see how much pride he has showing off the lasagna and homemade bread sticks.

I get Alison settled in her booster seat at the table, then take my place next to my husband while he serves everyone.

"This is incredible," he says after everyone has started.

"I got the recipe from Thalia," I tell him with a grin.

"The very same recipe that convinced you to stay with me all those years ago," he says softly.

"Yes, if it weren't for the lasagna, I would have been out of there," I tease.

"I'm thankful you stayed, angel," my sweet husband whispers, resting his hand on my thigh underneath the table.

"Me, too. Happy birthday, love."

"Love you with my whole heart, Allegra. Thank you for bringing so much joy to my life, not just today, but every day. You make life worth living."

I swallow through the tears clogging my throat and manage to give Armando a smile. "There you go again, always saying the perfect thing."

"I'm trying, angel. Anything I can do to keep you by my side."

"Anything?" I ask, raising an eyebrow in challenge. "I might have a few ideas for later…"

Armando's eyes turn dark, and a rush of liquid heat trickles down my spine.

"…And then uncle Romeo let us practice throwing darts and a picture of an old, wrinkly man in a suit!" Aaron says excitedly, pulling us out of the moment.

"He let you throw darts?" I ask in shock, looking over at my son. Aaron nods enthusiastically and mimics throwing a dart.

Armando chuckles, and I glare at him. He raises his hands in surrender, though he still has a grin plastered on his face. "I'll talk to him about letting the kids play with pointy objects," he promises, though he gives Aaron a wink.

Truthfully, I know Romeo, Dante, and Valentino love their families as well, and would never harm our kids. Still, someone has to keep these guys in check every once in a while.

Armando laces his fingers through mine once more, resting our joined hands in his lap. We listen to our kids tell us about their day, and I soak up everything about this moment. I have a family filled with love, two kids who laugh and smile all the time, and the sweetest husband in the world, despite his less-than normal career.

I had no idea life could be this good. When I look over at Armando, his hazel eyes meet mine, a spark of love and understanding buried deep inside. I know my husband is thinking the exact same thing.

I can't wait to see what our future holds.

* * *

THE END

VALENTINO

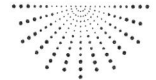

Blurb:

I stopped by the abandoned warehouse to check out some suspicious activity that had been reported recently. I thought we had a homeless person or a very stupid thief, but nothing could have prepared me for her. Katya, AKA, the mafia princess of our sworn enemies.

I should kidnap her and hold her for ransom, or possibly send her back to her scheming family with a message for them to back off. Instead, I scoop up the terrified yet determined young woman and tuck her into my bed. I even make hot chocolate for her for some stupid reason.

Katya is the last person I should be getting close to, but every moment in her presence undoes me little by little. I can't get enough of her sassy remarks and sweet kisses.

When my loyalty comes into question, will I be able to prove myself to the Di Salvos and still keep my princess safe?

CHAPTER ONE

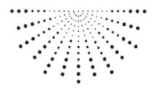

VALENTINO

"*W*hat now?" I grunt over the phone as I unlock my car. Slipping into the driver's seat, I sigh when our newest recruit tells me there's been another break-in by the docks. "And still no idea who it is?"

"No, Captain."

"You don't have to call me captain every time we talk," I tell Michael for the tenth time.

"Yes, Captain."

I roll my eyes but let it go. I remember what it was like starting from nothing in the Di Salvo crime family. In just over ten years, I went from lackey to foot soldier to Capo, charged with maintaining my own territory and commanding my own tier of soldiers. Not only that, but the Boss, Romeo, has trusted me enough to let me into the inner circle.

"Which facility did they hit up this time?" I ask, already frustrated that I'll have to make one last stop before going home for the night. Michael rattles off the address, and I hang up before pulling into New York City traffic.

The drive to the docks isn't horrible, it's just annoying.

For the last three days, my men have been reporting strange things going on around some of our properties. At first, it was petty complaints like missing snacks and lunches throughout the day. Then someone found a makeshift sleeping area in a rarely used storage closet, indicating we had a squatter.

Usually, I'd let someone else handle the riff-raff. This wouldn't be the first time a homeless person thought they found the perfect shelter. After scaring the shit out of them at gunpoint, the protocol is to set them up at one of our cheaper hotels for the night and send them off with an all-you-can-eat continental breakfast in the morning.

Of course, we also let them know if we see them on our property again, we'll shoot first and ask questions later. So far, no one has come back.

Everyone in the family is on high alert right now, however, this situation needs a more delicate touch. While I'm nearly one hundred percent certain it's another squatter, there's a small chance the Colombos, our rivals, are trying some shit again.

We know war is on the horizon, which means every detail matters. Including riff-raff.

I turn my headlights off before pulling into the alley leading to the warehouse in question. Parking in the shadows next to the building, I make sure I have my gun at my side and my knife secured to my ankle before stepping out and heading inside.

I debate whether or not to turn on the lights and scare the shit out of whoever is trying to sneak around, but ultimately decide to go the stealthy route. Grabbing a flashlight from the bench inside the door, I proceed to walk around the perimeter of the open room, shining the light into all the little hiding spots where someone could be lurking.

A macabre sense of power settles over me. I know it's

fucked up, but I enjoy these kinds of missions. For so long, I was the one who hid from monsters. Now, here I am, the monster other people run in fear from.

I suppose a sinister outlook on life is required for a made man such as myself. I don't mind. I've worked my ass off to get to where I am today, and if my dark, twisted heart helped pave the way, so be it.

A muffled sound catches my attention, and I freeze, waiting to hear it again. Silence stretches on for long moments, and I almost think I imagined it, but then I hear it again. Clearer this time.

A sneeze.

"Gotcha," I say under my breath as I stride toward the corner where the noise came from.

There's nowhere for the trespasser to go. Pallets filled with contraband to be sold are stacked fifteen feet high on one side, and on the other, a wide-open area leading to a locked and reinforced steel door. If they run, I'll sink a bullet into them long before they're able to escape.

Moving in closer, I see a few empty pallets leaning up against the wall at an angle, creating a makeshift barrier. I probably wouldn't have noticed it if not for the sneeze that drew me to this spot.

I creep along the side, keeping my flashlight pointed away until I get to the shadowed entrance. Then, all at once, I flash the bright, powerful light on the intruder and point my gun right between their eyes.

Round, golden irises blink up at me, catching me off-guard. It takes a second for my vision to adjust to the harsh light, but when I see the woman huddled on the ground with her legs tucked up and her arms around her knees, I feel like I might collapse. In fact, my knees shake, forcing me to squat down before toppling over.

What the fuck is happening to me?

I keep my gun trained on the woman, but I can't keep my eyes from wandering over her face, taking in her delicate features. Midnight black hair frames her large eyes and round cheeks, and her nose is slightly curved at the end, giving her a doll-like appearance.

Well, shit. I've never encountered a sweet little thing like her in a dark and dangerous place like this. It's usually delusional old drunks or meth addicts. I can tell by the clarity in her eyes she's not under the influence of drugs or alcohol, which only makes her presence here that much more puzzling.

"I-I'll come out," she says, her voice scratchy and barely above a whisper. "Please don't hurt me."

Jesus, why does my chest feel like it's caving in on itself at her words? I should be happy. This is going to be easier than I thought.

I grunt, lowering my weapon and nodding once. I'm about to stand from my position when the mysterious woman screeches and lunges at me, tackling me to the floor before scrambling off.

I jerk to the side and jump to my feet, cursing when I see my gun a few feet away from me on the ground.

"Don't even think about it," the woman says, causing me to whip my head in her direction.

She has a goddamn Glock pointed at me, and I'm not sure whether to be furious that she outsmarted me or impressed that this five-foot-nothing trespasser has me dead to rights within seconds of meeting me. Not many people can say they've gotten the drop on me. Actually, no one has, that I can remember.

I raise my hands, palms out, in surrender, as I take stock of my new situation. My gun is out of reach. My knife is on me, but I can't get to it without risking a bullet to the brain. Training my gaze on the threat, I notice the gun is shaking.

The woman is shaking, too. Trembling, in fact, from head to toe.

Her eyes tell a different story. I see a fierce look I recognize all too well; the animalistic need to survive. A golden flame flickers in her irises, a warning to anyone that her light won't easily be extinguished.

I have no idea who the hell this woman is, though the more I look at her, the more familiar she seems. Still, I know she's seen some shit. She's fought for her life from the moment she was born, and she managed to claw her way out, only to come face to face with a mafia captain and his gun. She's the exact kind of wild card with nothing to lose that I was at her age.

Maybe that's why I feel this inexplicable connection to her. She's young and terrified and angry at the world, and some part of me has the crazy urge to be the one person she can trust.

I take a step forward, my hands still up in surrender, and the woman shoves her weapon further toward me, though it slips from her sweaty grip slightly.

"You're going to hurt yourself more than me with that thing," I tell her, playing everything off like it's no big deal. She's desperate to project confidence and control, so letting her know I'm not phased is key.

"Bold, for someone with a gun pointed at their head," she quips. I'll give her credit, her voice is steady and full of venom.

"I hate to break it to you, princess, but this isn't the first time I've had a weapon drawn on me."

Her face turns pale, those round eyes growing impossibly bigger at something I said. "How did you…?"

I take advantage of her apparent confusion and move a few steps closer. "How did I what?" I ask smoothly.

"H-how did you know who I am?"

I raise an eyebrow and give her an enigmatic smile, not wanting to give away that I have no idea what she's talking about. I wish I knew who she was. The woman looks familiar and exotic at the same time. It's something to do with her eyes...

Princess.

The word pops into my head. I called her princess. I have no idea why I did that. It just came out of my mouth. Is that what she means? Her name is Princess?

Oh, fuck.

It hits me like a lead pipe to the sternum. Princess isn't her name, it's her *position.*

Katya Colombo, daughter of Marco Colombo, the head of the rival family we're on the brink of war with. She's a mafia princess. A sheltered one at that, presumably to keep prying eyes off her. There's no way this coddled woman knows how to load and shoot a gun.

In one swift and calculated move, I snag the weapon from her trembling hand, sliding it across the concrete floor a good hundred feet away or so. Grabbing my own piece from where she knocked it out of my hand, I point it at her, turning the tables once more.

"What the fuck are you doing here, Katya?" I spit out. I can't believe I felt sorry for her, though I shouldn't be surprised. Every woman I've ever known is only out for their own interests. They'll lie, cheat, steal, and manipulate anyone and everyone to further their agenda. Of course, Katya is no different.

"Not what you think," she answers, standing her ground.

She knows I won't kill her. Not yet, at least. Katya could be an important player in our war.

"Doesn't matter much what I think," I scoff. "But the Boss will be interested to know who our little trespasser is. Maybe we'll hold you for ransom or send you back with a message," I muse, though the words sound hollow to my ears.

Each one physically pains me, though I can't for the life of me understand why. She's the enemy. She's leverage. I shouldn't care about her safety, and I certainly shouldn't hesitate to call Romeo and tell him who I found.

And yet, I know deep down that I don't want anyone else to know. I don't want anyone else to touch her. Fuck me, these possessive feelings over another human are intense and unwelcome, and I'm not sure what to do about them.

"If you send me back to my family, I better be in a body bag," Katya says with a surprising amount of conviction. "I'm done with them. I want nothing to do with their plans, their wars, their agendas. I'm done being a pawn. So if you want to send a message, by all means, go for it. Sending my father my head on a platter would do the trick."

Katya further shocks me by spreading her arms out as if bracing for an execution shot. That's when I see blood soaking through her shirt, on her left side, right about where her ribs are.

The air drains from my lungs so quickly I grow light-headed. An unfamiliar sensation strikes at my core like a flash of lightning, electrocuting every nerve as I watch the red stain grow larger.

Fuck. Did I hurt her?

Panic courses through me as I lower my gun, followed quickly by guilt. Two things I haven't allowed myself to acknowledge since leaving home at eighteen.

"You're bleeding," I grit out, still confused as to why the thought of Katya in pain makes me angry.

"It's fine," she's quick to supply. "I patched it up a few days ago."

I grind my teeth together, my jaw tense as my nostrils flare. She's been wounded for days, and it clearly hasn't been properly tended to. She could get it infected if it isn't already.

Another thought rears its ugly head, just as confusing as the previous ones.

Who the fuck made her bleed in the first place? I'll do the same to them before ending their miserable life.

Jesus, I need to get it together.

"Not very well," I say, nodding to the blood on her shirt.

Katya looks down, wincing when she sees the stain. "Fuck," she says to herself, her hand instinctively coming up to cover the spot.

Her face contorts in pain, but she doesn't make a sound. I try not to let that bother me, but it doesn't sit right. How many times has she silently screamed, praying for someone to somehow hear her cries?

I shake my head of those thoughts, not liking the road they were taking me down. "You need stitches," I state.

"No," comes the automatic response.

"It's going to get infected."

"If I'm about to die, does it really matter?"

"We both know I'm not going to kill you."

Katya narrows her eyes at me, tearing me apart piece by piece. I'm not sure what she sees, but for the first time in my life, I worry about measuring up. Ridiculous, I know.

"Still. I'm not going to a hospital, and I sure as hell don't trust a Di Salvo doctor."

"Fair enough," I say with a nod. She's right, neither one of those options is a good one. For either of us. "I have an extensive first aid kit in my home. I'll take you there and stitch you up."

"Pass."

"Then I'll just take you to Romeo as is, I guess."

Katya glares at me, her jaw clenched and chin jutted out in defiance. I know that look, too. She's cornered. Trapped.

Forced to decide between two shitty outcomes. She doesn't know, however, that there's no way in hell I'm taking this injured, terrified woman straight to the lion's den. Fuck if I can explain why, I just know I need to get her to my place, where she'll be safe.

"Fine," Katya concedes, her shoulders drooping slightly.

"Good. Now, follow me out to my car, and don't try anything stupid." I try to sound like the gruff, no-nonsense Capo I am, but with Katya, everything comes out a little softer. I hate it.

"Can I at least know the name of my captor?" she mumbles, eyeing me warily.

"Valentino," I clip out.

Katya barely makes it three steps before doubling over, clutching her side as she hisses. I'm next to her in an instant, and before I even realize what's happening, she's in my arms, cradled against me. I ignore the feeling of something settling deep in my chest now that she's in my care.

"I'm fine," Katya whimpers, though I can feel her muscles jerking in pain with every step I take.

Why is it excruciating to see her suffer like this? I want to absorb her trauma, whatever it may be, and make it my own so she never has to feel this way again.

I'm fucking losing it.

We make it out to my car, where I carefully set her down, though I keep an arm around her waist. Opening the passenger door, I guide Katya to sit before taking off my suit jacket. She gives me a questioning look as I fold it up and hand it to her.

"Press it over the wound to help stop the bleeding," I tell her, nodding as she does what I say.

Katya makes a tiny sound of pain in the back of her throat, and my heart twists inside my chest, wanting to break free and comfort her. I grunt at my obsessive thoughts, then fasten Katya's seatbelt, careful to avoid her left side.

Climbing into the driver's seat, I start the car and slowly exit the gravel lot, trying to avoid the major potholes so as not to jostle Katya too much. Looking over at the confounding woman, my chest grows tight once more. Her eyes are squeezed shut, and her shoulders are hunched up to her ears as she holds my jacket against her side.

I have no clue what the fuck I got myself into, only that I need to patch this woman up and find out more of her story. Then I'll know what to do with her.

CHAPTER TWO

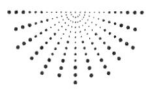

KATYA

*W*ell, this didn't go as planned.

Not that I had much of a plan when I was climbing through my third-story window at midnight three days ago. Still, I didn't think I'd find myself bleeding out in a car with a Di Salvo next to me, supposedly driving me to safety. I'll believe it when I see it.

The car hits a bump and I bite my lip to silence the scream fighting its way out. My left side burns as the stiff fabric rubs against my exposed wound, but I do my best to think of something else. Anything else.

Like how the last thing I ate was a stale, snack-sized bag of goldfish I found, and my stomach feels like it's dissolving into itself with hunger. Or the massive headache that's been residing behind my eyes for the last twenty-four hours. Could be from hunger, stress, illness, lack of sleep, or with any luck, a giant tumor that will render me unconscious soon. That has to be a better death than whatever the Di Salvos have in mind for me.

"Keep pressure on it," Valentino snaps, momentarily taking his eyes off the road to glare at me.

"Worried about me bleeding all over your leather seats?" I quip.

"No."

I raise my eyebrows in surprise, but the man doesn't elaborate any further. Surely he's not worried about *me*, so I'm confused why he cares.

The car in front of us honks, then slams on its breaks, causing Valentino to do the same. The seatbelt digs into my left side, right over the cut on my ribs. It feels like my skin is being flayed off one centimeter at a time, and I can't help the pathetic cry torn from my lips.

"Jesus Christ," Valentino curses.

At first, I think he's upset with me for making a scene. My father would be. But then Valentino's brown eyes rest on mine, and I'm left breathless at the concern I find in them. He looks angry, but this time, it's not directed at me. It seems to be directed at whatever or whoever hurt me.

His large hand covers mine, and together, we hold his jacket against my side.

"Who did this to you? One of my men?"

I blink up at him, still in shock. He looks like he's about to call every single mafia soldier he knows and line them up at gunpoint until someone confesses. That can't be right, though. This man has no reason to be protective of me.

"No."

He grunts in frustration, which I enjoy a little too much. Knowing nothing of Valentino aside from what little time we've spent together, I sense he's someone who always has an answer for everything. I also get the feeling he's used to getting answers from others as well, which must make me extra irritating to him.

"We're almost there," Valentino informs me, changing the subject.

A few moments later, we pull into a gorgeous home

tucked away on a decent-sized estate. The landscaping is flawless, and I find myself gaping at the trees and lush greenery as we wind our way up the long drive.

Valentino parks and jumps out of the car, hardly giving me time to take a breath before he opens my door. I swing my legs out and stand, only to be immediately scooped up in Valentino's arms. My body instinctively curls up against his, and despite knowing better, I cling to the massive man currently cradling me in his embrace. For just a moment, I soak up the strength and power emanating from him, letting myself feel safe and cared for.

When we get inside, the confusing man sets me down on his table. I make a move to jump down, but he gives me a stern look that has me feeling all sorts of unfamiliar emotions. Why does he have to be so... sexy?

Ugh, it's so dumb that I'm even aware of his looks, but it's hard not to notice when he's a foot taller than me, rippling with lean muscle, covered in ink, and giving me possessive glances with his deep brown eyes. It doesn't help that his nose and cheekbones are perfectly angled or that the slight stubble on his jaw makes him look impossibly gruff and refined at the same time.

"Here," he says, handing me a mug. I was too lost in my silly fantasy to notice Valentino grabbed a few things from the kitchen, including a first aid kit.

I take the mug, scrunching up my nose when I see the tiny amount of amber liquid inside.

"What is it?"

"Bourbon," he answers before taking a swig straight from the bottle. "You'll need it."

"I'm not old enough yet," I say for some stupid reason.

Valentino freezes, then slowly sets the bottle down. "How old are you, Katya?" he asks, his voice deeper than before.

"Twenty."

Something like relief spreads over his face, though he schools his features quickly. Weird.

"Close enough," he states, nodding to the mug in my hand.

"Not comforting words coming from the man who's about to give me stitches," I grumble. I swear I see the barest spark of amusement in his eyes, but it's gone before I can be sure.

I hold my breath and take the shot, frowning as the liquid burns its way down my throat and into my stomach.

"Good. Now lie back and lift your shirt." I balk at him, but he rolls his eyes. "Don't be weird about it. Just lift the hem enough to show me the wound."

I do as he says, resting my back against the cool tabletop and inching my shirt up. The cut is only a few inches below my bra line, and I hesitate slightly before taking the whole damn shirt off. Didn't think the first time someone saw me in my bra would be like this, but hey. For girls like me who come from families like mine, it's not the worst way for it to happen.

"Jesus," Valentino hisses, sitting down on a nearby chair and scooting it closer. He leans forward on the table, hovering his fingers above the three-inch cut. "What happened? Who did this to you?" he asks again.

"Does it matter?"

Valentino frowns at me but takes the hint. He gets to work disinfecting the wound, which isn't so bad. At least this pain is productive. When he presses on the wound and pushes my skin back together, however, I howl in pain.

"It's okay," he soothes.

"Easy for you to say," I grit out.

"It's not as bad as I thought. You'll just need some butterfly bandages and antibiotic cream."

"Told you I had it handled."

"You didn't let me finish," he scolds, returning his attention to my side. "It's not as bad as I thought, but left alone any longer, you'd risk infection. And a nasty scar."

"Wouldn't be the first one, doc."

He pauses, taking a second to let my response sink in. I don't know why I told him that. Thankfully, Valentino doesn't say anything.

"I'm not a doctor," he informs me as he takes out several small butterfly bandages and lines them up on the table. "But I learned how to take care of injuries at a young age. I had a lot of practice over the years on myself and my mom."

His confession is as heartbreaking as it is surprising. Valentino looks shocked and slightly embarrassed at what he just said.

Without thinking, I rest my hand over his, squeezing gently. "I'm so sorry," I whisper, meaning every word.

I understand more than he knows, and I hate he had to go through that. No one deserves to be treated that way, and I can't imagine being the kid in that situation, having to take care of your parent.

"I didn't mean to tell you that," he says, sounding flustered.

"It's not like my family is much better. I mean, you've met some of them, I assume."

This earns me a snort, which I'm considering a win. I wonder if Valentino ever smiles, or furthermore if he ever laughs. I have the sudden need to hear it. I bet it's contagious.

"Tell me what happened," he commands more than asks. "I told you something about me, it's only fair you do the same."

I glare at him right as he pinches my cut and secures it with the first butterfly bandage. I hiss and pound the table with my fist but manage not to whimper.

343

"It'll distract you from the pain," Valentino adds.

"Doubt it," I breathe, preparing for another pinch.

"Try," he tells me before repeating the process with a second bandage.

"My dad's business associate," I blurt out, hoping it covers up the cry of pain. "I met him for the first time four days ago." Valentino nods, encouraging me to continue as he works on my side. "My father called me into his office and told me to introduce myself to my new husband."

Valentino growls, his brown eyes fierce with something I can't quite make out. "Then what?" he rasps, focusing his attention on the next bandage.

"He said…" I bite my bottom lip, not wanting to relive the incident but knowing I have no choice. "He said he wanted to sample the goods," I murmur. "My dad was right there. Sitting in the corner," I say with more conviction. "He watched Raffe grab me and just… just sat there."

"Fucking bastard," Valentino snarls. "Did he… fuck, princess. I don't know how to ask this." Brown eyes meet mine, pleading with me to tell him the truth.

No one has ever cared this much about me, and it's perplexing and overwhelming to think it's coming from my family's sworn enemies.

"I didn't let him touch me," I whisper. "Not like that."

"Thank fuck," he says softly, true relief flooding his eyes. As if the rest of my statement is just catching up to him, Valentino's eyes turn from reassured to pure rage. "How did he touch you, then?"

I wave my hand over my side, showcasing the answer. "He wrapped his hand around my neck and tossed me into a side table. I broke a lamp and landed right on the biggest shard of ceramic."

"And your father just let it happen?" he asks as he places a large Band-Aid over the four butterfly bandages holding my cut together. Valentino helps me sit up, then takes a seat in his chair, his eyes locked on mine and waiting for an answer.

"He was concerned when I fell, but only because visible scars are unacceptable. If I cut my face, he probably would have sent me to a plastic surgeon."

"How can he just… Damnit," he grunts, taking a deep breath. "That's insane, Katya."

Indignation spikes my heart rate as it flows through my veins. "You seriously don't believe me?" I spit out. "I didn't even want to tell you in the first place, and now you're calling me crazy? How–"

"I believe you," Valentino says, cutting me off. He holds my gaze, those deep brown eyes lulling me into a sense of safety, almost against my will. "I believe you, Katya," he says again, his hand resting on my hip. I'm all too aware I'm only in my bra and pants, but there's nothing I can do about it now. The rough pad of his thumb caresses my bare skin in a calming gesture, and it feels far too good. I'm not sure he's even aware he's doing it. "I'm sorry you had to experience that."

For the tenth time today, I'm left speechless and bewildered by this man. He's apologizing for my pain?

Tears rush to the surface, and I try blinking them away before they drown me completely. I can't do this right now. I can't break down in front of Valentino. I can't feel these emotions, can't accept his kindness, can't do anything but force it all down and pretend nothing bothers me like I always do.

Only it's not working this time.

My teeth chatter as my eyes fill with tears, but still, Valentino never looks away. Slowly, so slowly, he lifts his hand toward my face, giving me plenty of time to back away. I don't want to, though. I'm desperate for more of his attention, more of his surprisingly tender touch.

Valentino cups my cheek, brushing away the first tear as it falls. "You're safe here," he murmurs.

I shake my head no, unable to believe him, even if I want to. "For how long?"

Something dark flashes across his eyes, followed quickly by a practiced look of indifference. I recognize it all too well. Valentino drops his hand from my cheek and stands, taking a step back as if being close to me is now dangerous.

"I'll check on the wound in the morning and change the Band-Aid," he says matter-of-factly.

He's back to being cold and business-like, which is probably for the best. We both shared some shit in the heat of the moment, but it's wiser to shut up and keep our distance.

"I won't be here in the morning," I point out, gingerly climbing down from the table. I ignore Valentino's hand as he reaches out to help.

"Of course, you will. You'll be staying here tonight. Your room is the second door on the left."

"Excuse me?" I question. I gather up my bloody shirt from the table, not wanting to put it back on but also not wanting to be this exposed. I ball the fabric up and hold it in front of my chest, attempting to cover as much skin as possible.

"Oh, did you have other plans tonight? Another warehouse with better accommodations, maybe?"

I narrow my eyes at the enigmatic man, who is vulnerable one minute and aloof the next.

"Fine," I concede. He's right. I have nowhere else to go.

"It's settled then. Bathroom is across the hall. Don't get your bandage wet, but you can clean up. I'll put some clothes outside."

I nod as my stomach lets out an embarrassing growl. Valentino stares at me, then drops his eyes to my belly, which I instinctively cover up.

"Dinner will be waiting for you in the microwave. Heat it

up when you're ready. I'll be retiring to my room for the night."

Without another word, he spins on his heel and stomps upstairs.

"I'll be retiring to my room for the night," I mimic under my breath in a mocking voice. Who says stuff like that?

I wait around the kitchen for a few moments, taking a look at the stainless-steel appliances and marble countertops. I want to give him plenty of time to brood before he *retires* for the night.

Despite the whiplash of emotions from Valentino, I feel... safe here. Just like he promised. Good things don't last, and I'm not expecting this to, either. I'll take advantage of the shower and warm bed for the night and be on my way tomorrow morning.

I'm sure I'll have figured out my next move by then.

CHAPTER THREE

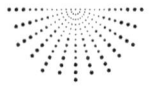

VALENTINO

"$\mathcal{D}$o you have an update on who's been sneaking around the docks?" Romeo asks over the phone.

Shit.

I pace from one side of my living room to the other, racking my brain for something to say. Why didn't I think about coming up with something before our call?

I know the answer before I'm even finished asking myself the question. I never thought I'd lie to the Boss. For the last fourteen years, my only goal has been to make him proud to have me in the family. When Romeo let me into his inner circle, I swore to myself I would never do anything to jeopardize my position in the family.

And then Katya burst into my life, quite literally, and everything I thought I valued was turned upside down. Without even realizing it, the little princess sleeping upstairs has become my new obsession.

So much so, I'm about to break the one rule I never thought I would.

"Valentino? I'm a busy man with three more calls to make this evening."

"Yes. Sorry, Boss. It was nothing to be alarmed about," I tell him, each word tasting like betrayal. "Someone was just hiding out from a bad situation." At least that's not a *total* lie.

Yeah, whatever helps you sleep at night, my brain unhelpfully adds.

"And you took care of it? Regular protocol?"

"Yes," I force out, gritting my teeth.

Romeo is silent for long moments, and I'm sure he's about to tell me I'm a fucking liar and strip me of my position, hell, even exile me completely. Except men like me, men at the top who know sensitive information, don't get exiled. We get executed.

My heart hammers away in my chest, though I manage to control my breathing. I've gotten quite talented at shutting down any emotion, including fear.

"Good," Romeo finally says. The panic clawing its way up my throat slowly recedes. "That's good to hear. I was concerned it was a fucking Colombo goon."

"Nope. Definitely not a goon." Another partial truth that does little to allay my guilt.

"Good," he states again, sounding a bit distracted. He's already moving on to the next phone call he needs to make, so we say our goodbyes.

I let out a relieved breath once he hangs up.

"Fuck me," I mutter under my breath.

What the hell am I going to do about Katya? I can't seem to let her go. Any outcome other than staying under my protection is unacceptable. No way in hell am I sending her back to her piece of shit father and the degenerate man he promised her to.

I also can't bring her in front of Romeo, not only because he'd know I was lying, but also because I don't want her to be a pawn in this war. She's been objectified and manipulated her entire life to be whatever her father wants. I can't explain it, but I'd rather take a sucker punch with brass knuckles than put Katya in a situation like that ever again.

A soft noise catches my attention, and I look in the direction of the stairs. Before I have a chance to comprehend what it might be, a guttural scream slices through the silence, striking me to my very core.

I bolt up the stairs two at a time, picking up my pace when I hear another agonizing cry from Katya's room. Without hesitation, I fling the door open, not sure how to comprehend what's happening.

She's thrashing around on the bed, her eyes squeezed shut even as tears stain her cheeks. "I'm sorry," she pleads, her voice scratchy from crying and yelling.

I approach the bed with caution, not wanting to scare her, but needing to fix this, to protect her, even from the nightmares in her own head.

"Katya," I say soothingly, climbing onto the bed with her. Her hair is matted down with sweat, her face blotchy and twisted in pain. "You're safe, princess. It's just a dream."

I try holding her hand to comfort her, but she shrinks away from my touch. Jesus, it hurts to see her afraid of me, but I know it's not intentional. Whatever dream she's having has swallowed her whole.

She jerks to the side, and that's when I see a blood stain on the shirt of mine she's wearing.

"Dammit," I rasp. She ripped her bandage off during all of this. I need to stop her before she hurts herself anymore.

I move closer to the terrified woman, then gather her tense body up in my arms, holding her against my chest. Jesus, she's trembling, and fear radiates off her in waves.

"Kayta, wake up," I whisper. "Wake up. It's not real."

She furrows her brows, and her movements become less jerky.

"You're safe," I continue, talking to her in soft, calming

tones. "I'm right here. I'll protect you from the whole goddamn world."

Katya stills in my arms, then opens her eyes, which are filled with confusion. "Wh-what happened?" she murmurs, sounding strained. "Oh, my god. Did I have a nightmare?" she whispers as her confusion gives way to shame.

I hate seeing her like this. I nod, not loosening my hold on her. She doesn't make a move to get out of my arms, so I keep her close. "It's nothing to be ashamed of, princess."

"It's a weakness," she all but whispers. "Other people can just, I don't know. They can just shove everything into a dark corner of their mind and lock it away. All the pain, all the memories, every scar, every lie. They just push all the trauma to the side and somehow move on. I've tried. God, I've tried. But at night…"

"All the monsters come out of that dark corner in your mind," I finish for her.

Katya hits me with her golden eyes, a heartbreaking look etched on her features. Without words, I know what she's thinking. She feels seen and understood for the first time in her life.

She nods, more tears gathering in her eyes. "Yeah," she says with a sniffle, adjusting herself to a more seated position in my lap.

I tuck some of her inky black hair behind her ears, moving slowly so I don't startle her. Cupping her cheek like I did yesterday, I wipe away her tears with the pad of my thumb. Her skin is silky smooth, and Katya tugs at my already shattered heart when she leans into my touch, nuzzling against the palm of my hand.

I guide her to rest against my shoulder, and she does, curling up and tucking her head in between my neck and shoulder. Combing my fingers through Katya's long hair, I hold her close, just letting my presence be enough.

Her quiet sniffles turn into sobs as she fists my shirt, her tears wetting my skin. I gently cup the back of her neck, keeping her close while stroking her back with my other hand. I have her all wrapped up so nothing can hurt her ever again.

"I-I can't," she chokes out.

"Can't what, baby?" I'm not sure where the term of endearment came from, but it fits.

"Can't cry," comes her muffled response.

"I don't know, you seem to be doing a good job of it right now," I tease.

Katya pops her head up from where it was buried in the side of my neck, glaring at me with her gorgeous eyes. "I didn't mean I couldn't *physically* cry," she says, narrowing her eyes even more. "I just meant…" Katya trails off, looking over my shoulder instead of meeting my gaze. "I mean, I can't handle it all crashing down. If I feel one thing, I have to feel them all, and, and, and… I can't. I just can't."

Her confession resonates with something deep inside me, and at this moment, it's just Katya and me, connecting on a level that's excruciatingly raw yet healing at the same time.

"The only way out of the fear is through," I whisper. "You can't avoid the bad, scary, and devastating things that happen to you. Not unless you want those memories to jump out and pull you under when you're most vulnerable."

"Like in my sleep?"

I nod. "Like in your sleep."

Katya takes a deep breath and exhales slowly, her muscles finally drained of the last of their tension. "And talking about it will help?" Again, I nod. "Well, shit."

This startles a laugh out of me. Katya's face instantly lights up, the most adorable smile gracing her lips. What did I do to earn such a precious gift?

"I like your laugh," she says, her eyes twinkling as she beams up at me.

It's not often I'm at a loss for words. Right now, however, I've got nothing.

"I need to change your bandage," I say, changing the subject before I do something stupid like kiss her and tell her to stay with me forever.

Katya's smile drops as she looks down at her side. "Sorry," she murmurs, holding her hand over the blood stain as though that would make it disappear.

It kills me that she's apologizing for her pain. It speaks volumes about what she's been through in her short life.

"Nothing to be sorry about, Katya," I tell her softly. "You did nothing wrong."

Golden eyes blink up at me in confusion and disbelief, but beneath the layers of insecurities and distrust, I see a tentative hope. I want to bring that out in her, to give her hope and joy and all the other shit I never thought I cared about. I may not deserve any of it, but Katya does. She deserves every good thing in this world, and for some reason I still can't comprehend, I need to be the one to give it to her.

"None of this is your fault," I whisper, running my fingertips up and down her arm in a calming gesture. "Now, let's get you cleaned up and back to bed, yeah?"

Katya nods, her eyes never leaving mine. It's intense, the way she looks at me. Like she's burrowing down into my very soul and making space for herself. She doesn't need to try so hard. I already know I'll never forget this woman.

I help her off the bed and half-carry her to the bathroom across the hall, sitting her down on the edge of the tub. After grabbing the first aid kit from the drawer next to the sink, I kneel down in front of Katya and begin to lift the hem of her shirt.

She immediately crosses her arms over her chest, and I

look up, lifting an eyebrow in question. "I have to see it so I know how to patch you up."

"I know, I just..." She trails off, looking to the side to avoid my gaze. Finally, Katya sighs and drops her arms to her sides. "I'm not wearing a bra," she whispers.

"Oh." At first, I'm not sure why that information is relevant. I didn't think about it, but it makes sense that she wouldn't sleep in a bra. "*Oh*," I say again once I realize what the issue is. She has to take off her shirt for me to have access, which means...

"It's fine, I mean, I know it's not a big deal," she rushes to say, her cheeks glowing red. "I just haven't ever shown anyone... I mean, it's not like I've even had... Oh my *god*, never mind." Katya finishes her outburst by covering her face with her hands.

What the hell just happened? What is she talking about?

Then it hits me. More like bludgeons me. *I've never shown anyone... I've never even had...*

Jesus. This woman is killing me. Never thought I had a possessive bone in my body until now, but hearing her admit she's never been with anyone? No one has touched her, kissed her, seen her naked curves...

"It's okay," I manage to say, hopefully not sounding as feral as I feel. "Nothing to be ashamed of." *In fact, I love it. More than I should.* "I'll turn around while you take the shirt off. You can, uh, cover what you need to cover as long as I have access to the cut."

I turn, giving her my back so she can undress in private. I'd much rather insist she goes topless, but no way in hell will I ever pressure her or disrespect her boundaries. This girl has had enough people trample all over her wants and needs, and I refuse to be another one.

"Valentino?" comes her soft voice. "I, um, I need help with the shirt. I think some of the blood dried, and... I trust you."

The last part is barely above a whisper, but I hear it as if it were a gunshot next to my ear. *She trusts me.*

I grab a washcloth and dampen it slightly before turning to face Katya. She's nibbling on her bottom lip, looking up at me with those wide, vulnerable eyes. Without saying a word, I gently press the damp cloth to her side, loosening the dried blood so it releases the bond between her skin and the fabric.

Tugging on the shirt slightly, I manage to lift it off of the wound fairly easily, thank God. I hate the thought of putting her through any more pain. Curling my fingers under the hem of the shirt, I slowly lift the fabric up, up, up her body, revealing creamy skin and round, firm breasts I don't allow myself to stare at.

Once the shirt is over her head, Katya captures my eyes. She's stunning but now isn't the time.

"You're beautiful, Katya," I find myself saying. "Now, let's get you cleaned up and back to bed."

I kneel once more, focusing all of my attention on cleaning her wound. Luckily, none of the butterfly bandages ripped off, just the large Band-Aid covering everything up. The skin around the cut is red, but the wound itself is actually healing up better than I hoped. With another few days of rest, it'll close and heal on its own.

For now, I put on another layer of antibiotic cream to help speed the process along. After covering the area with another bandage, I lightly trace my fingertips along the outside to make sure everything is secure.

Looking up at Katya, she gives me a tiny smile that lights up my world.

"I'll be right back," I tell her, dashing to my room to grab another shirt. "Here." I hold the shirt open above her head, and she understands, lifting her arms so I can slide the shirt over her gorgeous body.

"Thank you," she murmurs, tucking a few strands of hair

behind her ear. "For everything. I don't know what would have happened if someone else found me."

I grit my teeth, not liking the thought of that one bit. If it were someone else, she would be in a world of trouble.

"You're here now, that's all that matters." Another small smile graces her lips. I want to taste it, but that's so far beyond inappropriate for so many reasons. "Can I help you back to bed? Or do you want some water? A snack?"

Her head perks up, those damn eyes sparkling in a way that makes my chest tight. "Do you have hot chocolate?"

"Do I look like someone who has hot chocolate on hand?"

This earns me a quiet laugh and a shake of her head. "No, I suppose not," she says with a smile. "I'll be fine. Thank you again."

I don't know what to say to her, so I just offer my hand. She stands, and I lead her across the hall to her room, peeling back the covers so she can climb in. Once settled, I cover her with the blankets, tucking in the precious, strong, gorgeous princess.

I'm about to leave her when the question that's been burning in my mind all night comes spilling out without my permission.

"What was your nightmare about?"

Katya's eyes dim as she curls in on herself.

"Most of the time, it's flashes of conversations I've had with my father. His biting words take physical form and litter my skin with bruises. Sometimes he leaves me to bleed out in his office. Sometimes he carries my body to the river and tosses me in. Tonight…" She trails off, squeezing her eyes shut. "Tonight, he shot me in the face."

"Katya," I whisper, my hand finding hers beneath the blankets. "I will never let that happen," I vow.

"But how–"

"Never," I repeat. "You said you trusted me earlier. Is that still true?" She nods her head. "Then get some rest, princess."

I'm rewarded by a shy smile, that blush creeping into her cheeks once more. Only this time, I hope it's because she feels cared for and not ashamed.

"Goodnight, Valentino."

"Goodnight, Katya."

I step out of her room and shut the door, leaning against it.

What the fuck am I going to do now?

CHAPTER FOUR

KATYA

I've been awake for a while now, but I can't bring myself to get out of bed. Not yet. It's so soft and warm, and after three nights of sleeping on cement floors and hiding in crates, this mattress feels heavenly.

Rolling onto my back, memories of last night slowly rise to the surface. I was sound asleep, more at peace than I can ever remember, and then…

Oh, God. I had a nightmare.

Every muscle in my body tenses as the horrifying image of my father pulling a gun on me flashes across my mind. I remember crying out for someone, anyone, to help. It's never worked before, but this time, Valentino answered my call.

I cover my face with my hands, the embarrassment of being weak in front of Valentino too much to bear. He didn't make me feel fragile or silly for having a nightmare. In fact, the puzzling man held me in his arms and whispered surprisingly sweet things to me until I could breathe again.

More moments from our interaction last night bubble up, each one more vulnerable than the last. Valentino saw more of me than any man ever has, and what's more, he called me *beautiful.* Me. I don't think anyone has ever said that to me. Certainly not my parents.

My father never spared me a glance unless I could be a useful pawn in his latest scheme. His compliments always came with a bite. *Your dress is lovely. It would be even better if you dropped twenty pounds.* Or the classic, *You'd be so pretty if you smiled, Katya.*

My mother isn't much better. She started putting me on diets when I was eleven to "lose the baby fat." By the time I was in my teens, dear ol' Mom made a habit of making me stand in front of the mirror while she pointed out my "problem areas" and pinched the extra skin on my arms and waist.

I've known from an early age that I'm only worth what my father can get out of me. My role was to be the perfect doll, like my mom. I always fell short of their expectations, however. Too short, too chubby, too opinionated. Too much, yet never enough.

But when Valentino gently lifted up my shirt, I could see something close to reverence in his gaze. I thought I was making it up, but then he whispered that I was beautiful.

I was so caught off-guard that I didn't have time to respond before he got to work cleaning up my bandages. God, what a mess. I have no idea what Valentino is going to think of me this morning after everything that happened.

There's only one way to find out.

Swinging my legs over the edge of the bed, I take a deep breath and stand. I find a pair of socks and pull them on, smiling when they go halfway up my calves. I briefly think about finding some pants or shorts from Valentino, but I don't want to disturb him. Plus, the shirt I'm wearing is practically a dress.

I gather up my long black hair and twist it to the side, letting the strands flow over my left shoulder. Taking one last cleansing breath, I turn the doorknob and peek into the hallway, relieved to see I'm alone.

Tiptoeing out of my room, I head to the stairs and descend, pausing on the bottom step when I see Valentino in the kitchen. My palms grow sweaty and my heart kicks into high gear as I make my way in that direction.

He doesn't see me at first, giving me time to study his silhouette. Instead of a suit, Valentino is wearing joggers and a black t-shirt that stretches across his chest and showcases his thick biceps. He's casual today, which hopefully means he's starting to get more comfortable around me. I don't know what my future holds, but something tells me Valentino is going to be a very important person to me. He already is.

The far too sexy man pulls out a few boxes of something from a grocery bag, lining them up on the counter. Upon further inspection, I realize the boxes are different kinds of hot chocolate. My heart melts, even more so when Valentino opens another grocery bag and produces a huge bag of marshmallows.

"Will these do, princess?" he asks, startling me.

"You got me hot chocolate?" I whisper, looking between him and the boxes on the counter.

"I was thinking I might have some too, but yes."

I grin at him, and he returns it. Well, he tries to, anyway. It's going to take more than that to get a real smile out of him.

"I also picked up some clothes. I didn't know what to get, so the lady at the store just sort of filled my cart. The bags are in the living room."

"Valentino, I… You didn't have to do that," I whisper.

He shrugs, then looks away, concentrating heavily on the groceries instead of me. Is he embarrassed? It's kind of adorable. I take pity on him and bring the conversation back to the most important topic.

"There's just one problem," I say, tapping my chin as I look over the half-dozen varieties of hot chocolate. Valentino's brow furrows, making him look even more adorable. Not that I'd ever tell him that. "I prefer my hot chocolate with whipped cream and sprinkles. Like a princess," I tease, crossing my arms over my chest.

Valentino gives me a playful look, then empties the rest of the grocery bag onto the counter. He has three kinds of whipped cream, three different kinds of sprinkles, as well as mini chocolate chips, and mini butterscotch chips.

"Will this satisfy your sugar craving?" he asks, knowing full well he went above and beyond.

I nod once. "It will suffice," I declare, bringing a spark to Valentino's eyes. "Now, let's get to making some master-pieces," I say, rubbing my hands together as I survey my options.

Dark chocolate, white chocolate raspberry, milk chocolate and mint, caramel swirl, peanut butter chocolate, and candy cane hot chocolate all stare back at me. I open the dark chocolate box and pluck out a packet. Looking over my shoulder, I see Valentino standing there, shifting his weight from foot to foot.

"Which one do you want?" I ask, waving my hand in front of the selection.

"Uh, what do you recommend?"

"I mean, I like the dark chocolate, but you might be different. What have you had before? I can direct you to something similar."

Valentino looks up at the ceiling and lets out a sigh. "Can't say I've ever had hot chocolate," he admits.

"What?" I gasp in horror. My mouth drops as I stare at him. "Never?"

He shakes his head and shrugs. "I don't have room for such frivolous things in my life."

Ouch. Are we still talking about the hot chocolate? Or perhaps we've moved on to discussing me and how I need to get out of his hair.

"Right," I say after a beat of silence, hoping I don't sound too disappointed. "That makes sense."

"But then again, I've never tried to make room. Maybe hot chocolate would do me some good."

I can't contain the smile that stretches across my face. "Well, it certainly couldn't hurt."

Valentino flashes me a rare and radiant smile. I'll treasure it forever.

"Okay, then. I'll get to work on our drinks," I inform him, clapping my hands and rubbing them together. I need a hot chocolate concoction that will soften Valentino's defenses. No pressure.

He points to where the mugs are, along with a saucepan. I hum to myself as I heat up the milk on the stove, stirring constantly so it doesn't burn. Turning off the burner, I set the milk to the side to cool down a bit.

Pondering the perfect combination, I decide to stick with dark chocolate for both of us. We can branch out into the fancier flavors later. *If there is a later.* I shove that thought way down deep, unable to unpack why the thought of leaving physically pains me.

I stir the milk into the first mug, making sure to get rid of all the clumps of chocolate powder. Next, I grab the canned whipped cream and execute the perfect swirl right on top, followed by a dusting of rainbow sprinkles and a few strategically placed mini chocolate chips. I finish the decadent drink with a marshmallow nestled on top of the whipped cream, like a star on top of a Christmas tree.

I look over my shoulder to where Valentino is sitting at

the kitchen table, his eyes fixed on me. I should find it unnerving, but I like his attention. I want him to look at me, to praise me, to tell me I'm beautiful again.

As I approach the table, Valentino's gaze drops from mine to the beverage in my hand. His eyes go wide as I set it down in front of him, making me giggle.

"Holy shit," he mumbles.

"Too much?" I ask self-consciously, rocking back and forth on my heels.

Dammit. I should have scaled back, gone with something simpler. Of course, it's too–

"No," he's quick to respond. He sounds almost angry, but I don't think it's directed at me. Honestly, he sounds defensive, as if I'm going to take his drink away from him. That makes me light up from the inside. Valentino is so freaking cute, and he has no idea. "It's a masterpiece."

I'm sure my ecstatic smile is giving away all of my feelings for this man, but at this moment, I don't care. I watch intently as Valentino takes a sip, waiting for his approval.

"Sweetest thing I've ever tasted," he says.

"Is that… bad?"

"No. I expect nothing less from you, princess."

My eyebrows shoot up to my forehead at his words. What does that mean?

Valentino takes another sip, his eyes never leaving mine. I grin when he sets the mug down, pointing out his whipped cream mustache and dollop on the tip of his nose.

"Do I have something on my face?" he asks, a smirk pulling at his lips.

I nod, taking a step closer. Valentino scoots his chair back from the table and holds out his hand. I take it and let him draw me toward him until I'm standing in front of him, between his legs.

My heart thuds against my ribcage, each beat echoing throughout my chest and down my spine.

"Can you get it for me?" he rasps, never breaking eye contact.

I'm helpless to do anything other than obey. Reaching out, I swipe the cream off his nose and lick it off my finger without thinking about it. Valentino's eyes flash with something dark and fierce, but it's gone before I can be sure it was there in the first place.

My breathing grows shallow as I lift my hand to his face, and my fingers shake as they hover over his lips. I drag my thumb across his top lip, gathering up the whipped cream. Valentino surprises me by looping his fingers around my wrist and pulling my hand toward him.

His wicked gaze never leaves mine as he licks the whipped cream off of the tip of my thumb, grunting in approval before wrapping his lips around my digit and sucking.

"Valentino," I murmur, my breath caught in my throat.

"Katya," he growls, making me weak in the knees. "Come here, princess." He pats his lap and helps me straddle him, smoothing his hands up and down my bare thighs.

I steady myself with my hands on his shoulders, giggling when he bounces me once.

"God, what you do to me..." He trails off, sliding one hand up my spine until his fingers tangle in my hair. Tugging slightly, he pulls my head back, exposing my neck. Valentino ghosts his lips up and down my column, pausing to nip at an extra sensitive spot below my ear.

I squeeze my thighs around him, needing something. Needing everything, but not sure how to ask for it.

Valentino loosens his grip on my hair, dropping his hands to my hips and rocking me against his solid erection. I should be scandalized, right? But all I want is more. More of whatever this man has to offer.

"Need a taste," he says, his voice deep and gravelly.

I find myself nodding before he's finished his sentence. Leaning down, I meet him halfway, our lips finding each other in soft kisses until he drags my bottom lip through his teeth and dives into my mouth.

I moan as his tongue slides against mine and tickles the roof of my mouth. Each stroke winds me up tighter and tighter, and I grind my soaking wet center against his thick dick, a shudder running through me at how huge and hard it is.

We break for air, and Valentino rests his forehead on mine.

"Wow," I breathe. "That was… that was…"

"A mistake," he finishes for me.

A bucket of ice is thrown over me at his words. I scramble off of his lap and wrap my arms around my middle, protecting myself from him. Valentino looks angry and hurt at the same time.

"Do you really think that?" I whisper, trying to push back my tears until I'm alone.

"It doesn't matter what I think," he grits out. "It was wrong of me to take advantage. Inappropriate on all levels. Please accept my apology."

Double ouch.

I don't say anything, not trusting my voice at the moment. Valentino stands from his seat and clears his throat, adjusting himself so his erection isn't quite so prominent.

He clearly enjoyed himself, so what went wrong?

"Help yourself to anything in the kitchen," he says, the cold, aloof tone back in his voice. "I'm going to the gym downstairs and then off on an assignment. I probably won't see you the rest of the day."

I nod, blinking back tears.

"Listen, Katya…"

I hold my hand up, cutting him off. Valentino sighs, running a hand through his hair, then turns on his heel and stomps down the hallway, presumably toward the basement.

I'm left staring after Valentino, my fingers fluttering over my lips where I can still feel his kiss. I don't understand him at all. We made good progress with the hot chocolate, but then… I don't know. I honestly don't know what happened.

Maybe he's just as broken and scared as I am. Maybe it was intense for him, too. Like we shared more than just a kiss. He gave me a piece of his soul, and in return, Valentino kept a little piece of me.

Focusing on breakfast, I try to shake my head of those thoughts. Besides, I have my hot chocolate bar to devour. I'll just have to enjoy my time here for as long as it lasts.

CHAPTER FIVE

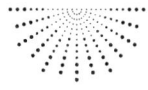

VALENTINO

I groan as hot water from the shower hits my skin, burning away the stress and confusion of the last few days. My muscles are sore, and not just from the grueling punishments I've put my body through at the gym several times a day. The pain is deeper than that. I ache everywhere, and I'm beginning to realize I won't feel better until I sort things out with Katya.

Goddamnit.

Pouring some body wash into the palm of my hand, I smooth it over my arms, chest, and torso, remembering the soft sweetness of her kiss. God, the way she gasped and moaned as I sipped from her lips, her luscious curves pressed against my hard muscles, her thighs spread out as she ground her hot little center over my…

Stop it, I shout at myself, though I know it won't help.

It's been three days since my world was flipped upside down with one little kiss. Three days since we've had a real conversation. Three days since I've touched, smelled or tasted her.

I successfully avoided Katya for the rest of that first day, though I worried about her having another nightmare. I set up camp outside her room until dawn, then caught a few hours of sleep before getting up for work.

Yesterday, Katya left the room any time I entered, refusing to make eye contact with me. Before leaving for the afternoon, I set out a fresh bandage and some vitamin E cream to help with scarring. I was half convinced she'd be gone when I came back. However, the bandage and lotion were gone from the table and the light was on in her room. There was evidence of freshly washed dishes drying in the rack as well. After a shower, I made my bed outside of her door again and settled in for another sleepless night.

I startled awake this morning around five when Katya got up to use the restroom. I barely made it back to my room before her door swung open. I don't know what I would have told her if she asked what the hell I was doing. When she was safely back in bed, I got dressed and slipped out of the house, needing to do something, anything other than deal with my thoughts and emotions.

Usually, throwing myself into work erases whatever bullshit is going on in my life. But Katya is different. The more I try to ignore her, the more she pops into my head. Her smile, those fierce golden eyes, her soft skin, and silky hair… She's all I can fucking think about, and it's messing with me.

Yes, she's exquisite. With olive skin, midnight black hair, and eyes the color of honey, Katya is like a goddess of beauty and grace. But her looks are only a fraction of why I'm obsessed with her.

Katya has been surprising me since the moment I laid eyes on her. From jumping me and holding me at gunpoint to confessing her horrible situation while I patched her up without any anesthesia. There's no denying she's strong as fuck and determined to survive. She's incredibly resilient, tender, and sweet, even after everything she's been through.

I finish up my shower, grabbing a towel and drying off before throwing on jeans and a t-shirt. I've been home for over an hour but still haven't seen Katya. It's almost dinner time, so maybe I can lure her out with a meal. We need to talk, though I'm not sure if I'm going to tell her to find a new place to stay or sweep her off her feet with another earth-shattering kiss.

Only one way to find out.

When I'm halfway down the stairs, I hear her rustling around in the kitchen. Good. I won't have to hunt her down and force her to eat with me. The aroma of creamy alfredo and seasoned chicken wafts past me as I reach the bottom step, and my mouth is watering by the time I get to the kitchen.

Katya is stirring a pot on the stove, sashaying her hips as she hums to herself. She hasn't seen me yet, which gives me the opportunity to study her. The dark orange and pink light from the setting sun streams in through the kitchen window, reflecting off her hair like glitter as she sways.

Yeah, there's no way I'm kicking this woman out. I very much want to kiss her again, but I forgot about the third option; fall to one knee and beg her to be mine forever.

Reel it in, goddamnit.

"Katya," I say, my voice much rougher than I intended.

She gasps and spins around, her feet slipping on the tiled floor. I'm next to her in a second, wrapping an arm around her back and steadying her before she falls. Katya peers up at me, those brilliant eyes searing me all the way down to my soul.

A million thoughts fly through my head as I stare into her golden depths. *Stay, be mine, let me protect you, let me worship you, let me be the one person you can trust.*

Instead of confessing any of that, I help Katya regain her balance, then take a step back. As much as I want to wrap her up in my arms, I need to respect her space. I haven't exactly been easy to deal with, so I'm not sure how she feels about my presence.

"You made dinner?" I ask after clearing my throat.

Katya nods, nibbling her bottom lip while looking away from me. I hate it, but I only have myself to blame.

"Chicken alfredo," she answers, her voice soft, almost shy.

Where is the woman who asked me to serve her head on a platter to her father? Fuck. I hurt her more than I thought by pushing her away. I'm about to thank her, but she talks before I get a chance.

"Go sit down, I'll dish us up."

Nodding, I follow her orders. Katya piles homemade fettuccine noodles onto a plate, followed by a perfectly seared chicken breast, and topped with a ladle of alfredo sauce.

"This looks incredible," I tell her as she sets the food down in front of me.

She smiles briefly, but her eyes never meet mine.

"Thank you," I try again.

Katya nods once, then flits away to grab her plate.

Once we're both seated at the table, I dig into the meal this gorgeous woman prepared. After three or four bites, I notice Katya isn't eating. Pausing, I set my utensils down and look at her, tilting my head to the side. She's tapping her foot and wringing her hands under the table. The old me would have assumed she poisoned my meal and her nerves were getting the better of her.

Sitting here, looking at the anxious mafia princess fidgeting in her chair, I know the cause of her restlessness is all my fault. I've been a dick by avoiding her after kissing her. No wonder she doesn't know how to act around me.

"Listen, Katya–"

"I was thinking–"

We both speak at the same time, talking over each other.

"You go first," I offer, trying to give her a smile. It's rusty as hell and might do more damage than good.

Katya takes a deep breath and straightens her shoulders, lifting her chin like the proper princess she was taught to be. "I was thinking it's probably time for me to get out of your hair," she starts. My heart squeezes up painfully inside my chest, but I let her continue. "You've already done so much for me, and I know this dinner doesn't even begin to make up for it, but I guess think of it as an audition?"

I furrow my brow, not understanding her. "Audition?"

"I'm not explaining this well at all," she says under her breath to herself. I don't like seeing her frustrated and doubting herself. Katya clears her throat and starts again. "The last favor I'll ever ask of you is if you could point me in the direction of a Di Salvo business and give me a good reference?" Before I can even say anything, she raises her hands in defense. "Don't worry, no one will know it's me. I'll bleach my hair and wear contacts. Change my name. I'm guessing a lot of your bars and restaurants pay in cash under the table? That's exactly what I'm looking for."

"Katya–"

"Just until I make enough money to pay you back and save some for a bus ticket somewhere else. I can sleep in one of the warehouses, as you know. I won't mess with anything or disturb anyone. I'll be gone before you know it."

She blinks at me, tears welling up in her eyes, though she doesn't let them fall. This woman is ruining me.

"Katya–"

"Please," she whispers, her voice cracking.

I can't take it anymore.

Standing from my chair, I close the distance between us, my eyes never leaving Katya's as I kneel in front of her.

"You can't leave," I tell her softly, gathering her hands in mine. "Somehow, you've become essential to my being, and I can't let you go." Brushing my lips over her knuckles, I kiss each one before guiding her to place her hands on my shoulders.

"But I thought..." Katya trails off, confusion filling her eyes. "I thought it was a mistake. Everything. The kiss, bringing me into your home, caring for my wound. I thought you were done with me."

"Fuck, princess, I'm so sorry. I know I'm difficult and confusing, but honestly, I've never met anyone like you. Never had these intense feelings, never needed someone's safety and happiness more than my own. I didn't know what to do with you, with myself, really. You make me feel... raw and vulnerable, and that scares me."

"I scare you?" she murmurs, lifting one eyebrow in question.

"With you in my life, I have someone to lose. Someone to let down. Someone to hurt, even if by accident."

"You would also have someone who cares about you. Someone to share in the joys and the sorrows of life. Someone to encourage and support, someone who wants the best for you. If you only look at the darkness, you'll never see the light."

"What if I don't deserve your light?" I rasp, gliding my hands up her legs until my fingers wrap around her hips. "What if the darkness is all I've ever known?"

"Then trust me enough to show you what you've been missing."

Hope sparks in her ethereal eyes and soothes something in my chest. Slowly, I pull Katya to the edge of her seat, then wrap my arms around her and settle her down into my lap. She giggles, and the sound warms me like a ray of sunshine.

"I do trust you, Katya," I tell her, resting my forehead on hers. "But can you trust me? I've already let you down."

She cups the side of my cheek, her thumb lightly brushing over my stubble. "We're both broken," she whispers. "But I think together, we could heal."

"I would like that very much. Can you forgive me for being an asshole the last few days?"

A wicked grin curls up the corners of her lips, making me want to kiss it right off of her face.

"With enough hot chocolate, forgiveness is definitely in your future." Katya's eyes sparkle as she smiles at me, and I can't hold back any longer.

Leaning forward, I pull Katya's bottom lip through my teeth, then whisper, "Can I start making it up to you?"

"What did you have in mind?" Her voice is low and breathy, and she has no idea how sexy she is right now.

"First," I murmur, "I'd like to kiss you until we can't breathe."

"Mmhm," she says with a nod, rubbing her nose against mine. "I like that plan."

"Then," I continue, pressing a kiss to that sensitive spot below her ear, "I'd like to kiss you everywhere if you'll let me."

"Everywhere?" she practically whimpers.

"Yes, princess. You need it, don't you? Need me to make the ache go away?"

Katya nods, a strangled sound stuck in her throat as she grinds down on my lap.

"Fuck," I growl, cupping the back of her neck and drawing her down for a kiss.

I'm instantly lost in everything she's offering. Kayta opens up for me, her tongue chasing mine and letting me know she wants this as much as I do. She breaks the kiss to breathe, but I can't get enough of her sweet skin. I drag my nose and lips down her throat, then lick and nip my way back up to her ear, where I whisper, "Need to get you naked."

"Yes," she whispers, her chest heaving with labored breaths.

I somehow manage to tear myself away from Katya long enough to grab the hem of her shirt and help her take it off. As soon as the offending garment is out of the way, I run my fingers up and down her torso, over her breasts, her nipples, anywhere and everywhere I can reach.

Pausing to gently trace the bandage on her side, I peer up at her, silently asking if she's in pain. Katya smiles and shakes her head, leaning close to capture my lips. "I'm feeling much better," she murmurs once we break apart. "I know you'd never hurt me."

"Damn right," I grunt, licking a stripe up her throat.

Katya's desperate moans spur me on as I gently lay her on the floor, spreading out her gorgeous body so I can consume every inch. I bend down and suck on her tits, licking one pebbled peak and then the other, alternating until I feel her tremble beneath me. Fuck, her skin tastes like warm vanilla and feels impossibly smooth, like porcelain. I nibble on the underside of her generous breasts, more than a handful, just like her juicy ass, and continue exploring her body with my mouth.

I drag my lips over her torso, careful to avoid her bandage. The wound itself is well on its way to healing, but I still need to be careful with my precious girl.

"Valentino... oh God, it feels... it feels..."

"How does it feel, princess?" I growl into the soft flesh of her stomach.

"Like... like..." Katya gasps and bucks her hips, thrusting up as I kiss my way down to her dripping center. I pause when I get to the waistband of my boxers that she's wearing, gripping it with my teeth and letting it snap against her skin.

"Tell me how it feels," I demand.

"Like my skin is on fire," she whispers.

"What else?" I murmur as my fingers dip into the waist-band and slowly pull the last piece of clothing down her legs, kissing her thighs and calves as I go.

"So much pressure. Valentino… please. It aches. I *ache* for you."

"Jesus," I breathe out through gritted teeth. "I can make the pain go away, Katya. Do you trust me?"

"I trust you, Valentino."

Her sweet words are surpassed only by the sweet scent of her pussy. I nuzzle into her dripping cunt, memorizing everything about how she feels, how she smells. Her soft curls tickle my nose, and the sensation makes my dick leak and throb in my pants. I dip my nose barely inside her wet slit. Goddamn, what this woman does to me, surrendering her sweet, innocent body to my sinful desires.

A strangled whimper falls from her lips, snapping the last thread of control I had. I lick up her sticky center, finding her swollen clit right away and lavishing it with attention. Her thighs snap against my head, but I pry them apart so I can taste more of her, all of her. It'll never be enough.

Katya twists and bucks her hips, trying to get me deeper. I lean back a bit and grin when she whines. Her protests die on her tongue when I drag a finger up and down her slit, circling her entrance.

I carefully push the tip of my middle finger inside her, groaning when her cunt squeezes and pulses around me. Jesus, fuck, she's *tight*. Holy hell.

"Valentino… oh! Ohmygod!"

I growl and lick her from top to bottom, flattening my tongue so I can taste and touch as much of her as possible. I feel her opening pulse underneath my tongue and more of her juices spill out.

She wants to be my dirty girl. I can feel it. Smell it. Taste it. Hear it in every ragged breath and broken cry. I swear I can see it written on her soul. She's mine. My innocent, filthy, perfect woman.

Katya tangles her fingers in my hair like she needs to steady herself. I slip my hands under her ass, gripping her cheeks and pulling her even closer to me while I eat out her little pussy in rough strokes and teasing bites.

"Something's happening... something is ha-happening to me."

"Let it happen," I growl, drawing her clit between my lips and sucking lightly. I let it go and bat it with the tip of my tongue and then lick. Hard.

"Ohmygod..." She presses her cunt into my mouth like she can't help it, rubbing her drenched folds all over my chin and tongue, whimpering like a sweet, confused angel. "It feels so good. And it aches, and... oh. *Oh!*"

She erupts in my mouth, her nails digging into my scalp as her trembles turn violent. Katya's throaty sobs of my name have me humping the goddamn floor to find some relief for my angry cock. I lap at her hungrily, not wanting a single drop of her pleasure to escape me. I made it. I own it. It's mine.

I shove one thick finger inside her, opening her up and giving her a taste of what's to come. Her pussy pulses around me, over and over, until I feel her relax on the floor completely. I remove my finger, chuckling as she gasps and shudders. I lick her essence off me and then gather her limp body into my arms, carrying her over to the couch.

I sit us down, then grab a blanket from the back of the couch, wrapping it around Katya's naked body. "Are you okay, princess?" I ask, kissing the top of her head.

"Oh my god, Valentino," she says in a raspy voice. "I've never... I mean, like... holy shit."

I chuckle at her response, loving her flushed cheeks and swollen lips. Her hair is mussed and her eyes shine with satisfaction and awe. I can't wait to see her like this again, only next time, she'll be spread out on my bed.

"So I can do that again?" I question, peering down at my worn-out, sexy-as-hell woman.

"Um, yes. Any time you want to… uh, do that, I would be appreciative," she slurs, tucking her head into the side of my neck.

I stroke her back, unable to help the smile stretching across my face. "Good," I murmur as her breathing grows steady and deep. "I'll need to start making up for lost time."

Katya doesn't answer, but I don't expect her to. Her cute little snores let me know she's resting after such an intense experience. I'll be right here when she wakes up.

CHAPTER SIX

KATYA

*T*he timer goes off, and I hop off the couch, eager to frost the cupcakes I made now that they are officially cool enough. I can't wait to see Valentino's face when he sees the dessert I made for tonight. I figured if he hadn't had hot chocolate until a few days ago, he'd probably been missing out on the amazingness of cupcakes as well.

He left this morning for a "meeting," aka, an assignment from the Boss. While I don't love that he's in the same line of work as my father, I know deep down in my soul that Valentino is different. For one, he could barely stomach the story behind the cut on my side. I know he'd be livid on my behalf if I told him the other ways I've been abused in the past.

Valentino has also taken better care of me than anyone I've ever met. He had no reason to patch me up and provide shelter. In fact, I'm sure he broke protocol by taking me into his home. As far as I know, he hasn't told anyone else in the family that I'm here.

I've never had anyone be so protective of me, and I won't lie, I kind of love it.

I spread buttercream frosting over one double chocolate cupcake, then move on to the next. After three cupcakes have been frosted, I stop to add a few sprinkles on top. I don't want the frosting to harden too much, otherwise the sprinkles won't stick.

Just as I'm finishing up the last cupcake, I hear Valentino's car pull up in the driveway. My stomach flips and dissolves into a thousand butterflies swirling around in my gut. After everything that happened last night, our confessions, our kisses, and God, the way he touched me, licked me, commanded my body…

I'm hoping for a repeat. Actually, I'm hoping we go further tonight. I want to give Valentino all of me. I want him to be my first, and I pray that he'll be my only. Is that crazy?

Yes. Definitely yes. That doesn't seem to matter, though. I crave more of him, more of his heart, more of his body, more of his painful secrets he's carried by himself for so long.

The front door swings open, and my eyes immediately find Valentino's as he stalks through the living room toward me. I grin at him, unable to contain the giddiness I feel whenever he's in the room.

Valentino steps up behind me and circles his arms around my waist, nuzzling into the back of my neck while I finish putting sprinkles on the last cupcake. I spin around in his arms, capturing his lips in a heated kiss. He groans, tightening his hold on me and pressing my body impossibly closer to his.

"Katya…" he breathes, sounding almost in pain. "Love everything you do to me."

I look up at him and smirk as a wicked idea passes through my mind. Valentino lifts an eyebrow in question, but before he can say anything, I start unbuttoning his shirt. He hums in approval, his voice deep and filled with desire as I trail my fingers up and down his chiseled abs and defined chest.

I slide his shirt down his powerful shoulders and dip my finger in the bowl of frosting sitting next to me on the counter. Valentino's eyes grow wide, but he doesn't say anything as I trail a line starting at his sternum and ending right above his belly button.

Flattening my tongue against his hard stomach, I lick up toward his chest, never breaking eye contact.

"Fuck," he grunts before winding his fingers in my hair and tipping my head back so he can devour me.

Valentino grips the hem of my t-shirt and I lift my arms so he can take it off, revealing my bare breasts. Deciding to have some fun of his own, Valentino dips his fingers in frosting and circles one nipple and then the other. I shiver at the cool cream and then moan when he sucks it off of me.

"Is this what you wanted, princess? You want to drive me insane?"

"I was hoping to seduce you," I breathe, my voice caught in my throat as he sucks on my other breast and bites my nipple.

Valentino stops in his tracks and looks at me. "You've been seducing me since the very first moment I held you in my arms."

"Well, then, how about I finish the job tonight?"

Before he can say anything else, I reach for his pants and get his belt undone.

"Are you sure, Katya?" he asks, his voice tight with restraint.

I loop my fingers in the waistband of his pants and tug him closer to me while looking up at him. "I'm sure, Valentino. I want everything with you, and I want it starting tonight."

His eyes somehow manage to go soft yet sharp with arousal at the same time.

"Thank fuck," he growls. "I can't stay away from you anymore, princess."

"Then don't."

I hardly get the words out of my mouth before Valentino slides my pants down my legs.

"Damn, Katya. You weren't wearing panties or a bra all day today?" he asks while kneeling in front of me and massaging up my legs.

I shrug and smile down at him.

"Dirty girl," he grunts, kissing a trail from my belly button to the top of my pussy.

In one swift move, Valentino stands up with me in his arms and deposits me on the counter. He stands between my legs and kisses me urgently. When we break apart, I see a playful gleam in his eyes.

"You don't know what kind of game you've started," he says, his voice low and gravelly and sexy as fuck.

"Show me then," I reply.

Valentino gathers up some frosting on his fingers and trails a lazy path between my breasts, down to circle my belly button. He lifts his fingers to my mouth and I suck the remnants of the sugary frosting off of his digits, swirling my tongue and nipping the pads of his fingers. I love watching his pupils dilate with every swipe of my tongue.

He withdraws his fingers from my mouth and leans in to pull my bottom lip between his teeth. He peppers hungry nips and bites down my neck and my collarbone and then begins cleaning up the trail of frosting with his tongue. I lean back with my hands behind me on the counter to give him better access. I swear I can feel every swipe of his tongue on my clit.

When he's done, Valentino stands and guides me so I'm

lying down on the counter all the way. He sets my heels on the edge, opening my legs wide for him to see all of me.

"Fucking beautiful," he whispers more to himself than to me. His hands are all over me then, cupping my breasts, tickling down my curves, squeezing my thighs.

Valentino kneels so his face is right in front of my pussy. I close my eyes when I feel his warm breath across my wet opening and gasp when cool frosting coats my folds. Before I can even process the different sensations, Valentino eats up the frosting, using every part of his mouth on my soft, tender skin.

He growls into my cunt and nips at my clit, making my inner muscles contract and my legs snap around his head. I feel Valentino's tongue circle around my tight little hole and slowly push inside. His wicked tongue darts in and out of me and then circles my clit, again and again, working me up into a frenzy.

I hold my breath as the muscles in my back all tense up. I buck my hips and moan every time Valentino's tongue hits me just right, sending jolts of electricity through my body. Slowly, one finger slides into my cunt, and I squeeze around it tightly, making Valentino groan.

"It's going to feel fucking incredible to be inside you, princess."

He keeps pumping his finger in and out of me while sucking on my clit. Then there are two fingers stretching my tight channel, and with a sudden flick of his wrist, Valentino hits some spot inside of my cunt that has my orgasm slamming into me, my entire body curling in and then exploding with uncontrollable waves of pleasure, so intense I can't breathe.

Valentino doesn't stop, he doesn't let up for one second, he just licks me right through it, pushing my orgasm beyond anything I've experienced so far. His ruthless tongue drags across my tender flesh, lapping at my release. He growls and sucks on my pussy, making wet, sloppy noises. I can't get enough. Neither can he.

My back bows off the counter as Valentino grunts into my still-convulsing pussy and guides my legs over his shoulders. His hands slip underneath my ass and bring me impossibly closer to his mouth so he can lick me clean. My bones are liquid by the time he's done.

I'm vaguely aware of being lifted in Valentino's arms and carried into his room. When he sets me down, Valentino kisses my forehead, nose, and lips so sweetly. He cups my cheeks and rests his forehead on mine.

"Are you sure about this, Katya?"

I nod and place my hands on the outsides of his, looking into those intense, brown eyes that have so quickly become my home. "I trust you, Valentino. I want you. I can't wait any longer.

"I know, kitten," he says, kissing me deeply, brutally, and yet reverently. "I'm gonna make you feel so good, I promise," he whispers into the side of my neck before kissing me there.

Valentino skims his hands down my body and walks us toward the bed, where he gently pushes me down so I'm spread out before him.

Seeing how his body reacts to mine, how his gaze darkens and his cock hardens even more in the confines of his pants, makes me feel sexy and confident. I spread my legs wide and offer myself to him.

"Jesus," he grunts, ridding himself of the rest of his clothing. "So goddamn gorgeous. My beautiful, sexy girl giving me her delicious body…"

Valentino stands in front of me completely naked, and God, how I've missed looking at all of him. Feeling all of him. I sit up and reach out for his thick dick, but he catches my wrist and pulls it away.

"I'm afraid you've got me right on the edge. I swear if you breathe on me, I'm going to come, and I want this to last longer than that."

"Oh…" I blush, not sure what to say to that. "So… now what?" I wince at my ignorance.

Valentino cups my face and traces his thumb over my jaw. "Now you let me enjoy you. Let me have control, kitten. Let me make your first time incredible."

I nod and lean back on the bed, opening myself up again for him. Valentino takes another moment to look me up and down. I feel the heat of his gaze over my skin, my nipples, my lips, and then he locks his eyes on mine.

Never breaking eye contact, Valentino crawls on top of me and settles between my legs, rubbing his cock up and down my slit while resting his weight on his forearm beside my head.

"Ready?" he asks.

I nod and squeeze my eyes shut, preparing for the pain of losing my virginity.

"Hey, look at me, Katya," Valentino says so softly.

I open my eyes and see Valentino looking at me with such longing, such desire, but beyond that, I see the kindness and patience of the man I'm falling in love with. "I'm ready," I whisper.

He kisses me sweetly and lines himself up with my entrance. I feel the head of his cock stretching me wide open, and he's hardly inside of me yet. I tense and hold my breath.

Valentino stops and nuzzles the side of my neck. "Breathe, princess," he whispers in my ear. "I promise I'll take good care of you."

I take a deep breath and turn my head to kiss him while he surges forward, stretching me with his massive cock. I cry out and cling to him as he splits my body open.

"I'm sorry, love. You're doing so good. Are you okay?" His

tone is equal parts concern on my behalf and pained that he can't move. I'm struck again at the self-control this man has over his body so I can be comfortable.

"I'm okay, Valentino. I'm so... full. It doesn't hurt much anymore."

"Yeah?" he croaks, resting his forehead on mine.

I wiggle my hips, trying to get used to the feeling of him inside me. I like it. Not only how he makes my skin light on fire and my pussy throb in ways I couldn't even imagine a few minutes ago, but I like knowing we're as connected, as close as two people can possibly be. I'm already losing track of where I end and he begins.

"Move, Valentino. I need you to move."

"Fuck," he groans. "I don't want to hurt you, Katya."

I buck my hips and wrap my legs around him, taking him impossibly deeper. We both cry out with the rush of sensations, and a wave of wetness flows out of me.

"Please," I beg, wiggling my hips again.

He crushes my lips with his and pulls out of me, only to push back inside, hitting me deep. Valentino growls and fists my hair, tugging my neck up so he can kiss and bite me there. "You feel so damn good. This pussy was made for me," he grunts while picking up the pace.

I moan when his mouth moves over my breast, his tongue flicking at one pebbled nipple and then the other. My fingers weave in his hair to hold him to my chest while I arch my back, wanting to feel more of him, all of him.

Valentino slides one hand to the curve of my ass and then squeezes roughly, lifting my lower half to meet him thrust for thrust. Each time he hits home, my muscles tense, and I let out a little whimper. The pleasure feels unreal. My pussy walls flutter, my muscles shake, and my eyes burn with the effort of keeping all of these sensations inside me.

"That's it, Katya, come on my big fucking cock," Valentino demands.

My orgasm rises to the surface. It starts deep inside me, a pinpoint of bright light trickling throughout my body. Each ragged breath and rough stroke adds to that bright light until my whole being is engulfed in pure energy. Valentino slams into me, shocking my body into an intense orgasm. It feels like my chest is being ripped open as I scream and convulse in his arms.

When I come back down, Valentino kisses my forehead so gently, then nuzzles my neck.

"Can your gorgeous body take any more, princess?" he asks before pulling my earlobe through his teeth.

"Fuck…" I exhale. "Fuck, yes."

Valentino growls and pulls out of me, flipping me on my stomach and pulling my hips back. He squeezes and massages my ass cheeks before pulling them apart and stroking his cock up and down my slit, from my clit all the way to my puckered asshole. I shudder at the thought of him taking me there.

I should be scandalized, right? But instead, I'm absolutely *dripping* at the thought. As if reading my mind, Valentino leans over me, his muscled chest covering my back, and kisses between my shoulder blades.

"Not today, love. But soon, I'm going to have every inch of you."

I whimper and nod, suddenly feeling empty without him filling me up in some way. "I need you, Valentino," I beg, not caring if that makes me wanton or weak or slutty. I'll be slutty for him any time.

"Need you too, kitten," he grunts, slapping my ass once and then thrusting all the way inside me.

"*Fuck,*" I yell, gasping for air and digging my fingers into the mattress. "Oh fuck, you're so deep, so deep…"

I trail off, unable to complete the thought as Valentino pistons in and out of me, hitting that special spot with each powerful stroke of his fat cock. I press my body back into him, increasing the friction and causing us both to moan.

Valentino slides one arm under my hips to keep me in place while he fucks me savagely. His other hand skims up my back, the softness of his fingertips tickling up my spine intensified by the hard pounding he's giving me.

Valentino twists his fingers in my hair, pulling my head to the side so he can lean down and kiss me. His abs flex and tense against my lower back as he stuffs me full of his dick and tongue at the same time.

I bite his lip and he snarls into my mouth, making me even wetter for him.

"I want to feel you come like this," he says in a gravelly whisper before kissing the spot between my neck and shoulder.

Before I can respond, Valentino pinches my clit and bites my shoulder, making my pussy snap almost painfully tight around him.

"God fucking damn, I love feeling you squeeze my cock," he rasps.

I think he's going to come too, but instead, he pulls out and flips me back over, entering me again in one swift motion.

"Valentino!" I scream, coming again, or maybe still. I claw at his back as my body jerks, every movement sparking a deep, insatiable need.

"Katya," he grunts, holding himself up on one hand beside my head. His other hand grips my hip and steadies my trembling body as he buries his massive dick inside me again and again, tearing me apart ruthlessly in the best way possible.

Each stroke winds me up, up, up, my pleasure mounting into an almost unbearable orgasm. Everything goes white as my climax ravishes me from the inside out. My back bows, pressing my tits up against Valentino's hard muscles, and then I curl up in his arms, burying my head in his chest right as he roars his own release.

His arms give out and Valentino collapses on top of me, his large, warm body blanketing mine and keeping me sheltered from the storm of emotions and sensations rushing through my body. He tries to roll away, but I cling to him, needing his skin on my skin just a little bit longer.

"I don't want to crush you, princess," he chuckles into the side of my neck before kissing me there.

Valentino rolls to the side but keeps me in his arms, pressing me close to his body. My eyes are closed and I'm still shaking from my multiple orgasms, but Valentino slowly calms me down with the gentle touch of his fingertips swirling over my skin.

When I open my eyes, I'm floored by the look of awe in his deep brown gaze.

"That was...Jesus, that was amazing."

I nod and grin at him, giggling when he kisses all over my face. He tucks my hair behind my ear and presses his lips to mine, just savoring our closeness.

We stay like that for a while, on our sides, facing one another. Valentino runs his hand up and down my curves, tracing my outline, drawing me into being, giving me shape and purpose and meaning.

Eventually, Valentino readjusts us so he can pull the covers over our naked bodies. I curl up against his side, feeling safer and more loved than I can ever remember.

CHAPTER SEVEN

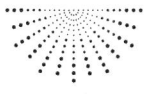

VALENTINO

"*W*hat the hell?" I mutter to myself as I pull the pan of what was supposed to be muffins out of the oven. Instead of having fluffy tops, these muffins are flat. How I managed to both burn the edges and undercook the center is a mystery to me.

So much for putting together a nice meal for Katya. She's made me hot chocolate, chicken alfredo, and cupcakes. It's only fair that I cook for her as well. Too bad I suck at anything culinary-related.

Growing up, my mom moved from one wealthy monster to another. We had chefs, so there was no need to learn how to cook. Once I escaped that prison at eighteen, I lived off whatever I could scrounge for until the Di Salvos picked me up and made me what I am today.

I'll just have to find a few easy recipes to start, then build my repertoire from there. I want to be able to provide my woman with everything, including her favorite meals.

I can't help the grin tugging at my lips. I sound like such a sap. I sound like someone I would have made fun of just a few short weeks ago. Actually, I remember telling our enforcer, Armando, that I couldn't understand his irrational attachment to Allegra. Seeing him, as well as Dante and Romeo find love was shocking and confusing to me. I didn't understand how one person could change your life so completely in the blink of an eye, or how priorities shift when you find someone worth keeping.

My situation is different from theirs, however. Katya is an enemy of the family, and a powerful one at that. She could be an important bargaining chip or give us intel on her father and his men. There are about a dozen things I should have done once I figured out who was squatting in the warehouse, but I couldn't bring myself to do any of them. I just... knew she was mine. Even back then, when I was fighting it with every cell in my body.

What the hell am I going to do? I've been wracking my mind for a solution, but can't seem to think of a way to keep Katya and my position within the family.

Usually, I'd talk to Armando about any problems I'm having, or Romeo himself if the occasion called for it. I trust both men with my life, and I wouldn't be in the inner circle if they didn't trust me with theirs.

I can't talk to anyone from the Di Salvos about this. Not until I have a plan.

Walking out of the kitchen, I peer up the stairs, listening for any sounds indicating Katya is awake. She was sleeping so soundly when I got up this morning, I couldn't bring myself to disturb her. She looked absolutely angelic with the golden morning light pouring over her soft skin and high-lighting her curves.

She must still be asleep, which makes me smirk. We wore each other out last night, and she deserves her rest.

Satisfied that I have a little while until she wakes up, I grab my phone from the counter and call one of two friends I have outside of the family. It rings a few times, and I pace

VALENTINO

around my kitchen, trying to decide if I should hang up and not bother with it.

"Val?" comes a raspy voice slurred with sleep.

Hawk is the only person who can call me that and get away with it. We've known each other for most of our lives, and everyone called me Val growing up. When I left that life, I left Val behind. I've been Valentino ever since.

"You there?" he asks.

"Yeah," I answer, clearing my throat.

"Everything okay? What fuckin' time is it?"

"Uh…"

"Seven-thirty in the morning? Not cool," he groans dramatically. I can just picture him running a hand through his messy hair as he flops back down on his bed. He never was a morning person, even before he joined the Savage Saints MC.

"Not all of us party at the clubhouse until three in the morning," I counter.

"I haven't lived that life for years and you know it," he grouses. "Besides, are you really trying to argue the moral high ground between the mafia and an outlaw MC?"

"No, I'm just giving you shit because you're easy to rile up."

"Remind me why I'm your friend?" he mutters, though I know he's mostly over it.

He doesn't stay upset for long. Despite being a high-ranking member of Savage Saints, Hawk is basically a golden retriever. Maybe that should have been his road name instead of Hawk.

"Because it's good to have friends in low places," I tease.

Hawk grunts then lets out a chuckle. "So what's up, Val? Why the early morning wake-up call?"

I sigh as I continue to circle around the kitchen restlessly.

"I have a… situation," I start. "A sensitive situation that I couldn't trust anyone else with."

My friend hums over the line, and I can tell he's focused on the conversation now. We give each other shit, but at the end of the day, we'll always have each other's back.

"There's a woman. She's… well, she's important to me. I think she's it. Like, the one or whatever sappy bullshit you want to call it."

I'm expecting Hawk to come in with a jab about falling in love, but he's surprisingly quiet. Strange.

"But she's also the daughter of our rivals. She ran away from her family, straight across enemy lines and into our territory. I should have called the Boss when I found her, but I just…"

"Couldn't let him decide her fate," Hawk finishes for me.

"Exactly. And now I don't know what the hell to do."

We're silent for a few moments, then Hawk clears his throat and whispers, "Believe it or not, I'm in a similar situation. Not the same, but there's this new waitress at the club-house, and she… Well, it's not about that right now," he cuts himself off. "Have you thought about telling the Boss? Maybe he'll understand."

"Are you going to tell the President of Savage Saints about your mysterious waitress situation?" I counter.

"I said it wasn't the same. Also, you're the one who called me, remember?"

I grunt in response, making Hawk laugh. "I need to figure out how to prove my loyalty and hat Katya is on our side. Tensions are high right now. We're on the razor's edge of an all-out war, and I've been harboring the enemy for over a week."

"Damn," he says, followed by a low whistle. "Have you talked to your woman about this? Katya, right?"

"Yeah. Well, no. I mean, she knows the situation, so what is there to talk about?"

"*This*," he answers emphatically. "This conversation. You know I appreciate your calls and your friendship, but these are the decisions you make as a couple. Share your fears and then figure out how to support each other and all that shit."

I chuckle. "I was calling for advice on handling my boss, and here you are, doling out relationship tips."

"Yeah, yeah, don't mention it," he jokes. "Just remember to send me an invite to the wedding. It's been a long time since I've visited NYC."

"Same to you and your waitress. Can't say I'll be thrilled to get gravel dust on my three-piece suit, but these are the kinds of sacrifices I make for our friendship."

Hawk laughs, and we say our goodbyes. No sooner do I set down the phone than the sweet, sleepy voice of my princess filters into the kitchen.

"Did you make breakfast?" she asks.

I spin around, my eyes roaming over Katya's body. She's in one of my shirts again, her hair a bit messy in the sexiest way, and a smile on her face that I'll never forget.

How is she this perfect combination of sweet, sassy, and drop-dead gorgeous? I don't know, but I'd like to spend the rest of my life figuring it out.

"I attempted to," I reply, tearing my gaze away from her to frown at the pan of ruined muffins. "But it turns out I'm not a baker."

Katya giggles, the sound lighter than air as it floats around the kitchen. She steps closer, rocking back and forth on her heels as those golden eyes meet mine. "I can teach you some things if you'd like," she says, leaning forward until her lips are barely an inch from mine.

"Only if I get to teach you a few things, too," I murmur, my tone deep and desperate.

"Like what?" Katya whispers, her breath tickling my lips.

I growl and take her hips in my hands, pulling her into my body and rubbing her soft belly up against my rock-hard cock. How is it possible to miss her already? I was inside of her less than eight hours ago, and yet everything in me is pulsing, panting, crying out for more.

"Like how much pleasure your curvy little body can handle and how many ways I can get you to come for me."

Katya moans and tilts her head back so I can bite and suck her sensitive skin. Her fingernails claw down my bare chest, and then she tugs at the waistband of my sweatpants to undress me, giving me permission to do the same to her.

I should slow down and make sure she's not too sore after last night, but one look in her hungry eyes lets me know she doesn't need my words, she needs my actions.

It's now my job to give Katya everything she's ever wanted, starting with my swollen fucking cock.

Gripping her hips, I spin her around so she's facing the kitchen counter. I nibble on her pulse point and lick away the sting before grazing my lips on the shell of her ear.

"Hands on the counter, princess. Bend over and show me that ass."

Katya moans and bends over, giving me permission to fulfill my deepest desire. I smooth my hands over the soft, porcelain skin of her ass, admiring everything about this goddess. She turns, looking at me over her shoulder. The image almost does me in, almost makes me burst on the spot.

"Are you going to fuck me, or just look at me?" Katya lifts a sassy eyebrow in challenge.

I remove my hands and then bring one down to smack her bare ass cheek, loving the way it jiggles and turns pink.

"Ah!" she yelps in surprise.

"That's for sassing me, Katya."

She glares at me, and I spank her again, watching her eyes

close and listening to the way her breath hitches when I make contact.

"You like that?" I grunt, massaging the sting away.

"Mmmm," she purrs as I continue to rub her heated flesh.

Sliding a hand down her front, I dip my fingers into her soaking wet pussy, chuckling darkly as I slowly circle her clit.

"Please, Valentino," she begs. "I need it. I need you."

Fuck, I need her too.

I whip out my dick and tease her entrance, running the head up and down her seam, collecting her sweet honey. Grabbing her hips, I position myself at her entrance and slam into her. Hard.

It takes everything in me not to come the instant I'm inside her. I pull out and thrust back inside one inch at a time, feeling the way her tight entrance stretches and pulses around me as I surge forward.

Katya bucks her hips, fucking me right back as we set a relentless pace. My hands slide from her hips and grab her ass cheeks, pulling them apart so I can see her pussy swallow my cock with each thrust. I keep rolling my hips, pounding into her as I feel my orgasm ready to rip through me.

I reach around and rub her clit, needing her to come first. Katya lets out a loud moan, her entire body tensing and spasming beneath me. I hook my other arm under her hips, holding her in place while I rut into her, barreling toward oblivion.

"Come on, baby," I grunt into the shell of her ear. "Come for me. Come so fucking hard."

I sink my teeth into her shoulder and she snaps, convulsing in my arms and shaking all over. Her pussy chokes my cock so fucking tight. It's amazing. I want to stay right here, on the edge of bliss, watching her convulse around my huge dick.

But I can't hang on another second. I thrust into her one

last time and explode, painting her pussy with my sticky cum. I continue to pump into her as she pulses around me again, my release triggering another earthquake inside her.

Katya's arms shake as she holds herself up on the counter, and I cover her with my body, placing my arms on either side of hers. We're both sweaty and panting as we slowly float back down to earth.

I tuck myself back inside my sweatpants, then turn Katya around, sliding her shirt over her arms and head. She's barely standing on her own, and I chuckle as I gather her limp body up and carry her over to the couch.

As soon as I sit down, my princess curls up against my chest, resting her head on my shoulder. I smooth her hair away from her face, then trail my fingertips across her neck, over her shoulder, and down her arm before reversing my path.

Katya relaxes completely, the tension draining from her muscles the longer I hold her.

"Valentino?" she whispers.

"Yes, princess?" I ask softly, continuing to stroke her side and neck.

"Earlier, when you were first bandaging me up, you said you learned at a young age how to take care of wounds." My breath catches in my throat, but I manage to swallow it down and give her a nod. "Can you tell me what happened? I just… I just want to know you. Everything about you."

She blinks up at me, and I'm struck by her purity, her goodness and light even though life hasn't been kind to her. Katya is dealing with so much, and yet she's making space to take on my burdens as well. She's truly incredible. I don't deserve her, but Katya is mine now, and I'm keeping her.

Leaning forward slightly, I press a kiss to her forehead and nose, savoring the connection before spilling my heart out to the only woman who has ever mattered to me.

"My dad took off when I was a kid, leaving me with my shallow, social-climbing mother. Her second husband was a bank president with a penchant for whiskey. He wasn't so bad, but his money ran out too quickly for my mother's growing appetite for the finer things."

I roll my eyes and scoff, remembering the day my mom and I moved out of the three-story mansion we'd been staying at for the last year. Katya runs her fingers over my collarbone, tracing my tattoos as she listens.

"She moved on to a hedge fund manager and strung him along for over a year, getting him to buy us a condo in Midtown while she cheated on him the entire time. After she milked him for all she could, dear ol' Mom was breaking her way into the upper echelons of society. That's when she doubled down on finding men who were richer than God and meaner than the devil."

"I'm so sorry," Katya whispers, her amber eyes peering into my very soul and comforting me on a deeper level than I knew possible.

I kiss her forehead before continuing. "I couldn't protect her when I was a kid. I tried, only to get tossed into a wall or beaten with a belt buckle. That's when I learned all I could about first aid. If I couldn't prevent the beatings, at least I could clean up the aftermath."

Katya gasps, her eyes filling with tears.

"Don't cry for me, sweet girl," I murmur. "I got my vengeance. After a decade of putting up with one abusive asshole after another, I beat the living shit out of the man we were living with at the time. I begged my mother to come with me, to leave the monstrous men of her past behind. But she refused. She told me... ah, fuck, princess. I don't mean to weigh you down with all of this."

"I want to know," she insists. "I asked, didn't I? Plus,

you've listened to all of my life problems for the last week. It's only fair to share some of yours."

I nod, then cup the back of her neck, pulling her in for a soft kiss. I hope she can feel how much this means to me, how our souls are now tied together forever.

Looking away from Katya, I take a deep breath and let out the last of my pitiful tale. "My mother told me everything in life comes at a price. Her highest goal was wealth, and she willingly sacrificed her health and safety to attain it."

"But *you* didn't have a choice!" Katya says with a surprising amount of anger. "Your mom had no right to sacrifice *your* safety for the sake of living the high life. How dare she?!"

I didn't think it was possible to smile after talking about such personal, painful things, but seeing my woman all worked up and ready to defend me has a grin pulling at my lips.

"I told her the exact same thing before walking away for good," I murmur. "My mother knows she can call me if and when she's ready to start a new life, but I'm not holding my breath."

Katya rests her forehead on mine, her hand coming up to cover my heart. "Thank you for sharing that with me," she whispers. "So, how did you end up with the Di Salvos?"

Gathering her hand up in mine, I kiss her knuckles before setting it back down on my chest. "I had nothing and no one, but I knew there was one place an Italian down on his luck could find work. Down by the docks."

She nods, knowing what I mean. That's where hopefuls line up to be recruited. If they complete an assignment quickly and efficiently, they get another one. And another. Until they're either proven too weak to stomach the life or promoted out of the rank of recruit.

"I got my first assignment when I was eighteen, promoted

to soldier at twenty, and then made Capo at twenty-five when I was given my own territory to manage. Last year, I joined the top-ranking officials in the inner circle. I…" I trail off, not sure why I said all of that.

"You've worked so hard to get to where you are today," Katya says softly. "And now…" she shrugs and looks away from me, but I'm not having any of that.

Cupping her chin, I gently turn her so she's facing me again. "And now?"

"I'm ruining everything," she chokes out, tears streaming down her cheeks. "I showed up and complicated your life, and now I'm ruining everything you've built. I'm sor–"

"Don't you dare apologize," I warn her, tucking a few strands of hair behind her ear. "You're not ruining anything. You have no idea how much you mean to me."

"But I'm the enemy. How can this possibly end well?"

"You're not the enemy," I growl, not liking those words coming out of her mouth. "I know things seem… unclear right now, but we'll figure it out."

"You'll lose everything, Valentino."

"The only way I could lose everything is if you walk away from me," I murmur, locking my eyes on hers. "I love you, Katya. I love everything about you. I love how strong you are in the face of danger and how selfless you are, even when you're hurting. I love your smile and laughter, the taste of your kisses, and your sinful curves. Princess, I'm afraid I can't let you go. I won't."

"You… love me?" she asks, disbelief evident in her gaze. Katya sniffles, her brow furrowing as she studies me.

"More than you could ever know," I promise.

A brilliant smile lights up her face, even with tears still falling down her cheeks. She's sunshine and rain and everything my dormant heart needs to grow.

"I love you, too, for the record."

"Say it again," I grunt, clenching my jaw as I stare at her lips.

"I love you, Valentino. I can't believe it's true, but I just… you make me feel so safe and wanted for the first time in my life. I don't think anyone has ever called me beautiful before. I didn't believe you when you said it to me the first time."

"Katya," I rasp, hating that she's had so little love and acknowledgment in her life. I vow to compliment her at least ten times a day until she starts to see herself through my eyes. And then I'll just keep on reminding her of her worth every single day for the rest of our lives.

"But you've shown me with your actions, your words, your entire being how much you care for me. I want to be the same for you. I love you."

I take her lips in a gentle kiss that turns heated quickly. Our tongues tangle, our breaths mingling as we pour out everything we can't say. Right as I start to slide my hands up Katya's shirt, my phone rings. I groan, breaking our kiss, while Katya continues to nibble my neck and chest.

"God, you feel so good," I breathe, hissing when she claws down my chest.

My phone rings again, and I know I need to answer it. Dante has been checking in on me a lot more the last few days. I'm trying not to be paranoid, but I'm starting to think he suspects me of betraying the family.

A third ring finally breaks my lustful haze enough to lean back and help Katya off my lap.

"Sorry, I should really take this."

She nods in understanding, but I know she's anxious.

By the time I reach my phone, the call went to voicemail. Shit.

A second later, a text pops up on the screen from Dante. *Come to the compound ASAP.*

Double shit.

"Everything okay?" Katya asks from her position on the couch.

"Yeah," I choke out. "Fine." She frowns at me. "I need to go into work. Important meeting just came up."

"Do you think…?"

She doesn't have to finish the sentence for me to know what she's asking. Do I think it's about us?

"No," I tell her, though I'm not so sure. I've taken off at odd hours the last week, and I know Dante keeps meticulous notes on all of that shit.

"For a made man, you kind of suck at lying," she sasses.

I grin at her and shake my head. "Whatever the meeting is about, I can handle it. Oh, I'll bring home breakfast for us since I screwed up the muffins."

Katya nods, though I can see the tension in her eyes. She's worried about me, and I can't say that's ever happened before.

I clean up and change into a suit in record time. The sooner I leave, the sooner I can get back to my woman. I know she'll be anxious the whole time I'm gone.

"Everything will be okay," I tell her before kissing the top of her head. She's still on the couch, wrapped up in a blanket. "Watch some TV and I'll be back before you know it."

"You better be," she says, trying to sound tough.

I give her one last kiss, keeping it brief, otherwise I'll strip both of us naked and take her again. There will be time for that when I get back. Hopefully.

CHAPTER EIGHT

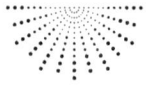

KATYA

*A*s soon as I hear Valentino's car pulling out of the driveway, I hop off the couch and sprint to the guest room I've been staying in. Rummaging around in the pile of clothes I came here in a week ago, I search for the nondescript notebook I stole from my father's office before sneaking out last week.

It was a last-minute decision, and I knew it was risky, but now I'm glad I made the effort. I'm positive he has no idea it was me, even if the timing matches up.

When my father wasn't yelling at me or teaching me a lesson with the back of his hand, he ignored me. I could be in the same room, sitting at the same table, and he would have no idea I was there. He didn't see me unless there was a problem. I spent most of my life resenting him for his heartlessness, but in this case, it worked out to my advantage.

I overheard him multiple times arguing with his second-in-command about keeping records. My father was insistent that there should be only one copy of the most important documents, and it would be handwritten. Otherwise, according to him, anyone could get their hands on it. No matter how many times they tried to tell him things were more secure than ever online, he never caved.

Pride comes before the fall, as they say. And what a fall it will be.

"Yes," I whisper to myself when my fingers graze across the cover of the small notebook. I tucked it in my bra for safe keeping, and luckily, was able to keep it hidden.

My stomach twists itself into knots at the thought of keeping a secret from Valentino. I hope when all is said and done, he'll understand why it had to be this way.

I quickly throw on a pair of leggings, a tank top, and a zip-up hoodie, slipping the notebook into the pocket of the oversized sweatshirt. I make my way downstairs, pausing in the kitchen where I saw a change jar tucked away in the corner of the counter. Dumping half of it out, I pick through the quarters until I have about twenty-five dollars. I'm hoping that will be enough to get me to the Di Salvo compound using public transportation.

A bus ride, a subway venture, and another bus ride later, I'm about a mile away from the compound. At least, I hope. My father has a section in his notebook for addresses and phone numbers of enemies, including the compounds of all the rival families in the city.

I'm not quite sure what my plan is, only that I have to do something. Valentino said he could handle the meeting on his own. He also said it wasn't about us, but I saw the doubt in his gaze as he told me both of those lies.

He's trying so hard to protect me, but who is going to protect him? I wish he would have talked to me about a plan for handling this instead of leaving me to take care of it himself.

I take calming breaths as I continue walking through the remote neighborhood containing the Di Salvo compound. The magnificent mansions grow farther and farther apart until I come across a large fortress surrounded by gates, cameras, and guards.

Bingo.

Shoring up the last of my courage, I straighten my spine, press my shoulders back, and lift my chin as I stride toward the front gate. The two guards out front take notice right away. One of them says something into the walkie-talkie attached to his shoulder while the other widens his stance and rests his hand on the gun tucked into his jacket.

I continue walking forward, my head held high, projecting a confidence I don't feel. I can see the moment they recognize me. Both men turn to each other, a look of disbelief and confusion shared between them.

I know they won't shoot me now they know I'm royalty. I'm too high up the food chain for them to pull the trigger without an order. Raising my hands in surrender, I continue moving forward until one of the men grabs my wrists, gathering them up in his large hand and holding them behind my back.

"What's a little Colombo princess doing so far away from her father's castle?" he sneers.

"That's between Romeo and me," I reply in a crisp tone.

The other man grunts, and the two exchange a glance and a nod. He stays put while the first guard shoves me forward, nearly making me fall on my face.

"Right this way, your highness," he says in a mocking tone.

I'm dragged through the house until I stand in front of a set of double doors made of solid oak and accented with gold. The guard pounds his fist on the door twice, then clears his throat.

"Boss? I've got a visitor here for you. You're going to want to talk to her."

"I don't have time," comes the harsh voice of who I assume is Romeo Di Salvo.

The guard is about to knock again, and I use the momentary distraction to pry my wrists from his death grip and lunge forward, grabbing the door handles and pulling them with all my might. The doors fly open, catching me off balance as I stumble inside the room.

My eyes are immediately drawn to Valentino, who jumps to his feet at the sight of me. Two other men I don't recognize are seated on the opposite side of the room. Before Valentino can say anything, I fix my gaze on Romeo, staring into his dark brown eyes and pleading with him to hear me out. "I'm Katya Colombo, and I ran away from my family over a week ago. I don't want anything to do with them anymore."

Romeo's eyebrows twitch upward slightly before he gains control of his features. Aside from that, his face is one of practiced indifference. "And why should we believe you?"

"Because–"

"I can vouch for her," Valentino says, stepping up next to me. I glare at him, and he glares back.

"I'm doing this to save you," I hiss at him. "Stop ruining it!"

Valentino doesn't back away. Instead, he wraps an arm around my waist and tucks me into his side. "If we go down, we go down together, princess."

"Someone better tell me what the fuck is going on," Romeo commands, his voice hard as granite.

"It's not Valentino's fault. Please don't blame him," I start, focusing on the Boss. "I ran away last week, and he found me."

"Katya," Valentino warns, but I keep going. I have no choice now. I jumped off the edge of a canyon, and I'm praying to every god I can think of that I land on the other side.

"Don't tell me she was the squatter in the warehouse," Romeo grits out, cutting a fierce glance at Valentino.

"I can explain," Valentino hedges.

"I was hurt," I jump in. "Bleeding real bad."

"My men roughed you up?" Romeo asks, some of the bite gone from his tone.

I'll never get used to people being upset over me getting hurt. Even though I'm part of a rival family, these men have a moral code not to harm me unnecessarily.

"No, the damage had already been done," I answer, looking away from him. I feel weak and stupid, but I press on, knowing that my mission is life or death. "By a man my father promised me to. I knew running away was risky, but I'd rather die fighting for my freedom than live with that abusive piece of shit day in and day out."

Valentino squeezes me closer to his side, turning his head so he can press his lips to my temple. I'm shaking from head to toe, but my man is right here with me, giving me the strength to continue.

"And you've been staying with…?"

"Me," Valentino responds. "I should have told you sooner, I just didn't know what to do," he says, bowing his head in deference to the Don. "She's already been through so much," he adds.

Romeo grunts, nodding his head once. "Why did you come here today, Katya? Why risk your life and your current set-up with Valentino? What's the advantage?"

"I couldn't live with myself if Valentino was harmed because he saved me, and it was only going to be a matter of time before the truth came out. But I have something important I hope you'll take in exchange for sparing Valentino."

"What?" Valentino whispers in my ear. "What are you doing, baby?"

"Something I should have done when you first found me," I whisper back. "I didn't know who I could trust, but I know now I should have trusted you. It's the only way I could think of to help."

Romeo clears his throat, and we both turn back to him.

I pull the little notebook out of my sweatshirt pocket, holding it out for Romeo to see. "I stole this before I left. My idiot father doesn't trust computers or the internet, so he keeps his most important notes written in here," I inform him, shaking the notebook for emphasis. "It's how I found your compound. It also contains numbers and addresses for numerous friends and foes, as well as coordinates for all kinds of weapons and storehouses."

The Boss raises an eyebrow, then holds out his hand.

I hold the notebook out slightly above his open palm, then stare at him directly in the eye. "If I give you this, you promise not to punish Valentino for being nice to me, right?"

"I'm not being nice to you," Valentino grumbles. "I fucking love you."

This startles the other two men in the room, as well as Romeo. For a brief moment, the infamous mafia boss looks surprised, followed by a flash of a smile, but he schools his face over before I can be sure what I saw.

"Usually, I don't negotiate," Romeo answers. "Especially with a Colombo."

Valentino growls softly, and I nudge him with my hip to shut up.

"And Valentino and I will need to have a chat about hiding things from me," Romeo continues. "But if what you say is true, and if Valentino's confession of love is real, then yes, we have a deal."

"Take me instead," I ramble, my mind still playing catch-up with the conversation. "Don't hurt Valentino. He's a good man."

"Katya, he said–"

"I'll lure my father out for you," I offer, scrambling to think of some way I can be valuable to Romeo. "I can–"

"Katya." This time, it's Romeo who says my name.

My eyes snap to his, my heart rattling around in my ribcage the longer I look at him.

"I said we had a deal."

"Wh-what? Really?" I blink at Romeo, not sure if this is all some cruel joke.

"Is that so hard to believe?"

"Yes," I answer truthfully. This earns me a smirk from Romeo. "I don't think anyone has ever listened to me."

Valentino kisses my temple again and whispers, "We're different from your family."

"That's a shame," Romeo finally says. "From what I can tell, you're brave, bold, and strong enough to fight for the life you want. You're clearly loyal to Valentino, even willing to offer your life for his. Those are excellent qualities for any mafioso to have."

A rush of emotions sweeps through me, stealing the breath from my lungs. "Thank you," I murmur, bowing my head at his compliment.

I place the notebook in Romeo's hand, then look over my shoulder at Valentino.

He spins me around in his arms and gathers me against his chest, nuzzling into the top of my head. "You should have told me what you were going to do," he whispers.

"You wouldn't have let me go through with it," I counter.

"Of course not."

"Well, goddamn," Romeo says, followed by a low whistle. He flips through a few more pages of the notebook, then looks around the room. "Jackpot, men. We have the location of their latest weapons haul."

He rattles off the address, and one of the men starts making notes on his laptop. I peer over at the other man who has been sitting in the corner, not saying a word. He has a goofy grin on his face, shaking his head at Valentino.

"Told you love would hit you in the chest like a lead pipe," the man says.

Valentino chuckles. "You also said not to fight it. Took me a little bit on that last part, but now that we're here…" He trails off, his gaze wandering back to me. "I wouldn't have it any other way."

I beam up at him, still not quite believing it all worked out. As if sensing my thoughts, Valentino hugs me closer, wrapping his arms around my back and stroking up and down my spine.

"We good here, Boss?" Valentino asks.

"What?" he grunts, his nose still buried in the notebook. "Oh. Yes, you two may go. Dante and I will go over the rest of these notes and have a plan of attack soon."

"Thank you," I say as Valentino takes my hand and starts pulling me toward the door.

Romeo nods. "Your loyalty will be tested in the days to come. This is a good start," he says, holding out the notebook.

"I won't back down," I tell him, clenching my jaw. "I'll fight beside you until every last one of my father's men is taken out."

"The hell you will," Valentino grunts.

I roll my eyes at him, which makes the other three men in the room laugh.

Without another word, Valentino tugs me the rest of the way out into the hall, then scoops me up in his arms, bridal style. I giggle and kick out my legs as he races toward the front door and down the porch steps.

"Where are we going?" I ask as he sets me down in front of his car. Valentino helps me into the passenger seat, then buckles my seatbelt before kissing my forehead.

"Need to get you home. Need to feel you, princess. All of you. Jesus, you scared me."

I cup his cheeks, drawing his face closer to mine. "I didn't mean to scare you. I just knew I had to do something."

"And now it's my turn to do something," he says with a wicked grin.

Valentino closes my door and hurries around to the driver's side, hopping in and peeling out of the Di Salvo compound.

CHAPTER NINE

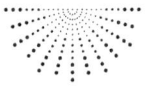

VALENTINO

*A*s soon as we get inside, I spin Katya around, pressing her against the closed door before crashing my lips down on hers. She grabs my shirt and pulls me closer as she sucks on my tongue, welcoming my kiss and fighting me for control.

"You shouldn't have put yourself at risk like that," I rasp before sucking on her neck.

"You would have done the same for me," Katya breathes, tipping her head back to give me more access to her creamy skin.

I glide my tongue over her flesh, nipping the sensitive spot below her ear before kissing away the sting. "It would have been a worthy sacrifice," I murmur, leaning back a bit to look her in the eyes. "But your life for mine? That doesn't make sense."

She furrows her brow in confusion, a heartbreaking look taking over her features. "Do you really think you're worth so little?"

"I… Well, I…" I look away from her, not sure how to answer.

Katya lays her palm gently against the side of my cheek, directing my gaze back to hers. "You're my whole world, Valentino. Whatever protective feelings you have for me, I also have them for you. Is that so hard to believe?"

"Yes," I answer truthfully, my voice hardly above a whisper. "But I believe you. I want to be the man you think I am. I want to be better for you, Katya."

"You're already so good to me," she says softly, her lips brushing against mine.

I welcome her kiss, letting her take the lead and falling under her spell once more. She writhes against my body, her nails digging into the back of my neck as she clings to me.

"Katya," I groan, resting my forehead against hers.

"Need you," she pleads, her voice breathy and laced with an undeniable urgency.

I growl into her lips, biting and nipping at her before licking into her mouth. My hands slide up the shirt she's wearing, pushing the fabric up as I feel every inch of her soft, porcelain skin. She moans and drags her hands down my chest, her fingers tugging at my belt and then working my button and zipper open. Katya grips my hard as fuck dick, pulling me out and pumping me roughly.

"Fuck," I groan, loving the fact that she's this needy, this turned-on, and this desperate for me. The thought makes me grunt possessively as I peel off her leggings, my hands finding the little lacy scrap of fabric covering her pussy. I rip it off her body and swallow her gasp as my fingers slide through her folds.

Goddamn, she's *soaked* for me, her cream dripping over my fingers and pooling in my hand. I circle her clit, the hard little pearl throbbing and swollen. Her legs shake, and I swear she's about to come from that one touch.

Without wasting any time, I grip her thighs and lift her up, pressing her against the door as she wraps her legs around my hips and digs her fingers into my shoulders. I look directly into her lust-filled eyes as I slam my cock inside her greedy little cunt.

Katya sucks in a breath and bites her lip to contain her scream. She comes as soon as I hit the end of her. I growl and hold myself deep inside her, feeling her orgasm from the inside out, wave after wave of ecstasy rippling from her core and dripping down my aching dick.

She buries her head in the side of my neck, panting and shaking and whimpering my name. It's more than I can take. I pull out of her pulsing, tight little pussy and push back inside, fucking her roughly, just like we both need.

"Valentino… oh fuck, Valentino… I-I-I'm…"

Holy shit. Is she...?

The goddess in my arms tangles her fingers in my hair and rips my head up, the sting shooting bliss straight to my cock, making it swell and stretch her out even more. Katya rests her sweaty forehead on mine, her chest heaving with each ragged breath as pained whimpers and grunts leave her mouth with each brutal thrust I give her.

"Come for me, princess," I growl.

My words unlock her orgasm, and Jesus, she comes so hard, shaking and sobbing out her release as her arms and legs squeeze me tightly. I grip her ass in both hands, holding her to me as I grind against her cunt and clit, keeping her right there, forcing her to feel it, feel me, feel every ounce of pleasure I'm giving her.

My balls are heavy with my pent-up orgasm, my dick throbbing and angry as fuck. But I want more. So much more. And I know exactly how I want it.

I set Katya down, her legs trembling much like the rest of her. She tilts her head up, peering at me through the fog of bliss surrounding her. I kiss her forehead, nose, and lips, allowing her to catch her breath.

And then I spin her around, pushing her forward so she has to brace herself with her hands on the door. I grip her cheeks, spreading her open for me so I can sink into her tight, wet little hole. With a feral roar, I snap my hips against her ass, stuffing her full of my thickness.

"S-s-so d-d-deep," Katya stutters out with a moan as her pussy contracts around me over and over.

I'm reduced to grunts and growls, tipping my head back and bouncing her off my dick. Every muscle in my body tenses and my balls draw up tight, my orgasm crawling down my spine and stealing the air from my lungs.

Sliding one arm beneath Katya's hips, I hold her still as I piston in and out of her. She claws at the door, then balls her hand up in a fist and pounds it against the wood as she succumbs to a final, vicious orgasm.

I slide my hand further down her body, rubbing her clit in furious circles as my other hand grabs a fistful of her silky black hair. She soaks my shaft with her cum and shudders in my arms. I bury my face between her neck and shoulder, breathing her in, feeling her shiver and pulse around me as I finally let go.

My orgasm barrels through me, clutching my muscles and making me shake uncontrollably as I come harder than I ever have. I shoot my release deep inside her still-throbbing core, each rope of cum forcing its way out in blissful, torturous waves.

It lasts forever, and yet it will never be enough. I know I'll want this woman wrapped around me as often as possible, chasing our pleasure and taking each other to heights unknown.

We both groan as I reluctantly pull out of her. I growl when I see our combined releases dripping down the insides of her thighs. I resist the urge to get on my knees and lick it up.

Katya leans against the door, pressing her forehead against the wood as she tries to control her breathing.

I smirk, knowing I gave her so many orgasms she can barely function. "Come here, baby," I say softly, holding out my hand.

Katya turns toward me, taking my hand and letting me gather her up in my arms.

"Love you so much," I whisper as I lift her and carry her to the couch.

"Love you, too," she mumbles, curling up on my chest once I sit down.

"I still can't believe you showed up at the Di Salvo compound to defend me," I tell her after a few moments of silence.

"I thought we already went over this, but I can give you a reminder if you need it." Katya lifts her head slightly, those golden eyes capturing mine as she smiles sweetly.

"I'm half-convinced I dreamt you up. There's no other explanation for why you want me."

My woman furrows her brow and flares her nostrils as she glares at me. "Valentino I-Don't-Know-Your-Middle-Name Rossi," she starts, her tone like that of a teacher scolding a disruptive child. "I don't want to hear you talk like that anymore. You're the most important person in my life, the only one who has ever given a damn about my well-being. You're selfless and fierce when it comes to protecting the things you love, and I take offense to your statement."

I can't help the smirk stretching across my face. She's so fucking adorable when she's all worked up like this, and over me, no less.

"I'm serious, mister!"

"I know you are, princess," I whisper, kissing her forehead and nose. "I'm still getting used to having someone care about me the way you do. It's humbling. I don't know what I did to deserve you, and I'm terrified I'm going to fuck it all up."

"I could say the same to you," she counters. "But instead of questioning our worth or worrying about the future, I say we just be thankful for what we've found. You're not going to fuck it up, Valentino."

"How do you know? What if I say something stupid or forget an important date or let the dishes pile up in the sink?"

"My love for you is bigger than all of that," she replies easily.

I grin, taking her lips in a tender kiss. "And my love is bigger than all of that as well," I whisper. "Thank you, Katya."

"For what?"

"For being you. For choosing me. For knowing how to soothe my dark places."

"Always," she murmurs, resting her forehead on mine.

"Always," I echo, cupping the side of her face to keep her close.

I soak up this moment with the love of my life, committing everything to memory. We'll be going to war soon, and knowing I have her waiting for me at home gives me the strength to do what I need to do. I will protect Katya and eliminate the threat of her family.

And then I'll come back and make sure Katya is mine forever.

CHAPTER TEN

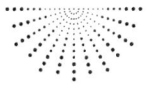

KATYA

"*How* ow many knives do you have?" I ask Valentino as he checks the magazine in his 9 mm handgun. "They're better for hand-to-hand combat."

Valentino pauses, looking at me with a raised eyebrow. "Is that so?" he asks with a grin.

"Yes," I tell him sternly, crossing my arms over my chest. "And stop smirking at me. You're heading into war, and I'm trying to give you some pointers."

His face softens slightly, those brown eyes finding mine and somehow imparting comfort and safety. We spent the rest of yesterday and last night in bed, with a few breaks for food and a shower. This morning, Romeo rounded up the troops and handed down orders. Valentino and the other men in the inner circle have been prepping all day, and now he's home to gather supplies before heading out to the Colombo warehouse.

"I've been doing this a long damn time, princess," he says, projecting confidence even though I see a hint of doubt in his deep brown eyes. No one else would notice, but I feel everything he's feeling.

"And I tackled your gun from your hands ten seconds after meeting you," I counter, lifting my chin and narrowing my eyes at the stupidly sexy man standing a few feet away from me.

Valentino smiles, then sets the gun down on the coffee table before holding his hand out to me. "Come here, Katya," he says soothingly.

I give him one last glare, then rest my hand in his open palm. He pulls me into his arms, pressing kisses to my temple, nose, cheek, and lips. Valentino circles his arms around my waist, drawing me closer as he rests his forehead on mine.

"I know you're worried," he starts, his voice washing over me like a cool breeze on a hot day. "But I promise you, I'll be right back here in your arms soon."

"But what if–"

"You can't think like that," Valentino whispers, smoothing his thumb over my cheek. "All the hypotheticals in the world won't make you feel better. Just trust that I have far too much to lose to do anything reckless. I have a job to do, and that's it."

"I could help," I plead for the tenth time today. "I can identify the major players in the family, help with attack strategy, or–"

"We've gone over this," he says, cutting me off. "I need you to stay here. Stay safe. I won't be able to concentrate if you're at risk."

I'm about to protest, but I know my words will fall on deaf ears. Taking a deep breath, I tilt my head up and close my eyes, trying to give voice to the sinking feeling I've had in the pit of my stomach all day.

"Something bad is going to happen," I whisper. "I can feel it."

"Something bad *is* going to happen. To the Colombos," he

says with a smirk.

I smack him on the shoulder. "I'm being serious. I love you, and I can't lose you. I won't." Tears burn the back of my eyes, but I don't let them fall.

Valentino's features turn serious, his hands coming up to cup my cheeks. "I love you too, Katya. I love you more with every day, every moment, every breath. You won't lose me. You have me forever, princess."

His lips find mine, and he leads us in a long, slow indulgent kiss, sweeping his tongue inside my mouth and making me forget about everything for a few blissful seconds. When we break apart, Valentino gathers up my hands in his, kissing my knuckles and then placing my hands on his chest, right over his heart.

"We'll be right back here, just like this, in a few hours." Brown eyes lock on mine, and I nod, wanting to believe him with every fiber of my being.

He gives me one last kiss, then steps back, slipping his gun into the inside of his jacket. Valentino strides to the door, and I wrap my arms around my torso, trying to hold myself together. He turns the handle, but right before he opens the door, Valentino looks at me over his shoulder.

"For the record, I have a knife strapped to my ankle, a switchblade in my pocket, brass knuckles, and two guns. Romeo will have bigger guns for us to use first, and we'll take every opportunity to snipe the enemy from a good distance before initiating hand-to-hand. Ideally, we just need to take out the guards and move the stockpile of weapons onto our trucks. They'll be distributed to our storage facilities, leaving the Colombos without the military power they are counting on to win this war."

Valentino holds my gaze as I nod, taking in his words. He's telling me the plan, trusting me with family secrets only the most loyal members have access to. It means more than he can comprehend. He's treating me as an equal, as someone worthy of trust.

"Thank you," I whisper.

He gives me a final nod, then steps outside, closing the door behind him.

Once again, I wait until I hear his car pull out of the driveway to jump into action. One day, my man will learn that I don't sit at home and wait very well. Until then, I'll have to keep surprising him.

I get dressed in a pair of black leggings and a black tank top, then I rummage through Valentino's closet until I find a dark long-sleeved t-shirt. Perfect.

Next, I pull open the bottom drawer of his dresser, just like I saw him do earlier this afternoon. Moving over the neatly folded shirts, I wedge my nail between the side of the wooden drawer and the false bottom, lifting up the piece of plywood to reveal a mini-armory.

There aren't any guns left, but I'm satisfied with a switch-blade and a dagger with a curved blade. I tuck the smaller one into my bra and the larger one up my sleeve. I finish up my thief-in-the-night look by gathering my hair into a bun at the base of my neck, then check the time.

Nine-thirty on the dot. Perfect.

Slipping out the front door, I make my way down the driveway and out onto the street, walking a few blocks before turning left. There, at the end of the block, is the cab I ordered when Valentino was in the shower earlier today. I feel a little guilty for charging his card, but not guilty enough to call it off. Besides, I wouldn't have had to do that if Valentino let me go with him in the first place.

I hurriedly open the back door of the car and greet the driver, hoping he's not chatty. The man barely acknowledges me, so that's a plus. He rattles off the address I gave him in the initial call—a club that's not too far from the warehouse in question. I confirm and then melt into the seat, going over everything in my head.

I'm not sure what exactly I'm doing, only that I have to be there. All day, I've had a needling feeling that something is off. Something we're not thinking about or some angle we've miscalculated. I knew Valentino wouldn't let me tag along, but I can't sit back and do nothing. Not when the man I love could end up dead.

The cab winds through the dark streets of the city, punctuated by streetlights and neon signs. I don't realize I've spaced out until the car stops and the cabbie clears his throat. "You're not really dressed for the club," he grunts, his eyes meeting mine in the rearview mirror.

"How do you know I'm not a bouncer?" I counter. "Maybe I'm packing heat." This earns me an amused snort, which I take as a good sign.

I thank the driver and get out of the cab, meandering to the back of the line of club-goers waiting to get in. No one pays me any mind as I fade into the shadows along the old brick wall, then slip out of line and down an alleyway.

"Left, right, forward, forward, forward, left, forward, right," I whisper to myself on repeat. I studied the city streets on a map earlier today and found a route from the club to the warehouse using mostly back roads and alleys. It seemed simple enough at the time, but now I'm beginning to doubt my brilliant plan.

After what feels like hours, I'm about ready to give up and admit that I'm lost. But then I hear it. That voice. I'll never forget that raspy tenor or the way it makes me want to vomit.

Raffe D'Angelo, AKA the man who attacked me in my father's office.

"Hello? Bruno? You missed the last check-in." A moment

of silence, then, "Goddamn lazy twat. Never shoulda' been put on guard duty," he mumbles.

I press my back against the wall of the building and slink forward, closer to the voice I've learned to hate. Peering out from my hiding spot in the alley, I take note of Raffe standing about ten feet away, frowning at the walkie-talkie in his hand.

"Yo, Bruno must be high on the job again," Raffe shouts to someone off in the distance. "I'm headed to the north side to tear him a new one."

The man turns, and I get a good look at his face for the first time since he tried to force himself on me. Something in me snaps. All the years of neglect, abuse, helplessness, and anger expand in my chest, clouding my vision and making me strike without a second thought.

As soon as Raffe is within three feet of my hiding spot, I jump out, dagger in one hand, switchblade in the other. I slash that motherfucker's big jowls, smiling like a psycho when crimson pours out of his wound.

"What the fu—"

I stab Raffe in the gut with the dagger in my other hand, twisting the knife before shoving the bastard backward. He collapses on the ground with a satisfying thud, and I stand over him, pressing my foot down on his chest as I watch the life drain from his eyes. Good riddance.

Wrapping my hand around the handle of the dagger, I'm about to pull it out when a horrid screech fills the air.

"Katya! Katya what the fuck?"

I freeze in place, not sure if I should run or try to fight him. Trembling from head to toe, I look up to see my father sprinting in my direction.

"Are you involved with this raid? How the fuck… Where the fuck…?"

He's panting as he approaches, and I quickly withdraw the knife from Raffe's side, holding it out in front of me.

"Really?" my father scoffs. "You think you can kill me? You're *mine*, Katya. My daughter. And you *will* submit to my authority."

"N-no," I say in a shaky voice.

My father sneers at me, taking a step closer. "Fucking ungrateful bitch. You killed one contender for your hand in marriage, but I've got a dozen lined up. You will fulfill your destiny of expanding my empire, child. One way or another."

Something catches my attention from the corner of my eye, behind my father, and off to the right. Without moving, I flick my gaze in that direction, and relief hits me square in the chest. Valentino is here. He puts his finger to his lips, and I blink in acknowledgment. Valentino tips his chin up, motioning for me to lead my father past where he's squatting behind a few wooden pallets.

"I will die before submitting to you or helping you in any way," I spit out.

My father's eyes grow wide with fury, and I take the opportunity to throw the dagger in his direction before taking off toward Valentino.

"Fucking cunt," my dad growls, dodging the blade and stumbling back while I sprint away.

I pump my legs as fast as I can, pushing myself until my muscles scream and my lungs burn. I'm vaguely aware of my father lumbering behind me, but I keep running, leading him straight to Valentino.

"You can't escape me, I'm–"

"Nothing to her," Valentino roars, seconds before tackling my father to the ground. "You selfish, worthless, tiny man," he continues, placing his boot on my dad's throat as he stands once more.

I turn, keeping my distance from their fight but staying

close enough to jump in if necessary. My dad tries fighting back, but he's no match for Valentino. I watch as my man pulls out a gun, aiming it directly at my father's forehead. He looks at me, silently asking permission.

I nod once, squeezing my eyes shut when I hear the gun go off.

All hell breaks loose at that one shot. Shouts, more gunshots, engines revving, tires squealing, and complete pandemonium surrounds me. It's all too much, and right before I curl into a ball and cover myself for protection, Valentino is by my side.

"Surprise?" I say weakly, not sure how upset he is with me.

Valentino shakes his head, then scoops me up in his arms. "I suppose me telling you how dangerous this was won't have any bearing on you doing it again?"

"Probably not," I confirm, resting my head on his shoulder as he carries me back through the alley I was hiding in originally.

He lets out a small chuckle, then kisses my forehead. "Let's get you home, princess."

CHAPTER ELEVEN

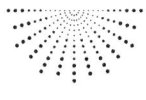

VALENTINO

*A*s soon as we make it back to my car, I get Katya settled in the passenger's seat and then peel out of the alley, heading straight to my home. Our home.

I grip the steering wheel and adjust in my seat, the adrenaline coursing through me and making it hard to sit still. Stealing a glance at Katya, I see she's staring out the window, her blank face reflected in the glass. She's shaking, her breaths fast and shallow.

Jesus, when I heard Marco Colombo scream Katya's name, my mind went blank. Nothing else mattered except getting to my woman. Everything had been going smoothly until one of the dead guard's walkie-talkies went off. We thought we took out everyone watching over the weapons stockpile, but apparently not. I was checking the perimeter for anyone we missed when Marco screamed.

There's no way I could have taken on the mob boss and his goon on my own, but thanks to Katya, I only had to handle her father. Even then, she led him right to me. I hate that she put herself at risk, again, might I add, but she wouldn't be the woman I fell in love with if she didn't fight tooth and nail to survive.

"Are you going to yell at me?" Katya asks.

I look over at her once more, those golden eyes finally resting on mine instead of out the window.

"No, baby. I should have known better than to tell you what to do."

My girl smiles at me, her hand finding mine on the center console. She weaves her fingers through mine, squeezing life back into every part of me.

We pull into the driveway of our home, and I waste no time bundling Katya up in my arms and carrying her inside.

"I can walk, you know," she tells me, even as she snuggles further into my embrace.

"This isn't for your benefit," I tell her. She gives me an adorably confused look, so I clarify. "I need you this close, Katya. I need to know you're here and we both made it out alive."

This makes Katya pop her head up from where she was resting it. "Oh my god, do we need to go back? We just left everyone there, and–"

"We're good, baby," I assure her as I make my way upstairs and into the bathroom. "We were almost done, and besides, you and I took out the big Boss. They can handle the clean-up."

"Are you sure?"

"I swear you almost look disappointed," I say, setting my woman down. Katya shrugs, which makes me smile, despite the crazy evening we've had. "Would you feel better if I gave him a call? I shot him a text right after…"

"Shooting my father?" Katya finishes for me.

I nod, still unsure of her feelings about everything. Yes, she gave me permission to end that piece of shit's life, but that doesn't mean she's not grieving.

"It's okay to say it," she whispers. "He deserved a lot worse."

I cup my hand around the back of her neck and pull her closer, pressing a kiss to the top of her head. "You're so strong," I murmur, kissing her one last time before stepping back. "You go ahead and get the water going while I call Romeo. Then I'll join you."

Katya nods, and I pull out my phone, dialing Romeo's number as I step out of the bathroom.

"Valentino," he answers, slightly out of breath. "It's over. Did you and Katya get home safe?"

"Yes, Boss. I wanted to check in. Well, Katya wanted me to check in."

Romeo chuckles. "I knew I was going to like her."

"So, what's the update? Did we lose any men?"

"Thankfully, no. We had already loaded up three of the four semis when Marco shouted for Katya. Is it true she killed Raffe D'Angelo? Or is Armando making shit up?"

"It's true," I confirm, pride welling up in my chest. "He was the prick who assaulted her. She got her revenge."

"Good," Romeo grunts before changing course. "We had snipers picking off the remnants of guards as the rest of us filled up the final semi. The Colombos have no armory and no leader. It will take years to rebuild and longer to retaliate."

"That's what I like to hear."

"You and me both. Now, go spend some time with your woman. I'll be indisposed for the next twenty-four hours, but we'll have a meeting after that."

"Thanks, Boss," I say with a chuckle. I'm sure Armando and Dante are spending the evening with their women as well.

Hanging up the phone, I toss it onto the kitchen table and then sprint upstairs to my Katya. The bathroom is practically a sauna, and I undress as quickly as possible, needing to see, touch, and feel everything about her.

When I pull back the curtain, I'm greeted with the sight of my precious, breathtaking woman dripping with water and surrounded by steam. She turns, holding her hand out for me. I take it, stepping inside our own little sanctuary of peace from the outside world.

"I can't believe you showed up tonight," I tell her as I smooth my hands over her curves.

"Really? It's kind of my signature move at this point," she teases.

I narrow my eyes at her, then nip the tip of her nose, making her giggle.

"I still can't comprehend why you'd put yourself in danger for me."

Katya's features grow serious, her magical eyes locked onto mine. "I love you, Valentino. Can't that be enough?"

"Yes," I choke out, cupping the sides of her neck with my hands. I brush my thumbs over her flushed cheeks, marveling at how soft she is. "I love you, Katya. More than I knew I was capable of."

I pull her closer, fusing our lips together as I tangle my fingers in her hair. My woman gives as much as she takes, her hands sliding up my back only to claw their way down.

When we break apart, Katya leans into me, resting her forehead on my chest. I keep her steady as I pour some body wash into my palm and slide my soapy hands all over her body. I massage Katya's sore muscles and take time to gently clean every inch of my fierce warrior goddess.

Katya returns the favor, soaping me up and running her hands up and down my torso, back, and legs. She trails kisses across my chest, and I tip my head back, closing my eyes and soaking up her gentle touches and sweet kisses.

"You feel incredible," I whisper, combing my fingers through her wet hair as she lavishes attention on me.

Katya takes a step back, and I tilt my head down, pouting at her. She grins, a mischievous glint in her golden eyes.

"I bet I can make you feel even better," she murmurs, biting her bottom lip.

Fuck me, how can I say no to that?

CHAPTER TWELVE

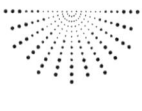

KATYA

e're a flurry of hands and lips and sloppy kisses as we make our way from the shower to the bed. The back of my knees hit the mattress, but Valentino grips my hips, not letting me fall backward. He breaks our kiss and trails his lips down my neck, sucking on my pulse point, my collarbone, lower, lower, until he's licking my nipples.

I arch my back, thrusting my breasts into his face, needing more of whatever he's willing to give me. Valentino grunts in approval, sucking on one breast while kneading the other in his massive hand. I rub up against him, feeling his hot, hard erection graze my center. We both groan at the contact. Valentino grinds into me and sucks my tits, working me over and hurtling my already amped-up body toward an orgasm.

I feel his teeth and tongue everywhere, even though he's only playing with my nipples. Each stroke and teasing bite echoes throughout my body and lands a devastating blow to my clit.

"V-Valentino, it's… I'm…"

He glides his thickness through my folds, holding me by my hips while he continues to worship my breasts. The head of his cock taps my clit just as he bites down on my nipple, and my pussy gushes for him. I hold my breath, waiting for my climax to hit, even though I don't want this to end yet.

The next thing I know, I'm falling backward, my climax and frustration mounting with no means of release.

"Valentino!" I growl in irritation. I can't focus on anything else except the ache between my thighs and my trembling muscles.

"Patience, princess," he purrs. Valentino is still standing, watching me squirm while fisting his massive cock. He glides his hand up and down in rough strokes. I'm mesmerized by the motion, so much so that I find the strength to sit up and grab a hold of him, mimicking what he's doing.

"Oh fuck, love, you feel so good," he groans.

I smile, finally feeling like I have the upper hand, so to speak. I lean forward and kiss the tip of his cock, grinning when it twitches.

"Christ," he hisses.

"My turn," I murmur in what I hope is a seductive voice.

It must work because he closes his eyes and tips his head back like he's lost to my touch. I lick the pearl of precum that leaks out of him, moaning at his salty, earthy flavor. Valentino wraps my hair around his fist and draws my head back so I'm looking right at him.

"You want to suck my cock, dirty girl?" he grits out.

I nod my head as much as I can and dart my tongue out, flicking it against his throbbing dick.

Valentino clenches his jaw and narrows his eyes at me like he's considering something. Then, he nods once and pushes me back onto the bed, crawling up next to me and settling on his back. "You can wrap those pretty little lips around me, love, but I need to taste you while you do."

"Oh. Um… how?" I know my face is flushed at my stupid question. I want to do everything with him, but I don't want to disappoint him with my inexperience.

One look in his molten eyes, however, puts all doubts and insecurities to rest.

"I'm going to love teaching you all the ways your sexy fucking body can feel pleasure," he growls. "Now turn around and straddle my face, princess. Ride me while you suck me off."

His filthy words spark the fire that never went out deep in my core. I scramble to get into position, then hesitate as a wave of vulnerability hits me square in the chest. I feel so much more exposed like this.

Valentino doesn't let me get stuck in my head for long. He grips my hips and pulls me down, sucking on my pussy and making me cry out. He growls and digs his fingers into my flesh while eating me out in sloppy strokes.

I focus on his massive cock once more, licking and kissing down his shaft before opening my mouth and seeing how much of him I can fit inside.

"Holy shit," he barks out, tearing his mouth from my cunt. "That's it, love, that's so fucking it."

I moan at his approval, taking more of him and sucking him down over and over. I reach out and cup his balls, surprised at how hot and heavy he feels in my hand. Valentino makes a tortured sound in the back of his throat and sucks on my clit, hard, before scraping his teeth against the pulsing little button.

I pop off his dick and drag air into my burning lungs. I rest my forehead on his thigh, trying to catch my breath and steady myself. My entire body trembles, my muscles tense, my pussy throbbing and soaking Valentino's face as he licks me over and over.

He continues sucking on my clit and circles my entrance

with the pad of his thumb before pressing it inside. I slap the mattress with one hand, then ball up my fist, clenching the sheet and twisting it around my fingers.

"V-Valentino…" I whimper as my hips start to buck. I can't stop. I need more. Need him to put me out of my misery.

He hums and shakes his head back and forth, nearly making me collapse. I widen my legs and press my convulsing cunt down on his mouth, not even caring how wanton and slutty that makes me. He did this to me. He drove me to the brink of insanity.

It's right there, so close to the surface I can taste it. My long-awaited orgasm claws at my insides the way I'm clawing at the bed, desperate with the need for release.

"Off," Valentino growls, pushing me off him and to the side. I land on my back with my legs spread out. Tension wraps itself around my body and pulls every muscle tighter, tighter, tighter, squeezing the air out of my lungs but never letting me find relief.

"No!" I whimper. The need to come is so painful I feel tears burning the back of my eyes. "Please, please, please…"

Valentino sits up and grabs my hand, guiding it over my quivering pussy lips. He drags my fingers through my soaking slit, making me suck in air when I touch my clit. He grunts and uses my hand to rub furious circles over my swollen bundle of nerves.

I can't concentrate on anything other than how my body is shrinking in on itself, becoming a tight, compact ball of pressure so dense I feel like I might implode and cease to exist. I draw in a huge breath and feel my heart thud against my ribcage once, twice, three times, and then…

Every ounce of tension releases as my body expands and contracts in waves of shuddering bliss. I sob out my orgasm and try to escape from the intensity of it all, but Valentino doesn't let me. He holds my hand down on my clit and continues to rub up and down, side to side, and then in slow circles.

"Again. Make yourself come again, Katya."

"Wh-what?" I stutter, confused by his words. I can't focus on anything except the scream caught in my throat and the unbelievable pressure building swiftly in the pit of my stomach.

I don't understand how it's even possible to be at the peak of one orgasm while another is barreling toward the surface, but when it hits, all the air drains from my lungs as I let out a guttural scream.

"Jesus," Valentino mutters, pressing my fingers against my clit, keeping me right there, forcing my orgasm to reach every empty space, every muscle, every cell before it finally crests and starts to fade.

Valentino helps me turn around so my head is next to his and we're on our sides, facing each other. He traces his fingertips over the curve of my hip and the dip in my waist, back and forth, while never breaking eye contact.

I sigh contentedly, then remember I left my man unsatisfied. I had the most incredible climax, but he never came. I was too wrapped up in what he was doing to me to finish him off. Reaching out, I wrap my hand around his rock-hard shaft, making him inhale sharply and dig his fingers into my hip.

"I want to give you what you just gave me," I whisper, gently pushing on his chest with my free hand so he's lying on his back.

"Katya," he groans. "You give me everything by existing."

I smile while I climb up his massive, muscled body, straddling him and running my hands up and down his torso. I start out with teasing touches, tracing the contours of his abs, pecs, and biceps. His muscles flex everywhere I touch, his skin heating as my pussy starts to pulse. He grunts when I score his flesh with my nails and rock against him, gliding my cunt up and down his thick dick.

"What if I want to give you more? What if I want more from you?" I bite my bottom lip and lift myself up on my knees, nestling his tip inside of my dripping opening.

"Fuck, take it, dirty girl. Take what you need. Feed that greedy pussy my cock until you come all over me."

My core clenches at his obscene words, making me tremble and suck in a breath. He can be filthy and brutal but also unbelievably sweet and tender.

Slowly, I ease my way down, feeling every inch of him invade me and fill me up. I know he feels it as his hands rest on my hips, holding me in place when I'm finally fully seated on him.

"Love being with you like this, Katya," he whispers, closing his eyes and breathing in deeply.

My pussy tightens around him as if agreeing with his statement. Valentino flexes his hips, wedging his cock deeper inside of me and making us both cry out. I grab his hands from where they are holding my hips and slide them up my body, placing them over my breasts. He takes the hint and squeezes my soft flesh, pinching my nipples.

I wrap my fingers around his wrists and grip him tightly, using his strength as leverage to buck my hips and grind down on him, testing to see what feels good for both of us. I angle my hips, hitting that spot inside me that drives me straight to the edge. I know it feels good for him when he squeezes my breasts roughly and growls.

Lifting myself up slightly, I drop down on him, hitting that same spot. I bounce on his cock, working us both up until we're sweating and shaking. I let go of his wrists and tangle my fingers in my hair, putting myself on display for my man. He makes me feel seen and loved and so desired. It makes me want to show myself off to him for his pleasure and mine.

"So fucking beautiful. So fucking mine," he growls, sliding his hands down my back to grip my ass.

He squeezes and separates my cheeks while thrusting his hips, fucking up into me so hard I fall forward. I catch myself on my hands, one on either side of his head.

"Valentino," I moan as he lifts my ass and then shoves me back down on his cock. He's so thick, so freaking long and hard, stretching me painfully, deliciously with each stroke.

My lips meet his in a frantic kiss, his teeth clashing, tongues tangling, breaths choppy and uneven as we get lost in our own rhythm. I snap my hips against his and bury my face into the side of his neck, unable to hold the weight of my head as a deep, drugging pleasure blankets and burns through me, destroying me in the best way possible.

"That's it, love," he groans. "So good, baby. So fucking good."

He slides one hand up my back and fists my hair, pulling my head up and holding it in place while he devours me. Each time he hits the end of me, sparks erupt and singe my nerves. My body feels heavy, swollen, and sensitive, but my head feels like it might float away on a cloud of bliss.

I tear my mouth from his, gulping down air while he fucks up into me in short, quick bursts. I match his movements as he spears me with his dick, over and over, breaking me apart one thrust at a time.

"Goddamn, look at us. Look at how well your tight little pussy takes my big cock."

I tilt my head down, looking between us. A wave of juices pours out of me, covering his dick. I whimper, loving the sight of him splitting me open.

"I can't hold on," I whisper, finally looking up at him.

Valentino's eyes are black with lust and the need for release. "I-I can't... I can't..."

Something inside me snaps and I lift my hips and slam my cunt down on him, grinding and swiveling my hips, fucking him desperately, racing toward my end. I can't stop. My body won't let me. My hips refuse to slow down.

I hold myself up with one hand and weave the fingers of my other hand in Valentino's hair, gripping it and forcefully yanking his head up so I can kiss him. His body responds to my manic, all-consuming, obsessive need to fuck hard and fast.

I cling to him as tightly as he's clinging to me, our bodies fusing together, grinding, rubbing, causing sweet, white-hot friction to spark a fire that blazes through us both.

"Fuck, fuck, fuck, little girl, need you to come for me. Need it, need, fuck, please..." he half groans, half growls.

Hearing this mountain of a man beg for me has my heart rattling around in my ribcage as lava floods my veins. I need to come so bad it scares me. I thought my last orgasm was the peak of pleasure, but the inferno threatening to swallow me whole is so much more intense. Flames lap at my nerves, and liquid heat courses through me, filling me up, then leaking out of my convulsing pussy.

"Let go, Katya. I'm here. I've got you," Valentino reassures me.

I make some undignified sound, then hold my breath, bracing myself for whatever lies on the other side of my release.

Valentino bites my shoulder and hits the very end of me in one brutal thrust. Flames engulf my body, burning me up from the inside out as I come, crying out his name. Tears well up and spill out of my eyes while sweat drips down my skin.

It's too much, yet not enough. I come again, but the ache

doesn't go away. Instead, it expands, seizing my lungs and heart, taking control of my limbs as I tremble violently. Valentino holds me close, his hands roaming up and down my back, my ass, my thighs, pressing my body impossibly closer to his like he wants to feel my orgasm with me.

My pleasure spikes again, this time unleashing a tidal wave inside of me. I'm embarrassed by how wet I am, but I can't stop. Every ounce of strength is wrung from my bones as heaving sobs wrack my body.

"Shit, you're squirting all over me. I feel it. Fuck, I feel it," he grunts.

I have no idea what he's talking about, but I don't have time to dwell on it. Valentino holds me still as he erupts inside of me. I feel his orgasm work its way through his body as he shudders against me. Thick ribbons of cum fill me up and spill out, joining my own release as it drips down my thighs and pools on the bed.

I don't know how long we're both suspended in our combined ecstasy, but when I finally come back into my body, I'm curled up into Valentino's side, my cheek pressed against his chest, right over his heart. I hear it thundering, his erratic heartbeat matching mine.

"Are you okay?" Valentino murmurs, placing a sweet kiss on the crown of my head.

"I'm perfect," I breathe out. "Blissful. Peaceful. Worn out." I lift my head, grinning at Valentino.

"You're definitely perfect," he says, his deep brown eyes peering down to the very depths of me. "And mine."

"Yours," I sigh contentedly. "Forever."

EPILOGUE

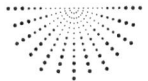

VALENTINO

"*H*appy birthday to you," everyone sings off-key, much to the delight of our seven-year-old daughter, Kaylee.

She rests her elbows on the table, clasping her little hands together as she looks around at her friends and family. Kaylee has her mother's golden eyes and strong spirit, which means she gets away with pretty much everything.

When the crowd finishes up their song, Kaylee's eyes grow wide as she takes in the cake Katya made especially for her birthday. It's a marble chocolate and strawberry cake with strawberry filling and chocolate frosting. My wife went all out, and I love that she found something she's passionate about.

After I put a ring on her finger and made her my wife, I encouraged Katya to go to college or explore hobbies and interests she was never able to when she lived with her father. She was hesitant at first, and it broke my heart when she confessed she's never let herself dream of a future where she gets to decide what she wants.

With some guidance and support, however, my princess

dove headfirst into the culinary arts, focusing on desserts and pastries. She runs a catering business on the side that's growing with each passing year. I couldn't be prouder of her and all of her accomplishments.

Claps and cheers echo around the dining room where we're hosting Kaylee's party, and then everyone scrambles for a piece of cake, knowing it will be incredible since Katya made it.

My phone buzzes in my pocket, and I'm about to shut it off when I see the name of a long-lost friend pop up on the screen.

Brewer Sullivan.

Stepping out into the kitchen for some privacy, I answer the call with more than a little curiosity. "Brewer? Is it really you?"

"Valentino," comes the gruff mountain man's voice. "Wasn't sure you'd pick up. Hell, I wasn't even sure this was still your number."

"It's been, what? Ten years? Twelve?" I muse.

"Therin about," he says, a slight country twang in his voice. "I hate to cut straight to the chase, but this is a time-sensitive matter."

"No problem," I reply. I'm not much for small talk anyway. "Is everything okay?"

"Is it too late to cash in that favor? You might not remember, but–"

"Of course, I remember. You saved my stupid ass on my first assignment."

I think back to the first time I met Brewer. He had just moved to New York City from his tiny mountain town in Nowhere, Idaho, and I was just starting out in the Di Salvo family, proving myself worthy.

I thought I'd get a gun from the Capo who gave me my first mission, but I found out real quick that weapons are earned. So there I was, barely nineteen, sent to deliver a package with no backup and no means of self-defense.

Long story short, I was tracked after making the hand-off and chased down by some crazy-ass motherfucker. Still don't know where he came from or what his problem was, but he got the jump on me before I even knew I was being chased. I could have handled one man on my own, but when three others showed up, I knew I was in bad shape.

That's when Brewer showed up. He grabbed one man by the back of his shirt and ripped him off of me, tossing him aside as if he weighed nothing more than a sack of flour. With that momentary distraction, I was able to scramble to my feet and help the stranger fight off the other bastards until they had had enough and ran away with their tails between their legs.

I had nothing to offer him at the time, so I promised him a favor to cash in once I was high enough in the ranks of the Di Salvo family. Looks like today is the day he's cashing it in.

"What do you need?" I ask after a moment of silence.

"There's a woman," he starts, making me smile. "More like an angel. A scared angel who has some secrets she thinks I can't handle."

"I can relate," I tell him, thinking of the first week with my Katya. We both had secrets and needed the safety of each other to confess them and heal.

"I need to know how to protect her. Can you look up information on people? I'm not sure what the scope of your influence is."

"Limitless."

Brewer chuckles. "Good. I'm going to need you to do some digging on her family and their business interests. And, uh, maybe you could gather some… other intel?"

"Something that could be used to blackmail someone, perhaps?"

"Exactly."

"Text me all the info you have and I'll run it through our networks. Might take a day or two."

"Thank you, Valentino. I mean it."

"I owe you more than looking up information. You saved my life."

"This is all I need. Keeping my angel safe is the most important thing to me."

"Well then how about I settle for an invite to the wedding?"

"Deal," Brewer grunts.

We say our goodbyes, and I head back into the dining room. My eyes are drawn to Katya, and I can't help but smile at how beautiful she is. Our three-year-old, Kira, is balanced on my wife's hip, sound asleep as sunlight from the bay window bathes both of them.

Katya returns my smile, weaving through the people to stand beside me.

"What are you thinking about?" she asks, gracing me with another smile.

"You, of course. It's always you."

Katya rolls her eyes, but I know she loves it. My woman went twenty years without hearing a single kind word, and it's my mission to make up for lost time.

I slip my hand into Katya's, weaving our fingers together as I lift her hand to my lips. "You're radiant today," I tell her, bending to kiss her temple.

"You always say that."

"It's always true," I counter.

My sweet girl blushes as she leans against me, resting her head on my shoulder. I wrap an arm around her waist and tuck her into my side, pressing a kiss to Kira's head and then Katya's. My heart is filled with pride and joy as I hold my wife and daughter and watch my other daughter obliterate her piece of cake the way only a child can.

"Love you," Katya sighs, her eyes fluttering closed.

"Love you more," I whisper.

Katya tips her head up, peeking one eye open. "Nope. Not possible. I'll fight you on this one, mister."

"I expect nothing less," I say with a chuckle.

My woman gives a satisfied nod before snuggling back into my embrace. I never thought I'd be this happy, never thought I deserved goodness in my life, but Katya changed everything.

I can't wait to spend the rest of my life showing her my gratitude.

* * *

THE END

Curious about Hawk & Savage Saints MC? Click here to find out more!

Want to know how Brewer's story ends? Get his book here!

ABOUT THE AUTHOR

Cameron Hart is a USA Today bestselling author of contemporary romance. She writes books with lots of heat, plenty of sweet, and just enough drama to keep things interesting.

Want to meet me? Check out events and book signings I'll be attending across the US: https://www.cameronhart.net/meet-me-in-person/

<u>**Sign up for my newsletter**</u> **and get a free novella!**

ALSO BY CAMERON HART

Check out my other popular series and books!

Mafia, MC, & Bodyguard Romance:

Moscatelli Crime Family Series

Di Salvo Crime Family Series

Savage Saints MC Series

Chaos MC series

Savage Ride

Ace

Watchdog Protection, Inc.

Mountain Man Romance:

Men of Blackthorne Mountain Series

Bear's Tooth Mountain Men Series

Curvy Girl Romance:

Curvy Temptations Boxset

Infinity

Claiming His Babygirl

Secret Temptations Boxset

At First Sight

Designed by Fate

My Heart & Soul

Finding Her Strength

1012 Curvy Way

Office Romance:

Boss Me Series

Beastly Brute

Executive Rule

Cowboy & Small Town Romance:

Roped in by Love Series

Sequoia Stud Farm

Small Town Love Boxset

Where I Belong

Seducing Sophia

Take Me Home

Forbidden Romance:

Secret Obsession

Secret Protector

Secret Desire

Holiday Romance:

Adored by Landon

Unwrapping His Package

Coming Down Her Chimney

His Christmas Angel

Hungry for Owen

Snow & Her Seven White Lies

Accidental Valentine

For Richer or Poorer

Printed in Great Britain
by Amazon